"Fascinating!"

—THE NEW YORKER

"Hauntingly evocative ... superb."

—THE NEW YORK TIMES

"Reading Ngaio Marsh's stories one becomes unconscious alike of printed pages and author's technique, and feels he is dealing with real people."

—Erle Stanley Gardner

"In her ironic and witty hands the mystery novel can be civilized literature ... style and atmosphere, humor which is never forced, characters who are fascinating and completely credible."

—Dorothy Cameron Disney

Also by Ngaio Marsh
from Jove

ARTISTS IN CRIME
BLACK AS HE'S PAINTED
CLUTCH OF CONSTABLES
COLOUR SCHEME
DEAD WATER
DEATH AND THE DANCING FOOTMAN
DEATH AT THE BAR
DEATH IN A WHITE TIE
DEATH IN ECSTASY
DEATH OF A PEER
DIED IN THE WOOL
ENTER A MURDERER
FALSE SCENT
FINAL CURTAIN
GRAVE MISTAKE
HAND IN GLOVE
KILLER DOLPHIN
LAST DITCH
LIGHT THICKENS
A MAN LAY DEAD
NIGHT AT THE VULCAN
THE NURSING HOME MURDER
OVERTURE TO DEATH
PHOTO FINISH
SCALES OF JUSTICE
SINGING IN THE SHROUDS
SPINSTERS IN JEOPARDY
TIED UP IN TINSEL
VINTAGE MURDER
WHEN IN ROME
A WREATH FOR RIVERA

NGAIO MARSH

Death of a Fool

JOVE BOOKS, NEW YORK

This Jove book contains the complete text of the original hardcover edition. It has been completely reset in a typeface designed for easy reading and was printed from new film.

DEATH OF A FOOL

A Jove Book / published by arrangement with Little, Brown and Company

PRINTING HISTORY
Little, Brown and Company edition published 1956
Four previous paperback printings
Jove edition / January 1978

ISBN: 0-515-07503-5

Jove Books are published by The Berkley Publishing Group, 200 Madison Avenue, New York, New York 10016.

PRINTED IN THE UNITED STATES OF AMERICA

20 19 18 17 16 15 14 13 12 11 10

For

JOHN *and* BEAR

with love

To anybody with the smallest knowledge of folklore it will be obvious that the Dance of the Five Sons is a purely imaginary synthesis combining in most unlikely profusion the elements of several dances and mumming plays. For information on these elements I am indebted, among many other sources, to *England's Dances*, by Douglas Kennedy, and *Introduction to English Folklore*, by Violet Alford.

Cast of Characters

Mrs. Bünz	
Dame Alice Mardian	*of Mardian Castle*
The Reverend Mr. Samuel Stayne	*Rector of East Mardian, her great-nephew by marriage*
Ralph Stayne	*her great-great-nephew and son of the Rector*
Dulcie Mardian	*her great-niece*
William Andersen	*of Copse Forge, blacksmith*
Daniel Andersen Andrew Andersen Nathaniel Andersen Christopher Andersen Ernest Andersen	*his sons*
Camilla Campion	*his grand-daughter*
Bill Andersen	*his grandson*
Tom Plowman	*landlord of the Green Man*
Trixie Plowman	*his daughter*
Dr. Otterly	*of Yowford, general practitioner*
Simon Begg	*of Simmy-Dick's Service Station*
Superintendent Carey	*of the Yowford Constabulary*
Police Sergeant Obby	*of the Yowford Constabulary*
Superintendent Roderick Alleyn Detective-Inspector Fox Detective-Sergeant Bailey Detective-Sergeant Thompson	*of the C.I.D., New Scotland Yard*

Contents

Death of a Fool

CHAPTER I Winter Solstice

OVER THAT PART of England the winter solstice came down with a bitter antiphony of snow and frost. Trees minutely articulate shuddered in the north wind. By four o'clock in the afternoon the people of South Mardian were all indoors.

It was at four o'clock that a small dogged-looking car appeared on a rise above the village and began to sidle and curvet down the frozen lane. Its driver, her vision distracted by wisps of grey hair escaping from a head scarf, peered through the fan-shaped clearing on her windscreen. Her woolly paws clutched rather than commanded the wheel. She wore, in addition to several scarves of immense length, a hand-spun cloak. Her booted feet tramped about over brake and clutch-pedal, her lips moved soundlessly and from time to time twitched into conciliatory smiles. Thus she arrived in South Mardian and bumped to a standstill before a pair of gigantic gates.

They were of wrought iron and beautiful, but they were tied together with a confusion of shopkeeper's twine. Through them, less than a quarter of a mile away, she saw on a white hillside the shell of a Norman castle, theatrically erected against a leaden sky. Partly encircled by this ruin was a hideous Victorian mansion.

The traveller consulted her map. There could be no doubt about it. This was Mardian Castle. It took some time in that deadly cold to untangle the string. Snow had mounted up the far side and she had to shove hard before she could open the gates wide enough to admit her car. Having succeeded and driven through, she climbed out again to shut them.

"'St. Agnes' Eve, ach, bitter chill it was!" she quoted in a faintly Teutonic accent. Occasionally, when fatigued or agitated, she turned her short *o*'s into long ones and transposed her *v*'s and *w*'s.

"But I see no sign," she added to herself, "of hare nor owl, nor of any living creature, godamercy." She was pleased with this improvisation. Her intimate circle had lately adopted "godamercy" as an amusing expletive.

There arose from behind some nearby bushes a shrill cachinnation and out waddled a gaggle of purposeful geese. They advanced upon her screaming angrily. She bundled herself into the car, slammed the door almost on their beaks, engaged her bottom gear and ploughed on, watched from the hillside by a pair of bulls. Her face was pale and calm and she hummed the air (from her Playford album) of "Sellinger's Round."

As the traveller drew near the Victorian house she saw that it was built of the same stone as the ruin that partly encircled it. "That is something, at least," she thought. She crammed her car up the final icy slope, through the remains of a Norman archway and into a courtyard. There she drew in her breath in a series of gratified little gasps.

The courtyard was a semicircle bounded by the curve of old battlemented walls and cut off by the new house. It was littered with heaps of rubble and overgrown with weeds. In the centre, puddled in snow, was a rectangular slab supported by two pillars of stone.

"Eureka!" cried the traveller.

For luck she groped under her scarves and fingered her special necklace of red silk. Thus fortified she climbed a flight of steps that led to the front door.

It was immense and had been transferred, she decided with satisfaction, from the ruin. There was no push-button, but a vast bell, demonstrably phoney and set about with cast-iron pixies, was bolted to the wall. She tugged at its chain and it let loose a terrifying rumpus. The geese, who had reappeared at close quarters, threw back their heads, screamed derisively and made for her at a rapid waddle.

With her back to the door she faced them. One or two made unsuccessful attempts to mount and she tried

Such was the din they raised that she did not hear the door open. "You are in trouble!" said a voice behind her. "Nip in, won't you, while I shut the door. Be off, birds."

The visitor was grasped, turned about and smartly pulled across the threshold. The door slammed behind her and she found herself face to face with a thin ginger-haired lady who stared at her in watery surprise.

"Yes?" said the lady. "Yes, well, I don't think—and in any case, what weather!"

"Dame Alice Mardian?"

"My great-aunt. She's ninety-four and I don't think—"

With an important gesture the visitor threw back her cloak, explored an inner pocket and produced a card.

"This is, of course, a suprise," she said. "Perhaps I should have written first, but I must tell you—frankly, frankly—that I was so transported with curiosity—no, not that, not curiosity—rather, with the zest of the hunter, that I could not contain myself. Not for another day. Another hour even!" She checked. Her chin trembled. "If you will glance at the card," she said. Dimly, the other did so.

Mrs. Anna Bünz

Friends of British Folklore
Guild of Ancient Customs
The Hobby-Horses

MORISCO CROFT
BAPPLE-UNDER-BACCOMB
WARWICKSHIRE

"Oh dear!" said the ginger-haired lady and added, "But in any case come in, of course." She led the way from a hall that was scarcely less cold than the landscape outside into a drawing-room that was, if anything, more so. It was jammed up with objects. Mediocre portraits reached from the ceiling to the floor, tables were smothered in photographs and ornaments, statuettes peered over each other's shoulders. On a vast hearth dwindled a shamefaced little fire.

"Do sit down," said the ginger-haired lady doubtfully, "Mrs.—ah—Buns."

to quell them, collectively, with an imperious glare.

"Thank you, but excuse me—Bünz. *Eü, eü,*" said Mrs. Bünz, thrusting out her lips with tutorial emphasis, "or if *eü* is too difficult, *Bins* or *Burns* will suffice. But nothing *edible!*" She greeted her own joke with the cordial chuckle of an old acquaintance. "It's a German name, of course. My dear late husband and I came over before the war. Now I am saturated, I hope I may say, in the very sap of old England. But," Mrs. Bünz added, suddenly vibrating the tip of her tongue as if she anticipated some delicious tid-bit, "to our muttons. To our muttons, Miss—ah—"

"Mardian," said Miss Mardian turning a brickish pink.

"Ach, that name!"

"If you wouldn't mind—"

"But of course. I come immediately to the point. It is this. Miss Mardian, I have driven three hundred miles to see your great-aunt."

"Oh dear! She's resting, I'm afraid—"

"You are, of course, familiar with the name of Rekkage."

"Well, there was old Lord Rekkage who went off his head."

"It cannot be the same."

"He's dead now. Warwickshire family near Bapple."

"It is the same. As to his sanity I feel you must be misinformed. A great benefactor. He founded the Guild of Ancient Customs."

"That's right. And left all his money to some too-extraordinary society."

"The Hobby-Horses. I see, my dear Miss Mardian, that we have dissimilar interests. Yet," said Mrs. Bünz lifting her voluminous chins, "I shall plod on. So much at stake. So much."

"I'm afraid," said Miss Mardian vaguely, "that I can't offer you tea. The boiler's burst."

"I don't take it. Pray, Miss Mardian, what are Dame Alice's interests? Of course, at her wonderfully great age—"

"Aunt Akky? Well, she likes going to sales. She picked up nearly all the furniture in this room at auctions. Lots of family things were lost when Mardian Place was burnt down. So she built this house of bits of the old castle and furnished it from sales. She likes doing that, awfully."

"Then there *is* an antiquarian instinct. Ach!" Mrs. Bünz exclaimed, excitedly clapping her hands and losing control of her accent. "Ach, sank Gott!"

"Oh crumbs!" Miss Mardian cried, raising an admonitory finger. "Here *is* Aunt Akky."

She got up self-consciously. Mrs. Bünz gave a little gasp of anticipation and, settling her cloak portentously, also rose.

The drawing-room door opened to admit Dame Alice Mardian.

Perhaps the shortest way to describe Dame Alice is to say that she resembled Mrs. Noah. She had a shapeless, wooden appearance and her face, if it was expressive of anything in particular, looked dimly jolly.

"What's all the row?" she asked, advancing with the inelastic toddle of old age. "Hullo! Didn't know you had friends, Dulcie."

"I haven't," said Miss Mardian. She waved her hands. "This is Mrs.—Mrs.—"

"Bünz," said that lady. "Mrs. Anna Bünz. Dame Alice, I am so inexpressibly overjoyed—"

"What about? How de do, I'm sure," said Dame Alice. She had loose-fitting false teeth which of their own accord chopped off the ends of her words and thickened her sibilants. "Don't see strangers," she added. "Too old for it. Dulcie ought to've told yer."

"It seems to be about old Lord Rekkage, Aunt Akky."

"Lor! Loony Rekkage. Hunted with the Quorn till

he fell on his head. Like you, Dulcie. Went as straight as the best, but mad. Don't you 'gree?" she asked Mrs. Bünz, looking at her for the first time.

Mrs. Bünz began to speak with desperate rapidity. "When he died," she gabbled, shutting her eyes, "Lord Rekkage assigned to me, as vice-president of the Friends of British Folklore, the task of examining certain papers."

"Have you telephoned about the boiler, Dulcie?"

"Aunt Akky, the lines are down."

"Well, order a hack and ride."

"Aunt Akky, we haven't any horses now."

"I keep forgettin'."

"But allow me," cried Mrs. Bünz, "allow me to take a message on my return. I shall be so delighted."

"Are you ridin'?"

"I have a little car."

"Motorin'? Very civil of you, I must say. Just tell William Andersen at the Copse that our boiler's burst, if you will. Much obliged. Me niece'll see you out. Ask you to 'scuse me."

She held out her short arm and Miss Mardian began to haul at it.

"No, no! Ach, *please*. I implore you!" shouted Mrs. Bünz, wringing her hands. "Dame Alice! Before you go! I have driven for two days. If you will listen for one minute. On my knees—"

"If you're beggin'," said Dame Alice, "it's no good. Nothin' to give away these days. Dulcie."

"But, no, no, no! I am not begging. Or only," urged Mrs. Bünz, "for a moment's attention. Only for von liddle vord."

"Dulcie, I'm goin'."

"Yes, Aunt Akky."

"Guided as I have been—"

"I don't like fancy religions," said Dame Alice, who with the help of her niece had arrived at the door and opened it.

"Does the winter solstice mean nothing to you? Does the Mardian Mawris Dance of the Five Sons mean nothing? Does—" Something in the two faces that confronted her caused Mrs. Bünz to come to a stop. Dame Alice's upper denture noisily capsized on its opposite number. In the silence that followed this mishap there was an outbreak from the geese. A man's voice shouted and a door slammed.

"I don't know," said Dame Alice with difficulty and passion, "I don't know who yar or what chupter. But you'll oblige me by takin' yerself off." She turned on her great-niece. "You," she said, "are a blitherin' idiot. I'm angry. I'm goin'."

She turned and toddled rapidly into the hall.

"Good evening, Aunt Akky. Good evening, Dulcie," said a man's voice in the hall. "I wondered if I—"

"I'm angry with you, too. I'm goin' upshtairs. I don't want to shee anyone. Bad for me to get fusshed. Get rid of that woman."

"Yes, Aunt Akky."

"And you behave yershelf, Ralph."

"Yes, Aunt Akky."

"Bring me a whishky-and-shoda to my room, girl."

"Yes, Aunt Akky."

"Damn theshe teeth."

Mrs. Bünz listened distractedly to the sound of two pairs of retreating feet. All by herself in that monstrous room she made a wide gesture of frustration and despair. A large young man came in.

"Oh, sorry," he said. "Good evening. I'm afraid something's happened. I'm afraid Aunt Akky's in a rage."

"Alas! Alas!"

"My name's Ralph Stayne. I'm her nephew. She's a bit tricky is Aunt Akky. I suppose, being ninety-four, she's got a sort of right to it."

"Alas! Alas!"

"I'm most frightfully sorry. If there's anything one could do?" offered the young man. "Only I might as well tell you I'm pretty heavily in the red myself."

"You are her nephew?"

"Her great-great-nephew actually. I'm the local parson's son. Dulcie's my aunt."

"My poor young man," said Mrs. Bünz, but she said it absentmindedly: there was speculation in her eye. "You could indeed help me," she said. "Indeed, indeed, you could. Listen. I will be brief. I have driven here from Bapple-under-Baccomb in Warwickshire. Owing partly to the weather, I must admit, it has taken me two days. I don't grudge them, no, no, no. But I digress. Mr. Stayne, I am a student of the folk dance, both central-European and—particularly—English. My little monographs on the Abram Circle Bush and the symbolic tea-pawt have been praised. I am a student, I say, and a performer. I can still cut a pretty caper, Mr. Stayne. Ach, yes, godamercy."

"I beg your pardon?"

"Godamercy. It is one of your vivid sixteenth-century English ejaculations. My little circle has revived it. For fun," Mrs. Bünz explained.

"I'm afraid I—"

"This is merely to satisfy you that I may in all humility claim to be something of an expert. My status, Mr. Stayne, was indeed of such a degree as to encourage the late Lord Rekkage—"

"Do you mean Loony Rekkage?"

"—to entrust no less than three Saratoga trunkfuls of precious, *precious* family documents to my care. It was one of these documents, examined by myself for the first time the day before yesterday, that has led me to Mardian Castle. I have it with me. You shall see it."

Ralph Stayne had begun to look extremely uncomfortable.

"Yes, well now, look here, Mrs.—"

"Bünz."

"Mrs. Burns, I'm most awfully sorry, but if you're heading the way I think you are, then I'm terribly afraid it's no go."

Mrs. Bünz suddenly made a magnificent gesture towards the windows.

"Tell me this," she said. "Tell me. Out there in the

courtyard, mantled in snow and surrounded at the moment by poultry, I can perceive, and with emotion I perceive it, a slightly inclined and rectangular shape. Mr. Stayne, is that object the Mardian Stone? The dolmen of the Mardians?"

"Yes," said Ralph. "That's right. It is."

"The document to which I have referred concerns itself with the Mardian Stone. And with the Dance of the Five Sons."

"Does it, indeed?"

"It suggests, Mr. Stayne, that unknown to research, to experts, to folk dancers and to the societies, the so-called Mardian Mawris (the richest immeasurably of all English ritual dance-plays) was being performed annually at the Mardian Stone during the winter solstice up to as recently as fifteen years ago."

"Oh," said Ralph.

"And not only that," Mrs. Bünz whispered excitedly, advancing her face to within twelve inches of his, "there seems to be no reason why it should not have survived to this very year, *this* winter solstice, Mr. Stayne—*this very week*. Now, do you answer me? Do you tell me if this is so?"

Ralph said, "I honestly think it would be better if you forgot all about it. Honestly."

"But you don't deny?"

He hesitated, began to speak and checked himself.

"All right," he said. "I certainly don't deny that a very short, very simple and not, I'm sure, at all important sort of dance-play is kept up once a year in Mardian. It is. We just happen to have gone on doing it."

"Ach, blessed Saint Use-and-Wont."

"Er—yes. But we have been rather careful not to sort of let it be known because everyone agrees it'd be too ghastly if the artsy-craftsy boys—I'm sure," Ralph said turning scarlet, "I don't mean to be offensive, but you know what can happen. Ye olde goings-on all over the village. Charabancs even. My family have all felt awfully strongly about it and so does the Old Guiser."

Mrs. Bünz pressed her gloved hands to her lips. "Did you, *did* you say 'Old Guiser'?"

"Sorry. It's a sort of nickname. He's William Andersen, really. The local smith. A perfectly marvellous old boy," Ralph said and inexplicably again turned scarlet. "They've been at the Copse Smithy for centuries, the Andersens," he added. "As long as we've been at Mardian, if it comes to that. He feels jolly strongly about it."

"The old man? The Guiser?" Mrs. Bünz murmured. "And he's a smith? And his forefathers perhaps made the hobby-horse?" Ralph was uncomfortable.

"Well—" he said and stopped.

"Ach! Then there is a hobby!"

"Look, Mrs. Burns, I—I do ask you as a great favour not to talk about this to anyone, or—or write about it. And for the love of Mike not to bring people here. I don't mind telling you I'm in pretty bad odour with my aunt *and* old William and, really, if they thought—look, I think I can hear Dulcie coming. Look, may I really *beg* you—"

"Do not trouble yourself. I am very discreet," said Mrs. Bünz with a reassuring leer. "Tell me, there is a pub in the district, of course? You see I use the word pub. Not inn or tavern. I am not," said Mrs. Bünz, drawing her hand-woven cloak about her, "what you describe as artsy-craftsy."

"There's a pub about a mile away. Up the lane to Yowford. The Green Man."

"The Green Man. A-a-ach! Excellent."

"You're *not* going to stay there!" Ralph ejaculated involuntarily.

"You will agree that I cannot immediately drive to Bapple-under-Baccomb. It is three hundred miles away. I shall not even start. I shall put up at the pub."

Ralph, stammering a good deal, said, "It sounds the most awful cheek, I know, but I suppose you wouldn't be terribly kind and—if you *are* going there—take a note from me to someone who's staying there. I—I—my car's broken down and I'm on foot."

"Give it to me."

"It's most frightfully sweet of you."

"Or I can drive you."

"Thank you most terribly, but if you'd just take the note. I've got it on me. I was going to post it." Still blushing he took an envelope from his breast-pocket and gave it to her. She stowed it away in a business-like manner.

"And in return," she said, "you shall tell me one more thing. What do you do in the Dance of the Five Sons? For you are a performer. I feel it."

"I'm the Betty," he muttered.

"A-a-a-ch! The fertility symbol, or in modern parlance—" she tapped the pocket where she had stowed the letter—"the love interest. Isn't it?"

Ralph continued to look exquisitely uncomfortable. "Here comes Dulcie," he said. "If you don't mind I really think it would be better—"

"If I made away with myself. I agree. I thank you, Mr. Stayne. Good evening."

Ralph saw her to the door, drove off the geese, advised her to pay no attention to the bulls as only one of them ever cut rough, and watched her churn away through the snow. When he turned back to the house Miss Mardian was waiting for him.

"You're to go up," she said. "What have you been doing? She's furious."

ii

Mrs. Bünz negotiated the gateway without further molestation from livestock and drove through what was left of the village. In all, it consisted only of a double row of nondescript cottages, a tiny shop, a church of little architectural distinction and a Victorian parsonage: Ralph Stayne's home, no doubt. Even in its fancy-dress of snow it was not a picturesque village. It would, Mrs. Bünz reflected, need a lot of pepping-up before it attracted the kind of people Ralph Stayne had talked about. She was glad of this because, in her own way, she too was a purist.

At the far end of the village itself and a little removed from it she came upon a signpost for East Mardian and Yowford and a lane leading off in that direction.

But where, she asked herself distractedly, was the smithy? She was seething with the zeal of the explorer and with an itching curiosity that Ralph's unwilling information had exacerbated rather than assuaged. She pulled up and looked about her. No sign of a smithy. She was certain she had not passed one on her way in. Though her interest was academic rather than romantic, she fastened on smithies with the fervour of a runaway bride. But no. All was twilight and desolation. A mixed group of evergreen and deciduous trees, the signpost, the hills and a great blankness of snow. Well, she would inquire at the pub. She was about to move on when she saw, simultaneously, a column of smoke rise above the trees and a short thickset man, followed by a dismal-looking dog, come round the lane from behind them.

She leant out and in a cloud of her own breath shouted: "Good evening. Can you be so good as to direct me to the Corpse?"

The man stared at her. After a long pause he said, "Ar?" The dog sat down and whimpered.

Mrs. Bünz suddenly realized she was dead-tired. She thought, "This frustrating day! So! I must now embroil myself with the village natural." She repeated her question. "Vere," she said speaking very slowly and distinctly, "is der corpse?"

" 'Oo's corpse?"

"Mr. William Andersen's."

" 'Ee's not a corpse. Not likely. 'Ee's my dad." Weary though she was she noted the rich local dialect. Aloud, she said, "You misunderstand me. I asked you where is the smithy. His smithy. My pronunciation was at fault."

"Copse Smithy be my dad's smithy."

"Precisely. Where is it?"

"My dad don't rightly fancy wummen."

"Is that it where the smoke is coming from?"

"Ar."

"Thank you."

As she drove away she thought she heard him loudly repeat that his dad didn't fancy women.

"He's going to fancy *me* if I die for it," thought Mrs. Bünz.

The lane wound round the copse and there, on the far side, she found that classic, that almost archaic picture—a country blacksmith's shop in the evening.

The bellows were in use. A red glow from the forge pulsed on the walls. A horse waited, half in shadow. Gusts of hot iron and seared horn and the sweetish reek of horse-sweat drifted out to mingle with the tang of frost. Somewhere in a dark corner beyond the forge a man with a lanthorn seemed to be bent over some task. Mrs. Bünz's interest in folklore, for all its odd manifestations, was perceptive and lively. Though now she was punctually visited by the, as it were, off-stage strains of "The Harmonious Blacksmith," she also experienced a most welcome quietude of spirit. It was as if all her enthusiasms had become articulate. This was the thing itself, alive and luminous.

The smith and his mate moved into view. The horseshoe, lunar symbol, floated incandescent in the glowing jaws of the pincers. It was lowered and held on the anvil. Then the hammer swung, the sparks showered and the harsh bell rang. Three most potent of all charms were at work—fire, iron and the horseshoe.

Mrs. Bünz saw that while his assistant was a sort of vivid enlargement of the man she had met in the lane and so like him that they must be brothers, the smith himself was a surprisingly small man: small and old. This discovery heartened her. With renewed spirit she got out of her car and went to the door of the smithy. The third man, in the background, opened his lanthorn and blew out the flame. Then, with a quick movement he picked up some piece of old sacking and threw it over his work.

The smith's mate glanced up but said nothing. The smith, apparently, did not see her. His branch-like arms, ugly and graphic, continued their thrifty gestures. He glittered with sweat and his hair stuck to his forehead in a white fringe. After perhaps half a dozen blows the young man held up his hand and the other stopped, his chest heaving. They exchanged roles. The young giant struck easily and with a noble movement that enraptured Mrs. Bünz.

She waited. The shoe was laid to the hoof and the smith in his classic pose crouched over the final task. The man in the background was motionless.

"Dad, you're wanted," the smith's mate said. The smith glanced at her and made a movement of his head. "Yes, ma-am?" asked the son.

"I come with a message," Mrs. Bünz began gaily. "From Dame Alice Mardian. The boiler at the castle has burst."

They were silent. "Thank you, then, ma-am," the son said at last. He had come towards her but she felt that the movement was designed to keep her out of the smithy. It was as if he used his great torso as a screen for something behind it.

She beamed into his face. "May I come in?" she asked. "What a wonderful smithy."

"Nobbut old scarecrow of a place. Nothing to see."

"Ach!" she cried jocularly, "but that's just what I like. Old things are by way of being my business, you see. You'd be—" she made a gesture that included the old smith and the motionless figure in the background—"you'd *all* be surprised to hear how much I know about blackschmidts."

"Ar, yes, ma-am?"

"For example," Mrs. Bünz continued, growing quite desperately arch, "I know *all* about those spiral irons on your lovely old walls there. They're fire charms, are they not? And, of course, there's a horseshoe above your door. And I see by your beautiful printed little notice that you are Anders*en*, not Anders*on*, and that tells me so exactly just what I want to know. Everywhere, there are evidences for me to read. Inside, I daresay—" she stood on tiptoe and coyly dodged her large head from side to side, peeping round him and making a mocking face as she did so—"I daresay there are all sorts of things—"

"No, there bean't then."

The old smith had spoken. Out of his little body had issued a great roaring voice. His son half turned and Mrs. Bünz, with a merry laugh, nipped past him into the shop.

"It's Mr. Andersen, Senior," she cried, "is it not? It is—dare I?—the Old Guiser himself? Now I *know* you don't mean what you've just said. You are much too modest about your beautiful schmiddy. And so handsome a horse! Is he a hunter?"

"Keep off. 'Er be a mortal savage kicker. See that naow," he shouted as the mare made a plunging movement with the near hind leg which he held cradled in his lap. "She's fair moidered already. Keep off of it. Keep aout. There's nobbut's men's business yur."

"And I had heard so much," Mrs. Bünz said gently, "of the spirit of hospitality in this part of England. Zo! I was misinformed it seems. I have driven over two hundred—"

"Blow up, there, you, Chris. Blow up! Whole passel's gone cold while she've been nattering. Blow up, boy."

The man in the background applied himself to the bellows. A vivid glow pulsed up from the furnace and illuminated the forge. Farm implements, bits of harness, awards won at fairs flashed up. The man stepped a little aside and, in doing so, he dislodged the piece of sacking he had thrown over his work. Mrs. Bünz cried out in German. The smith swore vividly in English. Grinning out of the shadows was an iron face, half-bird, half-monster, brilliantly painted, sardonic, disturbing and, in that light, strangely alive.

Mrs. Bünz gave a scream of ecstasy.

"The Horse!" she cried, clapping her hands like a

madwoman. "The Old Hoss. The Hooded Horse. I have found it. *Gott sei Dank*, what joy is mine!"

The third man had covered it again. She looked at their unsmiling faces.

"Well, that *was* a treat," said Mrs. Bünz in a deflated voice. She laughed uncertainly and returned quickly to her car.

CHAPTER II Camilla

UP IN her room at the Green Man, Camilla Campion arranged herself in the correct relaxed position for voice exercise. Her diaphragm was gently retracted and the backs of her fingers lightly touched her ribs. She took a long, careful deep breath and, as she expelled it, said in an impressive voice:

" 'Nine-men's morris is filled up with mud.' " This she did several times, muttering to herself, "On the breath, dear child, *on* the breath," in imitation of her speech-craft instructor, whom she greatly admired.

She glanced at herself in the looking-glass on the nice old dressing-table and burst out laughing. She laughed partly because her reflection looked so solemn and was also slightly distorted and partly because she suddenly felt madly happy and in love with almost everyone in the world. It was glorious to be eighteen, a student at the West London School of Drama and possibly in love, not only with the whole world, but with one young man as well. It was Heaven to have come along to Mardian and put up at the Green Man like a seasoned traveller. "I'm as free as a lark," thought Camilla Campion.

She tried saying the line about nine-men's morris with varying inflexions. It was *filled up* with mud. Then, it was filled up with *mud*, which sounded surprised and primly shocked and made her laugh again. She decided to give up her practice for the moment and, feeling rather magnificent, helped herself to a cigarette. In doing so she unearthed a crumpled letter from her bag. Not for the first time she re-read it.

Dear Niece,

Dad asked me to say he got your letter and far as he's concerned you'll be welcome up to Mardian.

There's accommodation at the Green Man. No use bringing up the past, I reckon, and us all will be glad to see you. He's still terrible bitter against your mother's marriage on account of it was to a R.C. so kindly do not refer to same although rightly speaking her dying ought to make all things equal in the sight of her Maker and us creatures here below.

Your affec. uncle,
Daniel Andersen

Camilla sighed, tucked away the letter and looked along the lane towards Copse Forge.

"I've got to be glad I came," she said.

For all the cold she had opened her window. Down below a man with a lanthorn was crossing the lane to the pub. He was followed by a dog. He heard her and looked up. The light from the bar windows caught his face.

"Hullo, Uncle Ernest," called Camilla. "You *are* Ernest, aren't you? Do you know who I am? Did they tell you I was coming?"

"Ar?"

"I'm Camilla. I've come to stay for a week."

"Our Bessie's Camilla?"

"That's me. Now do you remember?"

He peered up at her with the slow recognition of the mentally retarded. "I did yur tell you was coming. Does Guiser know?"

"Yes. I only got here an hour ago. I'll come and see him tomorrow."

"He doan't rightly fancy wummen."

"He will me," she said gaily. "After all, he's my grandfather! He *asked* me to come."

"Noa!"

"Yes, he did. Well—almost. I'm going down to the parlour. See you later."

It had begun to snow again. As she shut her window she saw the headlights of a dogged little car turn into the yard.

A roundabout lady got out. Her head was encased in

a scarf, her body in a mauve handicraft cape and her hands in flowery woollen gloves.

"Darling, what a make-up!" Camilla apostrophized under her breath. She ran downstairs.

The bar-parlour at the Green Man was in the oldest part of the pub. It lay at right angles to the Public, which was partly visible and could be reached from it by means of a flap in the bar counter. It was a singularly unpretentious affair, lacking any display of horse-brasses, warming-pans or sporting-prints. Indeed, the only item of anything but utilitarian interest was a picture in a dark corner behind the door: a faded and discoloured photograph of a group of solemn-faced men with walrus moustaches. They had blackened faces and hands and were holding up, as if to display it, a kind of openwork frame built up from short swords. Through this frame a man in clownish dress stuck his head. In the background were three figures that might have been respectively a hobby-horse, a man in a voluminous petticoat and somebody with a fiddle.

Serving in the private bar was the publican's daughter, Trixie Plowman, a fine ruddy young woman with a magnificent figure and bearing. When Camilla arrived there was nobody else in the Private, but in the Public beyond she again saw her uncle, Ernest Andersen. He grinned and shuffled his feet.

Camilla leant over the bar and looked into the Public. "Why don't you come over here, Uncle Ernie?" she called.

He muttered something about the Public being good enough for him. His dog, invisible to Camilla, whined.

"Well, fancy!" Trixie exclaimed. "When it's your niece after so long and speaking so nice."

"Never mind," Camilla said cheerfully. "I expect he's forgotten he ever had a niece."

Ernie could be heard to say that no doubt she was too upperty for the likes of them-all, anyhow.

"No, I'm not," Camilla ejaculated indignantly. "That's just what I'm *not*. Oh dear!"

"Never mind," Trixie said comfortably and made the

kind of face that alluded to weakness of intellect. Ernie smiled and mysteriously raised his eyebrows.

"Though, of course," Trixie conceded, "I must say it *is* a long time since we seen you," and she added with a countrywoman's directness, "Not since your poor mum was brought back and laid to rest."

"Five years," said Camilla, nodding.

"That's right."

"Ar," Ernie interjected loudly, "and no call for that if she'd bided homealong and wed one of her own. Too mighty our Bessie was, and brought so low's dust as a consequence."

"That may be one way of looking at it," Trixie said loftily. "I must say it's not mine. That dog of yours is stinky," she added.

"Same again," Ernie countered morosely.

"She wasn't brought as low as dust," Camilla objected indignantly. "She was happily married to my father, who loved her like anything. He's never really got over her death."

Camilla, as brilliantly sad as she had been happy, looked at Trixie and said, "They were in love. They married for love."

"So they did, then, and a wonderful thing it was for her," Trixie said comfortably. She drew a half-pint and pointedly left Ernie alone with it.

"Killed 'er, didn't it?" Ernie demanded of his boots. "For all 'is great 'oards of pelf and unearthly pride, 'e showed 'er the path to the grave."

"No. Oh, *don't!* How you can!"

"Never you heed," Trixie said and beckoned Camilla with a jerk of her head to the far end of the private bar. "He's queer," she said. "Not soft, mind, but queer. Don't let it upset you."

"I had a message from Grandfather saying I could come. I thought they wanted to be friendly."

"And maybe they do. Ernie's different. What'll you take, maid?"

"Cider, please. Have one yourself, Trixie."

There was a slight floundering noise on the stairs

outside followed by the entrance of Mrs. Bünz. She had removed her cloak and all but one of her scarves and was cozy in Cotswold wool and wooden beads.

"Good evening," she said pleasantly. "And *what* an evening! Snowing, again!"

"Good evening, ma-am," Trixie said, and Camilla, brightening up because she thought Mrs. Bünz such a wonderful "character make-up," said:

"I *know*. Isn't it *too* frightful!"

Mrs. Bünz had arrived at the bar and Trixie said, "Will you take anything just now?"

"Thank you," said Mrs. Bünz. "A noggin *will* buck me up. Am I right in thinking that I am in the mead country?"

Trixie caught Camilla's eye and then, showing all her white teeth in the friendliest of grins, said, "Us don't serve mead over the bar, ma-am, though it's made hereabouts by them that fancies it."

Mrs. Bünz leant her elbow in an easy manner on the counter. "By the Old Guiser," she suggested, "for example?"

She was accustomed to the singular little pauses that followed her remarks. As she looked from one to the other of her hearers she blinked and smiled at them and her rosy cheeks bunched themselves up into shiny knobs. She was like an illustration for a tale by the brothers Grimm.

"Would that be Mr. William Andersen you mean, then?" Trixie asked.

Mrs. Bünz nodded waggishly.

Camilla started to say something and changed her mind. In the Public, Ernie cleared his throat.

"I can't serve you with anything, then, ma-am?" asked Trixie.

"Indeed you can. I will take zider," decided Mrs. Bünz, carefully regional. Camilla made an involuntary snuffling noise and, to cover it up, said, "William Andersen's my grandfather. Do you know him?"

This was not comfortable for Mrs. Bünz, but she smiled and smiled and nodded and, as she did so, she told herself that she would never, never master the extraordinary vagaries of class in Great Britain.

"I have had the pleasure to meet him," she said. "This evening. On my way. A beautiful old gentleman," she added, firmly.

Camilla looked at her with astonishment.

"Beautiful?"

"Ach, yes. The spirit," Mrs. Bünz explained, waving her paws, "the raciness, the *élan!*"

"Oh," said Camilla dubiously, "I see." Mrs. Bünz sipped her cider and presently took a letter from her bag and laid it on the bar. "I was asked to deliver this," she said, "to someone staying here. Perhaps you can help me?"

Trixie glanced at it. "It's for you, dear," she said to Camilla. Camilla took it. Her cheeks flamed like poppies and she looked with wonder at Mrs. Bünz.

"Thank you," she said, "but I don't quite—I mean—are you—?"

"A chance encounter," Mrs. Bünz said airily. "I was delighted to help."

Camilla murmured a little politeness, excused herself and sat down in the inglenook to read her letter.

Dear, enchanting Camilla,

Don't be angry with me for coming home this week. I know you said I mustn't follow you because of the Mardian Morris and Christmas, but truly I had to. I shan't come near you at the pub and I won't ring you up. But please be in church on Sunday. When you sing I shall see your breath going up in little clouds and I shall puff away too like a train so that at least we shall be doing something *together. From this you will perceive that I love you.*

Camilla read this letter about six times in rapid succession and then put it in the pocket of her trousers. She would have liked to slip it under her thick sweater but was afraid it might fall out at the other end.

Her eyes were like stars. She told herself she ought to be miserable because after all she had decided it was no go about Ralph Stayne. But somehow the letter was an antidote to misery, and there went her heart singing like a lunatic.

Mrs. Bünz had retired with her cider to the far side of the inglenook, where she sat gazing—rather wistfully, Camilla thought—into the fire. The door of the Public opened. There was an abrupt onset of male voices—blurred and leisurely—unforced country voices. Trixie moved round to serve them and her father, Tom Plowman, the landlord, came in to help. There was a general bumble of conversation. "I had forgotten," Camilla thought, "what they sound like. I've never found out about them. Where do I belong?"

She heard Trixie say, "So she is, then, and setting in yonder."

A silence and a clearing of throats. Camilla saw that Mrs. Bünz was looking at her. She got up and went to the bar. Through in the Public on the far side of Trixie's plump shoulder she could see her five uncles—Dan, Andy, Nat, Chris and Ernie—and her grandfather, old William. There was something odd about seeing them like that, as if they were images in a glass and not real persons at all. She found this impression disagreeable and to dispel it called out loudly, "Hullo, there! Hullo, Grandfather!"

Camilla's mother, whose face was no longer perfectly remembered, advanced out of the past with the smile Dan offered his niece. She was there when Andy and Nat, the twins, sniffed at their knuckles as if they liked the smell of them. She was there in Chris's auburn fringe of hair. Even Ernie, strangely at odds with reality, had his dead sister's trick of looking up from under his brows.

The link of resemblance must have come from the grandmother whom Camilla had never seen. Old William himself had none of these signs about him. Dwarfed by his sons he was less comely and looked much more aggressive. His face had settled into a fixed churlishness.

He pushed his way through the group of his five sons and looked at his grand-daughter through the frame made by shelves of bottles.

"You've come, then," he said, glaring at her.

"Of course. May I go through, Trixie?"

Trixie lifted the counter flap and Camilla went into the Public. Her uncles stood back a little. She held out her hand to her grandfather.

"Thank you for the message," she said. "I've often wanted to come but I didn't know whether you'd like to see me."

"Us reckoned you'd be too mighty for your mother's folk."

Camilla told herself that she would speak very quietly because she didn't want the invisible Mrs. Bünz to hear. Even so, her little speech sounded a bit like a diction exercise. But she couldn't help that.

"I'm an Andersen as much as I'm a Campion, Grandfather. Any 'mightiness' has been on your side, not my father's or mine. We've always wanted to be friends."

"Plain to see you're as deadly self-willed and upperty as your mother before you," he said, blinking at her. "I'll say that for you."

"I am *very* like her, aren't I? Growing more so, Daddy says." She turned to her uncles and went on, a little desperately, with her prepared speech. It sounded, she thought, quite awful. "We've only met once before, haven't we? At my mother's funeral. I'm not sure if I know which is which, even." Here, poor Camilla stopped, hoping that they might perhaps tell her. But they only shuffled their feet and made noises in their throats. She took a deep breath and went on. ("Voice pitched too high," she thought.) "May I try and guess? You're the eldest. You're my Uncle Dan, aren't you, and you're a widower with a son. And there are Andy and Nat, the twins. You're both married but I don't know what families you've got. And then came Mummy. And then you, Uncle Chris, the one she liked so much and I don't know if you're married."

Chris, the ruddy one, looked quickly at Trixie, turned the colour of his own hair and shook his head.

"And I've already met Uncle Ernie," Camilla ended and heard her voice fade uneasily.

There seemed little more to say. It had been a struggle to say as much as that. There they were with their countrymen's clothes and boots, their labourers' bodies and their apparent unreadiness to ease a situation that they themselves, or the old man, at least, had brought about.

"Us didn't reckon you'd carry our names so ready," Dan said and smiled at her again.

"Oh," Camilla cried, seizing at this, "that was easy. Mummy used to tell me I could always remember your names in order because they spelt DANCE. Dan, Andy, Nat, Chris, Ernie. She said she thought Grandfather might have named you that way because of Sword Wednesday and the Dance of the Five Sons. Did you, Grandfather?"

In the inglenook of the Private, Mrs. Bünz, her cider half-way to her lips, was held in ecstatic suspension.

A slightly less truculent look appeared in old William's face.

"That's not a maid's business," he said. "It's men's gear, that is."

"I know. She told me. But we can look on, can't we? Will the swords be out on the Wednesday after the twenty-first, Grandfather?"

"Certain sure they'll be out."

"I be Whiffler," Ernie said very loudly. "Bean't I, chaps?"

"Hold your noise, then. Us all knows you be Whiffler," said his father irritably, "and going in mortal dread of our lives on account of it."

"And the Wing-Commander's 'Crack,' " Ernie said, monotonously pursuing his theme. "Wing-Commander Begg, that is. Old 'Oss, that is. 'E commanded my crowd, 'e did. I was 'is servant, I was. Wing-Commander Simon Begg, only we called 'im Simmy-Dick, we did. 'E'll be Old 'Oss, 'e will."

"Ya-a-as, ya-a-s," said his four brothers soothingly in unison. Ernie's dog came out from behind the door and gloomily contemplated its master.

"We can't have that poor stinking beast in here," Trixie remarked.

"Not healthy," Tom Plowman said. "Sorry, Ern, but there you are. Not healthy."

"No more 'tis," Andy agreed. "Send it back home, Ern."

His father loudly ordered the dog to be removed, going so far as to say that it ought to be put out of its misery, in which opinion his sons heartily concurred. The effect of this pronouncement upon Ernie was disturbing. He turned sheet-white, snatched up the dog and, looking from one to the other of his relations, backed towards the door.

"I'll be the cold death of any one of you that tries," he said violently.

A stillness fell upon the company. Ernie blundered out into the dark, carrying his dog.

His brothers scraped their boots on the floor and cleared their throats. His father said, "Damned young fool, when all's said." Trixie explained that she was as fond of animals as anybody, but you had to draw the line.

Presently Ernie returned, alone, and, after eying his father for some moments, began to complain like a child.

"A chap bean't let 'ave nothin' he sets his fancy to," Ernie whined. "Nor let do nothin' he's a notion to do. Take my case. Can't 'ave me dog. Can't do Fool's act in the Five Sons. I'm the best lepper and caperer of the lot of you. I'd be a proper good Fool, I would." He pointed to his father. "You're altogether beyond it, as the Doctor in 'is wisdom 'as laid it down. Why can't you heed 'im and let me take over?"

His father rejoined with some heat, "You're lucky to whiffle. Hold your tongue and don't meddle in what you don't understand. Which reminds me," he added, advancing upon Trixie. "There was a foreign wumman up along to Copse Forge. Proper old nosy besom. If so be—Ar?"

Camilla had tugged at his coat and was gesturing in the direction of the hidden Mrs. Bünz. Trixie mouthed distractedly. The four senior brothers made unhappy noises in their throats.

"In parlour is she?" William bawled. "Is she biding?"

"A few days," Trixie murmured. Her father said firmly, "Don't talk so loud, Guiser."

"I'll talk as loud as I'm minded. Us doan't want no fureignesses hereabouts—"

"Doan't, then, Dad," his sons urged him.

But greatly inflamed the Guiser roared on. Camilla looked through into the Private and saw Mrs. Bünz wearing an expression of artificial abstraction. She tiptoed past the gap and disappeared.

"Grandfather!" Camilla cried out indignantly. "She heard you! How you could! You've hurt her feelings dreadfully and she's not even English—"

"Hold your tongue, then."

"I don't in the least see why I should."

Ernie astonished them all by bursting into shouts of laughter.

"Like mother, like maid," he said, jerking his thumb at Camilla. "Hark to our Bessie's girl."

Old William glowered at his grand-daughter. "Bad blood," he said darkly.

"Nonsense! You're behaving," Camilla recklessly continued, "exactly like an over-played 'heavy.' Absolute ham, if you don't mind my saying so, Grandfather."

"What kind of loose talk's that!"

"Theatre slang, actually."

"Theatre!" he roared. "Doan't tell me you're shaming your sex by taking up with that trash. That's the devil's counting-house, that is."

"With respect, Grandfather, it's nothing of the sort."

"My grand-daughter!" William said, himself with considerable histrionic effect, "a play-actress! Ar, well! Us might have expected it, seeing she was nossled at the breast of the Scarlet Woman."

Chris and Andy with the occasional unanimity of twins groaned, "Ar, dear!"

The landlord said, "Steady, souls."

"I really don't know what you mean by that," Camilla said hotly. "If you're talking about Daddy's church you must know jolly well that it isn't mine. He and Mummy laid that on before I was born. I *wasn't* to be a Roman and if my brother had lived he *would* have been one. I'm C. of E."

"That's next door as bad," William shouted. "Turning your back on Chapel and canoodling with Popery."

He had come quite close to her. His face was scored with exasperation. He pouted, too, pushing out his lips at her and making a piping sound behind them.

To her own astonishment Camilla said, "No, honestly! You're nothing but an old baby after all," and suddenly kissed him.

"There now!" Trixie ejaculated, clapping her hands. Tom Plowman said, "Reckon that calls for one all round on the house."

The outside door was pushed open and a tall man in a duffle coat came in.

"Good evening, Mr. Begg," said Trixie.

"How's Trix?" asked Wing-Commander Simon Begg.

ii

Later on, when she had seen more of him, Camilla was to think of the first remark she heard Simon Begg make as completely typical of him. He was the sort of man who has a talent for discovering the Christian names of waiters and waitresses and uses them continually. He was powerfully built and not ill-looking, with large blue eyes, longish hair and a blond moustache. He wore an R.A.F. tie, and a vast woollen scarf in the same colours. He had achieved distinction (she was to discover) as a bomber-pilot during the war.

The elder Andersens, slow to recover from Camilla's kiss, greeted Begg confusedly, but Ernie laughed with pleasure and threw him a crashing salute. Begg clapped him on the shoulder. "How's the corporal?" he said. "Sharpening up the old whiffler, what?"

"Crikey!" Camilla thought, "he isn't half a cup-of-tea, is the Wing-Commander." He gave her a glance for which the word "practiced" seemed to be appropriate and ordered his drink.

"Quite a party to-night," he said.

"Celebration, too," Trixie rejoined. "Here's the Guiser's grand-daughter come to see us after five years."

"No!" he exclaimed. "Guiser! Introduce me, please."

After a fashion old William did so. It was clear that for all his affectation of astonishment, Begg had heard about Camilla. He began to ask her questions that contrived to suggest that they belonged to the same world. Did she live in "town"? Was it the same old show as ever? Did she by any chance know a little spot called "Phipps" near Shepherd Market—quite a bright little spot, really. Camilla, to whom he seemed almost elderly, thought that somehow he was also pathetic. She felt she was a failure with him and decided that she ought to slip away from the Public, where she now seemed out-of-place. Before she could do so, however, there was a further arrival: a pleasant-looking elderly man in an old-fashioned covert-coat with a professional air about him.

There was a chorus of " 'Evenin', Doctor." The newcomer at once advanced upon Camilla and said, "Why, bless my soul, there's no need to tell me who this is. I'm Henry Otterly, child. I ushered your mama into the world. Last time I spoke to her she was about your age and as like as could be. How very nice to see you."

They shook hands warmly. Camilla remembered that five years ago when a famous specialist had taken his tactful leave of her mother, she had whispered, "All the same, you couldn't beat Dr. Otterly up at Mardian." When she died, they carried her back to Mardian and Dr. Otterly had spoken gently to Camilla and her father.

She smiled gratefully at him now and his hand tightened for a moment round hers.

"What a lucky chap you are, Guiser," said Dr. Otterly, "with a grand-daughter to put a bit of warmth into your Decembers. Wish I could say as much for myself. Are you staying for Christmas, Miss Camilla?"

"For the winter solstice, anyway," she said. "I want to see the swords come out."

"Aha! So you know all about that."

"Mummy told me."

"I'll be bound she did. I didn't imagine you people nowadays had much time for ritual dancing. Too 'folksy'—is that the word?—or 'artsy-craftsy' or 'chi-chi.' Not?"

"Ah, no! Not the genuine article like this one," Camilla protested. "And I'm sort of specially interested because I'm working at a drama school."

"Are you, now?"

Dr. Otterly glanced at the Andersens, but they were involved in a close discussion with Simon Begg. "And what does the Guiser say to *that?*" he asked and winked at Camilla.

"He's livid."

"Ha! And what do you propose to do about it? Defy him?"

Camilla said, "Do you know, I honestly didn't think anybody was left who thought like he does about the theatre. He quite pitched into me. Rather frightening when you come to think of it."

"Frightening? Ah!" Dr. Otterly said quickly. "You don't really mean that. That's contemporary slang, I daresay. What did you say to the Guiser?"

"Well, I didn't *quite* like," Camilla confided, "to point out that after all *he* played the lead in a pagan ritual that is probably chock full of improprieties if he only knew it."

"No," agreed Dr. Otterly drily, "I shouldn't tell him that if I were you. As a matter of fact, he's a silly old fellow to do it at all at his time of life. Working himself into a fizz and taxing his ticker up to the danger-mark. I've told him so, but I might as well speak to the cat. Now, what do *you* hope to do, child? What roles do you dream of playing? Um?"

"Oh, Shakespeare if I could. If *only* I could."

"I wonder. In ten years' time? Not the giantesses, I fancy. Not the Lady M. nor yet the Serpent of Old Nile. But a Viola, now, or—what do you say to a Cordelia?"

"Cordelia?" Camilla echoed doubtfully. She didn't think all that much of Cordelia.

Dr. Otterly contemplated her with evident amusement and adopted an air of cozy conspiracy.

"Shall I tell you something? Something that to *me* at least is *immensely* exciting? I believe I have made a really significant discovery—*really* significant—about—you'd never guess—about *Lear*. There now!" cried Dr. Otterly with the infatuated glee of a White Knight. "What do you say to that?"

"A discovery?"

"About *King Lear*. And I have been led to it, I may tell you, through playing the fiddle once a year for thirty years at the winter solstice on Sword Wednesday for our Dance of the Five Sons."

"Honestly?"

"As honest as the day. And do you want to know what my discovery is?"

"Indeed I do."

"In a nutshell, this: here, my girl, in our Five Sons is nothing more nor less than a variant of the Basic Theme, Frazer's theme—the King of the Wood, the Green Man, the Fool, the Old Man Persecuted by His Young—the theme, by Guiser, that reached its full stupendous blossoming in *Lear*. Do you *know* the play?" Dr. Otterly demanded.

"Pretty well, I think."

"Good. Turn it over in your mind when you've seen

the Five Sons, and if I'm right you'd better treat that old grandpapa of yours with respect, because on the twenty-first, child, he'll be playing what I take to be the original version of *King Lear*. There now!"

Dr. Otterly smiled, gave Camilla a little pat and made a general announcement.

"If you fellows want to practice," he shouted, "you'll have to do it now. I can't give you more than half an hour. Mary Yeoville's in labour."

"Where's Mr. Ralph?" Dan asked.

"He rang up to say he might be late. Doesn't matter, really. The Betty's a free lance after all. Everyone else is here. My fiddle's in the car."

"Come on, then, chaps," said old William. "Into the barn." He had turned away and taken up a sacking bundle when he evidently remembered his granddaughter.

"If you bean't too proud," he said, glowering at her, "you can come and have a tell up to Copse Forge tomorrow."

"I'd love to. Thank you, Grandfather. Good luck to the rehearsal."

"What sort of outlandish word's that? We're going to practice."

"Same thing. May I watch?"

"You can *not*. 'Tis men's work, and no female shall have part nor passel in it."

"Just too bad," said Begg, "isn't it, Miss Campion? I think we ought to jolly well make an exception in this case."

"No. No!" Camilla cried. "I was only being facetious. It's all right, Grandfather. Sorry. I wouldn't dream of butting in."

"Doan't go nourishing and 'citing thik old besom, neither."

"No, no, I promise. Good-night, everybody."

"Good-night, Cordelia," said Dr. Otterly.

The door swung to behind the men. Camilla said good-night to the Plowmans and climbed up to her room. Tom Plowman went out to the kitchen.

Trixie, left alone, moved round into the bar-parlour to tidy it up. She saw the envelope that Camilla in the excitement of opening her letter had let fall.

Trixie picked it up and, in doing so, caught sight of the superscription. For a moment she stood very still, looking at it, the tip of her tongue appearing between her teeth as if she thought to herself, "This is tricky." Then she gave a rich chuckle, crumpled the envelope and pitched it into the fire. She heard the door of the public bar open and returned there to find Ralph Stayne himself staring unhappily at her.

"Trixie—?"

"I reckon," Trixie said, "you'm thinking you've got yourself into a terrible old pickle."

"Look—Trixie—"

"Be off," she said.

"All right. I'm sorry."

He turned away and was arrested by her voice, mocking him.

"I will say, however, that if she takes you, she'll get a proper man."

iii

In the disused barn behind the pub, Dr. Otterly's fiddle gave out a tune as old as the English calendar. Deceptively simply, it bounced and twiddled, insistent in its reiterated demand that whoever heard it should feel in some measure the impulse to jump.

Here, five men jumped—cleverly, with concentration and variety. For one dance they had bells clamped to their thick legs and, as they capered and tramped, the bells jerked positively with an overtone of irrelevant tinkling. For another, they were linked, as befitted the sons of a blacksmith, by steel: by a ring made of five swords. They pranced and leapt over their swords. They wove and unwove a concentric pattern. Their boots banged down the fiddle's rhythm and with each down-clamp a cloud of dust was bumped up from the floor. The men's faces were blank with concentration:

Dan's, Andy's, Nat's, Chris's and Ernie's. On the perimeter of the figure and moving round it, danced the Old Guiser, William Andersen. On his head was a rabbit-skin cap. He carried the classic stick-and-bladder. He didn't dance with the vigour of his sons but with dedication. He made curious, untheatrical gestures that seemed to have some kind of significance. He also chided his sons and sometimes called them to a halt in order to do so.

Independent of the Guiser but also moving as an eccentric satellite to the dance was "Crack," the Hobby-Horse, with Wing-Commander Begg inside him. "Crack" had been hammered out at Copse Forge, how many centuries ago none of the dancers could tell. His iron head, more bird-like than equine, was daubed with paint after the fashion of a witch-doctor's mask. It appeared through a great, flat, drum-like body: a circular frame that was covered to the ground with canvas and had a tiny horsehair tail stuck through it. "Crack" snapped his iron jaws and executed a solo dance of some intricacy.

Presently Ralph Stayne came in, shaking the snow off his hat and coat. He stood watching for a minute or two and then went to a corner of the barn where he found, and put on, a battered crinoline-like skirt. It was enormously wide and reached to the floor.

Now, in the character of man-woman, and wearing a face of thunder, Ralph, too, began to skip and march about in the Dance of the Five Sons. They had formed the Knot, or Glass—an emblem made by the interlacing of their swords. Dan and Andy displayed it, the Guiser approached, seemed to look in it at his reflection and then dashed it to the ground. The dance was repeated and the knot reformed. The Guiser mimed, with clumsy and rudimentary gestures, an appeal to the clemency of the Sons. He appeared to write and show his Will, promising this to one and that to another. They seemed to be mollified. A third time they danced and formed their knot. Now, mimed old William, there is no escape. He put his head in the knot. The swords were disengaged with a clash. He dropped his rabbit cap and fell to the ground.

Dr. Otterly lowered his fiddle.

"Sorry," he said. "I must be off. Quite enough anyway for you, Guiser. If I knew my duty I wouldn't let you do it at all. Look at you, you old fool, puffing like your own bellows. There's no need, what's more, for you to extend yourself like that. Yours is not strictly a dancing role. Now, don't go on after I've left. Sit down and play for the others if you like. Here's the fiddle. But no more dancing. Understand? 'Night, boys."

He shrugged himself into his coat and went out. They heard him drive away.

Ernie practiced "whiffling." He executed great leaps, slashing with his sword at imaginary enemies and making a little boy's spaceman noise between his teeth. The Hobby-Horse performed an extraordinary and rather alarming antic which turned out merely to be the preparatory manoeuvre of Simon Begg divesting himself of his trappings.

"Damned if I put this bloody harness on again tonight," he said. "It cuts my shoulders and it stinks."

"So does the Betty," said Ralph. "They must have been great sweaters, our predecessors. However, *toujours l'art*, I suppose."

"Anything against having them washed, Guiser?" asked Begg.

"You can't wash Old 'Oss," the Guiser pointed out. "Polish iron and leather and hop up your pail of pitch. Dip 'Crack's' skirt into it last thing as is what is proper and right. Nothin' like hot pitch to smell."

"True," Ralph said, "you have the advantage of me, Begg. I can't turn the Betty into a tar-baby, worse luck."

Begg said, "I'd almost forgotten the hot pitch. Queer sort of caper when you come to think of it. Chasing the lovely ladies and dabbing hot tar on 'em. Funny thing is, they don't run away as fast as all that, either."

"Padstow 'Oss," observed Chris, "or so I've 'eard

tell, catches 'em up and overlays 'em like a candle-snuff."

"'Eathen licentiousness," rejoined his father, "and no gear for us chaps, so doan't you think of trying it on, Simmy-Dick."

"Guiser," Ralph said, "you're superb. Isn't the whole thing heathen?"

"No, it bean't, then. It's right and proper when it's done proper and proper-done by us it's going to be."

"All the same," Simon Begg said, "I wouldn't mind twenty seconds under the old tar barrel with that very snappy little job you introduced to us to-night, Guiser."

Ernie guffawed and was instantly slapped down by his father. "You hold your noise. No way to conduct yourself when the maid's your niece. You should be all fiery hot in 'er defence."

"Yes, indeed," Ralph said quietly.

Begg looked curiously at him. "Sorry, old man," he said. "No offence. Only a passing thought and all that. Let's change the subject: when are you going to let us have that smithy, Guiser?"

"Never. And you might as well make up your mind to it. Never."

"Obstinate old dog, isn't he?" Begg said at large.

Dan, Chris and the twins glanced uncomfortably at their father.

Dan said, "Us chaps are favourable disposed as we're mentioned, Simmy-Dick, but the Dad won't listen to us, no more than to you."

"Look, Dad," Chris said earnestly, "it'd be in the family still. We know there's a main road going through in the near future. We know a service station'd be a little gold mine yur on the crossroads. We know the company'd be behind us. I've seen the letters that's been wrote. We can still *have* the smithy. Simmy-Dick can run the servicing side on his own to begin with. Ernie can help. Look, it's cast-iron—certain-sure." He turned to Ralph. "Isn't it? *Isn't it*?"

Before Ralph could answer, Ernie paused in his

whiffling and suddenly roared out, "I'd let you 'ave it, Wing-Commander, sir. So I would, too."

The Guiser opened his mouth in anger, but, before he could speak, Dan said, "We here to practice or not? Come on, chaps. One more dash at the last figure. Strike up for us, Dad."

The five brothers moved out into the middle of the floor. The Guiser, muttering to himself, laid the fiddle across his knees and scraped a preliminary call-in.

In a moment they were at it again. Down thumped their boots striking at the floor and up bounced the clouds of dust.

And outside in the snow, tied up with scarves, her hand-woven cloak enveloping her, head and all, Mrs. Bünz peered through a little cobwebby window, ecstatically noting the steps and taking down the tunes.

CHAPTER III Preparation

ALL THROUGH the following week snow and frost kept up their antiphonal ceremony. The two Mardians were mentioned in the press and on the air as being the coldest spots in England.

Up at the castle, Dame Alice gave some hot-tempered orders to what remained nowadays of her staff: a cook, a house parlour-maid, a cleaning woman, a truculent gardener and his boy. All of them except the boy were extremely old. Preparations were to be put in hand for the first Wednesday evening following the twenty-first of December. A sort of hot-cider punch must be brewed in the boiler house. Cakes of a traditional kind must be baked. The snow must be cleared away in the courtyard and stakes planted to which torches would subsequently be tied. A bonfire must be built. Her servants made a show of listening to Dame Alice and then set about these preparations in their own fashion. Miss Mardian sighed and may have thought all the disturbance a bit of a bore but took it, as did everybody else in the village, as a complete matter of course. "Sword Wednesday," as the date of the Dance of the Five Sons was sometimes called, made very little more stir than Harvest Festival in the two Mardians.

Mrs. Bünz and Camilla Campion stayed on at the Green Man. Camilla was seen to speak in a friendly fashion to Mrs. Bünz, towards whom Trixie also maintained an agreeable manner. The landlord, an easy man, was understood to be glad enough of her custom, and to be charging her a pretty tidy sum for it. It was learned that her car had broken down and the roads were too bad for it to be towed to Simon Begg's garage, an establishment that advertised itself as "Simmy-Dick's Service Station." It was situated at Yowford, a mile beyond East Mardian, and was believed to be doing not too well. It was common knowledge that Simon Begg wanted to convert Copse Forge into a garage and that the Guiser wouldn't hear of it.

Evening practices continued in the barn. In the bedrooms of the pub the thumping boots, jingling bells and tripping insistences of the fiddle could be clearly heard. Mrs. Bünz had developed a strong vein of cunning. She would linger in the bar-parlour, sip her cider and write her voluminous diary. The thumps and the scraps of fiddling would tantalize her almost beyond endurance. She would wait for at least ten minutes and then stifle a yawn, excuse herself and ostensibly go upstairs to bed. She had, however, discovered a backstairs by which, a few minutes later, she would secretly descend, a perfect mountain of hand-weaving, and let herself out by a side door into a yard. From here a terribly slippery brick path led directly to the near end of the barn which the landlord used as a storeroom.

Mrs. Bünz's spying window was partly sheltered by overhanging thatch. She had managed to clean it a little. Here, shuddering with cold and excitement, she stood, night after night, making voluminous notes with frozen fingers.

From this exercise she derived only modified rapture. Peering through the glass which was continually misted over by her breath, she looked through the storeroom and its inner doorway into the barn proper. Her view of the dancing was thus maddeningly limited. The Andersen brothers would appear in flashes. Now they would be out of her range, now momentarily within it. Sometimes the Guiser, or Dr. Otterly or the Hobby-Horse would stand in the doorway and obstruct her view. It was extremely frustrating.

She gradually discovered that there was more than one dance. There was a Morris, for which the men wore bells that jangled most provocatively, and there was also sword-dancing, which was part of a mime or play. And there was one passage of this dance-play which was always to be seen. This was when the

Guiser, in his role of Fool, or Old Man, put his head in the knot of swords. The Five Sons were grouped about him, the Betty and the Hobby-Horse were close behind. At this juncture, it was clear that the Old Man spoke. There was some fragment of dialogue, miraculously preserved, perhaps, from Heaven knew what ancient source. Mrs. Bünz saw his lips move, always at the same point and always, she was certain, to the same effect. Really, she would have given anything in her power to hear what he said.

She learnt quite a lot about the dance-play. She found that, after the Guiser had acted out his mock decapitation, the Sons danced again and the Betty and Hobby-Horse improvised. Sometimes the Hobby-Horse would come prancing and shuffling into the storeroom quite close to her. It was strange to see the iron beak-like mouth snap and bite the air on the other side of the window. Sometimes the Betty would come in, and the great barrel-like dress would brush up clouds of dust from the storeroom floor. But always the Sons danced again and, at a fixed point, the Guiser rose up as if resurrected. It was on this "act," evidently, that the whole thing ended.

After the practice they would all return to the pub. Once, Mrs. Bünz denied herself the pleasures of her peep show in order to linger as unobtrusively as possible in the bar-parlour. She hoped that, pleasantly flushed with exercise, the dancers would talk of their craft. But this ruse was a dead failure. The men at first did indeed talk, loudly and freely at the far end of the Public, but they all spoke together and Mrs. Bünz found the Andersens' dialect exceedingly difficult. She thought that Trixie must have indicated her presence because they were all suddenly quiet. Then Trixie, always pleasant, came through and asked her if she wanted anything further that evening in such a definite sort of way that somehow even Mrs. Bünz felt impelled to get up and go.

Then Mrs. Bünz had what she hoped at the time might be a stroke of luck.

One evening at half past five, she came into the bar-parlour in order to complete a little piece she was writing for an American publication on "The Hermaphrodite in European Folklore." She found Simon Begg already there, lost in gloomy contemplation of a small notebook and the racing page of an evening paper.

She had entered into negotiations with Begg about repairing her car. She had also, of course, had her secret glimpses of him in the character of "Crack." She greeted him with her particularly Teutonic air of camaraderie. "So!" she said, "you are early this evening, Wing-Commander."

He made a sort of token movement, shifting a little in his chair and eying Trixie. Mrs. Bünz ordered cider. "The snow," she said cozily, "continues, does it not?"

"That's right," he said, and then seemed to pull himself together. "Too bad we still can't get round to fixing that little bus of yours, Mrs.—er—er—Buns, but there you are! Unless we get a tow—"

"There is no hurry. I shall not attempt the return journey before the weather improves. My baby does not enjoy the snow."

"You'd be better off, if you don't mind my saying so, with something that packs a bit more punch."

"I beg your pardon?"

He repeated his remark in less idiomatic English. The merits of a more powerful car were discussed: it seemed that Begg had a car of the very sort he had indicated which he was to sell for an old lady who scarcely used it. Mrs. Bünz was by no means poor. Perhaps she weighed up the cost of changing cars with the potential result in terms of inside information on ritual dancing. In any case, she encouraged Begg, who became nimble in sales talk.

"It is true," Mrs. Bünz meditated presently, "that if I had a more robust motor-car I could travel with greater security. Perhaps, for example, I should be able to ascend in frost with ease to Mardian Castle—"

"Piece-of-cake," Simon Begg interjected.

"I beg your pardon?"

"This job I was telling you about laughs at a little stretch like that. Laughs at it."

"—I was going to say, to Mardian Castle on Wednesday evening. That is, if onlookers are permitted."

"It's open to the whole village," Begg said uncomfortably. "Open house."

"Unhappily—most unhappily—I have antagonized your Guiser. Also, alas, Dame Alice."

"Not to worry," he muttered and added hurriedly, "It's only a bit of fun, anyway."

"Fun? Yes. It is also," Mrs. Bünz added, "an antiquarian jewel, a precious survival. For example, five swords instead of six have I never before seen. Unique! I am persuaded of this."

"Really?" he said politely. "Now, Mrs. Buns, about this car—"

Each of them hoped to placate the óther. Mrs. Bünz did not, therefore, correct his pronunciation.

"I am interested," she said genially, "in your description of this auto."

"I'll run it up here to-morrow and you can look it over."

They eyed each other speculatively.

"Tell me," Mrs. Bünz pursued, "in this dance you are, I believe, the Hobby-Horse?"

"That's right. It's a wizard little number, you know, this job—"

"You are a scholar of folklore, perhaps?"

"*Me?* Not likely."

"But you perform?" she wailed.

"Just one of those things. The Guiser's as keen as mustard and so's Dame Alice. Pity, in a way, I suppose, to let it fold up."

"*Indeed, indeed.* It would be a tragedy. Ach! A sin! I am, I must tell you, Mr. Begg, an expert. I wish so much to ask you—" Here, in spite of an obvious effort at self-control, Mrs. Bünz became slightly tremulous. She leant forward, her rather prominent blue eyes misted with anxiety, her voice unconvincingly casual. "Tell me," she quavered, "at the moment of sacrifice, the moment when the Fool beseeches the Sons to spare him, something is spoken, is it not?"

"I say!" he ejaculated, staring at her, "you *do* know a lot about it, don't you?"

She began in a terrific hurry to explain that all European mumming had a common origin: that it was only reasonable to expect a little dialogue.

"We're not meant to talk out of school," Simon muttered. "I think it's all pretty corny, mind. Well, childish, really. After all, what the heck's it matter?"

"I *assure* you, I *beg* you to rest assured of my discretion. There is dialogue, no?"

"The Guiser sort of natters at the others."

Mrs. Bünz, clutching frantically at straws of intelligence on a high wind of slang, flung out her fat little hands at him.

"Ach, my good, kind young motor-salesman," she pleaded, reminding him of her potential as a customer, "of your great generosity, *tell* me what are the words he natters to the ozzers?"

"Honest, Mrs. Buns," he said with evident regret, "I don't know. Honest! It's what he's always said. Seems all round the bend to me. I doubt if the boys themselves know. P'raps it's foreign or something."

Mrs. Bünz looked like a cover-picture for a magazine called *Frustration.* "If it is foreign I would understand. I speak six European languages. *Gott in Himmel,* Mr. Begg—*What is it?*"

His attention had wandered to the racing edition on the table before him. His face lit up and he jabbed at the paper with his finger.

"Look at this!" he said. "Here's a turn-up! Could you beat it?"

"I have not on my glasses."

"Running next Thursday," he read aloud, "in the one-thirty. 'Teutonic Dancer by Subsidize out of Substitution'! Laugh that off."

"I do not understand you."

"It's a horse," he explained. "A race horse. Talk about coincidence! Talk about omens!"

"An omen?" she asked, catching at a familiar word.

"Good enough for me anyway. You're Teutonic, aren't you, Mrs. Buns?"

"Yes," she said patiently. "I am Teuton, yes."

"And we've been talking about *dancers*, haven't we? And I've suggested you *substitute* another car for the one you've got? And if you have the little job I've been telling you about, well, I'll be sort of *subsidized*, won't I? Look, it's uncanny."

Mrs. Bünz rummaged in her pockets and produced her spectacles.

"Ach, I understand. You will bet upon this horse?"

"You can say that again."

" 'Teutonic Dancer by Subsidize out of Substitution,' " she read slowly and an odd look came over her face. "You are right, Mr. Begg, it *is* strange. It may, as you say, be an omen."

ii

On the Sunday before Sword Wednesday, Camilla went after church to call upon her grandfather at Copse Forge. As she trudged through the snow she sang until the cold in her throat made her cough and then whistled until the frost on her lips made them too stiff. All through the week she had worked steadily at a part she was to play in next term's showing and had done all her exercises every day. She had seen Ralph in church. They had smiled at each other, after which the organist, who was also the village postman, might have been the progeny of Orpheus and Saint Cecilia, so heavenly sweet did his piping sound to Camilla. Ralph had kept his promise not to come near her, but she hurried away from church because she had the feeling that he might wait for her if he left before she did. And until she got her emotions properly sorted out, thought Camilla, that would never do.

The sun came out. She met a robin redbreast, two

sparrows and a magpie. From somewhere beyond the woods came the distant unalarming plop of a shot-gun. As she plodded down the lane she saw the spiral of smoke that even on Sundays wavered up over the copse from the hidden forge.

Her grandfather and his two unmarried sons would be home from chapel-going in the nearby village of Yowford.

There was a footpath through the copse making a short cut from the road to the smithy. Camilla decided to take it, and had gone only a little way into the trees when she heard a sound that is always most deeply disturbing. Somewhere, hidden in the wood, a grown man was crying.

He cried boisterously without making any attempt to restrain his distress and Camilla guessed at once who he must be. She hesitated for a moment and then went forward. The path turned a corner by a thicket of evergreens and, on the other side, Camilla found her uncle, Ernie Andersen, lamenting over the body of his mongrel dog.

The dog was covered with sacking, but its tail, horridly dead, stuck out at one end. Ernie crouched beside it, squatting on his heels with his great hands dangling, splay-fingered, between his knees. His face was beslobbered and blotched with tears. When he saw Camilla he cried, like a small boy, all the louder.

"Why, Ernie!" Camilla said, "you poor old thing."

He broke into an angry torrent of speech, but so confusedly and in such a thickened dialect that she had much ado to understand him. He was raging against his father. His father, it seemed, had been saying all the week that the dog was unhealthy and ought to be put down. Ernie had savagely defied him and had kept clear of the forge, taking the dog with him up and down the frozen lanes. This morning, however, the dog had slipped away and gone back to the forge. The Guiser, finding it lying behind the smithy, had shot it there and then. Ernie had heard the shot. Camilla pictured him, blundering through the trees, whimpering with anxiety. His father met him with his gun in his hand and told him to take the carcass away and bury it. At this point, Ernie's narrative became unintelligible. Camilla could only guess at the scene that followed. Evidently, Chris had supported his father, pointing out that the dog was indeed in a wretched condition and that it had been from motives of kindness that the Guiser had put it out of its misery. She supposed that Ernie, beside himself with rage and grief, had thereupon carried the body to the wood.

"It's God's truth," Ernie was saying, as he rubbed his eyes with the heels of his hands and became more coherent, "I tell 'e, it's God's truth I'll be quits with 'im for this job. Bad 'e is: rotten bad and so grasping and cruel's a blasted li'l old snake. Done me down at every turn: a murdering thief if ever I see one. Cut down in all the deathly pride of his sins, 'e'll be, if Doctor knows what he'm talking about."

"What on earth do you mean?" cried Camilla.

"I be a betterer guiser nor him. I do it betterer nor him: neat as pin on my feet and every step a masterpiece. Doctor reckons he'll kill hisself. By God, I hope 'e does."

"Ernie! Be quiet. You don't know what you're saying. Why do you want to do the Fool's act? It's an Old Man's act. You're a Son."

Ernie reached out his hand. With a finnicky gesture of his flat red thumb and forefinger, he lifted the tip of his dead dog's tail. "I got the fancy," he said, looking at Camilla out of the corners of his eyes, "to die and be rose up agin. That's why."

Camilla thought, "No, honestly, this is *too* mummerset." She said, "But that's just an act. It's just an old dance-play. It's like having mistletoe and plum-pudding. Nothing else happens, Ernie. Nobody dies."

Ernie twitched the sacking off the body of his dog. Camilla gave a protesting cry and shrank away.

"What's thik, then?" Ernie demanded. "Be thik a real dead corpse or bean't it?"

"Bury it!" Camilla cried out. "Cover it up, Ernie, and forget it. It's horrible."

She felt she could stand no more of Ernie and his dog. She said, "I'm sorry. I can't help you," and walked on past him and along the path to the smithy. With great difficulty she restrained herself from breaking into a run. She felt sick.

The path came out at a clearing near the lane and a little above the smithy.

A man was waiting there. She saw him at first through the trees and then, as she drew nearer, more clearly.

He came to meet her. His face was white and he looked, she couldn't help feeling, wonderfully determined and romantic.

"Ralph!" she said, "you mustn't! You promised. Go away, quickly."

"I won't. I can't, Camilla. I saw you go into the copse, so I hurried up and came round the other way to meet you. I'm sorry, Camilla. I just couldn't help myself, and, anyway, I've decided it's too damn silly not to. What's more, there's something I've got to say."

His expression changed. "Hi!" he said. "Darling, what's up? I haven't frightened you, have I? You look frightened."

Camilla said with a little wavering laugh, "I know it sounds the purest corn, but I've just seen something beastly in the copse and it's made me feel sick."

He took her hands in his. She would have dearly liked to put her head on his chest. "What did you see, poorest?" asked Ralph.

"Ernie," she said, "with a dead dog and talking about death."

She looked up at him and helplessly began to cry. He gave an inarticulate cry and gathered her into his arms.

A figure clad in decent blacks came out of the smithy and stood transfixed with astonishment and rage. It was the Guiser.

iii

On the day before Sword Wednesday, Dame Alice ordered her septuagenarian gardener to take his slasher and cut down a forest of dead thistles and briar that poked up through the snow where the Dance of the Five Sons was to be performed. The gardener, a fearless Scot with a will of iron and a sour disposition, at once informed her that the slasher had been ruined by unorthodox usage. "Dame," he said, for this was the way he chose to address his mistress, "it canna be. I'll no soil ma hands nor scald ma temper nor lay waste ma bodily health wi' any such matter."

"You can sharpen your slasher, man."

"It should fetch the blush of shame to your countenance to ask it."

"Send it down to William Andersen."

"And get insultit for ma pains? Yon godless old devil's altogether sunkit in heathen clamjamperies."

"If you're talkin' about Sword Wednesday, MacGlashan, you're talkin' bosh. Send down your slasher to the forge. If William's too busy one of the sons will do it."

"I'll hae nane but the smith lay hands on ma slasher. They'd ruin it. Moreover, they are as deep sunk in depravity as their auld mon."

"Don't you have sword dances in North Britain?"

"I didna come oot here in the caud at the risk o' ma ane demise to be insultit."

"Send the slasher to the forge and get the courtyard cleared. That will do, MacGlashan."

In the end, the slasher was taken down by Dulcie Mardian, who came back with the news that the Guiser was away for the day. She had given the slasher to Ernie with strict instructions that his father, and nobody else, was to sharpen it.

"Fancy, Aunt Akky, it's the first time for twenty years that William has been to Biddlefast. He got Dan Andersen to drive him to the bus. Everyone in the village is talking about it and wondering if he's gone to see Stayne and Stayne about his Will. I suppose Ralph would know."

"He's lucky to have somethin' to leave. I haven't and you might as well know it, Dulcie."

"Of course, Aunt Akky. But everybody says old William is really rich as possible. He hides it away, they say, like a miser. Fancy!"

"I call it shockin' low form, Dulcie, listenin' to village gossip."

"And, Aunt Akky, that German woman *is* still at the Green Man. She tries to pump everybody about the Five Sons."

"She'll be nosin' up here to see it. Next thing she'll be startin' some beastly guild. She's one of those stoopid women who turn odd and all that in their fifties. She'll make a noosance of herself."

"That's what the Old Guiser says, according to Chris."

"He's perfectly right. William Andersen is a sensible fellow."

"Could you turn her away, Aunt Akky, if she comes?"

Dame Alice merely gave an angry snap of her false teeth. "Is that young woman still at the Green Man?" she demanded.

"Do you mean William Andersen's grand-daughter?"

"Who the deuce else should I mean?"

"Yes, she is. Everyone says she's awfully nice and—well—you know—"

"If you mean she's a ladylike kind of creeter, why not say so?"

"One doesn't say that, somehow, nowadays, Aunt Akky."

"More fool you."

"One says she's a 'lidy.' "

"Nimby-pimby shilly-shallyin' and beastly vulgar into the bargain. Is the gel more of a Campion than an Andersen?"

"She's got quite a look of her mother, but, of course,

Ned Campion brought her up *as* a Campion. Good schools and all that. She went to that awfully smart finishing school in Paris."

"And learnt a lot more than they bargained for, I daresay. Is she keepin' up with the smithy?"

"She's quite cultivating them, it seems, and everybody says old William, although he pretends to disapprove, has really taken a great fancy to her. They say that she seems to like being with them. I suppose it's the common side coming out."

"Lor', what a howlin' snob you are, Dulcie. All the more credit to the gel. But I won't have Ralph gettin' entangled."

"What makes you think—"

Dame Alice looked at her niece with contempt. "His father told me. Sam."

"The rector?" Dulcie said automatically.

"Yes, he's the rector, Dulcie. He's also your brother-in-law. Are you goin' potty? It seems Ralph was noticed with the gel at Sandown and all that. He's been payin' her great 'tention. I won't have it."

"Have you spoken to Ralph, Aunt Akky?"

" 'Course I have. 'Bout that and 'bout somethin' else," said Dame Alice with satisfaction, "that he didn't know I'd heard about. He's a Mardian, is Master Ralph, if his mother *did* marry a parson. Young rake."

Dulcie looked at her aunt with a kind of dim, watery relish. "Goodness!" she said, "is Ralph a rake, Aunt Akky?"

"Oh, go and do yer tattin'," said Dame Alice contemptuously, "you old maiden."

But Dulcie paid little attention to this insult. Her gaze had wandered to one of the many clocks in her aunt's drawing-room.

"Sword Wednesday to-morrow," she said romantically, "and in twenty-four hours they'll be doing the Dance of the Five Sons. Fancy!"

iv

Their final practice over, the eight dancers contemplated each other with the steady complacency of men who have worked together in a strenuous job. Dr. Otterly sat on an upturned box, laid his fiddle down and began to fill his pipe.

"Fair enough," said old William. "Might be better, mind." He turned on his youngest son. "You, Ernie," he said, "you'm Whiffler, as us all knows to our cost. But that don't say you'm toppermost item. Altogether too much boistrosity in your whiffling. No need to lay about like a madman. Show me your sword."

"No, I won't, then," Ernie said. "Thik's mine."

"Have you been sharpening up again? Come on. Have you?"

"Thik's a sword, bean't 'er?"

Ernie's four brothers began to expostulate with him. They pointed out, angrily, that the function of the whiffler was merely to go through a pantomime of making a clear space for the dance that was to follow. His activities were purest make-believe. Ralph and Dr. Otterly joined in to point out that in other countries the whiffling was often done with a broom, and that Ernie, laying excitedly about him with a sword which, however innocuous at its point, had been made razor-sharp further down, was a menace at once to his fellow mummers and to his audience. All of them began shouting. Mrs. Bünz, at her lonely vigil outside the window, hugged herself in ecstasy. It was the ritual of purification that they shouted about. Immensely and thrillingly, their conversation was partly audible and entirely up her street. She died to proclaim her presence, to walk in, to join, blissfully, in the argument.

Ernie made no answer to any of them. He stared loweringly at his father and devotedly at Simon Begg, who merely looked bored and slightly worried. At last, Ernie, under pressure, submitted his sword for examination and there were further ejaculations. Mrs. Bünz could see it, a steel blade, pierced at the tip. A scarlet ribbon was knotted through the hole.

"If one of us 'uns misses the strings and catches hold be the blade," old Andersen shouted, "as a chap well might in the heat of his exertions, he'd be cut to the bloody bone. Wouldn't he, Doctor?"

"And I'm the chap to do it," Chris roared out. "I come next, Ern. I might get me fingers sliced off."

"Not to mention my yed," his father added.

"Here," Dr. Otterly said quietly, "let's have a squint at it."

He examined the sword and looked thoughtfully at its owner. "Why," he asked, "did you make it so sharp, boy?"

Ernie wouldn't answer. He held out his hand for the sword. Dr. Otterly hesitated and then gave it to him. Ernie folded his arms over it and backed away cuddling it. He glowered at his father and muttered and shuffled.

"You damned dunderhead," old William burst out, "hand over thik rapper. Come on. Us'll take the edge off of it afore you gets loose on it again. Hand it over."

"I won't, then."

"You will!"

"Keep off of me."

Simon Begg said, "Steady, Ern. Easy does it."

"Tell him not to touch me, then."

"Naow, naow, naow!" chanted his brothers.

"I think I'd leave it for the moment, Guiser," Dr. Otterly said.

"Leave it! Who's boss hereabouts! I'll not leave it, neither."

He advanced upon his son. Mrs. Bünz, peering and wiping away her breath, wondered, momentarily, if what followed could be yet another piece of histrionic folklore. The Guiser and his son were in the middle of her peep show, the other Andersens out of sight. In the background, only partially visible, their faces alternately hidden and revealed by the leading players, were Dr. Otterly, Ralph and Simon Begg. She heard Simon shout, "Don't be a fool!" and saw rather than heard Ralph admonishing the Guiser.

Then, with a kind of darting movement, the old man launched himself at his son. The picture was masked out for some seconds by the great bulk of Dan Andersen. Then arms and hands appeared, inexplicably busy. For a moment or two, all was confusion. She heard a voice and recognized it, high-pitched though it was, for Ernie Andersen's.

"Never blame me if you're bloody-handed. Bloody-handed by nature you are. What shows, same as what's hid. Bloody murderer, both ways, heart and hand."

Then Mrs. Bünz's peep show re-opened to reveal the Guiser, alone.

His head was sunk between his shoulders, his chest heaved as if it had a tormented life of its own. His right arm was extended in exposition. Across the upturned palm there was a dark gash. Blood slid round the edge of the hand and, as she stared at it, began to drip.

Mrs. Bünz left her peep show and returned faster than usual to her backstairs in the pub.

v

That night, Camilla slept uneasily. Her shallow dreams were beset with dead dogs that stood watchfully between herself and Ralph or horridly danced with bells strapped to their rigid legs. The Five Sons of the photograph behind the bar-parlour door also appeared to her, with Mrs. Bünz mysteriously nodding, and the hermaphrodite, who slyly offered to pop his great skirt over Camilla and carry her off. Then "Crack," the Hobby-Horse, came hugely to the fore. His bird-like head enlarged itself and snapped at Camilla. He charged out of her dream, straight at her. She woke with a thumping heart.

The Mardian church clock was striking twelve. A blob of light danced on the window curtain. Down in the yard somebody must be walking about with a lanthorn. She heard the squeak of trampled snow accompanied by a drag and a shuffle. Camilla, now wide awake, listened uneasily. They kept early hours at the Green Man. Squeak, squelch, drag, shuffle and still the light dodged on the curtain. Cold as it was, she sat up in bed, pulled aside the curtain and looked down.

The sound she made resembled the parched and noiseless scream of a sleeper. As well it might: for there below by the light of a hurricane lanthorn her dream repeated itself. "Crack," the Hobby-Horse, was abroad in the night.

CHAPTER IV The Swords Are Out

ON Sword Wednesday, early in the morning, there was another heavy fall of snow. But it stopped before noon and the sun appeared, thickly observable, like a live coal in the western sky.

There had been a row about the slasher. Nobody seemed to know quite what had happened. The gardener, MacGlashan, had sent his boy down to the forge to demand it. The boy had returned with a message from Ernie Andersen to say the Guiser wasn't working but the slasher would be ready in time and that, in any case, he and his brothers would come up and clear a place in the courtyard. The gardener, although he had objected bitterly and loudly to doing the job himself, instantly took offence at this announcement and retired to his noisomely stuffy cottage down in the village, where he began a long fetid sulk.

In the morning Nat and Chris arrived at Mardian Castle to clear the snow. MacGlashan had locked his toolshed, but, encouraged by Dame Alice, who had come down heavily on their side, they very quickly picked the lock and helped themselves to whatever they needed. Simon Begg arrived in his breakdown van with the other three Andersen brothers and a load of brushwood which they built up into a bonfire outside the old battlemented wall. Here it would be partially seen through a broken-down archway and would provide an extra attraction for the village when the Dance of the Sons was over.

Torches, made at the forge from some ancient receipt involving pitch, resin and tow, were set up round the actual dancing area. Later in the morning the Andersens and Simon Begg were entertained in the servants' hall with a generous foretaste of the celebrated

Sword Wednesday Punch, served out by Dame Alice herself, assisted by Dulcie and the elderly maids.

In that company there was nobody of pronounced sensibility. Such an observer might have found something disturbing in Simon Begg's attempts to detach himself from his companions, to show an ease of manner that would compel an answering signal from their hostesses. It was such a hopeless business. To Dame Alice (who if she could be assigned to any genre derived from that of Surtees) class was unremarkable and existed in the way that continents and races exist. Its distinctions were not a matter of preference but of fact. To play at being of one class when you were actually of another was as pointless as it would be for a Chinese to try to pass himself off as a Zulu. Dame Alice possessed a certain animal shrewdness but she was fantastically insensitive and not given to thinking of abstract matters. She was ninety-four and thought as little as possible. She remembered that Simon Begg's grandfather and father had supplied her with groceries for some fifty years and that he therefore was a local boy who went away to serve in the war and had, presumably, returned to do so in his father's shop. So she said something vaguely seignorial and unconsciously cruel to him and paid no attention to his answer except to notice that he called her Dame Alice instead of Madam.

To Dulcie, who was aware that he kept a garage and had held a commission in the Air Force, he spoke a language that was incomprehensible. She supposed vaguely that he preferred petrol to dry goods and knew she ought to feel grateful to him because of the Battle of Britain. She tried to think of remarks to make to him but was embarrassed by Ernie, who stood at his elbow and laughed very loudly at everything he said.

Simon gave Dulcie a meaning smile and patted Ernie's arm. "We're a bit above ourselves, Miss Mardian," he said. "We take ourselves very seriously over this little show tonight."

Ernie laughed and Dulcie said, "Do you?" not understanding Simon's playful use of the first person plural. He lowered his voice and said, "Poor old Ernie! Ernie was my batman in the old days, Miss Mardian. Weren't you, Corp? How about seeing if you can help those girls, Ernie?"

Ernie, proud of being the subject of his hero's attention, threw one of his crashing salutes and backed away. "It's pathetic, really," Simon said, "he follows me round like a dog. God knows why. I do what I can for him."

Dulcie repeated, "Do you?" even more vaguely and drifted away. Dan called his brothers together, thanked Dame Alice and began to shepherd them out.

"Here!" Dame Alice shouted. "Wait a bit. I thought you were goin' to clear away those brambles out there."

"So we are, ma-am," Dan said. "Ernie do be comin' up along after dinner with your slasher."

"Mind he does. How's your father?"

"Not feeling too clever to-day, ma-am, but he reckons he'll be right again for to-night."

"What'll you do if he can't dance?"

Ernie said instantly, "I can do Fool. I can do Fool's act better nor him. If he's not able, I am. Able and willing."

His brothers broke into their habitual conciliatory chorus. They eased Ernie out of the room and into the courtyard. Simon made rather a thing of his goodbye to Dame Alice and thanked her elaborately. She distressed him by replying, "Not 'tall, Begg. Shop doin' well, I hope? Compliments to your father."

He recovered sufficiently to look with tact at Dulcie, who said, "Old Mr. Begg's dead, Aunt Akky. Somebody else has got the shop."

Dame Alice said, "Oh? I'd forgotten," nodded to Simon and toddled rapidly away.

She and Dulcie went to their luncheon. They saw Simon's van surrounded by infuriated geese go past the window with all the Andersens on board.

The courtyard was now laid bare of snow. At its centre the Mardian dolmen awaited the coming of the Five Sons. Many brambles and thistles were still uncut.

By three o'clock Ernie had not returned with the slasher and the afternoon had begun to darken. It was at half-past four that Dulcie, fatigued by preparation and staring out of the drawing-room window, suddenly ejaculated, "Aunt Akky! Aunt Akky, they've left something on the stone."

But Dame Alice had fallen into a doze and only muttered indistinguishably.

Dulcie peered and speculated and at last went into the hall and flung an old coat over her shoulders. She let herself out and ran across the courtyard to the stone. On its slightly tilted surface which, in the times before recorded history, may have been used for sacrifice, there was a dead goose, decapitated.

ii

By eight o'clock almost all the village was assembled in the courtyard. On Sword Wednesday, Dame Alice always invited some of her neighbours in the county to Mardian, but this year, with the lanes deep in snow, they had all preferred to stay at home. They were unable to ring her up and apologize as there had been a major breakdown in the telephone lines. They told each other, rather nervously, that Dame Alice would "understand." She not only understood but rejoiced.

So it was entirely a village affair attended by not more than fifty onlookers. Following an established custom, Dr. Otterly had dined at the castle and so had Ralph and his father. The Honourable and Revernd Samuel Stayne was Dame Alice's great-nephew-in-law. Twenty-eight years ago he had had the temerity to fall in love with Dulcie Mardian's elder sister, then staying at the castle, and, subsequently, to marry her. He was a gentle, unwordy man who attempted to follow the teaching of the Gospels literally and was despised by Dame Alice not because he couldn't afford, but because he didn't care, to ride to hounds.

After dinner, which was remarkable for its lamentable food and excellent wine, Ralph excused himself. He had to get ready for the dance. The others sipped coffee essence and superb brandy in the drawing-room.

The old parlour-maid came in at a quarter to nine to say that the dancers were almost ready.

"I really think you'd better watch from the windows, you know," Dr. Otterly said to his hostess. "It's a devil of a cold night. Look, you'll see to perfection. May I?"

He pulled back the heavy curtains.

It was as if they were those of a theatre and had opened on the first act of some flamboyant play. Eight standing torches in the courtyard and the bonfire beyond the battlements flared into the night. Flames danced on the snow and sparks exploded in the frosty air. The onlookers stood to left and right of the cleared area and their shadows leapt and pranced confusedly up the walls beyond them. In the middle of this picture stood the Mardian dolmen, unencumbered now, glinting with frost as if, incongruously, it had been tinselled for the occasion.

"That youth," said Dame Alice, "has *not* cleared away the thistles."

"And I fancy," Dr. Otterly said, "that I know why. Now, how about it? You get a wonderful view from here. Why *not* stay indoors?"

"No, thankee. Prefer out."

"It's not wise, you know."

"Fiddle."

"All right! That's the worst of you young things: you're so damned headstrong."

She chuckled. Dulcie had begun to carry in a quantity of coats and shawls.

"Old William," Dr. Otterly went on, "is just as bad. He oughtn't to be out to-night with his heart what it is and he certainly oughtn't to be playing the Fool—by the way, Rector, has it ever occurred to you that the phrase probably derives from one of these mumming plays?—but, there you are. I ought to refuse to fiddle for the old goat. I would if I thought it'd stop him, but he'd fiddle and fool too, no doubt. If you'll excuse me I must join my party. Here are your programmes, by the way. That's *not* for me, I *trust*."

The parlour-maid had come in with a piece of paper on her tray. "For Dr. Otterly, madam," she said.

"*Now*, who the hell can be ill?" Dr. Otterly groaned and unfolded the paper.

It was one of the old-fashioned printed bills that the Guiser sent out to his customers. Across it was written in shaky pencil characters: *Cant mannage it young Ern will have to. W.A.*

"There now!" Dr. Otterly exclaimed. "He *has* conked out."

"The Guiser!" cried the Rector.

"The Guiser. I must see what's to be done. Sorry, Dame Alice. We'll manage, though. Don't worry. Marvellous dinner. 'Bye."

"Dear me!" the Rector said, "what *will* they do?"

"Dan Andersen's boy will come in as a Son," Dulcie said. "I know that's what they planned if it happened."

"And I 'spose," Dame Alice added, "that idiot Ernie will dance the Fool. What a bore."

"Poor Ernie, yes. A catastrophe for them," the Rector murmured.

"Did I tell you, Sam, he killed one of my geese?"

"We don't know it was Ernie, Aunt Akky."

"Nobody else dotty enough. I'll tackle 'em later. Come on," Dame Alice said. "Get me bundled. We'd better go out."

Dulcie put her into coat after coat and shawl after shawl. Her feet were thrust into fur-lined boots, her hands into mitts and her head into an ancient woollen cap with a pom-pom on the top. Dulcie and the Rector hastily provided for themselves and finally the three of them went out through the front door to the steps.

Here chairs had been placed with a brazier glowing in front of each. They sat down and were covered with rugs by the parlour-maid, who then retired to an upstairs room from which she could view the proceedings cozily.

Their breath rose up in three columns. The onlookers

below them were wreathed in mist. From the bonfire on the other side of the battlements smoke was blown into the courtyard and its lovely smell was mixed with the pungent odour of tar.

The Mardian dolmen stood darkly against the snow. Flanking it on either side were torches that flared boldly upon the scene which—almost of itself, one might have thought—had now acquired an air of disturbing authenticity.

Dame Alice, with a wooden gesture of her muffled arm, shouted, "Evenin', everybody." From round the sides of the courtyard they all answered raggedly, "Evening. Evening, ma-am," dragging out the soft vowels.

Behind the Mardian Stone was the archway in the battlements through which the performers would appear. Figures could be seen moving in the shadows beyond.

The party of three consulted their programmes, which had been neatly typed.

WINTER SOLSTICE

The Mardian Morris of the Five Sons

The Morris Side:	Fool	William Andersen
	Betty	Ralph Stayne
	Crack	Simon Begg
	Sons	Daniel, Andrew, Nathaniel, Christopher and Ernest (Whiffler) Andersen

The Mardian Morris, or perhaps, more strictly, Morris Sword Dance and Play, is performed annually on the first Wednesday after the winter solstice. It is probably the survival of an ancient fertility rite and combines, in one ceremony, the features of a number of other seasonal dances and mumming plays.

ORDER OF EVENTS

1.	General Entry		The Five Sons
2.	The Mardian Morris		
3.	Entry of the Betty and Crack		•
4.	Improvisation		Crack
5.	Entry of the Fool		
6.	First Sword Dance	(a) The Glass Is Broken	
		(b) The Will Is Read	
		(c) The Death	
7.	Improvisation		The Betty
8.	Solo		D. Andersen
9.	Second Sword Dance		
10.	The Resurrection of the Fool		

Dulcie put down her programme and looked round. "*Everybody* must be here, I should think," she said. "Look, Aunt Akky, there's Trixie from the Green Man and her father and that's old William's grand-daughter with them."

"Camilla?" the Rector said. "A splendid girl. We're all delighted with her."

"Trousers," said Dame Alice.

"Skiing trousers, I *think*, Aunt Akky. Quite suitable, really."

"Is that woman here? The German woman?"

"Mrs. Bünz?" the Rector said gently. "I don't *see* her, Aunt Akky, but it's rather difficult—She's a terrific enthusiast and I'm sure—"

"If I could have stopped her comin', Sam, I would. She's a pest."

"Oh, surely—"

"Who's this, I wonder?" Dulcie intervened.

A car was labouring up the hill in bottom gear under a hard drive and hooting vigorously. They heard it pull up outside the gateway into the courtyard.

"Funny!" Dulcie said after a pause. "Nobody's come in. Fancy!"

She was prevented from any further speculation by a

general stir in the little crowd. Through the rear entrance came Dr. Otterly with his fiddle. There was a round of applause, but the hand-clapping was lost in the night air.

Beyond the wall, men's voices were raised suddenly and apparently in excitement. Dr. Otterly stopped short, looked back and returned through the archway.

"Doctor's too eager," said a voice in the crowd. There was a ripple of laughter through which a single voice beyond the wall could be heard shouting something indistinguishable. A clock above the old stables very sweetly tolled nine. Then Dr. Otterly returned and this time, after a few preliminary scrapes, struck up on his fiddle.

The air for the Five Sons had never been lost. It had jigged down through time from one Mardian fiddler to another, acquiring an ornament here, an improvisation there, but remaining essentially itself. Nobody had rediscovered it, nobody had put it in a collection. Like the dance itself it had been protected by the commonplace character of the village and the determined reticence of generation after generation of performers. It was a good tune and well suited to its purpose. After a preliminary phrase or two it ushered in the Whiffler.

Through the archway came a blackamoor with a sword. He had bells on his legs and wore white trousers with a kind of kilt over them. His face was perfectly black and a dark cap was on his head. He leapt and pranced and jingled, making complete turns as he did so and "whiffling" his sword so that it sang in the cold air. He slashed at the thistles and brambles and they fell before him. Round and round the Mardian Stone he pranced and jingled while his blade whistled and glinted. He was the purifier, the acolyte, the precursor.

"That's why Ernie wouldn't clear the thistles," Dame Alice muttered.

"Oh, *dear!*" Dulcie said, "aren't they *queer?* Why not *say* so? I *ask* you." She stared dimly at the jigging blackamoor. "All the same," she said, "this can't be Ernie. He's the Fool now. Who is it, Sam? The boy?"

"Impossible to tell in that rig," said the Rector. "I would have thought from his exuberance that it *was* Ernie."

"Here come the rest of the Sons."

There were four of them dressed exactly like the Whiffler. They ran out into the torchlight and joined him. They left their swords by Dr. Otterly and with the Whiffler performed the Mardian Morris. Thump and jingle: down came their boots with a strike at the frozen earth. They danced without flourish but with the sort of concentration that amounts to style. When they finished there was a round of applause, sounding desultory in the open courtyard. They took off their pads of bells. The Whiffler threaded a scarlet cord through the tip of his sword. His brothers, whose swords were already adorned with these cords, took them up in their black hands. They waited in a strange rococo group against the snow. The fiddler's tune changed. Now came "Crack," the Hobby-Horse, and the Betty. Side by side they pranced. The Betty was a man-woman, black-faced, masculine to the waist and below the waist fantastically feminine. Its great hooped skirt hung from the armpits and spread like a bell-tent to the ground. On the head was a hat, half topper, half floral toque. There was a man's glove on the right hand and a woman's on the left, a boot on the left foot, a slipper on the right.

"Really," the Rector said, "how Ralph can contrive to make such an appalling-looking object of himself, I do not know."

"Here comes 'Crack.' "

"You don't need to tell us who's comin', Dulcie," Dame Alice said irritably. "We can see."

"I always like 'Crack,' " Dulcie said serenely.

The iron head, so much more resembling that of a fantastic bird than a horse, snapped its jaws. Beneath it the great canvas drum dipped and swayed. Its skirts left a trail of hot tar on the ground. The rat-like tail stuck up through the top of the drum and twitched busily.

"Crack" darted at the onlookers. The girls screamed unconvincingly and clutched each other. They ran into the arms of their boy friends and out again. Some of the boys held their girls firm and let the swinging canvas daub them with tar. Some of the girls, affecting not to notice how close "Crack" had come, allowed themselves to be tarred. They then put up a great show of indignation and astonishment. It was the age-old pantomime of courtship.

"Oh, *do* look, Aunt Akky! He's chasing the Campion girl and she's really *running*," cried Dulcie.

Camilla was indeed running with a will. She saw the great barbaric head snap its iron beak at her and she smelt hot tar. Both the dream and the reality of the previous night were repeated. The crowd round her seemed to have drawn itself back into a barrier. The cylindrical body of the horse swung up. She saw troused legs and a pair of black hands. It was unpleasant and, moreover, she had no mind to be daubed with tar. So she ran and "Crack" ran after her. There was a roar of voices.

Camilla looked for some way of escape. Torchlight played over a solid wall of faces that were split with laughter.

"No!" shouted Camilla. "No!"

The thing came thundering after her. She ran blindly and as fast as she could across the courtyard and straight into the arms of Ralph Stayne in his preposterous disguise.

"It's all right, my darling," Ralph said. "Here I am." Camilla clung to him, panting and half crying.

"Oh, I *see*," said Dulcie Mardian, watching.

"You don't see anythin' of the sort," snapped her great-aunt. "Does she, Sam?"

"I hope not," said the Rector worriedly.

"Here's the Fool," said Dulcie, entirely unperturbed.

iii

The Fool came out of the shadows at a slow jog-trot. On his appearance "Crack" stopped his horseplay and moved up to the near exit. The Betty released a flustered Camilla.

"Aunt Akky, do look at the German woman—"

"Shut up, Dulcie. I'm watchin' the Fool."

The Fool, who is also the Father, jogged quietly round the courtyard. He wore wide pantaloons tied in at the ankle and a loose tunic. He wore also his cap fashioned from a flayed rabbit with the head above his mask and the ears flopping. He carried a bladder on a stick. His head was masked. The mask was an old one, very roughly made from a painted bag that covered his head and was gathered and tied under his chin. It had holes cut for eyes and was painted with a great dolorous grin.

Dr. Otterly had stopped fiddling. The Fool made his round in silence. He trotted in contracting circles, a course that brought him finally to the dolmen. This he struck three times with the bladder. All his movements were quite undramatic and without any sense, as Camilla noted, of style. But they were not ineffectual. When he had completed his course, the Five Sons ran into the centre of the courtyard. "Crack" re-appeared through the back exit. The Fool waited beside the dolmen.

Then Dr. Otterly, after a warning scrape, broke with a flourish into the second dance: the Sword Dance of the Five Sons.

Against the snow and flames and sparks they made a fine picture, all black-faced and black-handed, down-beating with their feet as if the ground was a drum for their dancing. They made their ring of steel, each holding another's sword by its red ribbon, and they wove their knot and held it up before the Fool, who peered at it as if it were a looking-glass. "Crack" edged closer. Then the Fool made his undramatic gesture and broke the knot.

"Ernie's doing quite well," said the Rector.

The dance and its sequel were twice repeated. On the first repetition, the Fool made as if he wrote something and then offered what he had written to his Sons. On the second repetition, "Crack" and the Betty came forward. They stood to left and right of the Fool, who, this time, was behind the Mardian dolmen. The Sons, in front of it, again held up their knot of locked swords. The Fool leant across the stone and put his head within the knot. The Hobby-Horse moved in behind him and stood motionless, looking, in that flickering light, like some monstrous idol. The fiddling stopped dead. The onlookers were very still. Beyond the wall the bonfire crackled.

Then the Sons drew their swords suddenly with a great crash. Horridly the rabbit's head dropped on the stone. A girl in the crowd screamed. The Fool slithered down behind the stone and was hidden.

"Really," Dulcie said, "it makes one feel quite odd, don't you think, Aunt Akky?"

A kind of interlude followed. The Betty went round with an object like a ladle into which everybody dropped a coin.

"Where's it goin'?" Dame Alice asked.

"The belfry roof, this year," the Rector replied and such is the comfortable attitude of the Church towards the remnants of fertility ritual-dancing in England that neither he nor anybody else thought this at all remarkable.

Ralph, uplifted perhaps by his encounter with Camilla, completed his collection and began a spirited impromptu. He flirted his vast crinoline and made up to several yokels in his audience. He chucked one under the chin, tried to get another to dance with him and threw his crinoline over a third. He was a natural comedian and his antics raised a great roar of laughter. With an elaborate pantomime, laying his finger on his lips, he tiptoed up behind the Whiffler, who stood swinging his sword by its red ribbon. Suddenly Ralph snatched it away. The Hobby-Horse, who was behind the dolmen, gave a shrill squeak and went off. The

Betty ran and the Whiffler gave chase. These two grotesques darted here and there, disappeared behind piles of stones and flickered uncertainly through the torchlight. Ralph gave a series of falsetto screams, dodged and feinted and finally hid behind a broken-down buttress near the rear entrance. The Whiffler plunged past him and out into the dark. One of the remaining Sons now came forward and danced a short formal solo with great exactness and spirit.

"That'll be Dan," said Dulcie Mardian.

"He cuts a very pretty caper," said the Rector. From behind the battlemented wall at the back a great flare suddenly burst upwards with a roar and a crackle.

"They're throwin' turpentine on the fire," Dame Alice said. "Or somethin'."

"Very naughty," said the Rector.

Ralph, who had slipped out by the back entrance, now returned through an archway near the house, having evidently run round behind the battlements. Presently, the Whiffler, again carrying his sword, re-appeared through the back entrance and joined his brothers. The solo completed, the Five Sons then performed their final dance. "Crack" and the Betty circled in the background, now approaching and now retreating from the Mardian dolmen.

"This," said Dulcie, "is where the Old Man rises from the dead. Isn't it, Sam?"

"Ah—yes. Yes. Very strange," said the Rector, broad-mindedly.

"Exciting."

"Well—" he said uneasily.

The Five Sons ended their dance with a decisive stamp. They stood with their backs to their audience pointing their swords at the Mardian dolmen. The audience clapped vociferously.

"He rises up from behind the stone, doesn't he, Aunt Akky?"

But nobody rose up from behind the Mardian dolmen. Instead, there was an interminable pause. The swords wavered, the dancers shuffled awkwardly and at last lowered their weapons. The jigging tune had petered out.

"Look, Aunt Akky. Something's gone wrong."

"Dulcie, for God's sake, hold your tongue."

"My dear Aunt Akky."

"Be quiet, Sam."

One of the Sons, the soloist, moved away from his fellows. He walked alone to the Mardian dolmen and round it. He stood quite still and looked down. Then he jerked his head. His brothers moved in. They formed a semicircle and they too looked down: five glistening and contemplative blackamoors. At last their faces lifted and turned, their eyeballs showed white and they stared at Dr. Otterly.

His footfall was loud and solitary in the quietude that had come upon the courtyard.

The Sons made way for him. He stooped, knelt, and in so doing disappeared behind the stone. Thus, when he spoke, his voice seemed disembodied, like that of an echo.

"Get back! All of you. Stand away!"

The Five Sons shuffled back. The Hobby-Horse and the Betty, a monstrous couple, were motionless.

Dr. Otterly rose from behind the stone and walked forward. He looked at Dame Alice where she sat enthroned. He was like an actor coming out to bow to the Royal Box, but he trembled and his face was livid. When he had advanced almost to the steps he said loudly: "Everyone must go. At once. There has been an accident." The crowd behind him stirred and murmured.

"What's up?" Dame Alice demanded. "What accident? Where's the Guiser?"

"Miss Mardian, will you take your aunt indoors? I'll follow as soon as I can."

"I will if she'll come," said Dulcie, practically.

"Please, Dame Alice."

"I want to know what's up."

"And so you shall."

"Who is it?"

"The Guiser. William Andersen."

"But he wasn't dancing," Dulcie said foolishly. "He's ill."

"Is he dead?"

"Yes."

"Wait a bit."

Dame Alice extended her arm and was at once hauled up by Dulcie. She addressed herself to her guests.

"Sorry," she said. "Must 'pologize for askin' you to leave, but as you've heard there's bin trouble. Glad if you'll just go. Now. Quietly. Thankee. Sam, I don't want you."

She turned away and without another word went indoors followed by Dulcie.

The Rector murmured, "But what a shocking thing to happen! And so dreadful for his sons. I'll just go to them, shall I? I suppose it was his heart, poor old boy."

"Do you?" Dr. Otterly asked.

The Rector stared at him. "You look dreadfully ill," he said, and then, "What do you mean? For the love of Heaven, Otterly, what's happened?"

Dr. Otterly opened his mouth but seemed to have some difficulty in speaking.

He and the Rector stared at each other. Villagers still moved across the courtyard and the dancers were still suspended in immobility. It was as if something they all anticipated had not quite happened.

Then it happened.

The Whiffler was on the Mardian dolmen. He had jumped on the stone and stood there, fantastically against the snow. He paddled his feet in ecstasy. His mouth was redly open and he yelled at the top of his voice:

"What price blood for the stone? What price the Old Man's 'ead? Swords be out, chaps, and 'eads be off. What price blood for the stone?"

His sword was in his hand. He whiffled it savagely and then pointed it at someone in the crowd.

"Ax 'er," he shouted. "She knows. She'm the one what done it. Ax 'er."

The stragglers in the crowd parted and fell back from a solitary figure thickly encased in a multiplicity of hand-woven garments.

It was Mrs. Bünz.

CHAPTER V Aftermath

"HAS it ever occurred to you," Alleyn said, "that the progress of a case is rather like a sort of thaw? Look at that landscape."

He wiped the mist from their carriage window. Sergeants Bailey and Thompson, who had been taking gear from the rack, put on their hats, sat down again and stared out with the air of men to whom all landscapes are alike. Mr. Fox, with slightly raised brows, also contemplated the weakly illuminated and dripping prospect.

"Like icing," he said, "running off a wedding cake. Not that, I suppose, it ever does."

"Such are the pitfalls of analogy. All the same, there is an analogy. When you go out on our sort of job everything's covered with a layer of cagey blamelessness. No sharp outlines anywhere. The job itself sticks up like that partial ruin on the skyline over there, but even the job tends to look different under snow. Blurred."

Mr. Fox effaced a yawn. "So we wait for the thaw!"

"With luck, Br'er Fox, we produce it. This is our station."

They alighted on a platform bordered with swept-up heaps of grey slush. The train, which had made an unorthodox halt for them, pulled out at once. They were left with a stillness broken by the drip of melting snow. The outlines of eaves, gutters, rails, leaves, twigs slid copiously into the water.

A man in a belted mackintosh, felt hat and gumboots came forward.

"This'll be the Super," said Fox.

"Good morning, gentlemen," said the man.

He was a big chap with a serio-comic face that, when it tried to look grave, only succeeded in achieving an expression of mock solemnity. His name was Yeo Carey and he had a roaring voice.

The ceremonial handshaking completed, Superintendent Carey led the way out of the little station. A car waited, its wheels fitted with a suit of chains.

"Still need them, up to Mardians'," Carey said when they were all on board. "They're not thawed out proper thereabouts; though, if she keeps mild this way, they'll ease off considerably come nightfall."

"You must have had a nice turn-up with this lot," Fox said, indicating the job in hand.

"Terrible. Terrible! I was the first to say it was a matter for you gentlemen. We're not equipped for it and no use pretending we are. First capital crime hereabouts, I do believe, since they burned Betsey Andersen for a witch."

"What!" Alleyn ejaculated.

"That's a matter of three hundred years as near as wouldn't matter and no doubt the woman never deserved it."

"Did you say 'Andersen'?"

"Yes, sir, I did. There've been Andersens at Copse Forge for quite a spell in South Mardian."

"I understand," Fox said sedately, "the old man who was decapitated was called Andersen."

"So he was, then. He was one of them, was William."

"I think," Alleyn said, "we'll get you to tell us the whole story, Carey. Where are we going?"

"Up to East Mardian, sir. The Chief Constable thought you'd like to be as near as possible to the scene of the crime. They've got rooms for you at the Green Man. It's a case of two rooms for four men, seeing there's a couple of lodgers there already. But as they might be witnesses, we didn't reckon to turn them out."

"Fair enough. Where's your station, then?"

"Up to Yowford. Matter of two mile. The Chief Constable's sent you this car with his compliments. I've only got a motor-bike at the station. He axed me to say he'd have come hisself but is bedbound with influenza. We're anxious to help, of course. Every way we can."

"Everything seems to be laid on like central heating," Alleyn was careful to observe. He pointed to the building on the skyline that they had seen from the train. "What's that, up there?"

"Mardian Castle, Mr. Alleyn. Scene of crime."

"It looks like a ruin."

"So 'tis, then, in parts. Present residence is on 'tother side of those walls. Now, sir, shall I begin, to the best of my ability, to make my report or shall we wait till we're stationary in the pub? A matter of a few minutes only and I can then give my full attention to my duty and refer in order to my notes."

Alleyn agreed that this would be much the best course, particularly as the chains were making a great noise and the driver's task was evidently an exacting one. They churned along a deep lane, turned a corner and looked down on South Mardian: squat, unpicturesque, unremarkable and as small as a village could be. As they approached, Alleyn saw that, apart from its church and parsonage, it contained only one building that was not a cottage. This was a minute shop. BEGGS FOR EVERYTHING was painted vaingloriously in faded blue letters across the front. They drove past the gateway to Mardian Castle. A police constable with his motor-bicycle nearby stood in front of it.

"Guarding," explained Carey, "against sight-seers," and he waved his arm at the barren landscape.

As they approached the group of trees at the far end of the village, Carey pointed it out. "The Copse," he said, "and a parcel further on behind it, Copse Forge, where the deceased is assembled, Mr. Alleyn, in a lean-to shed, it being his own property."

"I see."

"We turn right, however, which I will now do, to the hamlet of East Mardian. There, sir, is your pub, ahead and on the right."

As they drove up, Alleyn glanced at the sign, a pleasant affair painted with a foliated green face.

"That's an old one, isn't it?" he said. "Although it looks as if it's been rather cleverly touched up."

"So it has, then. By a lady at present resident in the pub by the name of Buns."

"Mrs. Buns, the baker's wife," Alleyn murmured involuntarily.

"No, sir. Foreign. And requiring, by all 'counts, to be looked into."

"Dear me!" said Alleyn mildly.

They went into the pub leaving Bailey and Thompson to deal with their luggage. Superintendent Carey had arranged for a small room behind the private bar to be put at their disposal. "Used to be the missus's parlour," he explained, "but she's no further use for it."

"Are you sure?"

"Dead these five years."

"Fair enough," said Alleyn.

Trixie was there. She had lit a roaring fire and now put a dish of bacon and eggs, a plate of bread and cheese and a bottle of pickled onions on the table.

"Hour and a half till dinner," she said, "and you'm no doubt starved for a bite after travelling all night. Will you take something?"

They took three pints, which were increased to five on the arrival of Bailey and Thompson. They helped themselves to the hunks of food and settled down, finally, to Superintendent Carey's report.

It was admirably succinct.

Carey, it appeared, had been present at the Dance of the Five Sons. He had walked over from Yowford, more out of habit than enthusiasm and not uninfluenced, Alleyn gathered, by the promise of Dame Alice's Sword Wednesday Punch.

Like everybody else, he had heard rumours of the Guiser's indisposition and had supposed that the Fool was played by Ernie. When he heard Dr. Otterly's announcement, he concluded that the Guiser had, after all, performed his part and that on his mock decapitation, which Mr. Carey described vividly, he had died of a heart attack.

When, however, the Whiffler (now clearly recognizable as Ernie) had made his appalling announcement from the Mardian dolmen, Carey had gone forward and spoken to Dr. Otterly and the Rector. At the same time, Ernie's brothers had hauled him off the stone. He then, without warning, collapsed into a fit from which he was recovered by Dr. Otterly and, from then onwards, refused to speak to anybody.

After a word with the Doctor, Carey had ordered the stragglers off the place and had then, and not till then, walked round the dolmen and seen what lay on the ground beyond it.

At this point Carey, quite obviously, had to take a grip of himself. He finished his pint and squared his shoulders.

"I've seen things, mind," he said. "I had five years of it on active service and I didn't reckon to be flustered. But this flustered me, proper. Partly, no doubt, it was the way he was got up. Like a clown with the tunic thing pulled up. It'd have been over his head if—well, never mind. He didn't paint his face but he had one of these masks. It ties on like a bag and it hadn't fallen off. So he looked, if you can follow me, gentlemen, like a kind of doll that the head had come off of. There was the body, sort of doubled up, and there was the head two feet away, grinning, which was right nasty, until Rector took the bag off, which he did, saying it wasn't decent. And there was Old Guiser's face. And Rector put, as you may say, the pieces together, and said a prayer over them. I beg pardon, Mr. Alleyn?"

"Nothing. Go on."

"Now, Ernie Andersen had made this statement, which I have repeated to the best of my memory, about the German lady having 'done it.' I came out from behind where the remains was and there, to my surprise, the German lady stood. Kind of bewildered, if you can understand, she seemed to be, and axing *me* what had happened. 'What is it? What has happened? Is he ill?' she said.

"Now, Mr. Alleyn, this chap, Ernie Andersen, is not what you'd call right smart. He's a bit touched. Not simple exactly but not right. Takes funny turns. He was in a terrible state, kind of half frightened and half pleased with himself. *Why* he said what he did about Mrs. Buns, I can't make out, but *how* a lady of, say, fifty-seven or so could step out of the crowd and cut the head off a chap at one blow in full view of everybody and step back again without being noticed takes a bit of explaining. Still, there it was. I took a statement from her. She was very much put about."

"Well she might be."

"Just so. Denied knowing anything about it, of course. It seems she was latish getting to the castle. She's bought a new car from Simmy-Dick Begg up to Yowford and couldn't start it at first. Over-choked would be my bet. Everybody in the pub had gone early, Trixie, the barmaid, and the potboy having offered to help the Dame's maids. Well, Mrs. Buns started her car at last and, when she gets to the corner, who should she see but Old Guiser himself."

"Old Guiser?"

"That's what we called William Andersen hereabouts. There he was, seemingly, standing in the middle of the lane shaking his fist and swearing something ghastly. Mrs. Buns stops and offers a lift. He accepts, but with a bad grace, because, as everybody knows, he's taken a great unliking for Mrs. Buns."

"Why?"

"On account of her axing questions about Sword Wednesday. The man was in mortal dread of it getting made kind of public and fretted accordingly."

"A purist, was he?"

"That may be the word for it. He doan't pass a remark of any kind going up to the castle and, when she gets there, he bolts out of the car and goes round behind the ruins to where the others was getting ready to begin. She says she just walked in and stood in the crowd, which, to my mind, is no doubt what the woman did. I noticed her there myself, I remember, during the performance!"

"Did you ask her if she knew why Ernie Andersen said she'd done it?"

"I did, then. She says she reckons he's turned crazy-headed with shock, which is what seems to be the general view."

"Why was the Guiser so late starting?"

"Ah! Now! He'd been sick, had the Guiser. He had a bad heart and during the day he hadn't felt too clever. Seems Dr. Otterly, who played the fiddle for them, was against the old chap doing it at all. The boys (I call them boys but Daniel's sixty if he's a day) say their father went and lay down during the day and left word not to be disturbed. They'd fixed it up that Ernie would come back and drive his dad up in an old station-waggon they've got there, leaving it till the last so's not to get him too tired."

"Ernie again," Alleyn muttered.

"Well, axackly so, Mr. Alleyn. And when Ernie returns it's with a note from his dad which he found pinned to his door, that being the Old Guiser's habit, to say he can't do it and Ernie had better. So they send the note in to Dr. Otterly, who is having dinner with the Dame."

"What?" Alleyn said, momentarily startled by this apparent touch of transatlantic realism. "Oh, I see, yes. Dame Alice Mardian?"

"Yes, sir."

"Have you got the note?"

"The Doctor put it in his pocket, luckily, and I have."

"Good."

Carey produced the old-fashioned billhead with its pencilled message: *Cant mannage it young Ern will have to. W.A.*

"It's his writing all right," he said. "No doubt of it."

"And are we to suppose he felt better, and decided to play his part after all and hitch-hiked with the lady?"

"That's what his sons reckon. It's what they say he told them when he turned up."

"Do they, now!"

"Pointing out that there wasn't much time to say *anything*. Ernie was dressed up for his dad's part—it's what they call the Fool—so he had to get out of his clothes quick and dress up for his own part, and Daniel's boy, who was going to do Ernie's part, was left looking silly. So he went round and joined the onlookers. And he confirms the story. He says that's right, that's what happened when the old chap turned up."

"And it's certain the old man did dance throughout the show?"

"Must be, Mr. Alleyn, mustn't it? Certain sure. There they were, five Sons, a Fiddler, a Betty, a Hoss and a Fool. The Sons were the real sons all right. They wiped the muck off their faces while I was taking over. The Betty was the Dame's great-nephew: young Mr. Stayne. He's a lawyer from Biddlefast and staying with Parson, who's his father. The Hoss, they call it 'Crack,' was Simmy-Dick Begg, who has the garage up to Yowford. They all took off their silly truck there and then in my presence as soon's they had the wit to do so. So the Fool must have been the Guiser all the time, Mr. Alleyn. There's nobody left but him to be it. We've eight chaps ready to swear he dressed himself up for it and went out with the rest."

"And stayed there in full view until—"

Mr. Carey took a long pull at his tankard, set it down, wiped his mouth and clapped his palm on the table.

"There you are!" he declaimed. "Until they made out in their dance, or play, or whatever you like to call it, that they were cutting his head off. Cripes!" Mr. Carey added in a changed voice, "I can see him as if it was now. Silly clown's mask sticking through the knot of swords and then—k-r-r-ring—they've drawn their swords. Down drops the rabbit's head and down goes Guiser, out of sight behind the stone. You wouldn't credit it, would you? In full view of up to sixty persons."

"Are you suggesting—? No," Alleyn said, "you can't be."

"I was going to ask you, Super," Fox said. "You don't mean to say you think they may actually have beheaded the old chap then and there!"

"How could they!" Carey demanded angrily, as if Fox and Alleyn had themselves advanced this theory. "Ask yourself, Mr. Fox. The idea's comical. Of course they didn't. The thing is: when did they? If they did."

"They?" Alleyn asked.

"Well, now, no. No. It was done, so the Doctor says, and so a chap can see for himself if he's got the stomach to look, by one weapon with one stroke by one man."

"What about their swords? I'll see them, of course, but what are they like?"

"Straight. About two foot long. Wooden handle one end and a hole 'tother through which they stick a silly-looking bit of red cord."

"Sharp?"

"Blunt as a backside, all but one."

"Which one?" asked Fox.

"Ernie's," Alleyn said. "I'll bet."

"And you're dead right, sir. Ernie's it is and so sharp's a razor still, never mind how he whiffled down the thistles."

"So we are forced to ask ourselves if Ernie could have whiffled his old man's head off?"

"*And* we answer ourselves, no, he danged well couldn't of. For why? For because, after his old man dropped behind the stone, there was Ernie doing a comic act with the Betty: that is, Mr. Ralph Stayne, as I was telling you. Mr. Ralph, having taken up a collection, snatched Ernie's sword and they had a sort of chase round the courtyard and in and out through the gaps in the back wall. Ernie didn't get his sword back till Mr. Ralph give it him. After that, Dan Andersen did a turn on his own. He always does. You could tell it was Dan anyway on account of him being bowlegged. Then the Five Sons did another dance and that was when the Old Man should have risen up and didn't and there we are."

"What was the Hobby-Horse doing all this time?"

"Cavorting round chasing the maids. Off and on."

"And this affair," Fox said, "this man-woman-what-have-you-Betty, who was the clergyman's son, he'd collared the sharp sword, had he?"

"Yes, Mr. Fox, he had. And was swiping it round and playing the goat with it."

"Did he go near the stone?" Alleyn asked.

"Well—yes, I reckon he did. When Ernie was chasing him. No doubt of it. But further than that—well, it's just not believable," said Carey and added, "He must have given the sword back to Ernie because, later on, Ernie had got it again. There's nothing at all on the sword but smears of sap from the plants Ernie swiped off. Which seems to show it hadn't been wiped on anything."

"Certainly," said Alleyn. "Jolly well observed, Carey."

Mr. Carey gave a faint simper.

"Did any of them look behind the stone after the old man had fallen down?" Alleyn asked.

"Mr. Ralph—that's the Betty—was standing close up when he fell behind it and reckons he just slid down and lay. There's a kind of hollow there, as you'll see, and it was no doubt in shadow. Two of them came prancing back to the stone during the last dance—first Simmy-Dick and then Mr. Ralph—and they both think he was laying there then. Simmy-Dick couldn't see very clear because his face is in the neck of the horse and the body of the thing hides any object that's nearby on the ground. But he saw the whiteness of the Fool's clothing in the hollow, he says. Mr. Ralph says he did too, without sort of paying much attention."

"The head—?"

"They never noticed. They never noticed another thing till he was meant to resurrect and didn't. Then

Dan went to see what was wrong and called up his brothers. He says—it's a funny sort of thing *to* say, but—he says he thought, at first, it was some kind of joke and someone had put a dummy there and the head had come off. But, of course," Carey said, opening his extremely blue eyes very wide, "it was no such matter."

There was a long silence. The fire crackled; in a distant part of the pub somebody turned up the volume of a wireless set and turned it down again.

"Well," Alleyn said, "there's the story and very neatly reported if I may say so, Carey. Let's have a look at the place."

ii

The courtyard at Mardian Castle looked dismal in the thaw. The swept-up snow, running away into dirty water, was much trampled, the courtyard itself was greasy and the Mardian dolmen a lump of wet rock standing on two other lumps. Stone and mud glistened alike in sunlight that merely lent a kind of pallor to the day and an additional emphasis to the north wind. The latter whistled through the slits in the old walls with all the venom of the arrows they had originally been designed to accommodate. Eight burnt-out torches on stakes stood in a semi-circle roughly following that of the wall but set some twelve feet inside it. In the middle of this scene stood a police sergeant with his mackintosh collar turned up and his shoulders hunched. He was presented by Carey—"Sergeant Obby."

Taking in the scene, Alleyn turned from the semicircle of old wall to the hideous façade of the Victorian house. He found himself being stared at by a squarish wooden old lady behind a ground-floor window. A second lady, sandy and middle-aged, stood behind her.

"Who's that?" he asked.

"The Dame," said Carey. "And Miss Mardian."

"I suppose I ought to make a polite noise."

"She's not," Carey muttered, "in a wonderful good mood to-day."

"Never mind."

"And Miss Mardian's—well—er—well, she's just not right smart, Mr. Alleyn."

"Like Ernie?"

"No, sir. Not exactly. It may be," Carey ventured, "on account of in-breeding, which is what's been going on hot and strong in the Mardian family for a great time. Not that there's anything like that about the Dame, mind. She's ninety-four and a proper masterpiece."

"I'd better try my luck. Here goes."

He walked past the window, separated from the basilisk glare by two feet of air and a pane of glass. As he mounted the steps between dead braziers half full of wet ash, the door was opened by Dulcie.

Alleyn said, "Miss Mardian? I wonder if I may have two words with Dame Alice Mardian?"

"Oh, dear!" Dulcie said. "I don't honestly know if you can. I expect I ought to remember who you are, oughtn't I, but with so many new people in the county these days it's a bit muddly. Ordinarily I'm sure Aunt Akky would love to see you. She adores visitors. But this morning she's awfully upset and says she won't talk to anybody but policemen."

"I am a policeman."

"Really? How very peculiar. You are sure," Dulcie added, "that you are not just pretending to be one in order to find out about the Mardian Morris and all that?"

"Quite sure. Here's my card."

"Goodness! Well, I'll ask Aunt Akky."

As she forgot to shut the door Alleyn heard the conversation. "It's a man who says he's a policeman, Aunt Akky, and here's his card. He's a gent."

"I won't stomach these filthy 'breviations."

"Sorry, Aunt Akky."

" 'Any case you're talkin' rot. Show him in."

So Alleyn was admitted and found her staring at his card.

" 'Mornin' to yer," said Dame Alice. "Sit down."

He did so.

"This is a pretty kettle-of-fish," she said. "Ain't it?"

"Awful."

"What are you, may I ask? 'Tective?"

It wouldn't have surprised him much if she'd asked if he were a Bow Street Runner.

"Yes," he said. "A plain-clothes detective from Scotland Yard."

"Superintendent?" she read, squinting at the card.

"That's it."

"Ha! Are you goin' to be quick about this? Catch the feller?"

"I expect we shall."

"What'd yer want to see me for?"

"To apologize for making a nuisance of myself, to say I hope you'll put up with us and to ask you, at the most, six questions."

She looked at him steadily over the top of her glasses.

"Blaze away," she said at last.

"You sat on the steps there, last night during the performance."

"Certainly."

"What step exactly?"

"Top. Why?"

"The top. So you had a pretty good view. Dame Alice, could William Andersen, after the mock killing, have left the courtyard without being seen?"

"No."

"Not under cover of the last dance of the Five Sons?"

"No."

"Not if he crawled out?"

"No."

"As he lay there could he have been struck without your noticing?"

"No."

"No?"

"No."

"Could his body have been brought in and put behind the stone without the manoeuvre attracting your attention?"

"No."

"You're sure?"

"Yes."

He looked at Dulcie, who hovered uncertainly near the door. "You were with Dame Alice, Miss Mardian. Do you agree with what she says?"

"Oh, yes," Dulcie said a little vaguely and added, "Rather!" with a misplaced show of enthusiasm.

"Was anyone else with you?"

"Sam," Dulcie said in a hurry.

"Fat lot of good that is, Dulcie. She means the Rector, Sam Stayne, who's my great-nephew-in-law. Bit of a milksop."

"Right. Thank you so much. We'll bother you as little as possible. It was kind of you to see me."

Alleyn got up and made her a little bow. She held out her hand. "Hope you find," she said as he shook it.

Dulcie, astonished, showed him out.

There were three chairs in the hall that looked as if they didn't belong there. They had rugs safety-pinned over them. Alleyn asked Dulcie if these were the chairs they had sat on and, learning that they were, got her startled permission to take one of them out again.

He put it on the top step, sat in it and surveyed the courtyard. He was conscious that Dame Alice, at the drawing-room window, surveyed him.

From here, he could see over the top of the dolmen to within about two feet of its base and between its standing legs. An upturned box stood on the horizontal stone and three others, which he could just see, on the ground beyond and behind it. The distance from the dolmen to the rear archway in the old semi-circular wall—the archway that had served as an entrance and exit for the performers—was perhaps twenty-five feet. The other openings into the courtyard were provided at the extremities of the old wall by two further archways that joined it to the house. Each of these was about twenty feet distant from the dolmen.

There was, on the air, a tang of dead fire and, through the central archway at the back, Alleyn could see a patch of seared earth, damp now, but bearing the scar of heat.

Fox, who with Carey, Thompson, Bailey and the policeman was looking at the dolmen, glanced up at his chief.

"You have to come early," he remarked, "to get the good seats."

Alleyn grinned, replaced his chair in the hall and picked up a crumpled piece of damp paper. It was one of last night's programmes. He read it through with interest, put it in his pocket and went down into the courtyard.

"It rained in the night, didn't it, Carey?"

"Mortal hard. Started soon after the fatality. I covered up the stone and the place where he lay, but that was the best we could do."

"And with a team of morris-men, if that's what you call them, galumphing like baby elephants over the terrain there wouldn't be much hope anyway. Let's have a look, shall we, Obby?"

The sergeant removed the inverted box from the top of the dolmen. Alleyn examined the surface of the stone.

"Visible prints where Ernie stood on it," he said. "Rubber soles. It had a thin coat of rime, I should think, at the time. Hullo! What's this, Carey?"

He pointed a long finger at a small darkness in the grain of the stone. "Notice it? What is it?"

Before Carey could answer there was a vigorous tapping on the drawing-room window. Alleyn turned in time to see it being opened by Dulcie evidently under orders from her great-aunt, who, from within, leant forward in her chair, shouted, "If you want to know what that is, it's blood," and leant back again.

"How do you know?" Alleyn shouted in return. He had decided that his only hope with Dame Alice was to meet her on her own ground. "What blood?"

"Goose's. One of mine. Head cut off yesterday afternoon and left on the stone."

"Good Lord!"

"You may well say so. Guess who did it."

"Ernie?" Alleyn asked involuntarily.

"How yer know?"

"I guessed. Dame Alice, where's the body?"

"In the pot."

"Damn!"

"Why?"

"It doesn't matter."

"Shut the window, Dulcie."

Before Dulcie had succeeded in doing so, they heard Dame Alice say, "Ask that man to dinner. He's got brains."

"You've made a hit, Mr. Alleyn," said Fox.

Carey said, "My oath!"

"Did you know about this decapitated bird?"

"First I heard of it. It'll be one of that gang up on the hill there."

"Near the bulls?" Fox asked sombrely.

"That's right. You want to watch them geese, Mr. Fox," the sergeant said, "they so savage as lions and tricksy as snakes. I've been minded myself, off and on this morning, to slaughter one and all."

"I wonder," Alleyn said, "if it *was* Ernie. Get a shot of the whole dolmen, will you, Thompson, and some details of the top surface."

Sergeant Thompson moved in with his camera and Alleyn walked round to the far side of the dolmen.

"What," he asked, "are these black stains all over the place? Tar?"

"That's right, sir," Obby said, "off of old 'Crack's' skirts."

Carey explained. "Good Lord!" Alleyn said mildly and turned to the area behind the dolmen.

The upturned boxes that they had used to cover the ground here were bigger. Alleyn and Fox lifted them carefully and stood away from the exposed area. It was a shallow depression into which had collected a certain amount of the fine gravel that had originally been spread over the courtyard. The depression lay at right angles to the dolmen. It was six feet long and shelved up to the level of the surrounding area. At the end farthest from the dolmen there was a dark viscous patch, about four inches in diameter, overlying a little drift of gravel. A further patch, larger, lay about a foot from it, nearer the dolmen and still in the hollow.

"You know, Carey," Alleyn said under his breath and out of the sergeant's hearing, "he should never have been moved: never."

Carey, scarlet-faced, said loudly, "I know's well as the next man, sir, the remains didn't ought to have been shifted. But shifted they were before us chaps could raise a finger to stop it. Parson comes in and says, 'It's not decent as it is,' and, with 'is own 'ands, takes off mask and lays out the pieces tidy-like while Obby, 'ere, and I were still ordering back the crowd."

"You were here too, Sergeant?"

"Oh, ya-as, Mr. Alleyn. All through."

"And seeing, in a manner of speaking, the damage was done and rain setting in, we put the remains into his own car, which is an old station-waggon. Simmy-Dick and Mr. Stayne gave us a hand. We took them back to the forge. They're in his lean-to coach-house, Mr. Alleyn, locked up proper with a police seal on the door and the only other constable in five mile on duty beside it."

"Yes, yes," Alleyn said. "All right. Now, tell me, Carey, you did actually see how it was before the parson tidied things up, didn't you?"

"I did, then, and not likely to forget it."

"Good. How was it?"

Carey drew the back of his hand across his mouth and looked hard at the shallow depression. "I reckon," he said, "those two patches show pretty clear. One's blood from head and 'tother's blood from trunk."

Fox was squatting above them with a rule in his hands. "Twenty-three inches apart," he said.

"How was the body lying?" Alleyn asked. "Exactly."

"Kind of cramped up and on its left side, sir. Huddled. Knees to chin."

"And the head?"

"That was what was so ghassly," Carey burst out. "'Tother way round."

"Do you mean the crown of the head and not the neck was towards the trunk?"

"Just so, Mr. Alleyn. Still tied up in that there bag thing with the face on it."

"I reckoned," Sergeant Obby ventured, "that it must of been kind of disarranged in the course of the proceedings."

"By the dancers?"

"I reckoned so, sir. Must of been."

"In the final dance, after the mock beheading, did the Five Sons go behind the stone?"

There was a silence. The superintendent and the sergeant eyed each other.

"I don't believe they did, you know, Sarge," Carey said.

"Put it that way, no more don't I, then."

"But the other two. The man-woman and the hobby-horse?"

"They were every which-way," Carey said.

Alleyn muttered, "If they'd come round here they could hardly fail to see what was lying there. What colour were his clothes?"

"Whitish, mostly."

"There you are," Fox said.

"Well, Thompson, get on with it. Cover the area again. When he's finished we'll take specimens of the stains, Fox. In the meantime, what's outside the wall there?"

Carey took him through the rear archway. "They waited out here before the performance started," he said.

It was a bleak enough spot now: an open field that ran up to a ragged spinney and the crest of the hill. On the higher slopes the snow still lay pretty thick, but down near the wall it had melted and, to one side of the archway, there was the great scar left by the bonfire. It ran out from the circular trace of the fire itself in a blackened streak about fourteen feet long.

"And here," Alleyn said pointing his stick at a partially burnt-out drum, lying on its side in the fire-scar, "we have the tar barrel?"

"That's so, Mr. Alleyn. For 'Crack.' "

"Looks as if it caught fire."

"Reckon it might have got overturned when all the skylarking was going on between Mr. Ralph and Ernie. They ran through here. There was a mighty great blaze sprung up about then. The fire might have spread to it."

"Wouldn't the idea be to keep the fire as an extra attraction, though?"

"Maybe they lit it early for warmth. One of them may have got excited-like and poured tar on it."

"Ernie, for instance," Alleyn said patiently, and Carey replied that it was very likely.

"And this?" Alleyn went on. "Look at this, Carey."

Round the burnt-out scar left by the bonfire lay a fringe of green brushwood that had escaped complete destruction. A little inside it, discoloured and deadened by the heat, its wooden handle a mere blackened stump, was a steel blade about eighteen inches long.

"That's a slasher," Alleyn said.

iii

"That's Copse Forge," Carey said. "Stood there a matter of four hundred year and the smith's been an Andersen for as long as can be reckoned."

"Not so profitable," Fox suggested, "nowadays, would it be?"

"Nothing like. Although he gets all the shoeing for the Mardian and adjacent hunts and any other smith's jobs for miles around. Chris has got a mechanic's ticket and does a bit with cars. A big oil company's offered to back them if they convert to a service station. I believe Simmy-Dick Begg's very anxious to run it. The boys like the idea but the Guiser wouldn't have it at any price. There's a main road to be put through, too."

"Do they all work here?" Alleyn asked. "Surely not?"

"No, no. Dan, the eldest, and the twins, Andy and Nat, are on their own. Farming. Chris and Ernie work at the forge. Hullo, that's Dr. Otterly's car. I axed him to be here and the five boys beside. Mr. Ralph and Simmy-Dick Begg are coming up to the pub at two. If that suits, of course."

Alleyn said it did. As they drew up, Dr. Otterly got out of his car and waited for them. His tweed hat was pulled down over his nose and his hands were thrust deep in the pockets of his covert-coat.

He didn't wait to be introduced but came up and looked in at the window of their car.

" 'Morning," he said. "Glad you've managed to get here. 'Morning, Carey. Expect you are, too."

"We're damn' pleased to see *you*," Alleyn rejoined. "It's not every day you get police-officers and a medical man to give what almost amounts to eyewitnesses' evidence of a capital crime."

"There's great virtue in that 'almost,' however," Dr. Otterly said and added, "I suppose you want to have a look at him."

"Please."

"Want me to come?"

"I think so. Don't you, Carey?"

They went through the smithy. There was no fire that morning and no heart in the place. It smelt of cold iron and stale horse-sweat. Carey led the way out by a back door into a yard. Here stood a small ramshackle cottage and, alongside it, the lean-to coach-house.

"He lived in the cottage, did he?" Alleyn asked.

"Chris and Ern keep there. The old chap slept in a little room off the smithy. They all ate in the cottage, however."

"They're in there now," Dr. Otterly said. "Waiting."

"Good," Alleyn said. "They won't have to wait much longer. Will you open up, Carey?"

With some evidence of gratification, Carey broke the seal he had put on the double-doors of the coach-house and opened them wide enough to make an entry.

It was a dark place filled with every imaginable kind of junk, but a space had been cleared in the middle and an improvised bier made up from bóxes and an old door covered by a horse-cloth.

A clean sheet had been laid over the Guiser. When Dr. Otterly turned this down it was a shock, after the conventional decency of the arrangements, to see an old dead man in the dirty dress of a clown. For collar, there was a ragged bloodstained and slashed frill and this had been pulled up to hide the neck. The face was smudged with black on the nose, forehead, cheek bones and chin.

"That's burnt cork," Dr. Otterly said. "From inside his mask, you know. Ernie had put it on over his black make-up when he thought he was going to dance the Fool."

The Guiser's face under these disfigurements was void of expression. The eyes had been closed, but the mouth gaped. The old hands, chapped and furrowed, were crossed heavily over the breastbone. The tunic was patched with bloodstains. And above the Guiser, slung on wooden pins, were the shells of his fellow mummers. "Crack," the Hobby-Horse, was there. Its hinged jaw had dropped as if in burlesque of the head below it. The harness dangled over its flat drum-shaped carcass, which was propped against the wall. Nearby hung the enormous crinoline of the Betty and, above it, as if they belonged to each other, the Guiser's bag-like and dolorous mask, hanging upside down by its strings. It was stained darkly round the strings and also at the other end, at the apex of the scalp. This interested Alleyn immensely. Lower down, caught up on a nail, was the rabbit-cap. Further away hung the clothes and sets of bells belonging to the Five Sons.

From the doorway, where he had elected to remain, Carey said, "We thought best to lock all their gear in here, Mr. Alleyn. The swords are in that sacking there, on the bench."

"Good," Alleyn said.

He glanced up at Fox. "All right," he said, and Fox, using his great hands very delicately, turned down the rag of frilling from the severed neck.

"One swipe," Dr. Otterly's voice said.

"From slightly to the right of front centre to slightly left of back centre, would you say?" Alleyn asked.

"I would." Dr. Otterly sounded surprised. "I suppose you chaps get to know about things."

"I'm glad to say that this sort of thing doesn't come even our way very often. The blow must have fallen above the frill on his tunic and below the strings that tied the bag-mask. Would you say he'd been upright or prone when it happened?"

"Your Home Office man will know better than I about that. If it was done standing I'd say it was by somebody who was just slightly taller than the poor Old Guiser."

"Yes. Was there anybody like that in the team?"

"No. They're all much taller."

"And there you are. Let's have a look at that whiffler, Fox."

Fox went over to the bench. "The whiffler," Carey said from the door, "is rolled up separate. He didn't want to part with it, didn't Ernie."

Fox came back with Ernie's sword, holding it by the red cord that was threaded through the tip. "You can see the stains left by all that green-stuff," he said. "And sharp! You'd be astounded."

"We'd better put Bailey on it for dabs, though I don't fancy there's much future there. What do you think, Dr. Otterly? Could this be the weapon?"

"Without a closer examination of the wound, I wouldn't like to say. It would depend—but, no," Dr. Otterly said, "I can't give an opinion."

Alleyn had turned away and was looking at the garments hanging on the wall. "Tar over everything. On the Betty's skirt, the Sons' trousers and, I suppose, on a good many village maidens' stockings and shoes, to say nothing of their coats."

"It's a cult," Dr. Otterly said.

"Fertility rite?"

"Of course."

"See old Uncle Frazer and all," Alleyn muttered. He turned to the rabbit. "Recently killed and gutted with head left on. Strings on it. What for?"

"He wore it on his head."

"How very undelicious. Why?"

"Helped the decapitation effect. He put his head through the lock of swords, untied the strings and, as the Sons drew the swords, he let the rabbit's head drop. They do it in the Grenoside sword-dance too, I believe. It's quite startling—the effect."

"I daresay. In this case, rather over-shadowed by the subsequent event," Alleyn said drily.

"All right!" Dr. Otterly ejaculated with some violence. "I know it's beastly. All right."

Alleyn glanced at him and then turned to look at "Crack's" harness. "This must weigh a tidy lump. How does he wear it?"

"The head is on a sort of rod. His own head is inside the canvas neck. It was made in the smithy."

"The century before last?"

"Or before that. The body too. It hangs from the yoke. His head goes through a hole into the canvas tube, which has got a sort of window in it. 'Crack's' head is on top again and joined to the yoke by the flexible rod inside the neck. By torchlight it looks quite a thing."

"I believe you," Alleyn said absently. He examined the harness and then turned to the Betty's crinoline. "How does this go on? It's a mountain of a garment."

"It hangs from a kind of yoke too. But, in his case, the arms are free. The frame, as you see, is made of withies, like basket-work. In the old days, there used to be quite a lot of fairly robust fun with the Betty. The chap who was acting her would chase some smaller fellow round the ring and pop the crinoline thing right over him and go prancing off with the little chap hidden under his petticoats, as it were. Sometimes he collared a girl. You can imagine the sort of barracking that went on."

"Heaps of broad bucolic fun," Alleyn said, "was doubtless had by all. It's got a touch of the tar brush too, but not much."

"I expect Ralph kept clear of 'Crack' as well as he could."

"And the Guiser?" Alleyn returned to the bier and removed the sheet completely.

"A little tar on the front of the tunic and"—he stopped—"quite a lot on the hands," he said. "Did he handle the tar barrel do you know?"

"Earlier in the day perhaps. But no. He was out of action, earlier. Does it matter?"

"It might," Alleyn said. "It might matter very much indeed. Then again, not. Have you noticed this fairly recent gash across the palm of his right hand?"

"I saw it done." Dr. Otterly's gaze travelled to the whiffler, which Fox still held by the ribbons. He looked away quickly.

"With that thing," Alleyn asked, "by any chance?"

"Actually, yes."

"How did it happen?"

"It was nothing, really. A bit of a dust-up about it being too sharp. He—ah—he tried to grab it away from—well, from—"

"Don't tell me," Alleyn said. "Ernie."

iv

The shutters were down over the private bar and the room was deserted. Camilla went in and sat by the fire. Since last night she had felt the cold. It was as if some of her own natural warmth had deserted her. When the landlord had driven her and Trixie back to the pub from Mardian Castle, Camilla had shivered so violently that they had given her a scalding toddy and two aspirins and Trixie had put three stone hot-jugs in her bed. Eventually, she had dropped into a doze and was running away again from "Crack." He was the big drum in a band. Somebody beat him with two swords making a sound like a fiddle. His jaws snapped, dreadfully close. She experienced the dream of frustrated escape. His breath was hot on her neck and her feet were leaden. Then there was Ralph, with his arms strapped close about her, saying, "It's all right. I'll take care of you." That was Heaven at first, but even that wasn't quite satisfactory because Ralph was trying to stop her looking at something. In the over-distinct voice of nightmare, he said, "You don't want to watch Ernie because it's not most awfully nice." But Ernie jumped up on the dolmen and shouted at the top of his voice, "What price blood for the stone?" Then all the morris bells began to jingle like an alarm clock and she woke.

Awake, she remembered how Ralph had, in fact, run to where she and Trixie stood and had told them to go to the car at once. That was after Ernie had fainted and Dame Alice had made her announcement. The landlord, Tom Plowman, had gone up to the stone and had been ordered away by Dr. Otterly and Carey. He drove the girls back to the pub and, on the way, told them in great detail what he had seen. He was very excited and pleased with himself for having looked behind the stone. In one of her dreams during the night, Camilla thought he made her look too.

Now she sat by the fire and tried to get a little order into her thoughts. It was her grandfather who had been murdered, dreadfully and mysteriously, and it was her uncle who had exulted and collapsed. She herself, therefore, must be said to be involved. She felt as if she were marooned and deserted. For the first time since the event she was inclined to cry.

The door opened and she turned, her hand over her mouth. "Ralph!" she said.

He came to her quickly and dragged up a chair so that he could sit and hold both her hands.

"You want me now, Camilla," he said, "don't you?"

CHAPTER VI Copse Forge

RALPH had big hands. When they closed like twin shells over Camilla's her own felt imprisoned and fluttery, like birds.

She looked at his eyes and hair, which were black, at his face, which was lean, and at his ears, which were protuberant and, at that moment, scarlet. "I am in love with Ralph," thought Camilla.

She said, "Hullo, you. I thought we'd agreed not to meet again. After last Sunday."

"Thing of the past," Ralph said grandly.

"You promised your father."

"I've told him I consider myself free. Under the circs."

"Ralph," Camilla said, "you mustn't cash in on murder."

"Is that a very kind thing to say?"

"Perhaps it's not. I don't mean I'm not glad to see you—but—well, you know."

"Look," he said, "there are one or two things I've got to know. Important things. I've *got* to know them, Camilla. The first is: are you *terribly* upset about last night? Well, of course you are, but so much upset, I mean, that one just mustn't bother you about anything. Or are you—Oh, God, Camilla, I've never so much as kissed you and I do love you so much."

"Do you? No, never mind. About your first question: I just don't know *how* I feel about Grandfather and that's a fact. As far as it's a personal thing—well, I scarcely even knew him ten days ago. But, since I got here, we've seen quite a lot of each other and—this is what you may find hard to believe—we kind of clicked, Grandfather and I."

Ralph said on an odd inflexion, "You certainly did that," and then looked as if he wished he hadn't.

Camilla, frowning with concentration, unconsciously laced her fingers through his.

"You, of course," she said, "just think of him as a bucolic character. The Old Guiser. Wonderful old boy in his way. Not many left. Didn't have much truck with soap and water. Half of *me* felt like that about him: the Campion half. Smelly old cup-of-tea, it thought. But then I'd see my mother look out of his eyes."

"Of course," he said. "I know."

"Do you? You can't quite know, dear Ralph. You're all-of-a-piece: half Mardian, half Stayne. I'm an alloy."

"You're a terrible old inverted snob," he said fondly, but she paid no attention to this.

"But as for sorrow—personal grief," she was saying, "no. No. *Not* exactly that. It doesn't arise. It's the awful grotesquerie that's so nightmarish. It's like something out of Webster or Marlowe: horror-plus. It gives one the horrors to think of it."

"So you know what happened? Exactly, I mean?"

She made a movement of her head indicating the landlord. "He saw. He told us: Trixie and me."

She felt a stillness in his hands, almost as if he would draw them away, but he didn't do that. "The whole thing!" she exclaimed. "It's so outlandish and sickening and ghastly. The way he was dressed and everything. And then one feels such pity."

"He couldn't have known anything at all about it."

"Are you sure? How can you tell?"

"Dr. Otterly says so."

"And then—worst of all, unthinkably worst—the—what it was—the crime. You see, I can't use the word."

"Yes," Ralph said. "There's that."

Camilla looked at him with panic in her eyes. "The boys!" she said. "They couldn't. Any of them. Could they?" He didn't answer, and she cried out, "I know what you're thinking. You're thinking about Ernie and —what he's like. You're remembering what I told you about the dog. And what you said happened with his sword. Aren't you?"

"All right," Ralph said. "I am. No, darling. Wait a bit. Suppose, just suppose it *is* that. It would be quite dreadful and Ernie would have to go through a very bad time and probably spend several years in a criminal lunatic asylum. But there'd be no question of anything worse than that happening to him. It's perfectly obvious, if you'll excuse me, darling, that old Ernie's only about fifteen-and-fourpence in the pound."

"Well, I daresay it is," Camilla said, looking very white. "But to do that!"

"Look," he said, "I'm going on to my next question. Please answer it."

"I can guess—"

"All right. Wait a bit. I've told you I love you. You said you were not sure how you felt and wanted to get away and think about it. Fair enough. I respected that and I'd have held off and not waited for you on Sunday if it hadn't been for seeing you in church and—well, you know."

"Yes, well, we disposed of that, didn't we?"

"You were marvellously understanding. I thought everything was going my way. But then you started up *this* business. Antediluvian hooey! Because you're what you choose to call an 'alloy' you say it wouldn't do for us to marry. Did you, by any chance, come down here to see your mother's people with the idea of facing up to that side of it?"

"Yes," Camilla said, "I did."

"You wanted to glower out of the smithy at the county riding by."

"In effect. Though it's not the most attractive way of putting it."

"Do you love me, blast you?"

"Yes," Camilla said wildly. "I do. So shut up."

"Not bloody likely! Camilla, how marvellous! How frightfully, *frightfully* nice of you to love me. I can't get over it," said Ralph, who, from emotion and rapture, had also turned white.

"But I stick to my point," she said. "What's your great-aunt going to say? What's your father going to think? Ralph, can you look me in the eye and tell me they wouldn't mind?"

"If I look you in the eye I shall kiss you."

"Ah! You see? You can't. And now—now when this has happened! There'll be the most ghastly publicity, won't there? What about that? What sort of a fiancée am I going to be to a rising young county solicitor? Can you see the headlines? 'History Repeats Itself'! 'Mother Ran Away from Smithy to Marry Baronet'! 'Grand-daughter of Murdered Blacksmith Weds Peer's Grand-son'! 'Fertility Rite Leads to Engagement'! Perhaps—perhaps—'Niece of—' What are you doing?"

Ralph had got up and, with an air of determination, was buttoning his mackintosh. "I'm going," he said, "to send a telegraph to Auntie *Times*. Engagement announced between—"

"You're going to do nothing of the sort." They glared at each other. "Oh!" Camilla exclaimed, flapping her hands at him, "what *am* I going to do with you? And how *can* I feel so happy?"

She made an exasperated little noise and bolted into his arms.

Alleyn walked in upon this scene and, with an apologetic ejaculation, hurriedly walked out again.

Neither Ralph nor Camilla was aware either of his entry or of his withdrawal.

ii

When they had left Bailey and Thompson to deal with certain aspects of technical routine in the old coach-house, Alleyn and Fox, taking Carey and Dr. Otterly with them, had interviewed the Guiser's five sons.

They had found them crammed together in a tiny kitchen-living-room in the cottage next door to the coach-house. It was a dark room, its two predominant features being an immense iron range and a table covered with a plush cloth. Seated round this table in attitudes that were somehow on too large a scale for their environment were the five Andersen sons: Daniel, Andrew, Nathaniel, Christopher and Ernest.

Dr. Otterly had knocked and gone in and the others had followed him. Dan had risen; the others merely scraped their chair legs and settled back again. Carey introduced them.

Alleyn was greatly struck by the close family resemblance among the Andersens. Even the twins were scarcely more like to each other than to the other three brothers. They were all big, sandy, blue-eyed men with fresh colour in their cheeks: heavy and powerful men whose muscles bulged hard under their countrymen's clothing. Dan's eyes were red and his hands not perfectly steady. Andy sat with raised brows as if in a state of guarded astonishment. Nat looked bashful and Chris angry. Ernie kept a little apart from his brothers. A faint, foolish smile was on his mouth and he grimaced; not broadly, but with a portentous air as if he was possessed of some hidden advantage.

Alleyn and Fox were given a chair at the table. Carey and Dr. Otterly sat on a horsehair sofa against the wall and were thus a little removed from the central party.

Alleyn said, "I'm sorry to have to worry you when you've already had to take so much, but I'm sure that you'll want the circumstances of your father's death to be cleared up as quickly as possible."

They made cautious sounds in thier throats. He waited and, presently, Dan said, "Goes without saying, sir, we want to get to the bottom of this. We'm kind of addle-headed and over-set, one way and 'tother, and can't seem to take to *any* notion."

"Look at it how you like," Andy said, "it's fair fantastical."

There was a strong smell of stale tobacco-smoke in the room. Alleyn threw his pouch and a packet of cigarettes on the table. "Suppose we take our pipes to it," he said. "Help yourselves."

After a proper show of deprecation they did so: Ernie alone preferred a cigarette and rolled his own. He grimaced over the job, working his mouth and eyebrows. While they were still busy with their pipes and tobacco, Alleyn began to talk to them.

"Before we can even begin to help," he said, "we'll have to get as clear an account of yesterday's happenings as all of you can give us. Now, Superintendent Carey has already talked to you and he's given me a damn' good report on what was said. I just want to take up one or two of his points and see if we can carry them a bit further. Let's go back, shall we, to yesterday evening, about half an hour before the Dance of the Five Sons was due to start. All right?"

They were lighting their pipes now. They looked up at him guardedly and waited.

"I understand," Alleyn went on, "that would be about half past eight. The performers were already at Mardian Castle, with the exception of Mr. William Andersen himself and his youngest son, Mr. Ernest Andersen. That right?"

Silence. Then Dan, who looked like becoming the spokesman, said, "Right enough."

"Mr. William Andersen—may I for distinction use the name by which I'm told he was universally known—the Guiser? That means 'the mummer,' doesn't it?"

"Literally," Dr. Otterly said from the sofa, "it means 'the disguised one.' "

"Lord, yes! Of course. Well, the Guiser, at half past eight, was still down here at the forge. And Mr. Ernest Andersen was either here too, or shortly to return here, because he was to drive his father up to the castle. Stop me if I go wrong."

Silence.

"Good. The Guiser was resting in a room that opens off the smithy itself. When did he go there, if you please?"

"I can answer that one," Dr. Otterly said. "I looked in at midday to see how he was and he wasn't feeling too good. I told him that if he wanted to appear at all he'd have to take the day off—I said I'd come back later on and have another look at him. Unfortunately, I got called out on an urgent case and found myself running late. I dined at the castle and it doesn't do to be late there. I'd had a word with the boys about the Guiser and arranged to have a look at him when he arrived and—"

"Yes," Alleyn said. "Thank you so much. Can we just take it from there? So he rested all day in his room. Any of you go and see how he was getting on?"

"Not us!" Chris said. "He wouldn't have nobody anigh him when he was laying-by. Told us all to keep off."

"So you went up to the castle without seeing him?"

Dan said, "I knocked on the door and says, 'We're off then,' and, 'Hoping to see you later,' and Dad sings out, 'Send Ern back at half past. I'll be there.' So we all went up along and Ern drove back at half past like he'd said."

"Right." Alleyn turned to Ernie and found him leaning back in his chair with his cigarette in his mouth and his hands clasped behind his neck. There was something so strained in this attitude that it suggested a kind of clumsy affectation. "Now, will you tell us just what happened when you came back for your father?"

"A-a-a-aw!" Ernie drawled, without looking at him. "I dunno. Nuthin'."

"Naow, naow, naow!" counselled his brothers anxiously.

"Was he still in his room?"

"Reckon so. Must of been," Ernie said and laughed.

"Did you speak to him?"

"Not me."

"What did you do?"

Nat said, "Ernie seen the message—"

"Wait a bit," Alleyn said. "I think we'll have it from him, if we may. What did you do, Ernie? What happened? You went into the forge, did you—and what?"

"He'd no call," Ernie shouted astonishingly without changing his posture or shifting his gaze, "he'd no call to treat me like 'e done. Old sod."

"Answer what you're axed, you damned young fool," Chris burst out, "and don't talk silly." The brothers all began to tell Alleyn that Ernie didn't mean what he said.

Alleyn held up his hand and they stopped. "Tell me what happened," he said to Ernie. "You went into the forge and what did you see?"

"Ar?" He turned his head and looked briefly at Alleyn. "Like Nat says. I seen the message pinned to his door."

Alleyn drew from his coat pocket the copper-plate billhead with its pencilled message. It had been mounted between two sheets of glass by Bailey. He said, "Look at this, will you? Is this the message?"

Ernie took it in his hand and gave a great laugh. Fox took it away from him.

"What did you do then?" Alleyn asked.

"Me? Like what it says. 'Young Ern,' that's me, 'will have to.' There was his things hanging up ready: mask, clothes and old rabbity cap. So I puts 'em on; quick."

"Were you already dressed as the whiffling son?"

"Didn't matter. I put 'em on over. Quiet like. 'Case he heard and changed his mind. Out and away, quick. Into old bus and up the road. *Whee-ee-ee!*" Ernie gave a small boy's illustration of excessive speed. "I bet I looked right clever. I was the Fool, I was. Driving fast to the dance. Whee-ee-ee!"

Dan suddenly buried his face in his hands. " 'Tain't decent," he said.

Alleyn took them through the scene after Ernie's arrival. They said they had passed round the note and then sent it in to Dr. Otterly by Dan's young son, Bill, who was then dressed and black-faced in his role of understudy. Dr. Otterly came out. The brothers added some last-minute instructions to the boy. When the clock struck nine, Dr. Otterly went into the courtyard with his fiddle. It was at that moment they all heard Mrs. Bünz's car hooting and labouring up the drive. As they waited for their entrance-music, the car appeared round the outer curve of the old wall with the Guiser rampant in the passenger's seat. Dr. Otterly heard the subsequent rumpus and went back to see what had happened.

It appeared that, during the late afternoon, the Guiser had fallen deeply asleep and had woken refreshed and fighting fit, only to hear his son driving away without him. Speechless with rage, he had been obliged to accept a hitch-hike from his enemy, Mrs. Bünz.

"He was jibbering when he got to us," Otterly said, "and pretty well incoherent. He grabbed Ernie and began hauling his Fool's clothes off him."

"And how," Alleyn said to Ernie, "did you enjoy that?"

Ernie, to the evident perturbation of his brothers, flew into a retrospective rage. As far as Alleyn could make out, he had attempted to defy his father but had been hurriedly quelled by his brothers.

"Ern didn't want to whiffle," Dan said and they all confirmed this eagerly. Ernie had refused to dance if he couldn't dance the Fool. Simon Begg had finally prevailed on him.

"I done it for the Wing-Commander and not for another soul. He axed me and I done it. I went out and whiffled."

From here, what they had to tell followed without addition the account Alleyn had already heard from Carey. None of the five sons had, at any stage of their performance, gone behind the dolmen to the spot where their father lay hidden. They were all positive the Guiser could neither have left the courtyard nor returned to it, alive or dead. They were equally and mulishly positive that no act of violence could have been done upon him during the period begun by his mock fall and terminated by the discovery of his decapitated body. They stuck to this, loudly repeating their argument and banging down their great palms on the table. It was impossible.

"I take it," said Mr. Fox during a pause, "that we don't believe in fairies." He looked mildly round the table.

"Not at the bottom of this garden, anyway," Alleyn muttered.

"My dad did, then," Ernie shouted.

"Did what?" Alleyn asked patiently.

"Believe in fairies."

Fox sighed heavily and made a note.

"Did he," Alleyn continued, "believe in sacrifices too?"

The Guiser's five sons fidgeted and said nothing.

"The old idea, you know," Alleyn said. "I may have got it wrong, but in the earliest times didn't they sacrifice something—a bird, wasn't it—on some of these old stones? At certain times of the year?"

After a further and protracted silence, Dr. Otterly said, "No doubt they did."

"I take it that this morris dance—*cum*-sword-dance-*cum*-mumming play—forgive me if I've got the terms muddled—is a survival of some such practice?"

"Yes, yes, of course," Dr. Otterly said, impatiently, and yet with the air of a man whose hobby-horse is at the mounting-block. "Immeasurably the richest survival we have."

"Really? The ritual death of the Fool is the old mystery of sacrifice, isn't it, with the promise of renewal behind it?"

"Exactly."

"And, at one time, there would have been actual bloodshed? Or well might have been?"

To this there was no answer.

"Who," Alleyn asked, "killed Dame Alice's goose yesterday afternoon and put it on the dolmen?"

Through the pipe smoke that now hung thick over the table he looked round the circle of reddened faces. "Ernie," he said, "was it you?"

A slow grin stretched Ernie's mouth until he looked remarkably like a bucolic Fool himself.

"I whiffled 'im," he said.

iii

As Ernie was not concerned to extend this statement and returned very foolish answers to any further questions, Alleyn was obliged to listen to his brothers, who were eager in explanation.

Throughout yesterday morning, they said, while they erected the torches and prepared the bonfire, they had suffered a number of painful and determined assaults from Dame Alice's geese. One male, in particular, repeatedly placing himself in the van, had come hissing down upon them. Damaging stabs and sidelong slashes had been administered, particularly upon Ernie, who had greatly resented them. He had been sent up again in the afternoon with the gardener's slasher, which he had himself sharpened, and had been told to cut down the brambles on the dancing area. In the dusk, the gander had made a final assault and an extremely painful one. Irked beyond endurance, Ernie had swiped at him with the slasher. When they arrived in the evening the brothers were confronted with the corpse and taken to task by Miss Mardian. Subsequently, they had got the whole story out of Ernie. He now listened to their recital with a maddening air of complacency.

"Do you agree that is what happened?" Alleyn asked him and he clasped his hands behind his head, rocked to and fro and chuckled. "That's right," he said. "I whiffled 'im proper."

"Why did you leave the bird on the dolmen?"

Ernie said conceitedly, "You foreign chaps wouldn't rightly catch on. I know what for I done it."

"Was it blood for the stone?"

He ducked his head low between his shoulders and looked sideways at Alleyn. "Happen it was, then. And happen 'twasn't enough, however."

"Wanted more?" Alleyn asked and mentally crossed his thumbs.

"Wanted and got it, then."

("Naow, naow, naow!")

Ernie unclasped his hands and brought them down on the table. He gripped the edge so hard that the table quivered. "His own fault," he gabbled, "and not a soul else's. Blood axes for blood and always will. I told him. Look what he done on me, Sunday. Murdered my dog, he did, murdered my dog on me when my back was turned. What he done Sunday come home on him, Wednesday, and not a soul to answer for it but himself. Bloody murderer, he was, and paid in his own coin."

Chris Andersen reached out and gripped his brother's arm. "Shut your mouth," he said.

Dan said, "You won't stop him that fashion. Take thought for yourself, Ernie. You're not right smart in the head, boy. Your silly ways is well known: no blame to you if you're not so clear-minded as the rest of us. Keep quiet, then, or, in your foolishness, you'll bring shame on the family." His brothers broke into a confused chorus of approval.

Alleyn listened, hoping to glean something from the general rumpus, but the brothers merely reiterated their views with increased volume, no variation and little sense.

Ernie suddenly jabbed his forefinger at Chris. "You can't talk, Chrissie," he roared. "What about what happened yesterday? What about what you said you'd give 'im if he crossed you over—you know what—"

There was an immediate uproar. Chris and his three elder brothers shouted in unison and banged their fists down on the table.

Alleyn stood up. This unexpected movement brought about an instant quiet.

"I'm sorry, men," he said, "but from the way things are shaping, there can be no point in my keeping you round this table. You will stay either here or hereabouts, if you please, and we shall in due course see each of you alone. Your father's body will be taken to the nearest mortuary for examination, which will be made by the Home Office pathologist. As soon as we can allow the funeral to take place you will be told all about it. There will, of course, be an inquest which you'll be asked to attend. If you think it wise to do so, you may be legally represented, individually or as a family." He stopped, looked at each of them in turn and then said, "I'm going to do something that is unorthodox. Before I do so, however, I warn you that to conspire—that is, to act together and in collaboration for the purpose of withholding vital evidence—in a case of murder can be an extremely serious offence. I may be wrong, but I believe there is some such intention in your minds. You will do well to give it up. Now. Before more harm can come of it."

He waited but they said nothing.

"All right," said Alleyn, "we'll get on with it." He turned to Ernie. "Last night, after your father's body had been found, I'm told you leapt on the stone where earlier in the day you had put the dead gander. I'm told you pointed your sword at the German lady, who was standing not very far away, and you said, 'Ask her. She's the one that did it.' Did you do this?"

A half-smile touched Ernie's mouth, but he said nothing. "Did you?" Alleyn insisted.

"Ernie took a queer turn," Andy said. "He can't rightly remember after his turns."

"Let him answer for himself. Did you do this, Ernie?"

"I might and I might not. If they say so, I might of."

"Do you think the German lady killed your father?"

"*'Course* she didn't," Chris said angrily. "She couldn't."

"I asked Ernie if he thought she did."

"*I* dunno." Ernie muttered and laughed.

"Very well, then," Alleyn said and decided suddenly to treat them to a rich helping of ham. "Here, in the presence of you all—you five sons of a murdered father—I ask you, Ernest Andersen, if you cut off that father's head."

Ernie looked at Alleyn, blinked and opened his mouth: but whether to speak or horridly to laugh again would never be known. A shadow had fallen across the little room. A voice from the doorway said:

"I'd keep my mouth shut on that one if I were you, Corp."

It was Simon Begg.

iv

He came forward easily. His eyes were bright as if he enjoyed the effect he had made. His manner was very quietly tough. Alleyn wondered if it was based on some model that was second-rate but fully authentic.

"Sorry if I intrude," Simon said. "I'm on my way to the pub to be grilled by the cops and thought I'd look in. But perhaps you *are* the cops. Are you?"

"I'm afraid so," Alleyn said. "And you, I think, must be Mr. Simon Begg."

"He's my Wing-Commander, he is," Ernie cut in. "We was in the same crowd, him and me."

"O.K., boy, O.K.," Simon said and, passing round the table, put his hand on Ernie's shoulder. "You talk such a lot," he said good-naturedly. "Keep your great trap shut, Corp, and you'll come to no harm." He cuffed Ernie lightly over the head and looked brightly at Alleyn. "The Corp," he said, "is just a great big baby: not quite with us, shall we say. Maybe you like them that way. Anything I can do for you?"

Alleyn said, "If you'll go ahead we'll be glad to see you at the Green Man. Or—can we give you a lift?"

"Thanks, I've got my heap out there."

"We'll be hard on your heels, then."

Begg went through the motion of whistling.

"Don't wait for me," he said, "I'll follow you."

"No," Alleyn said very coolly, "you won't. You'll go straight on if you please."

"Is that an order or a threat, Mr.—I'm afraid I don't know your rank."

"We're not allowed to threaten. My rank couldn't matter less. Off you go."

Simon looked at him, raised his eyebrows, said, with a light laugh, "Well, *really!*" and walked out. They heard him start up his engine. Alleyn briefly surveyed the brothers Andersen.

"You chaps," he said, "had better reconsider your position a bit. Obviously you've talked things over. Now you'd do well to think them over, and jolly carefully at that. In the meantime, if any of you feel like making a sensible statement about this business I'll be glad to hear what it is." He moved to the door, where he was joined by Fox and Carey.

"By the way," he said, "we shall have to find out the terms of your father's Will, if he made one."

Dan, a picture of misery and indecision, scratched his head and gazed at Alleyn.

Andy burst out, "We was right fond of the old man. Stood together, us did, father and sons, so firm as a rock."

"A united family?"

"So we was, then," Nat protested. Chris added, "And so we are."

"I believe you," Alleyn said.

"As for his Will," Dan went on with great simplicity, "we can't tell you, sir, what we don't know our own selves. Maybe he made one and maybe not."

Carey said, "You haven't taken a look round the place at all, then?"

Andy turned on him. "It's our father what's been done to death, Mr. Carey. It's his body laying out there, not as an old man's did ought—peaceful and proper—but ghassly as a sacrifice and crying aloud for—for—" He looked round wildly, saw his youngest brother, hesitated and then broke down completely.

"—for justice?" Alleyn said. "Were you going to say?"

"He's beyond earthly justice," Nat put in. "Face to face with his Maker and no doubt proud to be there."

Superintendent Carey said, "I did hear tell he was up to Biddlefast on Tuesday to see lawyer Stayne."

"So he was, then, but none of us knows why," Chris rejoined.

"Well," Alleyn said, "we'll be off. I'm very sorry, but

I'm afraid we'll have to leave somebody here. Whoever it is will, I'm sure, be as considerate as possible. You see, we may have to poke back into the past. I can fully understand," he went on, talking directly to Andy, "how you feel about your father's death. It's been—of course it has—an appalling shock. But you will, no doubt, have a hunt round for any papers or instructions he may have left. I can get an expert search made or, if you'd rather, can just leave an officer here to look on. In case something turns up that may be of use to us. We really do want to make it as easy for you as we can."

They took this without much show of interest. "There'll be cash, no doubt," Dan said. "He was a great old one for putting away bits of cash. Proper old jackdaw, us used to call him." He caught back his breath harshly.

Alleyn said, "I'm sorry it has to be like this." Dan was the one nearest to him. "He's an elderly chap himself," Alleyn thought, and touched him lightly on the shoulder. "Sorry," he repeated and looked at Fox and Carey. "Shall we move on?"

"Do you want me again?" Dr. Otterly asked.

"If I can just have a word with you."

They all went out through the forge. Alleyn paused and looked round.

"What a place for a search! The collection of generations. There's the door, Fox, where Ernie says the note was pinned. And his room's beyond that."

He went down a narrow pathway between two heaped-up benches of litter and opened the door in the end wall. Beyond it was a tiny room with a bed that had been pulled together rather than made and gave clear evidence of use. The room was heaped up with boxes, piles of old newspapers and all kinds of junk. A small table had evidently served as a desk and bore a number of account books, files and the Guiser's old-fashioned copper-plate bills. *In Dr. to W. Andersen, Blacksmith, Copse Forge, South Mardian.* A pencil lay across a folded pile of blotting-paper.

"Hard lead," Alleyn said to Fox, who stood in the doorway. "The message was written with a hard point. Wonder if the paper lay here. Let's have a look."

He held the blotting-paper to the light and then took out his pocket lens. "Yes," he grunted, "it's there all right. A faint trace but it could be brought out. It's the trace of the note we've already got, my hearties. We'll put Bailey and Thompson on to this lot. Hullo!"

He had picked up a sheet of paper. Across it, in blue indelible pencil, was written, *Wednesday, W. Andersen. Kindly sharpen my slasher at once if not all ready done do it yourself mind and return by bearer to avoid further trouble as urgently require and oblige Jno. MacGlashan. P.S. I will have none but yourself on this job.*

"Carey!" Alleyn called out, and the Superintendent loomed up behind Fox. "Who's Jno. MacGlashan? Here, take a look at this. Will this be the slasher in question?"

"That'll be the one, surely," Carey agreed. "MacGlashan's the gardener up along."

"It was written yesterday. Who would the bearer be?"

"His boy, no doubt."

"Didn't they tell us Ernie sharpened the slasher? And took it up late yesterday afternoon? And whiffled the goose's head off with it?"

"That's right, sir. That's what they said."

"So the boy, if the boy was the bearer, was sent empty away."

"Must of been."

"And the slasher comes to a sticky end in the bonfire. Now, all of this," Alleyn said, rubbing his nose, "is hellish intriguing."

"Is it?" Fox asked stolidly.

"My dear old chap, of course it is. Nip back to the coach-house and tell Bailey and Thompson to move in here as soon as they're ready and do their stuff." Fox went sedately off and Alleyn shut the door of the bedroom behind him. "We'll have this room sealed, Carey.

And will you check up on the slasher story? Find out who spoke to the boy. And, Carey, I'll leave you in charge down here for the time being. Do you mind?"

Superintendent Carey, slightly bewildered by this mode of approach, said that he didn't.

"Right. Come on."

He led the way outside, where Dr. Otterly waited in his car.

Carey, hanging off and on, said, "Will I seal the room now, sir? Or what?"

"Let the flash and dabs chaps in first. Fox is fixing them. Listen as inconspicuously as you can to the elder Andersen boys' general conversation. How old is Dan, by the way? Sixty, did you say?"

"Turned sixty, I reckon."

"And Ernie?"

"He came far in the rear, which may account for him being not right smart."

"He's smart enough," Alleyn muttered, "in a way. Believe me, he's only dumb nor'-nor'-west and yesterday, I fancy, the wind was in the south."

"It shifted in the night," Carey said and stared at him. "Look, Mr. Alleyn," he burst out, "I can't help but ask. Do you reckon Ernie Andersen's our chap?"

"My dear man, *I* don't know. I think his brothers are determined to stop him talking. So's this man Begg, by the way. I could cheerfully have knocked Begg's grinning head off his shoulders. Sorry! Unfortunate phrase. But I believe Ernie was going to give me a straight answer, one way or the other."

"Suppose," Carey said, "Ernie lost his temper with the old chap, and gave a kind of swipe, or suppose he was just fooling with that murderous sharp whiffler of his and—and—well, without us noticing while the Guiser was laying doggo behind the stone—Ar, hell!"

"Yes," Alleyn said grimly, "and it'll turn out that the only time Ernie might have waltzed round behind the stone was the time when young Stayne had pinched his sword. And what about the state of the sword, Carey? Nobody had time to clean it and restain it with green sap, had they? And, my dear man, what about blood? Blood, Carey—which reminds me, we are keeping the doctor waiting. Leave Bailey and Thompson here while you arrange with Obby or that P.C. by the castle gates to take your place when you want to get off. I'll bring extra men in if we need them. I'll leave you the car and ask Dr. Otterly to take us up to the pub. O.K.?"

"O.K., Mr. Alleyn. I'll be up along later, then?"

"Right. Here's Fox. Come on, Foxkin. Otterly, will you give us a lift?"

Carey turned back into the forge and Alleyn and Fox got into Dr. Otterly's car.

Dr. Otterly said, "Look here, Alleyn, before we go on I want to ask you something."

"I bet I know what it is. Do we or do we not include you in our list of suspects?"

"Exactly so," Otterly said rather stuffily. "After all, one would prefer to know. Um?"

"Of course. Well, at the moment, unless you can explain how you fiddled unceasingly in full view of a Superintendent of Police, a P.C., a Dame of the British Empire, a parson and about fifty other witnesses during the whole of the period when this job must have been done and, at the same time, *did* it, you don't look to be a likely starter."

"Thank you," said Dr. Otterly.

"On the other hand, you look to be a damn' good witness. Did you watch the dancers throughout?"

"Never took my eyes off 'em. A conscientious fiddler doesn't."

"Wonderful. Don't let's drive up for a moment, shall we? Tell me this. Would you swear that it was in fact the Guiser who danced the role of Fool?"

Dr. Otterly stared at him. "Good Lord, of course it was! I thought you understood. I'd gone out to start proceedings, I heard the rumpus, I went back and found him lugging his clothes off Ernie. I had a look at him, not a proper medical look, because he wouldn't let me, and I told him if he worked himself up any more he'd probably crack up anyway. So he calmed down, put on the Fool's clothes and the bag-mask, and, when he was ready, I went out. Ernie followed and did his whiffling. I could see the others waiting to come on. The old man appeared last, certainly, but I could see him just beyond the gate, watching the others. He'd taken his mask off and only put it on at the last moment."

"Nobody, at any stage, could have taken his place?"

"Utterly impossible," Otterly said impatiently.

"At no time could he have gone offstage and swapped with somebody?"

"Lord, Lord, Lord, how many more times! *No!*"

"All right. So he danced and lay down behind the stone. You fiddled and watched and fiddled and watched. Stayne and Ernie fooled and Stayne collared Ernie's sword. Begg, as the Hobby-Horse, retired. These three throughout the show were all over the place and dodged in and out of the rear archway. Do you know exactly when and for how long any of them was out of sight?"

"I do not. I doubt if they do. Begg dodged out after his first appearance when he chivvied the girls, you know. It's damn' heavy, that gear he wears, and he took the chance, during the first sword-dance, to get the weight off his shoulders. He came back before they made the lock. He had another let-up after the 'death.' Ralph Stayne was all over the shop. In and out. So was Ernie during their interlude."

"Right. And at some stage Stayne returned the sword to Ernie. Dan did a solo. The Sons danced and then came the denouement. Right?"

"It hasn't altered," Dr. Otterly said drily, "since the last time you asked."

"It's got to alter sometime, somehow," Fox observed unexpectedly.

"Would you also swear," Alleyn said, "that at no time did either Ernie or Ralph Stayne prance round behind the stone and make one more great swipe with the sword that might have done the job?"

"I know damn' well neither of them did."

"Yes? Why?"

"Because, my dear man, as I've told you, I never took my eyes off them. I knew the old chap was lying there. I'd have thought it a bloody dangerous thing to do."

"Is there still another reason why it didn't happen that way?"

"Isn't it obvious that there is?"

"Yes," Alleyn said, "I'd have thought it was. If anybody had killed in that way he'd have been smothered in blood?"

"Exactly."

"But, all the same, Otterly, there could be one explanation that would cover that difficulty."

Dr. Otterly slewed round in his seat and stared at Alleyn. "Yes," he said. "Yes, you're right. I'd thought of it, of course. But I'd still swear that neither of them did."

"All the same it is, essentially, I'm sure, the explanation nearest to the truth."

"And, in the meantime," Mr. Fox observed, "we still go on believing in fairies."

CHAPTER VII The Green Man

BEFORE they set off for the Green Man, Alleyn asked Dr. Otterly if he could arrange for the Guiser's accommodation in a suitable mortuary.

"Curtis, the Home Office man, will do the P.M.," Alleyn said, "but he's two hundred-odd miles away across country, and the last time I heard of him he was held up on a tricky case. I don't know how or when he'll contrive to get here."

"Biddlefast would offer the best facilities. It's twenty miles away. We've a cottage hospital at Yowford where we could fix him up straightaway—after a fashion."

"Do, will you? Things are very unsatisfactory as they are. Can we get a mortuary van or an ambulance?"

"The latter. I'll fix it up."

"Look," Alleyn said, "I want you to do something else, if you will. I'm going now to talk to Simon Begg, young Stayne, the German lady and the Guiser's granddaughter, who, I hear, is staying at the pub. Will you sit in on the interviews? Will you tell me if you think anything they may say is contrary to the facts as you observed them? Will you do that, Otterly?"

Dr. Otterly stared at the dripping landscape and whistled softly through his teeth. "I don't know," he said at last.

"Don't you? Tell me, if this is deliberate homicide, do you want the man run in?"

"I suppose so." He pulled out his pipe and opened the door to knock it out on the running-board. When he re-appeared he was very red in the face. "I may as well tell you," he said, "that I disapprove strongly and vehemently of the McNaughton Rules and would never voluntarily bring anybody who was mentally a borderline case under their control."

"And you look upon Ernie Andersen as such a case."

"I do. He's an epileptic. *Petit mal.* Very rare attacks, but he had one, last night, after he saw what had happened to his father. I won't fence with you, but I tell you that, if I thought Ernie Andersen stood any chance of being hanged for the murder of his father, I wouldn't utter a syllable that might lead to his arrest."

"What would you do?"

"Bully a couple of brother-medicos into certifying him and have him put away."

Alleyn said, "Why don't you chaps get together and make a solid medical front against the McNaughton Rules? But never mind that now. Perhaps if I tell you exactly what I'm looking for in this case, you'll feel more inclined to sit in. Mind you, I may be looking for something that doesn't exist. The theory, if it can be graced with the title, is based on such slender evidence that it comes jolly close to being guesswork and, when you find a cop guessing, you kick him in the pants. Still, here, for what it's worth, is the line of country."

Dr. Otterly stuffed his pipe, lit it, threw his head back and listened. When Alleyn had finished, he said, "By God, I wonder!" and then, "All right. I'll sit in."

"Good. Shall we about it?"

It was half past twelve when they reached the pub. Simon and Ralph were eating a snack at the bar. Mrs. Bünz and Camilla sat at a table before the parlour fire, faced with a meal that Camilla, for her part, had been quite unable to contemplate with equanimity. Alleyn and Fox went to their private room, where they found that cold meat and hot vegetables awaited them. Dr. Otterly returned from the telephone to say he had arranged for the ambulance to go to Copse Forge and for his partner to take surgery alone during the early part of the afternoon.

While they ate their meal, Alleyn asked Dr. Otterly to tell him something of the history of the Dance of the Five Sons.

"Like most people who aren't actively interested in

folklore, I'm afraid I'm inclined to associate it with flushed ladies imperfectly braced for violent exercise and bearded gentlemen dressed like the glorious Fourth of June gone elfin. A Philistine's conception, I'm sure."

"Yes," Dr. Otterly said, "it is. You're confusing the 'sports' with the true generic strain. If you're really interested, ask the German lady. Even if you don't ask, she'll probably tell you."

"Couldn't you give me a succinct résumé? Just about this particular dance?"

"Of course I could. I don't want any encouragement, I assure you, to mount on my hobby-horse! And there, by the way, you are! Have you thought how many everyday phrases derive from the folk drama? Mounting one's hobby-horse! Horseplay! Playing the fool! Cutting capers! Midsummer madness! Very possibly 'horn mad,' though I recognize the more generally known application. This pub, the Green Man, gets its name from a variant of the Fool, the Robin Hood, the Jack-in-the-Green."

"What does the whole concept of the ritual dance go back to? Frazer's King of the Sacred Grove?"

"Certainly. And the Dionysian play about the Titans who killed their old man."

"Fertility rite-*cum*-sacrifice-death and resurrection?"

"That's it. It's the oldest manifestation of the urge to survive and the belief in redemption through sacrifice and resurrection. It's as full of disjointed symbolism as a surrealist's dream."

"Maypoles, corn-babies, ladles—all that?"

"Exactly. And, being a folk manifestation, the whole thing changes all the time. It's full of cross-references. The images overlap and the characters swap roles. In the few places in England where it survives in its traditional form, you get, as it were, different bits of the kaleidoscopic pattern. The lock of the swords here, the rabbit-cap there, the blackened faces somewhere else. Horns at Abbots Bromely, Old Hoss in Kent and Old Tup in Yorkshire. But always, however much debased and fragmentary, the central idea of the death and resurrection of the Fool, who is also the Father, Initiate, Medicine Man, Scapegoat and King. At its lowest, a few scraps of half-remembered jargon. At its highest—"

"Not—by any chance—*Lear?*"

"My dear fellow," Dr. Otterly cried, and actually seized Alleyn by the hand, "you don't mean to say you've spotted that! My dear fellow, I really am *delighted* with you. You must let me bore you again and at greater length. I realize, now is *not* the time for it. No. No, we must confine ourselves for the moment to the Five Sons."

"You're far from boring me, but I'm afraid we must. Surely," Alleyn said, "this particular dance-drama is unusually rich? Doesn't it present a remarkable number of elements?"

"I should damn' well say it does. Much the richest example we have left in England and, luckily for us, right off the beaten track. Generally speaking, traditional dancing and mumming (such of it as survives) follows the line of the original Danish occupation, but here we're miles off it."

"The spelling of the Andersen name, though?"

"Ah! There you are! In my opinion, they're a Danish family who, for some reason, drifted across to this part of the world and brought their winter-solstice ritual with them. Of course, the trade of smith has always been particularly closely associated with folklore."

"And, originally, there was an actual sacrifice?"

"Of some sort, I have no doubt."

"Human?"

Dr. Otterly said, "Possibly."

"This lock, or knot, of swords, now. Five swords—you'd expect it to be six."

"So it is everywhere else that I know of. Another element that makes the Five Sons unique."

"How do they form it?"

"While they dance. They've got two methods. The combination of a cross interwoven with an A and a sort of monogram of an X and an H. It takes quite a bit of doing."

"And Ernie's was as sharp as hell."

"Absolutely illicit, but it was."

"I wonder," Alleyn said, "if Ernie expected his particular Old Man to resurrect."

Dr. Otterly laid down his knife and fork. "*After* what happened?" He gave a half-laugh. "I wouldn't be surprised."

"What's their attitude to the dance? All of them? Why do they go on with it, year after year?"

Dr. Otterly hesitated. "Come to that, Doctor," Fox said, "why do you?"

"Me? I suppose I'm a bit of a crank about it. I've got theories. Anyway, I enjoy fiddling. My father and his before him and his before that have been doctors at Yowford and the two Mardians and we've all fiddled. Before that, we were yeomen and, before that, tenant farmers. One in the family has always been a fiddler. I try not to be cranky. The Guiser was a bigger crank in his way than I. I can't tell you *why* he was so keen. He just inherited the Five Sons' habit. It runs in his blood like poaching does in old Moley Moon's up to Yowford Bridge or hunting in Dame Alice Mardian's, or doctoring, if you like, in mine."

"Do you think any of the Andersens pay much attention to the ritualistic side of the thing? Do you think they believe, for instance, that anything tangible comes of the performance?"

"Ah. Now! You're asking me just how superstitious they are, you know." Dr. Otterly placed the heels of his well-kept hands against the edge of his plate and delicately pushed it away. "Hasn't every one of us," he asked, "a little familiar shamefaced superstition?"

"I daresay," Alleyn agreed. "Cossetted but reluctantly acknowledged. Like the bastard sons of Shaksperian papas."

"Exactly. I know, *I've* got a little Edmund. As a man of science, I scorn it; as a countryman, I give it a kind of heart-service. It's a particularly ridiculous notion for a medical man to harbour."

"Are we to hear what it is?"

"If you like. I always feel it's unlucky to see blood. Not, may I hasten to say, to see it in the course of my professional work, but fortuitously. Someone scratches a finger in my presence, say, or my own nose bleeds. Before I can stop myself I think, 'Hullo. Trouble coming.' No doubt it throws back to some childish experience. I don't let it affect me in the slightest. I don't believe in it. I merely get an emotional reflex. It's—" He stopped short. "How very odd," he said.

"Are you reminded that the Guiser cut his hand on Ernie's sword during your final practice?"

"I was, yes."

"Your hunch wasn't so far wrong that time," Alleyn observed. "But what are the Andersens' superstitious reflexes? Concerning the Five Sons?"

"I should say pretty well undefined. A feeling that it would be unlucky not to do the dance. A feeling, strong perhaps in the Guiser, that, in doing it, something is placated, some rhythm kept ticking over."

"And in Ernie?"

Dr. Otterly looked vexed. "Any number of crackpot notions, no doubt," he said shortly.

"Like the headless goose on the dolmen?"

"I am persuaded," Dr. Otterly said, "that he killed the goose accidentally and in a temper and put it on the dolmen as an afterthought."

"Blood, as he so tediously insists, for the stone?"

"If you like. Dame Alice was furious. She's always been very kind to Ernie, but this time—"

"He's killed the goose," Fox suggested blandly, "that lays the golden eggs?"

"You're in a bloody whimsical mood, aren't you?" Alleyn inquired idly and then, after a long silence, "What a very disagreeable case this is, to be sure. We'd better get on with it, I suppose."

"Do you mind," Dr. Otterly ventured, "my asking if you two are typical C.I.D. officers?"

"I am," Alleyn said. "Fox is a sport."

Fox collected their plates, stacked all the crockery neatly on a tray and carried it out into the passage, where he was heard to say, "A very pleasant meal, thank you, miss. We've done nicely."

"Tell me," Alleyn asked, "is the Guiser's granddaughter about eighteen with dark reddish hair cut short and very long fingers? Dressed in black skiing trousers and a red sweater?"

"I really can't tell you about the fingers, but the other part's right. Charming child. Going to be an actress."

"And is young Stayne about six feet? Dark? Long back? Donegal tweed jacket with a red fleck and brown corduroy bags?"

"That's right, I think. He's got a scar on his cheekbone."

"I couldn't see his face," Alleyn said. "Or hers."

"Oh?" Dr. Otterly murmured. "Really?"

"What's her name?"

"Camilla Campion."

"Pretty," Alleyn said absently. "Nice name."

"Isn't it?"

"Her mum was the Guiser's daughter, was she?"

"That's right."

"There's a chap," Alleyn ruminated, "called Camillo Campion who's an authority on Italian primitives. Baronet. Sir Camillo."

"Her father. Twenty years ago, his car broke an axle coming too fast down Dame Alice's drive. He stopped at Copse Forge, saw Bess Andersen, who was a lovely creature, fell like a plummet and married her."

"Lor'!" said Fox mildly, returning from the passage. "Sudden!"

"She had to run away. The Guiser wouldn't hear of it. He was an inverted snob and a bigoted nonconformist and, worst of all, Campion's a Roman Catholic."

"I thought I remembered some story of that kind," Alleyn said. "Had he been staying at Mardian Castle?"

"Yes. Dame Alice was livid because she'd made up her mind he was to marry Dulcie. Indeed, I rather fancy there was an unofficial engagement. She never forgave him and the Guiser never forgave Bess. She died in childbirth five years ago. Campion and Camilla brought her back here to be buried. The Guiser didn't say a word to them. The boys, I imagine, didn't dare. Camilla was thirteen and like enough to her mama at that age to give the old man a pretty sharp jolt."

"So he ignored her?"

"That's right. We didn't see her again for five years and then, the other day, she turned up, determined to make friends with her mother's people. She managed to get round him. She's a dear child, in my opinion."

"Let's have her in," said Alleyn.

ii

When they had finished their lunch, of which Camilla ate next to nothing and Mrs. Bünz, who normally had an enormous appetite, not much more, they sat, vis-à-vis, by the parlour fire and found very little to say to each other. Camilla was acutely conscious of Simon Begg and, in particular, of Ralph Stayne, consuming their counter lunches in the public bar. Camilla had dismissed Ralph with difficulty when Mrs. Bünz came in. Now she was in a rose-coloured flutter only slightly modified by the recurrent horror of her grandfather's death. From time to time, gentle Camilla reproached herself with heartlessness and as often as she attempted this pious exercise the memory of Ralph's kisses made nonsense of her scruples.

In the midst of her preoccupations, she noticed that Mrs. Bünz was much quieter than usual and seemed, in some indefinable way, to have diminished in size. She noticed, too, that Mrs. Bünz had a monstrous cold, characterized by heavy catarrhal noises of a most irritating nature. In addition to making these noises, Mrs. Bünz sighed very often and kept moving her shoulders uneasily as if her clothes prickled them.

Trixie came round occasionally from the public bar into the private. It was Trixie who had been entrusted by Alleyn with the message that the police would be obliged if Mrs. Bünz and Miss Campion would keep the early afternoon free.

"Which was exactly the words he used," Trixie said. "A proper gentleman, if a policeman, and a fine deep voice, moreover, with a powerful kind of a smack in it."

This was not altogether re-assuring.

Mrs. Bünz said unexpectedly, "It is not pleasant to be told to await the police. I do not care for policemen. My dear husband and I were anti-Nazi. It is better to avoid such encounters."

Camilla, seeing a look of profound anxiety in Mrs. Bünz's eyes, said, "It's all right, Mrs. Bünz. They're here to take care of us. That's what we keep them for. Don't worry."

"Ach!" Mrs. Bünz said, "you are a child. The police do not look after anybody. They make investigations and arrests. They are not sympathetic. Da," she added, making one of her catarrhal noises.

It was upon this sombre note that Inspector Fox came in to say that if Miss Campion had finished her luncheon, Mr. Alleyn would be very pleased to have a word with her.

Camilla told herself it was ridiculous to feel nervous, but she continued to do so. She followed the enormous bulk of Mr. Fox down the narrow passage. Her throat became dry and her heart thumped. "Why?" she thought. "What have I got to get flustered about? This is ridiculous."

Fox opened the door into the little sitting-room and said, "Miss Campion, Mr. Alleyn." He beamed at Camilla and stepped aside for her. She walked in and was immeasurably relieved to find her friend, Dr. Otterly. Beyond him, at the far side of a table, was a tall dark man who stood up politely as she came in.

"Ah!" Dr. Otterly said, "here's Camilla."

Alleyn came round the table and Camilla found herself offering him her hand as if they had been introduced at a party.

"I hope," he said, "you don't mind giving us a few minutes."

"Yes," murmured Camilla. "I mean, no."

Alleyn pushed forward a chair.

"Don't worry," he said, "it won't be as bad as all that and Dr. Otterly's here to see fair play. The watchword is 'routine.' "

Camilla sat down. Like a good drama student, she did it beautifully without looking at the chair. "If I could pretend this was a mood-and-movement exercise," she thought, "I'd go into it with a good deal more poise."

Alleyn said, "We're checking the order of events before and during the Dance of the Five Sons. You were there, weren't you, for the whole time? Would you be very patient and give us an account of it? From your point of view?"

"Yes, of course. As well as I can. I don't expect I'll be terribly good."

"Let's see, anyway," he suggested comfortably. "Now: here goes."

Her account tallied in every respect with what he had already been told. Camilla found it easier than she would have expected and hadn't gone very far before she had decided, with correct professional detachment, that Alleyn had "star-quality."

When she arrived at the point where Simon Begg as "Crack," the Hobby-Horse, did his improvisation, Camilla hesitated for the first time and turned rather pink.

"Ah, yes," Alleyn said. "That was the tar-baby thing after the first general entrance, wasn't it? What exactly *is* 'Crack's' act with the tar?"

"It's all rather ham, I'm afraid," Camilla said grandly. "Folksy hokum." She turned a little pinker still and then said honestly, "I expect it isn't, really. I expect it's quite interesting, but I didn't much relish it because he came thundering after me and, for some ridiculous reason, I got flustered."

"I've seen the head. Enough to fluster anybody in that light, I should imagine."

"It did me, anyway. And I wasn't all that anxious to have my best skiing trousers ruined. So I ran. It came roaring after me. I couldn't get away because of all the people. I felt kind of cornered and faced it. Its body swung up—it hangs from a frame, you know. I could see his legs: he was wearing lightish-coloured trousers."

"Was he?" Alleyn said with interest.

"Yes. Washed-out cords. Almost white. He always wears them. It *was* silly," Camilla said, "to be rattled. Do you know, I actually yelled. Wasn't it shaming? In front of all those village oafs." She checked herself. "I don't mean that. I'm half village myself and I daresay that's why I yelled. Anyway, I did."

"And then?"

"Well," Camilla said, half laughing, "well, then I kind of made a bee-line for the Betty, and that was all right because it was Ralph Stayne, who's not at all frightening."

"Good," Alleyn said, smiling at her. "And he coped with the situation, did he?"

"He was just the job. Masterful type: or he would have been if he hadn't looked so low-comedy. Anyway, I took refuge in his bombazine bosom and 'Crack' sort of sloped off."

"Where to?"

"He went sort of cavorting and frisking out at the back and everybody laughed. Actually, Begg does get pretty well into the skin of that character," Camilla said with owlish professionalism.

Alleyn led her through the rest of the evening and was told nothing that he hadn't already heard from Dr. Otterly. It was oddly touching to see how Camilla's natural sprightliness faltered as she approached the moment of violence in her narrative. It seemed to Alleyn she was still so young that her spirit danced away from any but the most immediate and direct shock. "She's vulnerable only to greenstick fracture of the emotion," he thought. But, as they reached the point when her grandfather failed to reappear and terror came upon the five sons, Camilla turned pale and pressed her hands together between her knees.

"I didn't know in the slightest what had happened, of course. It was queer. One sort of felt there was something very much amiss and yet one didn't exactly know, one felt it. Even when Dan called them and they all went and looked I—it was so silly, but I think I sort of wondered if he'd just gone away."

"Ah!" Alleyn said quickly. "So he could have gone away during the dance and you mightn't have noticed?"

Dr. Otterly sighed ostentatiously.

"Well—no," Camilla said. "No, I'm sure he couldn't. It would have been quite impossible. I was standing right over on the far side and rather towards the back of the stage. About O.P. second entrance, if you know where that is."

Alleyn said he did. "So you actually could see behind the stone?"

"Sort of," Camilla agreed and added in a worried voice, "I must stop saying 'sort of.' Ralph says I do it all the time. Yes, I could see behind the stone."

"You could see him lying there?"

She hesitated, frowning. "I saw him crouch down after the end of the dance. He sat there for a moment, and then lay down. When he lay down, he sort—I mean, I really couldn't see him. I expect that was the idea. He meant to hide. I think he must have been in a bit of a hollow. So I'd have noticed like anything if he'd got up."

"Or, for the sake of argument, if anybody had offered him any kind of violence?"

"Good Heavens, yes!" she said, as if he'd suggested the ridiculous. "Of *course*."

"What happened immediately after he sank out of sight? At the end of the dance?"

"They made a stage picture. The Sons had drawn their swords out of the lock. 'Crack' stood behind the stone looking like a sort of idol. Ralph stood on the prompt side and the Sons separated. Two of them stood on one side, near me, and two on the other and the fifth, the Whiffler—I knew afterwards it was Ernie—wandered away by himself. Ralph went round with the collecting thing and then Ralph snatched Ernie's sword away and they had a chase. Ralph's got a rather nice sense of comedy, actually. He quite stole the show. I remember 'Crack' was behind the dolmen about then so he ought to be able to tell you if there was anything—anything—wrong—"

"Yes. What did he do while he was there?"

"Nothing. He just stood. Anyway," Camilla said rapidly, "he couldn't do anything much, could he, in that harness? Nothing—nothing that would—"

"No," Alleyn said, "he couldn't. What *did* he do, in fact?"

"Well, he sort of played up to Ralph and Ernie. He gave a kind of falsetto scream—meant to be a neigh, I expect—and he went off at the back."

"Yes? And then?"

"Then Ralph pretended to hide. He crouched down behind a heap of rubble and he'd still got Ernie's sword. And Ernie went offstage looking for him."

"You're sure all this is in the right order?"

"I think so. One looked at it in terms of theatre," said Camilla. "So, of course, one wouldn't forget."

"No," Alleyn agreed with careful gravity, "one wouldn't, would one? And then?"

"Then Uncle Dan did his solo and I rather think that was when the bonfire flared up." She looked at Dr. Otterly. "Do you?"

"It was then. I was playing 'Lord Mardian's Fancy,' which is Dan's tune."

"Yes. And Ralph came out of his hiding place and went off at the back. He must have returned his sword to Ernie and walked round behind the wall because he came on at the O.P. entrance. I *call* it 'O.P.' "

"Precisely."

"And I think, at about the same time, Ernie and

'Crack' must have come back together through the centre entrance at the back."

"And Ernie had got his sword?"

"Yes, he had. I remember thinking, 'So Ralph's given him back his sword,' and, anyway, I'd noticed that Ralph hadn't got it any longer."

Camilla had a very direct way of looking at people. She looked, now, straight at Alleyn and frowned a little. Then, a curious thing happened to her face. It turned ashen white without changing its expression. "About the sword," she said. "About the sword—?"

"Yes?"

"It wasn't—it couldn't have been—could it?"

"There's no saying," Alleyn said gently, "what the weapon was. We're just clearing the ground, you know."

"But it couldn't. No. Nobody went near with the sword. I swear nobody went near. I swear."

"Do you? Well, that's a very helpful thing for us to know."

Dr. Otterly said, "I do, too, you know, Alleyn."

Camilla threw a look of agonized gratitude at him and Alleyn thought, "Has she already learnt at her drama school to express the maximum of any given emotion at any given time? Perhaps. But she hasn't learnt to turn colour in six easy lessons. She was frightened, poor child, and now she's relieved and it's pretty clear to me she's fathoms deep in love with Master Stayne."

He offered Camilla a cigarette and moved round behind her as he struck a match for it.

"Dr. Otterly," he said, "I wonder if you'd be terribly kind and ring up Yowford about the arrangements there? I've only just thought of it, fool that I am. Fox will give you the details. Sorry to be such a bore."

He winked atrociously at Dr. Otterly, who opened his mouth and shut it again.

"There, now!" said Mr. Fox, "and I'd meant to remind you. 'T, 't, 't! Shall we fix it up now, Doctor? No time like the present."

"Come back," Alleyn said, "when it's all settled, won't you?"

Dr. Otterly looked fixedly at him, smiled with constraint upon Camilla and suffered Mr. Fox to shepherd him out of the room.

Alleyn sat down opposite Camilla and helped himself to a cigarette.

"All wrong on duty," he said, "but there aren't any witnesses. *You* won't write a complaint to the Yard, will you?"

"No," Camilla said and added, "Did you send them away on purpose?"

"How did you guess?" Alleyn asked admiringly.

"It had all the appearance of a piece of full-sized hokum."

"Hell, how shaming! Never mind, I'll press on. I sent them away because I wanted to ask you a personal question and having no witnesses makes it unofficial. I wanted to ask you if you were about to become engaged to be married."

Camilla choked on her cigarette.

"Come on," Alleyn said. "Do tell me, like a nice comfortable child."

"I don't know. Honestly I don't."

"Can't you make up your mind?"

"There's no reason that *I* can see," Camilla said, with a belated show of spirit, "why I should tell you anything at all about it."

"Nor there is, if you'd rather not."

"Why do you want to know?"

"It makes it easier to talk to people," Alleyn said, "if you know about their preoccupations. A threatened engagement is a major preoccupation, as you will allow and must admit."

"All right," Camilla said. "I'll tell you. I'm not engaged but Ralph wants us to be."

"And you? Come," Alleyn said, answering the brilliant look she suddenly gave him. "You're in love with him, aren't you?"

"It's not as easy as all that."

"Isn't it?"

"You see, my mother was Bess Andersen. She was the feminine counterpart of Dan and Andy and Chris and Nat, and talked and thought like them. She was their sister. I loved my mother," Camilla said fiercely, "with all my heart. And my father, too. We should have been a happy family and, in a way, we were: in our attachment for each other. But my mother wasn't really happy. All her life she was homesick for South Mardian and she never learnt to fit in with my father's setting. People tell you differences of that sort don't matter any more. Not true. They matter like hell."

"And that's the trouble?"

"That's it."

"Anything more specific?"

"Look," Camilla said, "forgive my asking, but did you get on in the Force by sheer cheek or sheer charm or what?"

"Tell me your trouble," Alleyn said, "and I'll tell you the secret of my success-story. Of course, there's your pride, isn't there?"

"All right. Yes. And there's also the certainty of the past being rehashed by the more loathsome daily newspapers in the light of this ghastly crime. I don't know," Camilla burst out, "how I can *think* of Ralph, and I *am* thinking all the time of him, after what has happened."

"But why shouldn't you think of him?"

"I've told you. Ralph's a South Mardian man. His mother was a Mardian. His aunt was jilted by my papa when he ran away with my mum. My Mardian relations are the Andersen boys. If Ralph marries me, there'd be hell to pay. Every way there'd be hell. He's Dame Alice's heir, after his aunt, and, although I agree that doesn't matter so much—he's a solicitor and able to make his own way—she'd undoubtedly cut him off."

"I wonder. Talking of Wills, by the way, do you know if your grandfather made one?"

Camilla caught back her breath. "Oh, God!" she whispered. "I hope not. Oh, I *hope* not."

Alleyn waited.

"He talked about it," Camilla said, "last time I saw him. Four days ago. We had a row about it."

"If you'd rather not tell me, you needn't."

"I said I wouldn't touch a penny of his money, ever, and that, if he left me any, I'd give it to the Actors' Benevolent Fund. That rocked him."

"He'd spoken of leaving you something?"

"Yes. Sort of backhandedly. I didn't understand, at first. It was ghastly. As if I'd come here to—ugh!—to sort of worm my way into his good books. Too frightful it was."

"The day before yesterday," Alleyn said, watching her, "he visited his solicitors in Biddlefast."

"He *did?* Oh, my goodness me, how awful. Still, perhaps it was about something else."

"The solicitors are Messrs. Stayne and Stayne."

"That's Ralph's office," Camilla said instantly. "How funny. Ralph didn't say anything about it."

"Perhaps," Alleyn suggested lightly, "it was a secret."

"What do you mean?" she said quickly.

"A professional secret."

"I see."

"Is Mr. Ralph Stayne your own solicitor, Miss Campion?"

"Lord, no," Camilla said. "I haven't got one."

The door opened and a dark young man, wearing a face of thunder, strode into the room.

He said in a magnificent voice, "I consider it proper and appropriate for me to be present at any interviews Miss Campion may have with the police."

"Do you?" Alleyn said mildly. "In what capacity?"

"As her solicitor."

"My poorest heavenly old booby!" Camilla ejaculated, and burst into peals of helpless laughter.

"Mr. Ralph Stayne," Alleyn said, "I presume."

iii

The five Andersens, bunched together in their cold smithy, contemplated Sergeant Obby. Chris, the belligerent brother, slightly hitched his trousers and placed himself before the sergeant. They were big men and of equal height.

"Look yur," Chris said, "Bob Obby. Us chaps want to have a tell. Private."

Without shifting his gaze, which was directed at some distant object above Chris's head, Obby very slightly shook his own. Chris reddened angrily and Dan intervened:

"No harm in that now, Bob; natural as the day, seeing what's happened."

"You know us," the gentle Andy urged. "Soft as doves so long's we're easy-handled. Harmless."

"But mortal set," Nat added, "on our own ways. That's us. Come on, now, Bob."

Sergeant Obby pursed his lips and again slightly shook his head.

Chris burst out, "If you're afraid we'll break one of your paltry by-laws you can watch us through the bloody winder."

"But out of earshot, in simple decency," Nat pursued. "For ten minutes you're axed to shift. Now!"

After a longish pause and from behind an expressionless face, Obby said, "Can't be done, souls."

Ernie broke into aimless laughter.

"Why, you damned fool," Chris shouted at Obby, "what's gone with you? D'you reckon one of us done it?"

"Not for me to say," Obby primly rejoined, "and I'm sure I hope you're all as innocent as newborn babes. But I got my duty, which is to keep observation on the whole boiling of you, guilty or not, as the case may be."

"We got to talk PRIVATE!" Chris shouted. "We got to." Sergeant Obby produced his notebook.

"No 'got' about it," he said. "Not in the view of the law."

"To oblige, then?" Andy urged.

"The suggestion," Obby said, "is unworthy of you, Andrew."

He opened his book and licked his pencil.

"What's that for?" Chris demanded.

Obby looked steadily at him and made a note.

"Get out!" Chris roared.

"That's a type of remark that does an innocent party no good," Obby told him. "Let alone a guilty."

"What the hell d'you mean by that?"

"Ax yourself."

"Are you trying to let on you reckon one of us is a guilty party? Come on. Are you?"

"Any such caper on my part would be dead against the regulations," Obby said stuffily.

"Then why do you pick on me to take down in writing? What 'ave I done?"

"Only yourself and your Maker," Obby remarked, "knows the answer to that one."

"And me," Ernie announced unexpectedly. "*I* know."

Sergeant Obby became quite unnaturally still. The Andersens, too, seemed to be suspended in a sudden, fierce attentiveness. After a considerable pause, Obby said, "What might you know, then, Ernest?"

"Ar-ar-ar! That'd be telling!"

"So it would," Chris said shortly. "So shut your big silly mouth and forget it."

"No, you don't, Christopher," Obby rejoined. "If Ern's minded to pass a remark, he's at liberty to do so. Speak up, Ernest. What was you going to say? You don't," Obby added hastily, "*have* to talk, but if you want to, I'm here to see fair play. What's on your mind, Ernest?"

Ernie dodged his head and looked slyly at his brothers. He began to laugh with the grotesquerie of his kind. He half shut his eyes and choked over his words. "What price Sunday, then? What price Chrissie and the Guiser? What price you-know-who?"

He doubled himself up in an ecstasy of bucolic enjoyment. "How's Trix?" he squeaked and gave a shrill catcall. "Poor old Chrissie," he exulted.

Chris said savagely, "Do you want the hide taken off of you?"

"When's the wedding, then?" Ernie asked, dodging behind Andy. "Nothing to hold you now, is there?"

"By God—!" Chris shouted and lunged forward. Andy laid his hands on Chris's chest.

"Steady, naow, Chris, boy, steady," Andy begged him.

"And you, Ernie," Dan added, "you do like what Chris says and shut your mouth." He turned on Obby. "You know damn' well what he's like. Silly as a sheep. You didn't ought to encourage him. 'Tain't neighbourly."

Obby completed his notes and put up his book. He looked steadily from one of the Andersens to another. Finally, he addressed himself to them collectively.

"Neighbourliness," he said, "doesn't feature in this job. I don't say I like it that way, but that's the way it is. I don't say if I could get a transfer at this moment I wouldn't take it and pleased to do so. But I can't, and that being so, souls, here I stick according to orders." He paused and buttoned his pocket over his notebook. "Your dad," he said, "was a masterpiece. Put me up for the Lodge, did your dad. Worth any two of you, if you'll overlook the bluntness. And, unpleasant though it may be to contemplate, whoever done him in, ghastly and brutal, deserves what he'll get. I said 'whoever,' " Sergeant Obby repeated with sledgehammer emphasis and let his gaze dwell in a leisurely manner first on Ernest Andersen and then on Chris.

"All right. *All* right," Dan said disgustedly. "Us all knows you're a monument."

Nat burst out, "What d'you think *we* are, then? Doan't you reckon we're all burning fiery hot to lay our hands on the bastard that done it? Doan't you?"

"Since you ax me," Sergeant Obby said thoughtfully, "no. Not all of you. No, I don't."

iv

"I am not in the least embarrassed," Ralph said angrily. "You may need a solicitor, Camilla, and, if you do, you will undoubtedly consult me. My firm has acted for your family—ah—for many years."

"There you are!" Alleyn said cheerfully. "The point is, did your firm act for Miss Campion's family in the person of her grandfather, the day before yesterday?"

"That," Ralph said grandly, "is neither here nor there."

"Look," Camilla said, "darling. I've told Mr. Alleyn that Grandfather intimated to me that he was thinking of leaving me some of his cash and that I said I wouldn't have it at any price."

Ralph glared doubtfully at her. It seemed to Alleyn that Ralph was in that degree of love which demands of its victim some kind of emphatic action. "He's suffering," Alleyn thought, "from in-growing knight-errantry. And I fancy he's also very much worried about something." He told Ralph that he wouldn't at this stage press for information about the Guiser's visit but that, if the investigation seemed to call for it, he could insist.

Ralph said that, apart from professional discretion and propriety, there was no reason at all why the object of the Guiser's visit should not be revealed, and he proceeded to reveal it. The Guiser had called on Ralph, personally, and told him that he wished to make a Will. He had been rather strange in his manner, Ralph thought, and beat about the bush for some time.

"I gathered," Ralph said to Camilla, "that he felt he wanted to atone—although he certainly didn't put it like that—for his harshness to your mama. It was clear enough you had completely won his heart and I must say," Ralph went on in a rapid burst of devotion, "I wasn't surprised at that."

"Thank you, Ralph," said Camilla.

"He also told me," Ralph continued, addressing himself with obvious difficulty to Alleyn, "that he believed Miss Campion might refuse a bequest and it turned out that he wanted to know if there were some legal method of tying her up so that she would be obliged to accept it. Of course I told him there wasn't." Here Ralph looked at Camilla and instantly abandoned Alleyn. "I said—I knew, dear—I knew you would want me to—that it might be better for him to think it over and that, in any case, his sons had a greater claim, surely, and that you would never want to cut them out."

"Darling, I'm terribly glad you said that."

"Are you? I'm so glad."

They gazed at each other with half-smiles. Alleyn said, "To interrupt for a moment your mutual rejoicing—" and they both jumped slightly.

"Yes," Ralph said rapidly. "So then he told me to draft a Will on those lines, all the same, and he'd have a look at it and then make up his mind. He also wanted some stipulation made about keeping Copse Forge on as a smithy and not converting it into a garage, which the boys, egged on by Simon Begg, rather fancy. He asked me if I'd frame a letter that he could sign, putting it to Miss Campion—"

"Darling, I have *told* Mr. Alleyn we're in love, only not engaged on account of I've got scruples."

"Camilla, darling! Putting it to her that she ought to accept for his ease of spirit, as it were, and for the sake of the late Mrs. Elizabeth Campion's memory."

"My mum," Camilla said in explanation.

"And then he went. He proposed, by the way, to leave Copse Forge to his sons and everything else to Camilla."

"Would there be much else?" Alleyn asked, remembering what Dan Andersen had told him. Camilla answered him almost in her uncle's words. "All the Andersens are great ones for putting away. They used to call Grandfather an old jackdaw."

"Did you, in fact, frame a draft on those lines?" Alleyn asked Ralph.

"No. It was only two days ago. I was a bit worried about the whole thing."

"Sweetest Ralph, why didn't you ask *me?*"

"Darling: (a) because you'd refused to see me at all and (b) because it would have been grossly unprofessional."

"Fair enough," said Camilla.

"But you already knew, of course," Alleyn pointed out, "that your grandfather was considering this step?"

"I told you. We had a row about it."

"And you didn't know he'd gone to Biddlefast on Tuesday?"

"No," she said, "I didn't go down to the forge on Tuesday. I didn't know."

"All right," Alleyn said and got up. "Now I want to have a word or two with your young man, if I'm allowed to call him that. There's no real reason why you should leave us, except that I seem to get rather less than two fifths of his attention while you are anywhere within hail." He walked to the door and opened it. "If you see Inspector Fox and Dr. Otterly," he said, "would you be very kind and ask them to come back?"

Camilla rose and walked beautifully to the door.

"Don't you want to discover Ralph's major preoccupation?" she asked and fluttered her eyelashes.

"It declares itself abundantly. Run along and render love's awakening. Or don't you have that one at your drama school?"

"How did you know I went to drama school?"

"I can't imagine. Star-quality, or something."

"What a heavenly remark!" she said.

He looked at Camilla. There she was: loving, beloved, full of the positivism of youth, immensely vulnerable, immensely resilient. "Get along with you," he said. No more than a passing awareness of something beyond her field of observation seemed to visit Camilla. For a moment she looked puzzled. "Stick to your own preoccupation," Alleyn advised her, and gently propelled her out of the room.

Fox and Dr. Otterly appeared at the far end of the passage. They stood aside for Camilla, who, with great charm, said, "Please, I was to say you're wanted."

She passed them. Dr. Otterly gave her an amiable buffet. "All right, Cordelia?" he asked. She smiled brilliantly at him. "As well as can be expected, thank you," said Camilla.

When they had rejoined Alleyn, Dr. Otterly said, "An infallible sign of old age is a growing inability to understand the toughness of the young. I mean toughness in the nicest sense," he added, catching sight of Ralph.

"Camilla," Ralph said, "is quite fantastically sensitive."

"My dear chap, no doubt. She is a perfectly enchanting girl in every possible respect. What I'm talking about is a purely physiological matter. Her perfectly enchanting little inside mechanisms react youthfully to shock. My old machine is in a different case. That's all, I assure you."

Ralph thought to himself how unamusing old people were when they generalized about youth. "Do you still want me, sir?" he asked Alleyn.

"Please. I want your second-to-second account of the Dance of the Five Sons. Fox will take notes and Dr. Otterly will tell us afterwards whether your account tallies with his own impressions."

"I see," Ralph said, and looked sharply at Dr. Otterly.

Alleyn led him along the now-familiar train of events and at no point did his account differ from the others. He was able to elaborate a little. When the Guiser ducked down after the mock beheading, Ralph was quite close to him. He saw the old man stoop, squat and then ease himself cautiously down into the depression. "There was nothing wrong with him," Ralph said. "He saw me and made a signal with his hand and I made an answering one, and then went off to take up the collection. He'd planned to lie in the hollow because he thought he would be out of sight there."

"Was anybody else as close to him as you were?"

"Yes, 'Crack'—Begg, you know. He was my opposite number just before the breaking of the knot. And after that, he stood behind the dolmen for a bit and—" Ralph stopped.

"Yes?"

"It's just that—no, really, it's nothing."

"May I butt in?" Dr. Otterly said quickly from the fireside. "I think perhaps I know what Ralph is thinking. When we rehearsed, 'Crack' and the Betty—Ralph—stood one on each side of the dolmen and then, while Ralph took up the collection, 'Crack' was meant to cavort round the edge of the crowd repeating his girl-scaring act. He didn't do that last night. Did he, Ralph?"

"I don't think so," Ralph said and looked very disturbed. "I don't, of course, know which way your mind's working, but the best thing we can do is to say that, wearing the harness he does, it'd be quite impossible for Begg to do—well, to do what must have been done. Wouldn't it, Dr. Otterly?"

"Utterly impossible. He can't so much as see his own hands. They're under the canvas body of the horse. Moreover, I was watching him and he stood quite still."

"When did he move?"

"When Ralph stole Ernie Andersen's sword. Begg squeaked like a neighing filly and jogged out by the rear exit."

"Was it in order for him to go off then?"

"Could be," Ralph said. "The whole of that part of the show's an improvisation. Begg probably thought Ernie's and my bit of fooling would do well enough for him to take time off. That harness is damned uncomfortable. Mine's bad enough."

"You, yourself, went out through the back exit a little later, didn't you?"

"That's right," Ralph agreed very readily. "Ernie chased me, you know, and I hid. In full view of the audience. He went charging off by the back exit, hunting me. I thought to myself, Ernie *being* Ernie, that the joke had probably gone far enough, so I went out too, to find him."

"What *did* you find, out there? Behind the wall?"

"What you'd expect. 'Crack' squatting there like a great clucky hen. Ernie looking absolutely furious. I gave him back his sword and he said—" Ralph scratched his head.

"What did he say?"

"I think he said something about it being too late to be any use. He was pretty bloody-minded. I suppose it *was* rather a mistake to bait him, but it went down well with the audience."

"Did Begg say anything?"

"Yes. From inside 'Crack.' He said Ernie was a bit rattled and it'd be a good idea if I left him alone. I could see that for myself, so I went off round the outside wall and came through the archway by the house. Dan finished his solo. The Sons began their last dance. Ernie came back with his sword and 'Crack' followed him."

"Where to?"

"Just up at the back somewhere, I fancy. Behind the dancers."

"And you, yourself? Did you go anywhere near the dolmen on your return?"

Ralph looked again at Dr. Otterly and seemed to be undecided. "I'm not sure," he said. "I don't really remember."

"Do you remember, Dr. Otterly?"

"I think," Otterly said quietly, "that Ralph did make a round trip during the dance. I suppose that would bring him fairly close to the stone."

"Behind it?"

"Yes. Behind it."

Ralph said, "I remember now. Damn' silly of me. Yes, I did a trip round."

"Did you notice the Guiser lying in the hollow?"

Ralph lit himself a cigarette and looked at the tip. He said, "I don't remember."

"That's a pity."

"Actually, at the time, I was thinking of something quite different."

"Yes?"

"Yes. I'd caught sight of Camilla," said Ralph simply.

"Where was she?"

"At the side and towards the back. The left side, as you faced the dancing arena. O.P., she calls it."

"By herself?"

"Yes. Then."

"But not earlier? Before she ran away from 'Crack'?"

"No." Ralph's face slowly flooded to a deep crimson. "At least, I don't think so."

"Of course she wasn't," Dr. Otterly said in some surprise. "She came up with the party from this pub. I remember thinking what a picture the two girls made, standing there together in the torchlight."

"The *two* girls?"

"Camilla was there with Trixie and her father."

"Was she?" Alleyn asked Ralph.

"I—ah—I—yes, I believe she was."

"Mr. Stayne," Alleyn said, "you will think my next question impertinent and you may refuse to answer it. Miss Campion has been very frank about your friendship. She has told me that you are fond of each other but that, because of her mother's marriage and her own background, in its relation to yours, she feels an engagement would be a mistake."

"Which is most utter and besotted bilge," Ralph said hotly. "Good God, what age does she think she's living in! Who the hell cares if her mum was a blacksmith's daughter?"

"Perhaps she does."

"I never heard such a farrago of unbridled snobbism."

"All right. I daresay not. You said, just now, I think, that Miss Campion had refused to see you. Does that mean you haven't spoken to each other since you've been in South Mardian?"

"I really fail to understand—"

"I'm sure you don't. See here, now. Here's an old man with his head off, lying on the ground behind a sacrificial stone. Go back a bit in time. Here are eight men, including the old man, who performed a sort of play-dance as old as sin. Eight men," Alleyn repeated and vexedly rubbed his nose. "Why do I keep wanting to say 'nine'? Never mind. On the face of it, the old man never leaves the arena, or dance-floor, or stage, or whatever the hell you like to call it. On the face of it, nobody offered him any violence. He dances in full view. He has his head cut off in pantomime and in what, for want of a better word, we must call fun. But it isn't really cut off. You exchanged signals with him after the fun, so we know it isn't. He hides in a low depression. Eight minutes later, when he's meant to resurrect and doesn't, he is found to be genuinely decapitated. That's the story everybody gives us. Now, as a reasonably intelligent chap and a solicitor into the bargain, don't you think that we want to know every damn' thing we can find out about those eight men and anybody connected with them?"

"You mean—just empirically. Hoping something will emerge?"

"Exactly. You know very well that where nothing apropos does emerge, nothing will be made public."

"Oh, no, no, no," Ralph ejaculated irritably. "I suppose I'm being tiresome. What was this blasted question? Have I spoken to Camilla since we both came to South Mardian? All right, I have. After church on Sunday. She'd asked me not to, but I did because the sight of her in church was too much for me."

"That was your only reason?"

"She was upset. She'd come across Ernie howling over a dead dog in the copse."

"Bless my soul!" Alleyn ejaculated. "What next in South Mardian? Was the dog called Keeper?"

Ralph grinned. "I suppose it is all a bit Brontë. The Guiser had shot it because he said it wasn't healthy, which was no more than God's truth. But Ernie cut up uncommonly rough and it upset Camilla."

"Where did you meet her?"

"Near the forge. Coming out of the copse."

"Did you see the Guiser on this occasion?"

After a very long pause, Ralph said, "Yes. He came up."

"Did he realize that you wanted to marry his granddaughter?"

"Yes."

"And what was his reaction?"

Ralph said, "Unfavourable."

"Did he hold the same views that she does?"

"More or less."

"You discussed it there and then?"

"He sent Camilla away first."

"Will you tell me exactly all that was said?"

"No. It was nothing to do with his death. Our conversation was entirely private."

Fox contemplated the point of his pencil and Dr. Otterly cleared his throat.

"Tell me," Alleyn said abruptly, "this thing you wear as the Betty—it's a kind of Stone Age crinoline to look at, isn't it?"

Ralph said nothing.

"Am I dreaming it, or did someone tell me that it's sometimes used as a sort of extinguisher? Popped over a girl so that she can be carried off unseen? Origin," he suggested facetiously, "of the phrase 'undercover girl'? Or 'undercover man,' of course."

Ralph said quickly and easily, "They used to get up to some such capers, I believe, but I can't see how they managed to carry anybody away. My arms are *outside* the skirt thing, you know."

"I thought I noticed openings at the sides."

"Well—yes. But with the struggle that would go on—"

"Perhaps," Alleyn said, "the victim didn't struggle."

The door opened and Trixie staggered in with two great buckets of coal.

"Axcuse me, sir," she said. "You-all must be starved with cold. Boy's never handy when wanted."

Ralph had made a movement towards her as if to take her load, but had checked awkwardly.

Alleyn said, "That's much too heavy for you. Give them to me."

"Let be, sir," she said, "no need."

She was too quick for him. She set one bucket on the hearth and, with a sturdy economy of movement, shot half the contents of the other on the fire. The knot of reddish hair shone on the nape of her neck. Alleyn was reminded of a Brueghel peasant. She straightened herself easily and turned. Her face, blunt and acquiescent, held, he thought, its own secrets and, in its mode, was attractive.

She glanced at Ralph and her mouth widened.

"You don't look too clever yourself, then, Mr. Ralph," she said. "Last night's ghastly business has overset us all, I reckon."

"I'm all right," Ralph muttered.

"Will there be anything, sir?" Trixie asked Alleyn pleasantly.

"Nothing at the moment, thank you. Later on in the day sometime, when you're not too busy, I might ask for two words with you."

"Just ax," she said. "I'm willing if wanted."

She smiled quite broadly at Ralph Stayne. "Bean't I, Mr. Ralph?" she asked placidly and went away, swinging her empty bucket.

"Oh, *God!*" Ralph burst out, and, before any of them could speak, he was gone, slamming the door behind him.

"Shall I—?" Fox said and got to his feet.

"Let him be."

They heard an outer door slam.

"*Well!*" Dr. Otterly exclaimed with mild concern, "I must say I'd never thought of *that!*"

"And nor, you may depend upon it," Alleyn said, "has Camilla."

CHAPTER VIII Question of Fact

WHEN afternoon closing-time came, Trixie pulled down the bar shutters and locked them. Simon Begg went into the Private. There was a telephone in the passage outside the Private and he had put a call through to his bookmaker. He wanted, if he could, to get the results of the 1.30 at Sandown. Teutonic Dancer was a rank outsider. He'd backed it both ways for a great deal more than he could afford to lose and had already begun to feel that, if he did lose, it would in some vague way be Mrs. Bünz's fault. This was both ungracious and illogical.

For many reasons, Mrs. Bünz was the last person he wanted to see and, for an equal number of contradictory ones, she was the first. And there she was, the picture of uncertainty and alarm, huddled, snuffling, over the parlour fire with her dreadful cold and her eternal notebooks.

She had bought a car from Simon, she might be his inspiration in a smashing win. One way and another, they had done business together. He produced a wan echo of his usual manner.

"Hullo-'llo! And how's Mrs. B. today?" asked Simon.

"Unwell. I have caught a severe cold in the head. Also, I have received a great shawk. Last night in the pawk was a terrible, terrible shawk."

"You can say that again," he agreed glumly, and applied himself to the *Sporting News*.

Suddenly, they both said together, "As a matter of fact—" and stopped, astonished and disconcerted.

"Ladies first," said Simon.

"Thank you. I was about to say that, as a matter of fact, I would suggest that our little transaction—Ach! How shall I say it?—should remain, perhaps—"

"Confidential?" he ventured eagerly.

"That is the word for which I sought. Confidential."

"I'm all for it. Mrs. B. I was going to make the same suggestion myself. Suits me."

"I am immensely relieved. Immensely. I thank you, Wing-Commander. I trust, at the same time—you do not think—it would be so shawkink—if—"

"Eh?" He looked up from his paper to stare at her. "What's that? No, no. no. Mrs. B. Not to worry. Not a chance. The idea's laughable."

"To me it is not amusink but I am glad you find it so," Mrs. Bünz said stuffily. "You read something of interest, perhaps, in your newspaper?"

"I'm waiting. Teutonic Dancer. Get me? The one-thirty?"

Mrs. Bünz shuddered.

"Oh, well!" he said. "There you are. I follow the form as a general thing. Don't go much for gimmicks. Still! Talk about coincidence! You couldn't go past it, really, could you?" He raised an admonitory finger. The telephone had begun to ring in the passage. "My call," he said. "This is it. Keep your fingers crossed, Mrs. B."

He darted out of the room.

Mrs. Bünz, left alone, breathed uncomfortably through her mouth, blew her nose and clocked her tongue against her palate. "Dar," she breathed.

Fox came down the passage past Simon, who was saying, "Hold the line, please, miss, for Pete's sake. Hold the line," and entered the parlour.

"Mrs. Burns?" he asked.

Mrs. Bünz, though she eyed him with evident misgivings, rallied sufficiently to correct him. "*Eü, eü, eü,*" she demonstrated windily through her cold. "Bünz."

"Now that's *very* interesting," Fox said beaming at her. "That's a noise, if you will excuse me referring to it as such, that we don't make use of in English, do we? Would it be the same, now, as the sound in the French *eu?*" He arranged his sedate mouth in an agonized pout. "*Deux diseuses,*" said Mr. Fox by way of illustration. "Not that I get beyond a very rough approximation, I'm afraid."

"It is not the same at all. *Bünz.*"

"Bünz," mouthed Mr. Fox.

"Your accent is not perfect."

"I know that," he agreed heavily. "In the meantime, I'm forgetting my job. Mr. Alleyn presents his compliments and wonders if you'd be kind enough to give him a few minutes."

"Ach! I too am forgetting. You are the police."

"You wouldn't think so, the way I'm running on, would you?"

(Alleyn had said, "If she was an anti-Nazi refugee, she'll think we're ruthless automatons. Jolly her along a bit.")

Mrs. Bünz gathered herself together and followed Fox. In the passage, Simon Begg was saying, "Look, old boy, *all* I'm asking for is the gen on the one-thirty. Look, old boy—"

Fox opened the door of the sitting-room and announced her.

"Mrs. Bünz," he said quite successfully.

As she advanced into the room Alleyn seemed to see, not so much a middle-aged German, as the generalization of a species. Mrs. Bünz was the lady who sits near the front at lectures and always asks questions. She has an enthusiasm for obscure musicians, stands nearest to guides, keeps handicraft shops of the better class and reads Rabindranath Tagore. She weaves, forms circles, gives talks, hand-throws pots and designs book-plates. She is sometimes a vegetarian, though not always a crank. Occasionally, she is an expert.

She walked slowly into the room and kept her gaze fixed on Alleyn. "She is afraid of me," he thought.

"This is Mr. Alleyn, Mrs. Bünz," Dr. Otterly said.

Alleyn shook hands with her. Her own short stubby hand was tremulous and the palm was damp. At his invitation, she perched warily on a chair. Fox sat down behind her and palmed his notebook out of his pocket.

"Mrs. Bünz," Alleyn said, "in a minute or two I'm going to throw myself on your mercy."

She blinked at him.

"Zo?" said Mrs. Bünz.

"I understand you're an expert on folklore and, if ever anybody needed an expert, we do."

"I have gone a certain way."

"Dr. Otterly tells me," Alleyn said, to that gentleman's astonishment, "that you have probably gone as far as anyone in England."

"Zo," she said, with a magnificent inclination towards Otterly.

"But, before we talk about that, I suppose I'd better ask you the usual routine questions. Let's get them over as soon as possible. I'm told that you gave Mr. William Andersen a lift—"

They were off again on the old trail, Alleyn thought dejectedly, and not getting much further along it. Mrs. Bünz's account of the Guiser's hitch-hike corresponded with what he had already been told.

"I was so delighted to drive him," she began nervously. "It was a great pleasure to me. Once or twice I attempted, tactfully, to a little draw him out, but he was, I found, angry, and not inclined for cawnversation."

"Did he say anything at all, do you remember?"

"To my recollection he spoke only twice. To begin with, he invited me by gesture to stop and, when I did so, he asked me in his splendid, *splendid* rich dialect, 'Be you goink up-alongk?' *On* the drive, he remarked that when he found Mr. Ernie Andersen he would have the skin off of his body. Those, however, were his only remarks."

"And when you arrived?"

"He descended and hurried away."

"And what," Alleyn asked, "did you do?"

The effect of the question, casually put, upon Mrs. Bünz was extraordinary. She seemed to flinch back into her clothes as a tortoise into its shell.

"When you got there, you know," Alleyn gently prompted her. "What did you do?"

Mrs. Bünz said in a cold-thickened voice, "I became a spectator. Of course."

"Where did you stand?"

Her head sank a little further into her shoulders.

"Inside the archway."

"The archway by the house as you come in?"

"Yes."

"And, from there, you watched the dance?"

Mrs. Bünz wetted her lips and nodded.

"That must have been an absorbing experience. Had you any idea of what was in store for you?"

"Ach! No! No, I swear it! No!" she almost shouted.

"I meant," Alleyn said, "in respect of the dance itself."

"The dance," Mrs. Bünz said in a strangulated croak, "is unique."

"Was it all that you expected?"

"But, of course!" She gave a little gasp and appeared to be horror-stricken. "Really," Alleyn thought, "I seem to be having almost too much success with Mrs. Bünz. Every shy a coconut."

She had embarked on an elaborate explanation. All folk dance and drama had a common origin. One expected certain elements. The amazing thing about the Five Sons was that it combined so rich an assortment of these elements as well as some remarkable features of its own. "It has everythink. But everythink," she said and was plagued by a Gargantuan sneeze.

"And did they do it well?"

Mrs. Bünz said they did it wonderfully well. The best performance for sheer execution in England. She rallied from whatever shock she had suffered and began to talk incomprehensibly of galleys, split-jumps and double capers. Not only did she remember every move of the Five Sons and the Fool in their twice-repeated dance, but she had noted the positions of the Betty and Hobby. She remembered how these two pranced round the perimeter and how, later on, the Betty chased the young men and flung his skirts over their heads and the Hobby stood as an image behind the dolmen. She remembered everything.

"This is astonishing," he said, "for you to retain the whole thing, I mean, after seeing it only once. Extraordinary. How do you do it?"

"I—I—have a very good memory," said Mrs. Bünz and gave an agonized little laugh. "In such matters my memory is phenomenal." Her voice died away. She looked remarkably uncomfortable. He asked her if she took notes and she said at once she didn't, and then seemed in two minds whether to contradict herself.

Her description of the dance tallied in every respect with the accounts he had already been given, with one exception. She seemed to have only the vaguest recollection of the Guiser's first entrance when, as Alleyn had already been told, he had jogged round the arena and struck the Mardian dolmen with his clown's bladder. But, from then onwards, Mrs. Bünz knew everything right up to the moment when Ralph stole Ernie's sword. After that, for a short period, her memory seemed again to be at fault. She remembered that, somewhere about this time, the Hobby-Horse went off, but had apparently forgotten that Ernie gave chase after Ralph and only had the vaguest recollection, if any, of Ralph's improvised fooling with Ernie's sword. Moreover, her own uncertainty at this point seemed to embarrass her very much. She blundered about from one fumbled generalization to another.

"The solo was interesting—"

"Wait a bit," Alleyn said. She gulped and blinked at him. "Now look here, Mrs. Bünz. I'm going to put it to you that from the time the first dance ended with the mock death of the Fool until the solo began, you didn't watch the proceedings at all. Now, is that right?"

"I was not interested—"

"How could you know you wouldn't be interested if you didn't even look? *Did* you look, Mrs. Bünz?"

She gaped at him with an expression of fear. She was elderly and frightened and he supposed that, in her mind, she associated him with monstrous figures of her past. He was filled with compunction.

Dr. Otterly appeared to share Alleyn's feeling. He walked over to her and said, "Don't worry, Mrs. Bünz. Really, there's nothing to be frightened about, you know. They only want to get at the facts. Cheer up."

His large doctor's hands fell gently on her shoulders.

She gave a falsetto scream and shrank away from him.

"Hullo!" he said good-humouredly, "what's all this? Nerves? Fibrositis?"

"I—yes—yes. The cold weather."

"In your shoulders?"

"*Ja.* Both."

"Mrs. Bünz," Alleyn said, "will you believe me when I remind you of something I think you must already know? In England the Police Code has been most carefully framed to protect the public from any kind of bullying or overbearing behaviour on the part of investigating officers. Innocent persons have nothing to fear from us. Nothing. Do you believe that?"

It was difficult to hear what she said. She had lowered her head and spoke under her breath.

" . . . because I am German. It does not matter to you that I was anti-Nazi; that I am naturalized. Because I am German, you will think I am capable. It is different for Germans in England."

The three men raised a little chorus of protest. She listened without showing any sign of being at all impressed.

"They think I am capable," she said, "of anything."

"You say that, don't you, because of what Ernie Andersen shouted out when he stood last night on the dolmen?"

Mrs. Bünz covered her face with her knotty little hands.

"You remember what that was, don't you?" Alleyn asked.

Dr. Otterly looked as if he would like to protest but caught Alleyn's eye and said nothing.

Alleyn went on. "He pointed his sword at you, didn't he, and said, 'Ask her. She knows. She's the one that did it.' Something like that, wasn't it?" He waited for a moment, but she only rocked herself a little with her hands still over her face.

"Why do you think he said that, Mrs. Bünz?" Alleyn asked.

In a voice so muffled that they had to strain their ears to hear her, she said something quite unexpected.

"It is because I am a woman," said Mrs. Bünz.

ii

Try as he might, Alleyn could get no satisfactory explanation from Mrs. Bünz as to what she implied by this statement or why she had made it. He asked her if she was thinking of the exclusion of women from ritual dances and she denied this with such vehemence that it was clear the question had caught her on the raw. She began to talk rapidly, excitedly and, to Mr. Fox at least, embarrassingly about the sex element in ritual dancing.

"The man-woman!" Mrs. Bünz shouted. "An age-old symbol of fertility. And the Hobby, also, without a doubt. There must be the Betty to lover him and the Hobby to—"

She seemed to realize that this was not an acceptable elucidation of her earlier statement and came to a halt. Dr. Otterly, who had heard all about her arrival at Copse Forge, reminded her that she had angered the Guiser in the first instance by effecting an entrance into the smithy. He asked her if she thought Ernie had some confused idea that, in doing this, she had brought ill-luck to the performance.

Mrs. Bünz seized on this suggestion with feverish intensity. "Yes, yes," she cried. That, no doubt, was what Ernie had meant. Alleyn was unable to share her enthusiasm and felt quite certain it was assumed. She eyed him furtively. He realized, with immense distaste, that any forbearance or consideration that he might show her would probably be taken by Mrs. Bünz for weakness. She had her own ideas about investigating officers.

Furtively, she shifted her shoulders under their layers of woollen clothes. She made a queer little arrested gesture as if she were about to touch them and thought better of it.

Alleyn said, "Your shoulders *are* painful, aren't they? Why not let Dr. Otterly have a look at them? I'm sure he would."

Dr. Otterly made guarded professional noises, and Mrs. Bünz behaved as if Alleyn's suggestion was tantamount to the Usual Warning. She shook her head violently, became grey-faced and speechless and seemed to contemplate a sudden break-away.

"I won't keep you much longer," Alleyn said. "There are only one or two more questions. This is the first: at any stage of the proceedings last night did the Hobby-Horse come near you?"

At this she did get up, but slowly and with the unco-ordinated movements of a much older woman. Fox looked over the top of his spectacles at the door. Alleyn and Dr. Otterly rose and on a common impulse moved a little nearer to her. It occurred to Alleyn that it would really be rather a pleasant change to ask Mrs. Bünz a question that did *not* throw her into a fever.

"*Did* you make any contact at all with the Hobby?" he insisted.

"I think. Once. At the beginning, during his chasinks." Her eyes were streaming, but whether with cold or distress, it was impossible to say. "In his flirtinks he touched me," she said. "I think."

"So you have, no doubt, got tar on your clothes?"

"A liddle on my coat. I think."

"Do the Hobby and Betty rehearse, I wonder?"

Dr. Otterly opened his mouth and shut it again.

"I know nothing of that," Mrs. Bünz said.

"Do you know where they rehearsed?"

"Nothingk. I know nothingk."

Fox, who had his eye on Dr. Otterly, gave a stentorian cough and Alleyn hurried on.

"One more question, Mrs. Bünz, and I do ask you very seriously to give me a frank answer to it. I beg you to believe that, if you are innocent of this crime, you can do yourself nothing but good by speaking openly and without fear. Please believe it."

"I am combletely, *combletely* innocent."

"Good. Then here is the question: did you after the end of the first morris leave the courtyard for some reason and not return to it until the beginning of the solo dance? *Did you*, Mrs. Bünz?"

"No," said Mrs. Bünz very loudly.

"Really?"

"No."

Alleyn said after a pause, "All right. That's all. You may be asked later on to sign a statement. I'm afraid I must also ask you to stay in East Mardian until after the inquest." He went to the door and opened it. "Thank you," he said.

When she reached the door, she stood and looked at him. She seemed to collect herself and, when she spoke, it was with more composure than she had hitherto shown.

"It is the foolish son who had done it," she said. "He is epileptic. Ritual dancing has a profound effect upon such beings. They are carried back to their distant origins. They become excited. Had not this son already cut his father's hand and shed his blood with his sword? It is the son."

"How do you know he had already cut his father's hand?" Alleyn asked.

"I have been told," Mrs. Bünz said, looking as if she would faint.

Without another word and without looking at him again, she went out and down the passage.

Alleyn said to Fox, "Don't let her talk to Begg. Nip out, Fox, and tell him that, as we'll be a little time yet, he can go up to his garage and we'll look in there later. Probably suit him better, anyway."

Fox went out and Alleyn grinned at Dr. Otterly.

"You can go ahead now," he said, "if you want to spontaneously combust."

"I must say I feel damn' like it. What's she up to, lying right and left? Good God, I never heard anything like it! Not know when we rehearsed. Good God! They could hear us all over the pub."

"Where did you rehearse?"

"In the old barn at the back, here."

"Very rum. But I fancy," Alleyn muttered, "we know why she went away during the show."

"Are you sure she did?"

"My dear chap, yes. She's a fanatic. She's a folklore hound with her nose to the ground. She remembered the first and last parts of your programme with fantastic accuracy. *Of course*, if she'd been there she'd have watched the earthy antics of the comics. If they are comics. Of course. She'd have been on the look-out for all the fertility fun that you hand out. If she'd been there she'd have looked and she'd have remembered in precise detail. She doesn't remember because she didn't look and she didn't look because she wasn't there. I'd bet my boots on it and I bet I know why."

Fox returned, polishing his spectacles, and said, "Do you know what I reckon, Mr. Alleyn? I reckon Mrs. B. leaves the arena, just after the first dance, is away from it all through the collection and the funny business between young Mr. Stayne and daft Ernie and gets back before Dan Andersen does a turn on his own. Is that your idea?"

"Not altogether, Br'er Fox. If my tottering little freak of an idea is any good, she leaves her observation post *before* the first dance."

"Hey?" Fox ejaculated. "But it's the first dance that she remembers so well."

"I must say—" Dr. Otterly agreed and flapped his hands.

"Exactly," Alleyn said. "I know. Now, let me explain."

He did so at some length and they listened to him with the raised eyebrows of assailable incredulity.

"Well," they said, "I suppose it's possible." And, "It might be, but how'll you prove it?" And, "Even so, it doesn't get us all that much further, does it?" And, "How are you to find out?"

"It gets us a hell of a lot further," Alleyn said hotly, "as you'd find out pretty quickly if you could take a peep at Mrs. Bünz in the rude nude. However, since that little treat is denied us, let's visit Mr. Simon Begg and see what he can provide. What was he up to, Fox?"

"He was talking on the telephone about horse-racing," Fox said. "Something called 'Teutonic Dancer' in the one-thirty at Sandown. That's funny," Mr. Fox added. "I never thought of it at the time. Funny!"

"Screamingly. You might see if Bailey and Thompson are back, Fox, and if there's anything. They'll need a meal, poor devils. Trixie'll fix that, I daresay. Then we'll take a walk up the road to Begg's garage."

While Fox was away Alleyn asked Dr. Otterly if he could give him a line on Simon Begg.

"He's a local," Dr. Otterly said. "Son of the ex-village-shopkeeper. Name's still up over the shop. He did jolly well in the war with the R.A.F.—bomber-pilot. He was brought down over Germany, tackled a bunch of Huns single-handed and got himself and two of his crew back through Spain. They gave him the D.F.C. for it. He'd been a bit of a problem as a lad but he took to active service like a bird."

"And since the war?"

"Well—in a way, a bit of a problem again. I feel damn' sorry for him. As long as he was in uniform with his ribbons up he was quite a person. That's how it was with those boys, wasn't it? They lived high, wide and dangerous and they were everybody's heroes. Then he was demobilized and came back here. You know what country people are like: it takes a flying bomb to put a dent in their class-consciousness, and then it's only temporary. They began to say how ghastly the

R.A.F. slang was and to ask each other if it didn't rock you a bit when you saw them out of uniform. It's quite true that Simon bounded sky high and used an incomprehensible and irritating jargon and that some of his waist-coats were positively terrifying. All the same."

"I know," Alleyn said.

"I felt rather sorry for him. Neither fish, nor flesh nor stockbroker's Tudor. That was why I asked him to come into the Sword Wednesday show. Our old Hobby was killed in the raids. He was old Begg from Yowford, a relation of Simon's. There've been Beggs for Hobbies for a very long time."

"So this Begg has done it—how many times?"

"About nine. Ever since the war."

"What's he been up to all that time?"

"He's led rather a raffish kind of life for the last nine years. Constantly changing his job. Gambling pretty high, I fancy. Hanging round the pubs. Then, about three years ago his father died and he bought a garage up at Yowford. It's not doing too well, I fancy. He's said to be very much in the red. The boys would have got good backing from one of the big companies if they could have persuaded the Guiser to let them turn Copse Forge into a filling station. It's at a cross-roads and they're putting a main road through before long, more's the pity. They were very keen on the idea and wanted Simon to go in with them. But the Guiser wouldn't hear of it."

"They may get it—now," Alleyn said without emphasis. "And Simon may climb out of the red."

"He's scarcely going to murder William Andersen," Dr. Otterly pointed out acidly, "on the off-chance of the five sons putting up five petrol pumps. Apart from the undoubted fact that, wherever Begg himself may have got to last night, the Guiser certainly didn't leave the stage after he walked on to it and I defy you to perform a decapitation when you're trussed up in 'Crack's' harness. Besides, I *like* Begg; ghastly as he is, I like him."

"All right. I know. I didn't say a thing."

"You are not, I hope," Dr. Otterly angrily continued, "putting on that damned superior-sleuth act: 'you have the facts, my dear—' whatever the stooge's name is."

"Not I."

"Well, you've got some damned theory up your sleeve, haven't you?"

"I'm ashamed of it."

"*Ashamed?*"

"Utterly, Otterly."

"Ah, hell!" Dr. Otterly said in disgust.

"Come with us to Begg's garage. Keep on listening. If anything doesn't tally with what you remember, don't say a word unless I tip you the wink. All right? Here we go."

iii

In spite of the thaw, the afternoon had grown deadly cold. Yowford Lane dripped greyly between its hedgerows and was choked with mud and slush. About a mile along it, they came upon Simmy-Dick's Service Station in a disheartened-looking shack with Begg's car standing outside it. Alleyn pulled up at the first pump and sounded his horn.

Simon came out, buttoning up a suit of white overalls with a large monogram on the pocket: witness, Alleyn suspected, to a grandiloquent beginning. When he saw Alleyn, he grinned sourly and raised his eyebrows.

"Hullo," Alleyn said. "Four, please."

"Four what? Coals of fire?" Simon said, and moved round to the petrol tank.

It was an unexpected opening and made things a good deal easier for Alleyn. He got out of the car and joined Simon.

"Why coals of fire?" he asked.

"After me being a rude boy this morning."

"That's all right."

"It's just that I know what a clot Ernie can make of himself," Simon said, and thrust the nose of the hosepipe into the tank. "Four, you said?"

"Four. And this *is* a professional call, by the way."

"I'm not all that dumb," Simon grunted.

Alleyn waited until the petrol had gone in and then paid for it. Simon tossed the change up and caught it neatly before handing it over. "Why not come inside?" he suggested. "It's bloody cold out here, isn't it?"

He led the way into a choked-up cubby-hole that served as his office. Fox and Dr. Otterly followed Alleyn and edged in sideways.

"How's the Doc?" Simon said. "Doing a Watson?"

"I'm beginning to think so," said Dr. Otterly. Simon laughed shortly.

"Well," Alleyn began cheerfully, "how's the racing-news?"

"Box of birds," Simon said.

"Teutonic Dancer do any good for herself?"

Simon looked sharply at Fox. "Who's the genned-up type?" he said. "You?"

"That's right, Mr. Begg. I heard you on the telephone."

"I see." He took out his cigarettes, frowned over lighting one and then looked up with a grin. "I can't keep it to myself," he said. "It's the craziest thing. Came in at twenty-seven to one. Everything else must have fallen down."

"I hope you had something on."

"A wee flutter," Simon said and again the corners of his mouth twitched. "It was a dicey do, but was it worth it! How's the Doc?" he repeated, again aware of Dr. Otterly.

"Quite well, thank you. How's the garage proprietor?" Dr. Otterly countered chillily.

"Box of birds."

As this didn't seem to be getting them anywhere, Alleyn invited Simon to give them his account of the Five Sons.

He started off in a very business-like way, much, Alleyn thought, as he must have given his reports in his bomber-pilot days. The delayed entrance, the arrival of the Guiser, "steamed-up" and roaring at them all. The rapid change of clothes and the entrance. He described how he began the show with his pursuit of the girls.

"Funny! Some of them just about give you the go-ahead signal. I could see them through the hole in the neck. All giggles and girlishness. Half-windy, too. They reckon it's lucky or something."

"Did Miss Campion react like that?"

"The fair Camilla? I wouldn't have minded if she *had*. I made a very determined attempt, but not a chance. She crash-landed in the arms of another bod. Ralphy Stayne. Lucky type!"

He grinned cheerfully round. "*But*, still!" he said. It was a sort of summing up. One could imagine him saying it under almost any circumstances.

Alleyn asked him what he did after he'd finished his act and before the first morris began. He said he had gone up to the back archway and had a bit of a breather.

"And during the morris?"

"I just sort of bummed around on my own."

"With the Betty?"

"I think so. I don't remember exactly. I'm not sort of officially 'on' in that scene."

"But you didn't go right off?"

"No, I'm meant to hang round. I'm the animal-man. God knows what it's all in aid of, but I just sort of trot round on the outskirts."

"And you did that last night?"

"That's the story."

"You didn't go near the dancers?"

"I don't think so."

"Nor the dolmen?"

"No," he said sharply.

"You couldn't tell me, for instance, exactly what the Guiser did when he slipped down to hide?"

"Disappeared as usual behind the stone, I suppose, and lay doggo."

"Where were you at that precise moment?"

"I don't remember exactly."

"Nowhere near the dolmen?"

"Absolutely. Nowhere near."

"I see," Alleyn said, and was careful not to look at Dr. Otterly. "And then? After that? What did you do?"

"I just hung round for a bit and then wandered up to the back."

"What was happening in the arena?"

"The Betty did an act and after that Dan did his solo."

"What was the Betty's act?"

"Kind of ad lib. In the old days, they tell me, 'she' used to hunt down some bod in the crowd and tuck him under her petticoats. Or she'd come on screeching and, presently, there'd be a great commotion under the crinoline and out would pop some poor type. You can imagine, a high old time was had by all."

"Mr. Stayne didn't go in for that particular kind of clowning?"

"Who—Ralphy? Only very mildly. He's much too much the gentleman, if you know what I mean."

"What *did* he do?" Alleyn persisted.

"Honest, I've forgotten. I didn't really watch. Matter of fact, I oozed off to the back and had a smoke."

"When did you begin to watch again?"

"After Dan's solo. When the last dance began. I came back for that."

"And then?"

After that, Simon's account followed the rest. Alleyn let him finish without interruption and was then silent for so long that the others began to fidget and Simon Begg stood up.

"Well," he said, "if that's all—"

"I'm afraid it's nothing like all."

"Hell!"

"Let us consider," Alleyn said, "your story of your own movements during and immediately after the first dance—this dance that was twice repeated and ended with the mock decapitation. Why do you suppose that your account of it differs radically from all the other accounts we have had?"

Simon glanced at Dr. Otterly and assumed a tough and mulish expression.

"Your guess," he said, "is as good as mine."

"We don't want to guess. We'd like to know. We'd like to know, for instance, why you say you trotted round on the outskirts of the dance and that you didn't go near the dancers or the dolmen. Dr. Otterly here and all the other observers we have consulted say that, as a matter of fact, you went up to the dolmen at the moment of climax and stood motionless behind it."

"Do they?" he said. "I don't remember everything I did. Perhaps they don't either. P'r'aps you've been handed a lot of duff gen."

"If that means," Dr. Otterly said, "that I may have laid false information, I won't let you get away with it. I am absolutely certain that you stood close behind the dolmen and therefore so close to where the Guiser lay that you couldn't fail to notice him. Sorry, Alleyn. I've butted in."

"That's all right. You see, Begg, that's what they all say. Their accounts agree."

"Too bad," Simon said.

"If, in fact, you did stand behind the dolmen when he hid behind it you must have seen exactly what the Guiser did."

"I didn't see what the Guiser did. I don't remember being behind the stone. I don't think I was near enough to see."

"Would you make a statement, on oath, to that effect?"

"Why not?"

"And that you don't remember exactly what the clowning act was between the Betty and Ernest Andersen?"

"Didn't he and Ralphy have a row about his whiffler? Come to think of it, I believe I oozed off before they got going."

"No, you didn't. Sorry, Alleyn," said Dr. Otterly.

"We are told that 'Crack,' who was watching them,

gave a sort of neighing sound before he went off by the rear archway. Did you do that?"

"I might have. Daresay. Why the heck should I remember?"

"Because, up to the point when you finished tarring the village maidens and the dance-proper began, you remember everything very clearly. Then we get this period when you're overtaken by a sort of mental miasma, a period that covers the ritual of the Father and the Five Sons culminating in the mock death. Everybody else agrees about where you were at the moment of the climax: behind the dolmen, they tell us, standing stock still. You insist that you don't remember going near the dolmen."

"That's right," Simon said very coolly and puckered his lips in a soundless whistle. "To the best of my remembrance, you know."

"I think I'd better tell you that, in my opinion, this period, from the end of your improvisation until your return (and, incidentally, the return of your memory) covers the murder of William Andersen."

"I didn't hand him the big chop," Simon said. "Poor old bastard."

"Have you any notion who did?"

"No."

"I do *wish*," Alleyn said vexedly, "you wouldn't be such an ass—if you are being an ass, of course."

"Will that be all, Teacher?"

"No. How well do you know Mrs. Bünz?"

"I never met her till she came down here."

"You've sold her a car, haven't you?"

"That's right."

"Any other transactions?"

"What the hell do you mean?" Simon asked very quietly.

"Did you come to any understanding about Teutonic Dancer?"

Simon shifted his shoulders with a movement that reminded Alleyn of Mrs. Bünz herself. "Oh," he said. "That." He seemed to expand and the look of irrepressible satisfaction appeared again. "You might say the old dear brought me that bit of luck. I mean to say: could you beat it? Teutonic Dancer by Subsidize out of Substitution? Piece of cake!"

"Subsidize?"

"Yes. Great old sire, of course, but the dam isn't so hot."

"Did they give you any other ideas?"

"Who?"

"Subsidize and Substitution?"

"I don't," Simon said coolly, "know what you mean."

"Let it go, then. What clothes did you wear last night?"

"Clothes? Oldest I've got. By the time the party was over, I looked pretty much like the original tar-baby myself."

"What were they?"

"A heavy R.A.F. sweater and a pair of old cream slacks."

"Good," Alleyn said. "May we borrow them?"

"Look here, I don't much like this. Why?"

"Why do you think? To see if there's any blood on them."

"Thanks," said Simon turning pale, "very much!"

"We'll be asking for everybody's."

"Safety in numbers?" He hesitated and then looked again at Dr. Otterly. "Not my job," he muttered, "to try and teach the experts. I know that. All the same—"

"Come on," Alleyn said. "All the same, what?"

"I just happen to know. Anybody buys his bundle that way, there isn't just a *little* blood."

"I see. How do you happen to know?"

"Show I was in. Over Germany."

"Can you elaborate a bit?"

"It's not all that interesting. We got clobbered and I hit the silk the same time as she exploded."

"His bomber blew up and they parachuted down," Dr. Otterly translated drily.

"That's the story," Simon agreed.

"Touch and go?" Alleyn hazarded.

"You can say that again." Simon drew his brows together. His voice was unemphatic and without dramatic values, yet had the authentic colour of vivid recollection.

"I could see the Jerries before I hit the deck. Soon as I did they bounced me. Three of them. Two went the hard way. But the third, a little old tough-looking type he was, with a hedge-cutter, came up behind while I was still busy with his cobs. I turned and saw him. Too late to cope. I'd have bought it if one of my own crew hadn't come up and got operational. He used his knife." Simon made an all too graphic gesture. "That's how I know," he said. "O.K., isn't it, Doc? Buckets of blood?"

"Yes," Dr. Otterly agreed. "There would be."

"Yes. Which ought to make it a simple story," Simon said and turned to Alleyn. "Oughtn't it?"

"The story," Alleyn said, "would be a good deal simpler if everyone didn't try to elaborate it. Now, keep still. I haven't finished with you yet. Tell me this: as far as I can piece it out, you were either up at the back exit or just outside it when Ernie Andersen came backstage."

"Just outside it's right."

"What happened?"

"I told you. After the morris, I left Ralphy to it. I could hear him squeaking away and the mob laughing. I had a drag at a gasper and took the weight off the boots. Then the old Corp—that's Ernie, he was my batman in the war—came charging out in one of his tantrums. I couldn't make out what was biting him. After a bit, Ralphy turned up and gave Ernie his whiffler. Ralphy started to say, 'I'm sorry,' or something like that, but I told him to beat it. So he did."

"And then?"

"Well, then it was just about time for me to go back. So I did. Ernie went back, too."

"Who threw tar on the bonfire?"

"Nobody. I knocked the drum over with the edge of 'Crack's' body. It's a dirty big clumsy thing. Swings round. I jolly nearly went on fire myself," Simon reflected with feeling. "By God, I did."

"So you went back to the arena? You and Ernie?"

"That's the story."

"Where exactly did you go?"

"I don't know where Ernie got to. Far as I remember, I went straight in." He half shut his eyes and peered back through the intervening hours. "The boys had started their last dance. I think I went fairly close to the dolmen that time because I seem to remember it between them and me. Then I sheered off to the right and took up my position there."

"Did you notice the Guiser lying behind the dolmen?"

"Sort of. Poor visibility through the hole in that canvas neck. And the body sticks out like a great shelf just under your chin. It hides the ground for about three feet all round you."

"Yes, I see. Do you think you could have kicked anything without realizing you'd done it?"

Simon stared, blinked and looked sick. "Nice idea I *must* say," he said with some violence.

"Do you remember doing so?"

He stared at his hands for a moment, frowning.

"God, I don't know. I don't know. I *hadn't* remembered."

"Why did you stop Ernie Andersen answering me when I asked if he'd done this job?"

"Because," Simon said at once, "I know what Ernie's like. He's not more than nine-and-fivepence in the pound. He's queer. I sort of kept an eye on him in the old days. He takes fits. I knew. I fiddled him in as a batman." Simon began to mumble. "You know, same as the way he felt about his ghastly dog, I felt about him, poor old bastard. I know him. What happened last night got him all worked up. He took a fit after it happened, didn't he, Doc? He'd be just as liable to say he'd done it as not. He's queer about blood and he's got some weird ideas about this dance and the stone and what-have-you. He's the type that rushes in and confesses to a murder he hasn't done just for the hell of it."

"Do you think he did it?" Alleyn said.

"I do not. How could he? Only time he might have had a go, Ralphy had pinched his whiffler. I certainly do not."

"All right. Go away and think over what you've said. We'll be asking you for a statement and you'll be subpoenaed for the inquest. If you'd like, on consideration, to amend what you've told us, we'll be glad to listen."

"I don't *want* to amend anything."

"Well, if your memory improves."

"Ah, hell!" Simon said disgustedly and dropped into his chair.

"You never do any good," Alleyn remarked, "by fiddling with the facts."

"Don't you just," Simon rejoined with heartfelt emphasis and added, "You lay off old Ern. He hasn't got it in him: he's the mild one in that family."

"Is he? Who's the savage one?"

"They're all mild," Simon said, grinning. "As mild as milk."

And on that note they left him.

When they were in the car, Dr. Otterly boiled up again.

"What the devil does that young bounder think he's up to! I never heard such a damned farrago of lies. By God, Alleyn, I don't like it. I don't like it at all."

"Don't you?" Alleyn said absently.

"Well, damn it, do you?"

"Oh," Alleyn grunted. "It sticks out a mile what Master Simon's up to. Doesn't it, Fox?"

"I'd say so, Mr. Alleyn," Fox agreed cheerfully.

Dr. Otterly said, "Am I to be informed?"

"Yes, yes, of course. Hullo, who's this?"

In the hollow of the lane, pressed into the bank to make way for the oncoming car, were a man and a woman. She wore a shawl pulled over her head and he a woollen cap and there was a kind of intensity in their stillness. As the car passed, the woman looked up. It was Trixie Plowman.

"Chris hasn't lost much time," Dr. Otterly muttered.

"Are they engaged?"

"They were courting," Dr. Otterly said shortly. "I understood it was all off."

"Because of the Guiser?"

"I didn't say so."

"You said Chris hadn't lost much time, though. Did the Guiser disapprove?"

"Something of the sort. Village gossip."

"I'll swap Simon's goings-on for your bit of gossip."

Dr. Otterly shifted in his seat. "I don't know so much about that," he said uneasily. "I'll think it over."

They returned to the fug and shadows of their room in the pub. Alleyn was silent for some minutes and Fox busied himself with his notes. Dr. Otterly eyed them both and seemed to be in two minds whether or not to speak. Presently, Alleyn walked over to the window. "The weather's hardening. I think it may freeze tonight," he said.

Fox looked over the top of his spectacles at Dr. Otterly, completed his notes and joined Alleyn at the window.

"Woman," he observed. "In the lane. Looks familiar. Dogs."

"It's Miss Dulcie Mardian."

"Funny how they will do it."

"What?"

"Go for walks with dogs."

"She's coming into the pub."

"All that fatuous tarradiddle," Dr. Otterly suddenly fulminated, "about where he was during the triple sword-dance! Saying he didn't go behind the dolmen. Sink me, he *stood* there and squealed like a colt when he saw Ralph grab the sword. I don't understand it and I don't like it. Lies."

Alleyn said, "I don't think Simon lied."

"What!"

"He says that during the first dance, the triple

sword-dance, he was nowhere near the dolmen. I believe that to be perfectly true."

"But, rot my soul, Alleyn—*I* swear—"

"Equally, I believe that he didn't see Ralph Stayne grab Ernest Andersen's sword."

"Now, look here—"

Alleyn turned to Dr. Otterly. "Of *course* he wasn't. He was well away from the scene of action. He'd gone offstage to keep a date with a lady-friend."

"A *date*? What lady-friend, for pity's sake?"

Trixie came in.

"Miss Dulcie Mardian," she said, "to see Mr. Alleyn, if you please."

CHAPTER IX

Question of Fancy

ALLEYN found it a little hard to decide quite how addle-pated Dulcie Mardian was. She had a strange vague smile and a terribly inconsequent manner. Obviously, she was one of those people who listen to less than half of what is said to them. Yet, could the strangeness of some of her replies be attributed only to this?

She waited for him in the tiny entrance hall of the Green Man. She wore a hat that had been mercilessly sat upon, an old hacking waterproof and a pair of down-at-heel Newmarket boots. She carried a stick. Her dogs, a bull-terrier and a spaniel, were on leashes and had wound them round her to such an extent that she was tied up like a parcel.

"How do you do," she said. "I won't come in. Aunt Akky asked me to say she'd be delighted if you'd dine to-night. Quarter past eight for half past and don't dress if it's a bother. Oh, yes, I nearly forgot. She's sorry it's such short notice. I hope you'll come because she gets awfully cross if people don't, when they're asked. Good-bye."

She plunged a little but was held firmly pinioned by her dogs and Alleyn was able to say, "Thank you very much," collect his thoughts and accept.

"And I'm afraid I can't change," he added.

"I'll tell her. *Don't*, dogs."

"May I—?"

"It's all right, thank you. I'll kick them a little."

She kicked the bull-terrier, who rather half-heartedly snapped back at her.

"I suppose," Dulcie said, "you ran away to be a policeman when you were a boy."

"Not exactly."

"Isn't it awful about old William? Aunt Akky's furious. She was in a bad mood anyway because of Ralph and this has put her out more than ever."

Trixie came through the passage and went into the public bar.

"Which reminds me," Dulcie said, but didn't elucidate which reminded her of what. It was much too public a place for Alleyn to pursue the conversation to any professional advantage, if there was any to be had. He asked her if she'd come into their improvised office for a few minutes and she treated the suggestion as if it were an improper advance.

"No, thank you," she said, attempting to draw herself up but greatly hampered by her dogs. "Quite impossible, I'm afraid."

Alleyn said, "There are one or two points about this case that we'd like to discuss with you. Perhaps, if I come a little early to-night? Or if Dame Alice goes to bed early, I might—"

"I go up at the same time as my aunt. We shall be an early party, I'm afraid," Dulcie said, stiffly. "Aunt Akky is sure you'll understand."

"Of course, yes. But if I might have a word or two with you in private—"

He stopped, noticing her agitation.

Perhaps her involuntary bondage to the bull-terrier and the spaniel had put into Dulcie's head some strange fantasy of jeopardized maidenhood. A look of terrified bravado appeared on her face. There was even a trace of gratification.

"You don't," Dulcie astoundingly informed him, "follow with the South Mardian and Adjacent Hunts without learning how to look after yourself. No, by Jove!"

The bull-terrier and the spaniel had begun to fight each other. Dulcie beat them impartially and was forced to accept Alleyn's help in extricating herself from a now quite untenable position.

"Hands off," she ordered him brusquely as soon as it was remotely possible for him to leave her to her own devices. "Behave yourself," she advised him, and was suddenly jerked from his presence by the dogs.

Alleyn was left rubbing his nose.

When he rejoined the others, he asked Dr. Otterly how irresponsible he considered Miss Mardian to be.

"Dulcie?" Dr. Otterly said. "Well—"

"In confidence."

"Not certifiable. No. Eccentric, yes. Lot of in-breeding there. She took a bad toss in the hunting-field about twenty years ago. Kicked on the head. Never ridden since. She's odd, certainly."

"She talked as if she rode to hounds every day of the week."

"Did she? Odd, yes. Did she behave as if you were going to make improper proposals?"

"Yes."

"She does that occasionally. Typical spinster's hallucination. Dame Alice thinks she waxes and wanes emotionally with the moon. I'd give it a more clinical classification, but you can take your choice. And now, if you don't mind, Alleyn, I really am running terribly late."

"Yes, of course."

"I won't ask you for an explanation of your extraordinary pronouncement just now. Um?"

"Won't you? That's jolly big of you."

"You go to hell," Dr. Otterly said without much rancour and took himself off.

Fox said, "Bailey and Thompson have rigged up a workroom somewhere in the barn and got cracking on dabs. Carey saw the gardener's boy from the castle. He went down yesterday with the note from the gardener himself about the slasher. He didn't see the Guiser. Ernie took the note in to him and came back and said the Guiser would do the job if he could."

"I thought as much."

"Carey's talked to the lad who was to stand in for Ernie: Dan's boy, he is. He says his grand-dad arrived on the scene at the last moment. Ernie was dressed up in the Guiser's clothes and this boy was wearing

Ernie's. The Guiser didn't say much. He grabbed Ernie and tried to drag the clothes off of him. Nobody explained anything. They just changed over and did the show."

"Yes, I see. Let's take another dollop of fresh air, Fox, and then I think I'll have a word with the child of nature."

"Who? Trixie?"

"That, as Mr. Begg would say, is the little number. A fine, cheerful job straight out of the romps of Milkwood. Where's the side door?"

They found it and walked out into the back yard.

"And there," Alleyn said, "is the barn. They rehearsed in here. Let's have a look, shall we?"

They walked down the brick path and found themselves by a little window in the rear of the barn. A raincoat had been hung over it on the inside. "Bailey's," Alleyn said. "They'll be hard at it."

He stood there, filling his pipe and looking absently at the small window. "Somebody's cleaned a peephole on the outside," he said. "Or it looks like a peephole."

He stooped down while Fox watched him indulgently. Between the brick path and the wall of the barn there was a strip of unmelted snow.

"Look," Alleyn said and pointed.

Mrs. Bünz had worn rubber overboots with heels. Night after night she had stood there and, on the last night, the impressions she made had frozen into the fresh fall of snow. It was a bitterly cold, sheltered spot and the thaw had not yet reached it. There they were, pointing to the wall, under the window: two neat footprints over the ghosts of many others.

"Size six. Not Camilla Campion and Trixie's got smallish feet, too. I bet it was the Teutonic folklorist having a sly peep at rehearsals. Look here, now. Here's a nice little morsel of textbook stuff for you."

A naked and ragged thornbush grew by the window. Caught up on one of its twigs was a tuft of grey-blue woollen material.

"Hand-spun," Alleyn said, "I bet you."

"Keen!" Fox said, turning his back to a razor-like draught.

"If you mean the lady," Alleyn rejoined, "you couldn't be more right, Br'er Fox. As keen as a knife. A fanatic, in fact. Come on."

They moved round to the front of the barn and went in. The deserted interior was both cold and stuffy. There was a smell of sacking, cobwebs and perhaps the stale sweat of the dancers. Cigarettes had been trodden out along the sides. The dust raised by the great down-striking capers had settled again over everything. At the far end, double-doors led into an inner room and had evidently been dragged together by Bailey and Thompson, whose voices could be heard on the other side.

"We won't disturb them," Alleyn said, "but, if those doors were open, as I should say they normally are, there'd be a view into this part of the barn from the little window."

"It'd be a restricted view, wouldn't it?"

"It'd be continually interrupted by figures coming between the observer and the performers and limited by the size of the opening. I tell you what, Foxkin," Alleyn said, "unless we can 'find,' as the Mardian ladies would say, pretty damn' quickly, we'll have a hell of a lot of deadwood to clear away in this case."

"Such as?"

"Such as the Andersen boys' business instincts, for one thing. And tracking down Master Ralph's peccadillos, for another. And the Bünz, for a third. And just what Ernie got up to before the show. And Chris's love pangs. All that and more and quite likely none of it of any account in the long run."

"None?"

"Well—there's one item that I think may ring the bell."

Bailey, hearing their voices, wrenched open one of the double-doors and stuck his head out.

"No dabs anywhere that you wouldn't expect, Mr. Alleyn," he reported. "A few stains that look like blood on the Andersens' dancing pants and sleeves. Nothing on their swords. They handled the body, of coures. The slasher's too much burnt for anything to show and the harness on the horse affair's all mucked up with tar."

Bailey was a man of rather morose habit, but when he had this sort of report to make he usually grinned. He did so now. "Will I get Begg's clothes off him?" he asked.

"Yes. I've told him we want them. You may have the car for the next hour."

Bailey said, "The local sergeant looked in. Obby. Pretty well asleep in his boots. He says when you left this morning the Andersens had a bit of a set-to. Seems Ernie reckons there was something about Chris Andersen. He kept saying, 'What about Chris and the Guiser and you-know-who?' Obby wrote it all down and left his notes. It doesn't sound anything much."

"I'll look at it," Alleyn said and, when Bailey produced the notebook, read it carefully.

"All right," he said. "Carry on finding out nothing you wouldn't expect. Glad you're enjoying yourself."

Bailey looked doubtful and withdrew his head.

"I'm going to see Trixie," Alleyn announced.

"If you get frightened," Mr. Fox said, "scream."

"I'll do that, Fox. Thank you."

ii

Trixie was behind the shutter tidying the public bar. Tucked away behind the shelves of bottles, she had a snuggery with a couple of chairs and an electric fire. Into this retreat she invited Alleyn, performed the classic gesture of dusting a chair and herself sat down almost knee-to-knee with him, calmly attentive to whatever he might choose to say.

"Trixie," Alleyn began, "I'm going to ask you one or two very personal questions and you're going to think I've got a hell of a cheek. If your answers are no help to us, then I shall forget all about them. If they are of help, we shall have to make use of them, but, as far as possible, we'll treat them as confidential. All right?"

"I reckon so," Trixie said readily.

"Good. Before we tackle the personalities, I want you to tell me what you saw last night, up at the castle."

Her description of the dance tallied with Dr. Otterly's except at moments when her attention had obviously strayed. Such a moment had occurred soon after the entry of the Guiser. She had watched "Crack's" antics and had herself been tarred by him. "It's lucky to get touched," Trixie said with her usual broad smile. She had wonderfully strong white teeth and her fair skin had a kind of bloom over it. She remembered in detail how "Crack" had chased Camilla and how Camilla had run into the Betty's arms. But, at the moment when the Guiser came in, it seemed, Trixie's attention had been diverted. She had happened to catch sight of Mrs. Bünz.

"Were you standing anywhere near her?" Alleyn asked.

"So I was, then, but she was powerful eager to see and get tar-touched and crept in close."

"Yes?"

"But after Guiser come in I see her move back in the crowd and, when I looked again, she wasn't there."

"Not anywhere in the crowd?"

"Seemingly."

Knowing how madly keen Mrs. Bünz was to see the dance, Trixie was good-naturedly concerned and looked round for her quite persistently. But there was no sign of her. Then Trixie herself became interested in the performance and forgot all about Mrs. Bünz. Later on, when Dan was already embarked on his solo, Trixie looked round again and, lo and behold, there was Mrs. Bünz after all, standing inside the archway and looking, Trixie said, terribly put-about. After that, the account followed Dr. Otterly's in every respect.

Alleyn said, "This has been a help. Thank you, Trixie. And now, I'm afraid, for the personalities. This afternoon when you came into our room and Mr. Ralph Stayne was there, I thought from your manner and from his that there had been something—some understanding—between you. Is that right?"

Trixie's smile widened into quite a broad grin. A dimple appeared in her cheek and her eyes brightened.

"He's a proper lad," she said, "is Mr. Ralph."

"Does he spend much time at home, here?"

"During the week he's up to Biddlefast lawyering, but most week-ends he's to home." She chuckled. "It's kind of slow most times hereabouts," said Trixie. "Up to rectory it's so quiet's a grave. No place for a high-mettled chap."

"Does he get on well with his father?"

"Well enough. I reckon Passon's no notion what fancies lay hold on a young fellow or how powerful strong and masterful they be."

"Very likely not."

Trixie smoothed her apron and, catching sight of her reflection in a wall-glass, tidied her hair. She did this without coquetry and yet, Alleyn thought, with a perfect awareness of her own devastating femininity.

"And so—?" he said.

"It was a bit of fun. No harm come of it. Or didn't ought to of. He's a proper good chap."

"Did something come of it?"

She giggled. "Sure enough. Ernie seen us. Last spring 'twas, one evening up to Copse Forge." She looked again at the wall-glass but abstractedly, as if she saw in it not herself as she was now but as she had been on the evening she evoked. " 'Twasn't nothing for him to fret hisself over, but he's a bit daft-like, is Ern."

"What did he do about it?"

Nothing, it seemed, for a long time. He had gaped at them and then turned away. They had heard him stumble down the path through the copse. It was Trixie's particular talent not so much to leave the precise character of the interrupted idyll undefined as to suggest by this omission that it was of no particular importance. Ernie had gone, Ralph Stayne had become uneasy and embarrassed. He and Trixie parted company and that was the last time they had met, Alleyn gathered, for dalliance. Ralph had not returned to South Mardian for several week-ends. When summer came, she believed him to have gone abroad during the long vacation. She answered all Alleyn's questions very readily and apparently with precision.

"In the end," Alleyn suggested, "did Ernie make mischief, or what?"

"So he did, then. After Camilla came back, 'twas."

"Why then, particularly?"

"Reckon he knew what was in the wind. He's not so silly but what he doesn't notice. Easy for all to see Mr. Ralph's struck down powerful strong by her."

"But were they ever seen together?"

"No, not they."

"Well, then—"

"He'd been courting her in London. Maids up to castle heard his great-auntie giving him a terrible rough-tonguing and him saying if Camilla would have him he'd marry her come-fine-or-foul."

"But where," Alleyn asked patiently, "does Ernie come in?"

Ernie, it appeared, was linked up with the maids at the castle. He was in the habit of drifting up there on Sunday afternoon, when, on their good-natured sufferance, he would stand inside the door of the servants' hall, listening to their talk and, occasionally, contributing an item himself. Thus he had heard all about Dame Alice's strictures upon her great-nephew's attachment to Camilla. Ernie had been able, as it were, to pay his way by describing his own encounter with Ralph and Trixie in the copse. The elderly parlourmaid, a gossip of Trixie's, lost no time in acquainting her of the whole conversation. Thus the age-old mechanics of village intercommunication were neatly demonstrated to Alleyn.

"Did you mind," he asked, "about this tittle-tattle?"

"Lor', no," she said. "All they get out of life, I reckon, them old maidens."

"Did anyone else hear of these matters?"

She looked at him with astonishment.

"Certain-sure. Why wouldn't they?"

"Did the Guiser know, do you think?"

"He did, then. And was so full of silly notions as a baby, him being Chapel and terrible narrow in his views."

"Who told him?"

"Why," she said, "Ernie, for sure. He told, and his dad went raging and preachifying to Dame Alice and to Mr. Ralph saying he'd tell Passon. Mr. Ralph come and had a tell with me, axing me what he ought to do. And I told him, 'Pay no 'tention: hard words break no bones and no business of Guiser's, when all's said.' 'Course," Trixie added, "Mr. Ralph was upset for fear his young lady might get to hear of it."

"Did she?"

"I don't reckon she did, though if she had, it mightn't have made all that differ between them. She'm a sensible maid, for all her grand bringing-up: a lovely nature, true's steel and a lady. But proper proud of her mother's folk, mind. She's talked to me since she come back: nobody else to listen, I dessay, and when a maid's dizzy with love, like Camilla, she's a mighty need to be talking."

"And you don't really think she knew about you and Mr. Ralph?"

"Not by my reckoning, though Mr. Ralph got round to thinking maybe he should tell her. Should he make a clean breast of it to Camilla and I dunno what else beside. I told him it were best left unsaid. Anyway, Camilla had laid it down firm they was not to come anigh each other. But, last Sunday, he seen her in church and his natural burning desire for the maid took a-hold of him and he followed her up to Copse Forge and kissed her and the Guiser come out of the smithy and seen them. Camilla says he ordered her off and Mr. Ralph told her it would be best if she went. So she did and left them together. I reckon Guiser gave Mr.

Ralph a terrible tonguing, but Camilla doesn't know what 'twas passed between them."

"I see. Do you think the Guiser may have threatened to tell Camilla about you?"

Trixie thought this extremely likely. It appeared that, on the Monday, the Guiser had actually gone down to the Green Man and tackled Trixie herself, declaiming that Ralph ought to make an honest woman of her. For this extreme measure, Trixie said, perhaps a thought ambiguously, there was no need whatever. The Guiser had burst into a tirade, saying that he wouldn't hear of his grand-daughter marrying so far "above her station," and repeating the improper pattern of her mother's behaviour. It could lead, he said, to nothing but disaster. He added, with superb inconsistency, that, anyway, Ralph was morally bound to marry Trixie.

"What did you say to all that?" Alleyn asked her.

"I said I'd other notions."

He asked her what had been the outcome of her interview with the Guiser and gathered that a sort of understanding had been arrived at between them. An armed neutrality was to be observed until after Sword Wednesday. Nobody could do the Betty's act as well as Ralph and for the Guiser this was a powerful argument. Towards the end of their talk, the old man had become a good deal calmer. Trixie could see that a pleasing thought had struck him.

"Did you discover what this was?"

"So I did, then. He was that tickled with his own cunning, I reckon he had to tell me."

"Yes?"

"He said he'd make his Will and leave his money to Camilla. He said he'd make Mr. Ralph do it for him and that'd stop his nonsense."

"But why?"

"Because he'd make him lay it down that she'd only get the money if she didn't marry him," said Trixie.

There was a long silence.

"Trixie," Alleyn said at last. "Do you mind telling me if you were ever in love with Ralph Stayne?"

She stared at him and then threw back her head. The muscles in her neck swelled sumptuously and she laughed outright.

"Me! He's a nice enough young fellow and no harm in him, but he's not my style and I'm not his. It were a bit of fun, like I said, and natural as birds in May: no offence taken either side."

Thinking, evidently, that the interview was over, she stood up and, setting her hands at her waist, pulled down her dress to tidy it.

"Have you got a man of your own?" Alleyn asked.

"So I have, then, and a proper man, too."

"May I know who he is?"

"I don't see why for not," she said slowly. "It's Chris Andersen. Reckon you saw us a while back in the lane."

"What did the Guiser have to say about that?"

For the first time since he spoke to her, Trixie looked uneasy. An apple-blossom blush spread over her face and faded, Alleyn thought, to an unusual pallor.

"You tell me," he said, "that the Guiser thought Mr. Stayne should marry you. Did the Guiser know about Chris?"

She hesitated and then said, "Reckon he knew, all right."

"And objected?"

"He wasn't all that pleased, no doubt," she said.

"Did he have an argument about it with Chris?"

She put her hand over her mouth and would say no more.

Alleyn said, "I see you can keep things to yourself and I hope you'll decide to do so now. There's something else I want you to do."

Trixie listened. When he'd finished she said, "I reckon I can but try and and try I will."

He thanked her and opened the door for her to go out.

"A remarkable young woman," he thought.

iii

Fox, who had enjoyed a substantial high-tea, sat on the edge of the bed, smoked his pipe and watched his chief get ready for his dinner-party.

"The water's hot," Alleyn said. "I'll say that for the Green Man or Trixie or whoever stokes the boilers."

"What happened, if it's not indiscreet, of course, with Trixie?"

Alleyn told him.

"Fancy!" Fox commented placidly. "So the old boy asks the young solicitor to make out the Will that's planned to put the kibosh on the romance. What a notion!"

"I'm afraid the Guiser was not only a bloody old tyrant but a bloody old snob into the bargain."

"And the young solicitor," Mr. Fox continued, following his own line of thought, "although he talks to us quite freely about the proposed Will, doesn't mention this bit of it. Does he?"

"He doesn't."

"Ah!" said Fox calmly. "I daresay. And how was Trixie, Mr. Alleyn?"

"From the point of view of sex, Br'er Fox, Trixie's what nice women call a-moral. That's what *she* is."

"Fancy!"

"She's a big, capable, good-natured girl with a code of her own and I don't suppose she's ever done a mean thing in her life. Moreover, she's a generous woman."

"So it seems."

"In every sense of the word."

"That's right, and this morning," Fox continued, "Ernie let on that there were words between Chris and the old man. On account of Trixie, would you think?"

"I wouldn't be surprised."

"Ah! Before you go up to the castle, Mr. Alleyn, would there be time for a quick survey of this case?"

"It'll have to be damn' quick. To put it your way, Fox, the case is going to depend very largely on a general refusal to believe in fairies. We've got the Guiser alive up to the time he ducks down behind the dolmen and waves to Ralph Stayne (if, of course, he did wave). About eight minutes later, we've got him still behind the dolmen, dead and headless. We've got everybody swearing blue murder he didn't leave the spot and offering to take Bible oaths nobody attacked him. And, remember, the presumably disinterested on-lookers, Carey and the sergeant, agree about this. We've got to find an answer that will cover their evidence. I can only think of one and it's going to be a snorter to ring home."

"You're telling me."

"Consider the matter of bloodstains, for instance, and I wish to hell Curtis would get here and confirm what we suppose. If the five brothers, Begg, Otterly, and Stayne had blood all over their clothes it wouldn't get us much nearer because that old ass Carey let them go milling round the corpse. As it is, Bailey tells me they've been over the lot and can't find anything beyond some smears on their trousers and sleeves. Begg, going on his own cloak-and-dagger experience in Germany, points out that the assailant in such cases is well-enough bloodied to satisfy the third murderer in *Macbeth.* And he's right, of course."

"Yes, but we think we know the answer to that one," said Fox. "Don't we?"

"So we do. But it doesn't get us any closer to an arrest."

"Motive?"

"I *despise* motive. (Why, by the way, don't we employ that admirable American usage?) I *despise* it. The case is lousy with motive. Everybody's got a sort of motive. We can't ignore it, of course, but it won't bring home the bacon, Br'er Fox. Opportunity's the word, my boy. Opportunity."

He shrugged himself into his jacket and attacked his head violently with a pair of brushes.

Fox said, "That's a nice suit, Mr. Alleyn, if I may say so. Nobody'd think you'd travelled all night in it."

"It ought to be Victorian tails and a red silk handkerchief for the Dame of Mardian Castle. What'll you do, Fox? Could you bear to go down to the forge and see if the boys have unearthed the Guiser's wealth? Who's on duty there, by the way?"

"A fresh P.C. Carey got up by the afternoon bus from Biddlefast. The ambulance is coming from Yowford for the remains at nine. I ought to go down and see that through."

"Come on, then. I'll drop you there."

They went downstairs and, as they did so, heard Trixie calling out to some invisible person that the telephone lines had broken down.

"That's damn' useful," Alleyn grumbled.

They went out to their car, which already had a fresh ledge of snow on it.

"Listen!" Alleyn said and looked up to where a lighted and partially opened window glowed theatrically beyond a light drift of falling snow. Through the opening came a young voice. It declaimed with extraordinary detachment and great attention to consonants:

" '*Nine-men's morris is filled up with mud.*' "

"Camilla," Alleyn said.

"*What's* she saying!" Fox asked, startled. Alleyn raised a finger. The voice again announced:

" '*Nine-men's morris is filled up with mud.*' "

"It's a quotation. 'Nine-men's morris.' Is that why I kept thinking it ought to be nine and not eight? Or did I—"

The voice began again, using a new inflexion.

" '*Nine-men's morris is filled up with MUD.*' "

"So was ours this morning," Alleyn muttered.

"I thought, the first time, she said 'blood,' " Fox ejaculated, greatly scandalized.

"Single-track minds: that's what's the matter with us." He called out cheerfully, "You can't say, 'The human mortals want their winter here,' " and Camilla stuck her head out of the window.

"Where are you off to?" she said. "Or doesn't one ask?"

"One doesn't ask. Good-night, Titania. Or should it be Juliet?"

"Dr. Otterly thinks it ought to be Cordelia."

"He's got a thing about her. Stick to your fairy-tales while you can," Alleyn said. She gave a light laugh and drew back into her room.

They drove cautiously down the lane to the cross-roads. Alleyn said, "We've got to get out of Ernie what he meant by his speech from the dolmen, you know. And his remark about Chris and the old man. If a propitious moment presents itself, have a shot."

"Tricky, a bit, isn't it?"

"Very. Hullo! Busy night at the smithy."

Copse Forge was alert in the snowbound landscape. The furnace glowed and the lights moved about in the interior: there was a suggestion of encrusted Christmas cards that might open to disclose something more disturbing.

When Alleyn and Fox arrived, however, it was to discover Simon Begg's car outside and a scene of semi-jubilant fantasy within. The five Andersen brothers had been exceedingly busy. Lanthorns, lighted candles and electric torches were all in play. A trestle-table had been rigged up in the middle of the smithy and, on it, as if they bore witness to some successful parish fete, were many little heaps of money. Copper, silver, paper: all were there; and, at the very moment of arrival, Alleyn and Fox found Dan Andersen with his brothers clustered round him shining their torches on a neat golden pile at one end of the table.

"Sovereigns," Dan was saying. "Eleven golden sovereigns. There they be! Can you believe your eyes, chaps?"

"Gold," Ernie said loudly, "ain't it? Gold."

"It'll've been the Grand-dad's, surely," Andy said solemnly. "He were a great saver and hoarder and the Dad after him: so like's two cherry stones. As has always been recognized."

A little worshipful chorus mounted above the totem brightness of the sovereigns. A large policeman moved nearer the table, and out of the shadows behind the forge came Simon Begg, wearing the broad and awkward smile of an onlooker at other people's good fortune.

They heard Alleyn and Fox and they all looked up, preoccupied and perhaps a little wary.

Dan said, "Look at this, sir. This is what we've found and never thought to see. My father's savings and his dad's before him and no doubt his'n before that. There's crown pieces here with a king's head on them and sovereigns and bank notes so old and dirty it's hard to say what they're worth. We're flabbergasted."

"I'm not surprised," Alleyn said. "It's a fabulous sight. Where did you find it all?"

Dan made a comprehensive sweep of his arm.

"Everywhere. Iron boxes under his bed. Mouldy old tins and pots along the top shelves. Here it's been, as you might say, laughing at us, I dun know how many years. We've not touched on the half of it yet, however. No doubt there'll be lashings more to come."

"I can't credit it!" Andy said. "It's unnatural."

"We're made men, chaps," Nat said doubtfully. "Bean't we?"

"Have you found a Will?" Alleyn asked.

"So we have, then," they chanted. They were so much alike in appearance and in manner that, again, Alleyn couldn't help thinking of them as chorus to the action.

"May I see it?"

Dan produced it quite readily. It had been found in a locked iron box under the bed and was twenty years old.

Andy, who was gradually emerging as the least rugged and most sentimental of the Andersens, embarked, with some relish, on a little narrative.

"April the second, 1936. That was the day our Bess ran away to marry. Powerful angered he was that night. Wouldn't go to bed. Us could hear him tramping about in yur, all hours."

"Stoked up the fire, he did," Dan chipped in and he

also adopted the story-teller's drone, "and burnt all her bits of finery and anything else she left behind. Ah-huh!"

Ernie laughed uproariously and hit his knees.

Chris said, "He must of wrote it that night. Next day when two chaps come in with a welding job, he axed 'em into his room and when they come out I yurd 'em laughing and telling each other they didn't reckon what the old chap left would make a millionaire of nobody. There's their names put to it in witness."

"More fools them, as it turns out," Dan said amiably. "Not to say 'millionaire,' mind, but handsome."

They all murmured together and the policeman from Biddlefast cleared his throat.

Simon said, "Funny how things work out, though, isn't it?"

Alleyn was reading the Will. It was a very short document: the whole of the Guiser's estate was to be divided equally among his sons, " 'on condition that they do not give any to my daughter Elizabeth or to any child she may bear, on account of what she done this day.' Signed 'W. Andersen.' "

"Terrible bitter," Andy pointed out and sighed heavily.

Nat, addressing himself to Alleyn, asked anxiously, "But how do us chaps stand, sir? Is this here document a proper testyment? Will it hold up afore a coroner? Is it *law?*"

Alleyn had much ado not to reply, " 'Aye, marry is't. Crowner's quest law!' " so evocative of those other countrymen were the Andersens, peering up at him, red-faced and bright-eyed in the lamplight.

He said, "Your solicitor will be the man to talk to about that. Unless your father made a later Will, I should think this one ought to be all right."

"And then us'll have enough to turn this old shop into a proper masterpiece of a garridge, won't us, chaps?" Ernie demanded excitedly.

Dan said seriously, "It's not the occasion to bring that up, now, Ern. It'll come due for considering at the proper time."

Chris said, "Why not consider it now? It's at the back of what we're thinking. And with all this great heap of cash—well!"

Andy said, "I don't fancy talking about it, knowing how set he was agin it." He turned to Alleyn. "Seems to me, sir, we ought to be axing you what's the right thing to do with all this stuff."

"You should leave everything as it is until the Will is proved. But I don't really know about these things and I've got to be off. Inspector Fox will stay here until the ambulance comes. I'd suggest that when your—your astonishing search is completed, you do very carefully count and lock away all this money. Indeed, if I may say so, I think you should keep a tally as you go. Good-night."

They broke into a subdued chorus of acknowledgment. Alleyn glanced at Fox and turned to go out. Simon said, "Don't do anything you wouldn't do if I was watching you, all you bods. Cheery-ho-ho," and accompanied Alleyn to the cars. Fox walked down with them.

"Like a lot of great kids, really, aren't they?" Simon said.

Alleyn was non-committal.

"Well, Ern is, anyway," Simon said defensively. "Just a great big kid." He opened the door for Alleyn and stood with his hand still on it. He looked at his boots and kicked the snow, at the moment rather like a small boy, himself.

"You all seem to pick on the old Corp," Simon mumbled.

"We only want the facts from him, you know. As from everybody else."

"But he's not *like* everybody else. He'll tell you *anything*. Irresponsible."

("He's going to say it again," Alleyn thought.)

"Just like a great big kid," Simon added punctually.

"Don't worry," Alleyn said. "We'll try not to lose our heads."

Simon grinned and looked at him sideways.

"It's nice for them, all the same," he said. He rubbed his fingers and thumb together.

"Oh!" Alleyn said, "the Guiser's hoard. Yes. Grand, for them, isn't it? I must get on."

He started his engine. It was cold and sluggish and he revved it up noisily. Ernie appeared in the pool of light outside the smithy door. He came slowly towards the car and then stopped. Something in his demeanor arrested Alleyn.

"Hi-ya, Corp," Simon called out cheerfully. It was characteristic of him to bestow perpetual greetings.

Alleyn suddenly decided to take a chance. "See here," he said hurriedly to Simon. "I want to ask Ernie something. I could get him by himself, but I've a better chance of a reasonable answer if you stand by. Will you?"

"Look here, though—"

"Ernie," Alleyn called, "just a second, will you?" Ernie moved forward.

"If you're trying to catch him out—" Simon began.

"Do you suggest there's anything to catch?"

"No."

"Ernie," Alleyn said, "come here a moment." Ernie walked slowly towards them, looking at Simon.

"Tell me," Alleyn said, "why did you say the German lady killed your father?"

Chris Andersen had come into the smithy doorway. Ernie and Simon had their backs turned to him.

Ernie said, "I never. What I said, she *done* it."

"Ah, for Pete's sake!" Simon ejaculated. "Go on! Go right ahead. I daresay he knows, and, anyway, it couldn't matter less. Go on."

But Ernie seemed to have been struck by another thought. "Wummen!" he observed. "It's them that's the trouble, all through, just like what the Guiser reckoned. Look at our Chris."

The figure standing in the over-dramatic light from the smithy turned its head, stirred a little and was still again.

"What about him?" Alleyn asked very quietly and lifted a warning finger at Simon.

Ernie assumed a lordly off-hand expression. "You can't," he said, "tell me nothing I don't know about them two," and incontinently began to giggle.

Fox suddenly said, "Is that so? Fancy!"

Ernie glanced at him. "Ar! That's right. Him and Trix."

"And the Guiser?" Alleyn suggested under his breath.

Ernie gave a long affirmative whistle.

Chris moved down towards them and neither Simon nor Ernie heard him. Alleyn stamped in the snow as if to warm his feet, keeping time with Chris.

Simon appealed to Alleyn. "Honest to God," he said, "I don't know what this one's about. Honest to God."

"What's it all about, Corp?" Simon began obediently. "Where did the Guiser come into it? What's the gen? Come on."

Ernie, always more reasonable with Simon than with anyone else, said at once, "Beg pardon, sir. I was meaning about Trix and what I told the Guiser I seen. You know. Her and Mr. Ralph."

Simon said, "Hell!" and to Alleyn, "I can't see this is of any interest to you, you know."

Chris was close behind his brother.

"Was there a row about it?" Alleyn asked Ernie. "On Sunday?"

Ernie whistled again, piercingly.

Chris's hand closed on his brother's arm. He twisted Ernie round to face him.

"What did I tell you?" he said, and slapped him across the face.

Ernie made a curious sound, half whimper, half giggle. Simon, suddenly very tough indeed, shouldered between them.

"Was that necessary?" he asked Chris.

"You mind your own bloody business," Chris rejoined. He turned on his heel and went back into the smithy. Fox, after a glance at Alleyn, followed him.

"By God!" Simon said thoughtfully. He put his arm across Ernie's shoulders.

"Forget it, Corp," he said. "It's like what I said: nobody argues with the dumb. You talk too much, Corp." He looked at Alleyn. "Give him a break, sir," Simon said. "Can't you?"

But Ernie burst out in loud lamentation. "Wummen!" he declared. "There you are! Like what the old man said. They're all the same, that lot. Look what the fureigness done on us. Look what she done."

"All right." Alleyn said. "What *did* she do?"

"Easy on, easy, now, Corp. What did I tell you?" Simon urged very anxiously and looked appealingly at Alleyn. "Have a heart," he begged. He moved towards Ernie and checked abruptly. He stared at something beyond the rear of Alleyn's car.

Out of range of the light from the smithy, but visible against the background of snow and faintly illuminated by a hurricane lanthorn that one of them carried, were three figures. They came forward slowly into the light and were revealed.

Dr. Otterly, Mrs. Bünz and Ralph Stayne.

iv

Mrs. Bünz's voice sounded lonely and small on the night air and had no more endurance than the jets of frozen breath that accompanied it. It was like the voice of an invalid.

"What is he saying about me? He is speaking lies. You must not believe what he tells you. It is because I was a German. They are in league against me. They think of me as an enemy, still."

"Go on, Ernie," Alleyn said.

"No!" Ralph Stayne shouted, and then, with an air that seemed to be strangely compounded of sheepishness and defiance, added:

"She's right. It's not fair."

Dr. Otterly said, "I really do think, Alleyn—"

Mrs. Bünz gabbled, "I thank you. I thank you, gentlemen." She moved forward.

"You keep out of yur," Ernie said and backed away from her. "Don't you go and overlook us'ns."

He actually threw up his forearm as if to protect himself, turned aside and spat noisily.

"There you are!" Simon said angrily to Alleyn. "That's what *that* all adds up to."

"All right, all right," Alleyn said.

He looked past Simon at the smithy. Fox had come out and was massively at hand. Behind him stood the rest of the Andersen brothers, fitfully illuminated. Fox and one of the other men had torches and, whether by accident or design, their shafts of light reached out like fingers to Mrs. Bünz's face.

It was worth looking at. As the image from a lantern slide that is being withdrawn may be momentarily overlaid by its successor, so alarm modulated into fanaticism in Mrs. Bünz's face. Her lips moved. Out came another little jet of breath. She whispered, "*Wunderbar!*" She advanced a pace towards Ernie, who at once retired upon his brothers. She clasped her hands and became lyrical.

"It is incredible," Mrs. Bünz whispered, "and it is very, *very* interesting and important. He believes me to have the Evil Eye. It is remarkable."

Without a word, the five brothers turned away and went back into the smithy.

"You are determined, all of you," Alleyn said with unusual vehemence, "to muck up the course of justice, aren't you? What are you three doing here?"

They had walked down from the pub, it appeared. Mrs. Bünz wished to send a telegram and to buy some eucalyptus from the village shop, which she had been told would be open. Ralph was on his way home. Dr. Otterly had punctured a tyre and was looking for an Andersen to change the wheel for him.

"I'm meant to be dining with you at the castle," he said. "Two nights running, I may tell you, which is an acid test, metaphorically and clinically, for any elderly stomach. I'll be damn' late if I don't get moving."

"I'll drive you up."

"Like me to change your wheel, Doc?" Simon offered.

"I didn't expect you'd be here. Yes, will you, Begg? And do the repair? I'll pick the car up on my way back and collect the wheel from your garage to-morrow."

"Okey-doke, sir," Simon said. "I'll get cracking, then." He tramped off, whistling self-consciously.

"Well," Ralph Stayne said from out of the shadows behind Alleyn's car, "I'll be off, too, I think. Good-night."

They heard the snow squeak under his boots as he walked away.

"I also," said Mrs. Bünz.

"Mrs. Bünz," Alleyn said, "do you really believe it was only the look in your eye that made Ernie say what he did about you?"

"But yes. It is one of the oldest European superstitions. It is fascinating to find it. The expression 'over-looking' proves it. I am immensely interested," Mrs. Bünz said rather breathlessly.

"Go and send your telegram," Alleyn rejoined crossly. "You are behaving foolishly, Mrs. Bünz. Nobody, least of all the police, wants to bully you or dragoon you or brain-wash you, or whatever you're frightened of. Go and get your eucalyptus and snuff it up and let us hope it clears your head for you. *Guten Abend,* Mrs. Bünz."

He walked quickly up the path to Fox.

"I'll hand you all that on a plate, Fox," he said. "Keep the tabs on Ernie. If necessary, we'll have to lock him up. What a party! All right?"

"All right, Mr. Alleyn."

"Hell, we must go! Where's Otterly? Oh, there you are. Come on."

He ran down the path and slipped into the car. Dr. Otterly followed slowly.

Fox watched them churn off in the direction of Mardian Castle.

CHAPTER X Dialogue for a Dancer

THE elderly parlour-maid put an exquisite silver dish filled with puckered old apples on the table. Dame Alice, Dulcie, Alleyn and Dr. Otterly removed their mats and finger bowls from their plates. Nobody helped themselves to apples.

The combined aftermath of pallid soup, of the goose that was undoubtedly the victim of Ernie's spleen and of Queen Pudding lingered in the cold room together with the delicate memory of a superb red wine. The parlour-maid returned, placed a decanter in front of Dame Alice and then withdrew.

"Same as last night," Dame Alice said. She removed the stopper and pushed the decanter towards Dr. Otterly.

"I can scarcely believe my good fortune," he replied. He helped himself and leant back in his chair. "We're greatly honoured, believe me, Alleyn. A noble wine."

The nobility of the port was discussed for some time. Dame Alice, who was evidently an expert, barked out information about it, no doubt in much the same manner as that of her male forebears. Alleyn changed down (or up, according to the point of view) into the appropriate gear and all the talk was of vintages, body and aroma. Under the beneficent influence of the port even the dreadful memory of wet Brussels sprouts was gradually effaced.

Dulcie, who was dressed in brown velveteen with a lace collar, had recovered her usual air of vague acquiescence, though she occasionally threw Alleyn a glance that seemed to suggest that she knew a trick worth two of his and could look after herself if the need arose.

In the drawing-room, Alleyn had seen an old copy of one of those publications that are dedicated to the profitable enshrinement of family relationships. Evidently, Dame Alice and Dulcie had consulted this work with reference to himself. They now settled down to a gruelling examination of the kind that leaves not a second-cousin unturned nor a collateral unexplored. It was a pastime that he did not particularly care for and it gave him no opportunity to lead the conversation in the direction he had hoped it would take.

Presently, however, when the port had gone round a second time, some execrable coffee had been offered and a maternal great-aunt of Alleyn's had been tabulated and dismissed, the parlour-maid went out and Dame Alice suddenly shouted:

"Got yer man?"

"Not yet," Alleyn confessed.

"Know who did it?"

"We have our ideas."

"Who?"

"It's a secret."

"Why?"

"We might be wrong and then what fools we'd look."

"I'll tell yer who I'd back for it."

"Who?" asked Alleyn in his turn.

"Ernest Andersen. He took the head off that goose you've just eaten and you may depend upon it he did as much for his father. Over-excited. Gets above himself on Sword Wednesday, always. Was it a full moon last night, Otters?"

"I—yes, I rather think—yes. Though, of course, one couldn't see it."

"There yar! All the more reason. They always get worst when the moon's full. Dulcie does, don't you, Dulcie?" asked her terrible aunt.

"I'm sorry, Aunt Akky, I wasn't listening."

"There yar! I said you always get excited when the moon's full."

"Well, I think it's awfully *pretty*," Dulcie said, putting her head on one side.

"How," Alleyn intervened rather hurriedly, "do you think Ernie managed it, Dame Alice?"

"That's for you to find out."

"True."

"Pass the port. Help yerself."

Alleyn did so.

"Have you heard about the great hoard of money that's turned up at Copse Forge?" he asked.

They were much interested in this news. Dame Alice said the Andersens had hoarded money for as long as they'd been at the forge, a matter of four centuries and more, and that Dan would do just the same now that his turn had come.

"I don't know so much about that, you know," Dr. Otterly said, squinting at his port. "The boys and Simon Begg have been talking for a long time about converting the forge into a garage and petrol station. Looking forward to when the new road goes through."

This, as might have been expected, aroused a fury in Dame Alice. Alleyn listened to a long diatribe, during which her teeth began to play up, against new roads, petrol pumps and the decline of proper feeling in the artisan classes.

"William," she said (she pronounced it Will'm), "would never've had it. Never! He told me what his fools of sons were plottin'. Who's the feller that's put 'em up to it?"

"Young Begg, Aunt Akky."

"Begg? Begg? What's he got to do with it? He's a grocer."

"No, Aunt Akky, he left the shop during the war and went into the Air Force and now he's got a garage. He was here yesterday."

"You don't have to tell me that, Dulcie. Of course I know young Begg was here. I'd have given him a piece of my mind if you'd told me what he was up ter."

"When did you see William Andersen, Dame Alice?"

"What? When? Last week. I sent for 'im. Sensible old feller, Will'm Andersen."

"Are we allowed to ask why you sent for him?"

"Can if yer like. I told 'im to stop his grand-daughter makin' sheep's eyes at my nephew."

"Goodness!" Dulcie said, "was she? Did Ralph like it? Is that what you meant, Aunt Akky, when you said Ralph was a rake?"

"No."

"If you don't mind my cutting in," Dr. Otterly ventured, "I don't believe little Miss Camilla made sheep's eyes at Ralph. She's a charming child with very nice manners."

"Will'm 'greed with me. Look what happened when his girl 'loped with young Campion. That sort of mix-up never answers and he knew it."

"One can't be too careful, can one, Aunt Akky," Dulcie said, "with men?"

"Lor', Dulcie, what a stoopid gel you are. When," Dame Alice asked brutally, "have you had to look after yerself, I'd like to know?"

"Ah-ha, Aunt Akky!"

"Fiddlesticks!"

The parlour-maid re-appeared with cigarettes and, surprisingly, a great box of cigars.

"I picked 'em up," Dame Alice said, "at old Tim Comberdale's sale. We'll give you ten minutes. You can bring 'em to the drawin'-room. Come on, Dulcie."

She held out her arm. Dulcie began to collect herself.

"Let me haul," Alleyn said, "may I?"

"Thanks. Bit groggy in the fetlocks, these days. Go with the best, once I'm up."

He opened the door. She toddled rapidly towards it and looked up at him.

"Funny world," she said. "Ain't it?"

"Damned odd."

"Don't be too long over your wine. I've got a book to show you and I go up in half an hour. Don't keep 'im now, Otters."

"Wouldn't dream of it," Dr. Otterly said. When the door had shut he placed his hand on his diaphragm and muttered, "By Heaven, that was an athletic old gander. But what a cellar, isn't it?"

"Wonderful," Alleyn said abstractedly.

He listened to Dr. Otterly discoursing on the Mardian family and its vanished heyday. "Constitutions of oxes and heads of cast-iron, the lot of them," Dr. Otterly declared. "And arrogant!" He wagged a finger. " 'Nuff said." It occurred to Alleyn that Dr. Otterly's head was not perhaps of the same impregnability as the Mardians'.

"Join the ladies?" Dr. Otterly suggested, and they did so.

Dame Alice was established in a bucket-shaped armchair that cut her off in some measure from anybody that wasn't placed directly in front of her. Under her instructions, Alleyn drew up a hideous Edwardian stool to a strategic position. Dulcie placed a newspaper parcel on her great-aunt's knee. Alleyn saw with some excitement a copy of the *Times* for 1871.

"Time someone got some new wrappin' for this," Dame Alice said and untied the tape with a jerk.

"By Heaven," Dr. Otterly said, waving his cigar, "you're highly favoured, Alleyn. By Heaven, you are!"

"There yar," said Dame Alice. "Take it. Give him a table, Dulcie, it's fallin' to bits."

Dr. Otterly brought up a table and Alleyn laid down the book she had pushed into his hands. It was of the kind that used to be called "commonplace" and evidently of a considerable age. The leather binding had split down the back. He opened it and found that it was the diary of one "Ambrose Hilary Mardian of Mardian Place, nr. Yowford, written in the year 1798."

"My great-grandfather," said Dame Alice. "I was born Mardian and married a Mardian. No young. Skip to the Wednesday before Christmas."

Alleyn turned over the pages. "Here we are," he said.

The entry, like all the others, was written in an elaborate copper-plate. The ink had faded to a pale brown.

" 'Sword Wednesday,' " he read, " '1798. A note on

the Mardian Morris of Five Sons.' " Alleyn looked up for a second at Dame Alice and then began to read.

This evening being the occasion of the Mardian Mumming or Sword Dance (which is perhaps the more proper way of describing it than as a morisco or morris) I have thought to set down the ceremony as it was performed in my childhood, for I have perceived since the death of old Yeo Andersen at Copse Forge there has been an abridgement of the doggerel which I fear either through indifference, forgetfulness or sheepishness on the part of the morris side—if morris or morisco it can be named—may become altogether neglected and lost. This were a pity as the ceremony is curious and I believe in some aspects unique. For in itself it embraces divers others, as the mummers' play in which the father avoids death from his sons by breaking the glass, or knot, and then by showing his Will and the third time is in mockery beheaded. Also from this source is derived the Sword Dance itself in three parts and from yet another the quaint device of the rabbit cap. Now, to leave all this, my purpose here is to set down what was always said by Yeo Andersen the smith and his forebears who have enacted the part of the Fool. Doubtless the words have been changed as time goes by but here they are, as given to me by Yeo. These words are not spoken out boldly but rather are they mumbled under the breath. Sorry enough stuff it is, no doubt, but perhaps of interest to those who care for these old simple pastimes of our country people.

At the end of the first part of the Sword Dance, as he breaks the glass, the Fool says:

"Once for a looker and all must agree
If I bashes the looking-glass so I'll go free."

At the end of the second part he shews them his Will and says:

"Twice for a Testament. Read it and see
If you look at the leavings then so I'll go free."

At the end of the third part, he puts his head in the Lock and says:

"Here comes the rappers to send me to bed
They'll rapper my head off and then I'll be dead."

And after that he says:

"Betty to lover me
Hobby to cover me
If you cut off my head
I'll rise from the dead."

N.B. I believe the word "rapper" to be a corruption of "rapier," though in other parts it is used of wooden swords. Some think it refers to a practice of rapping or hitting with them after the manner of Harlequin in his dancing. Yet in the Mardian dance the swords are of steel pierced for cords at the point.

There the entry for Sword Wednesday ended.

"Extraordinarily interesting," Alleyn said. "Thank you." He shut the book and turned to Dr. Otterly. "Did the Guiser speak any of this verse?"

"I believe he did, but he was very cagey about it. He certainly used to mutter something at those points in the dance, but he wouldn't tell anybody what it was. The boys were near enough to hear, but they don't like talking about it, either. Damn' ridiculous when you come to think of it," Dr. Otterly said, slightly running his words together. "But interesting, all the same."

"Did he ever see this diary, Dame Alice?"

"I showed it to him. One of the times when he'd come to mend the boiler. He put on a cunnin' look and said he knew all about it."

"Would you think these lines, particularly the last

four, are used in other places where folk dancing thrives?"

"Definitely not," Dr. Otterly said, perhaps rather more loudly than he had intended. "They're not in the Revesby text nor anywhere else in British ritual mumming. Purely local. Take the word 'lover' used as a verb. You still heard it hereabouts when I was a boy, but I doubt if it's ever been found elsewhere in England. Certainly not in that context."

Alleyn put his hand on the book and turned to his hostess. "Clever of you," he said "to think of showing me this. I congratulate you." He got up and stood looking at her. She turned her Mrs. Noah's face up to him and blinked like a lizard.

"Not goin', are yer?"

"Isn't it your bedtime?"

"Most certainly it is," said Dr. Otterly, waving his cigar.

"Aunt Akky, it's after ten."

"Fiddlededee. Let's have some brandy. Where's the grog-tray? Ring the bell, Otters."

The elderly parlour-maid answered the bell at once, like a servant in a fairy-tale, ready-armed with a tray, brandy-glasses and a bottle of fabulous cognac.

"I 'fer it at this stage," Dame Alice said, "to havin' it with the coffee. Papa used to say, 'When dinner's dead in yer and bed is still remote, ring for the brandy.' Sound advice in my 'pinion."

It was eleven o'clock when they left Mardian Castle.

Fox, running through his notes with a pint of beer before the fire, looked up over his spectacles when his chief came in. There was an unusual light in Alleyn's eyes.

"You're later than I expected, sir," said Fox. "Shall I order you a pint?"

"Not unless you feel like carrying me up to bed after it. I've been carousing with the Dame of Mardian Castle. She may be ninety-four, Fox, but she carries her wine like a two-year-old, does that one."

"God bless my soul! Sit down, Mr. Alleyn."

"I'm all right. I must say I wonder how old Otterly's managing under his own steam. He was singing the 'Jewel Song' from *Faust* in a rousing falsetto when we parted."

"What did you have for dinner? To eat, I mean."

"Ernie's victim and sodden Brussels sprouts. The wine, however, was something out of this world. Laid down by one of the gods in the shape of Dame Alice's papa. But the *pièce de résistance*, Br'er Fox, the wonder of the evening, handed to me, as it were, on a plate by Dame Alice herself, was—what do you suppose?"

"I *don't* suppose, sir," Fox said, smiling sedately.

"The little odd golden morsel of information that clicks down into the pattern and pulls it together. The key to the whole damn' set-up, my boy. Don't look scandalized, Br'er Fox, I'm not so tight that I don't know a crucial bit of evidence when it's shoved under my nose. Have you heard the weather report?"

Mr. Fox began to look really disturbed. He cleared his throat and said warmer and finer weather had been predicted.

"Good," Alleyn cried and clapped him on the back. "Excellent. You're in for a treat."

"What sort of treat," Mr. Fox said, "for Heaven's sake?"

"A touch of the sword and fiddle, Br'er Fox. A bit of hey-nonny-no. A glimpse of Merrie England with bells on. Nine-men's morris, mud and all. Repeat, *nine.*"

"Eh?"

"We're in for a reconstruction, my boy, and I'll tell you why. Now, listen."

ii

The mid-winter sun smiled faint as an invalid over South and East Mardian on the Friday after Sword Wednesday. It glinted on the breakfast tables of the Reverend Mr. Samuel Stayne and of his great-aunt, Dame Alice Mardian. It touched up the cruet-stand and the britannia metal in the little dining-room at the Green Man and an emaciated ray even found its way to the rows of bottles in the bar and to the anvil at Copse Forge. A feeble radiance it was, but there was something heartening about it, nevertheless. Up at Yowford, Dr. Otterly surveyed the scene with an uplifting of his spirit that he would have found hard to explain. Also at Yowford, Simon Begg, trundling out Dr. Otterly's wheel with its mended puncture, remembered his winning bet, assured himself that he stood a fair chance now of mending his fortunes with an interest in a glittering petrol station at Copse Forge, reminded himself it wouldn't, under the circumstances, look nice to be too obviously pleased about this and broke out, nevertheless, into a sweet and irresponsibly exultant whistling.

Trixie sang and the potboy whistled louder but less sweetly than Simon. Camilla brushed her short hair before her open window and repeated a voice-control exercise. "Bibby bobby bounced a ball against the wall." She thought how deeply she was in love and, like Simon, told herself it wasn't appropriate to be so obviously uplifted. Then the memory of her grandfather's death suddenly flooded her thoughts and her heart was filled with a vast pity and love, not only for him but for all the world. Camilla was eighteen and a darling.

Dame Alice woke from a light doze and felt for a moment quite desperately old. She saw a robin on her windowsill. Sharp as a thorn were its bright eyes and quick as thought the turn of its sun-polished head. Down below, the geese were in full scream. Dulcie would be pottering about in the dining-room. The wave of depression receded. Dame Alice was aware of her release but not, for a moment, of its cause. Then she remembered her dinner-party. Her visitor had enjoyed himself. It was, she thought, thirty years—more—since she had been listened to like that. He was a pretty fellow, too. By "pretty" Dame Alice meant "dashing." And what was it he'd said when he left? That with her permission they would revive the Mardian Morris that afternoon. Dame Alice was not moved by the sort of emotions that the death of the Guiser had aroused in younger members of Wednesday's audience. The knowledge that his decapitated body had been found in her courtyard did not fill her with horror. She was no longer susceptible to horror. She merely recognized in herself an unusual feeling of anticipation and connected it with her visitor of last night. She hadn't felt so lively for ages.

"Breakfast," she thought and jerked at the tapestry bell-pull by her bed.

Dulcie in the dining-room heard the bell jangling away in the servants' hall. She roused herself, took the appropriate dishes off the hot plate and put them on the great silver tray. Porridge. Kedgeree. Toast. Marmalade. Coffee. The elderly parlour-maid came in and took the tray up to Dame Alice.

Dulcie was left to push crumbs about the tablecloth and hope that the police wouldn't find the murderer too soon. Because, if they did, Mr. Alleyn, to whom she had shown herself as a woman of the world, would go somewhere else.

Ralph Stayne looked down the table at his father, who had, he noticed, eaten no breakfast.

"You're looking a bit poorly, Pop," he said. "Anything wrong?"

His father stared at him in pale bewilderment.

"My dear chap," he said, "no. Not with me. But the—the events of the night before last—"

"Oh!" Ralph said, "that! Yes, of course. As long as it's only that—I mean," he went on hurriedly, answering the look in his father's eye, "as long as it's not anything actually *wrong* with you. Yes, I *know* it was ghastly about the poor Old Guiser. It was quite frightful."

"I can't get it out of my head. Forgive me, old boy, but I really don't know how you contrive to be so—so resilient."

"I? I expect this sounds revoltingly tough to you—but, you see, Pop, if one's seen rather a lot of that particular kind of horror—well, it's a hell of a sight different. I have. On the deck of a battleship, among other places. I'm damn'—blast, I keep swearing!—I couldn't be sorrier about the Guiser, but the actual look of the thing wasn't all that much of a horror to me."

"I suppose not. I suppose not."

"One'd go mad," Ralph said, "if one didn't get tough. When there's a war on. Simmy-Dick Begg would agree. So would Ernie and Chris. Although it *was* their father. Any returned chap would agree."

"I suppose so."

Ralph got up. He squared his shoulders, looked steadily at his father and said, "Camilla's the one who really did get an appalling shock."

"I know. Poor child. I wondered if I should go and see her, Ralph."

"Yes," Ralph said. "I wish you would. I'm going now, and I'll tell her. She'll be awfully pleased."

His father, looking extremely disturbed, said, "My dear old man, you're not—?"

"Yes, Pop," Ralph said, "I'm afraid I am. I've asked Camilla to marry me."

His father got up and walked to the window. He looked out on the dissolving whiteness of his garden.

"I wish this hadn't happened," he said. "Something was suggested last night by Dulcie that seemed to hint at it. I—as a churchman, I hope I'm not influenced by—by—well, my dear boy, by any kind of snob's argument. I'm sure I'm not. Camilla is a dear child and, other things being equal, I should be really delighted." He rubbed up his thin hair and said ruefully, "It'll worry Aunt Akky most awfully."

"Aunt Akky'll have to lump it, I'm afraid," Ralph said and his voice hardened. "She evidently heard that I've been seeing a good deal of Camilla in London. She's already tried to bulldoze me about it. But, honestly, Pop, what, after all, has it got to do with Aunt Akky? I know Aunt Akky's marvellous. I adore her. But I refuse to accept her as a sort of animated tribal totem, though I admit she looks very much like one."

"It's not only that," his father said miserably. "There's—forgive me, Ralph, I really detest having to ask you this, but isn't there—someone—"

Mr. Stayne stopped and looked helplessly at his son. "You see," he said, "I've listened to gossip. I tried not to, but I listened."

Ralph said, "You're talking about Trixie Plowman, aren't you?"

"Yes."

"Who gossiped? Please tell me."

"It was old William Andersen."

Ralph drew in his breath. "I was afraid of that," he said.

"He was genuinely worried. He thought it his duty to talk to me. You know how adamant his views were. Apparently Ernie had seen you and Trixie Plowman together. Old William was the more troubled because, on last Sunday morning—"

"It appears to be my fate," Ralph said furiously, "to be what the Restoration dramatists call 'discovered' by the Andersens. It's no good trying to explain, Pop. It'd only hurt you. I know you would look on this Trixie thing as—well—"

"As a sin? I do, indeed."

"But—it was so brief and so much outside the general stream of my life. And hers—Trixie's. It was just a sort of natural thing; a little kindness of hers."

"You can't expect me to take that view of it."

"No," Ralph said. "I'll only sound shallow or something."

"It's not a question of how you sound. It's a question of wrong-doing, Ralph. There's the girl—Trixie herself."

"She's all right. Honestly. She's going to be tokened to Chris Andersen."

The Rector momentarily shut his eyes. "Oh, Ralph!" he said and then, "William Andersen forbade it. He spoke to Chris on Sunday."

"Well, anyway, *now* they can," Ralph said, and then looked rather ashamed of himself. "I'm sorry, Pop. I shouldn't have put it like that, I suppose. Look: it's all *over*, that thing. It was before I knew Camilla. I did regret it very much, after I loved Camilla. Does that help?"

The Rector made a most unhappy gesture. "I am talking to a stranger," he said. "I have failed you, dreadfully, Ralph. It's quite dreadful."

A bell rang distantly.

"They've fixed the telephone up," the Rector said.

"I'll go."

Ralph went out and returned looking bewildered.

"It was Alleyn," he said. "The man from the Yard. They want us to go up to the castle this afternoon."

"To the *castle?*"

"To do the Five Sons again. They want you too, Pop."

"Me? But why?"

"You were an observer."

"Oh, *dear!*"

"Apparently, they're calling everybody up: Mrs. Bünz included."

Ralph joined his father in a kind of half-companionable dissonance and looked across the rectory tree-tops towards East Mardian, where a column of smoke rose gracefully from the pub.

Trixie had done her early chores and seen that the fires were burning brightly.

She had also taken Mrs. Bünz's breakfast up to her.

At this moment, Trixie was behaving oddly. She stood with a can of hot water outside Mrs. Bünz's bedroom door, intently listening. The expression on her face was not at all sly, rather it was grave and attentive. On the other side of the door, Mrs. Bünz clicked her knife against her plate and her cup on its saucer. Presently, there was a more complicated clatter as she put her tray down on the floor beside her bed. This was followed by the creak of a wire mattress, a heavy thud and the pad of bare feet. Trixie held her breath, listened feverishly and, then, without knocking, quickly pushed open the door and walked in.

"I'm sure I do ax your pardon, ma-am," Trixie said.

"Axcuse, me, please." She crossed the room to the washstand, set down her can of water, returned past Mrs. Bünz and went out again. She shut the door gently behind her and descended to the back parlour, where Alleyn, Fox, Thompson and Bailey had finished their breakfasts and were setting their course for the day.

"Axcuse me, sir," Trixie said composedly.

"All right, Trixie. Have you any news for us?"

"So I have, then." She crossed her plump arms and laid three fingers of each hand on the opposite shoulder. "So broad's that," she said, "and proper masterpieces for a colour: blue and red and yaller and all puffed up angry-like, either side."

"You're a clever girl. Thank you very much."

"Have you in the force yet, Miss Plowman," Fox said, beaming at her.

Trixie gave them a tidy smile, cleared the breakfast things away, asked if that would be all and left the room.

"Pity," Thompson said to Bailey, "there isn't the time."

Bailey, who was a married man, grinned sourly.

"Have we got through to everybody, Fox?" Alleyn asked.

"Yes, Mr. Alleyn. All set for four o'clock at the castle. The weather report's still favourable, the telephone's working again and Dr. Curtis has rung up to say he hopes to get to us by this evening."

"Good. Before we go any further, I think we'd better have a look at the general set-up. It'll take a bit of time, but I'll be glad of a chance to try and get a bit of shape out of it."

"It'd be a nice change to come up against something unexpected, Mr. Alleyn," Thompson grumbled. "We haven't struck a thing so far."

"We'll see if we can surprise you. Come on."

Alleyn put his file on the table, walked over to the fireplace and began to fill his pipe. Fox polished his spectacles. Bailey and Thompson drew chairs up and produced their notebooks. They had the air of men who had worked together for a long time and who understood each other's ways.

"You know," Alleyn said, "if this case had turned up three hundred years ago, nobody would have had any difficulty in solving it. It'd have been regarded by the villagers, at any rate, as an open-and-shut affair."

"Would it, now?" Fox said placidly. "How?"

"Magic."

"Hell!" Bailey said, and looked faintly disgusted.

"Ask yourselves. Look how the general case echoes the pattern of the performance. Old Man. Five Sons. Money. A Will. Decapitation. The only thing that doesn't tally is the poor old boy's failure to come to life again."

"You reckon, do you, sir," Thompson asked, "that, in the olden days, they'd have taken a superstitious view of the death?"

"I do. The initiates would have thought that the god was dissatisfied, or that the gimmick had misfired, or that Ernie's offering of the goose had roused the blood lust of the god, or that the rites had been profaned and the Guiser punished for sacrilege. Which again tallies, by the way."

"Does it?" Bailey asked, and added, "Oh, yes. What you said, Mr. Alleyn. That's right."

"The authorities, on the other hand," Alleyn went on, "would have plumped at once for witchcraft and the whole infamous machinery of seventeenth-century investigation would have begun to tick over."

"Do you reckon," Thompson said, "that any of these chaps take the superstitious view? Seems hardly credible but—well?"

"Ernie?" Fox suggested rather wearily.

"He's dopey enough, isn't he, Mr. Fox?"

"He's not so dopey," Alleyn said strongly, "that he can't plan an extremely cunning leg-pull on his papa, his four brothers, Simon Begg, Dr. Otterly and Ralph Stayne. And jolly nearly bring it off, what's more."

"Hul-*lo*," Bailey said under his breath to Thompson. "Here comes the 'R.A.' touch."

Fox, who overheard him, bestowed a pontifical but not altogether disapproving glance upon him. Bailey, aware of it, said, "Is this going to be one of your little surprises, Mr. Alleyn?"

Alleyn said, "Damn' civil of you to play up. Yes, it is, for what it's worth. Bring out that chit the Guiser's supposed to have left on his door, saying he wouldn't be able to perform."

Bailey produced it, secured between two sheets of glass and clearly showing a mass of finger prints where he had brought them up.

"The old chap's prints," he said, "and Ernie's. I got their dabs after you left yesterday afternoon. Nobody objected, although I don't think Chris Andersen liked it much. He's tougher than his brothers. There's a left and right thumb of Ernie's on each side of the tack hole, and all the rest of the gang. Which is what you'd expect, isn't it, if they handed it round?"

"Yes," Alleyn said. "And do you remember where Ernie said he found it?"

"Tacked to the door. There's the tack hole."

"And where are the Guiser's characteristic prints? Suppose he pushed the paper over the head of the existing tack, which the nature of the hole seems to suggest? You'd get a right and left thumb print on each side of the hole, wouldn't you? And what *do* you get? A right and left thumb print, sure enough. But whose?"

Bailey said, "Ah, *hell!* Ernie's."

"Yes. Ernie's. So Ernie shoved it over the tack. But Ernie says he found it there when he came down to get the Guiser. So what's Ernie up to?"

"Rigging the old man's indisposition?" Fox said.

"I think so."

Fox raised his eyebrows and read the Guiser's message aloud.

" 'Cant mannage it young Ern will have to. W.A.' "

"It's the old man's writing, isn't it, Mr. Alleyn?" Thompson said. "Wasn't that checked?"

"It's his writing all right, but, in my opinion, it wasn't intended for his fellow mummers, it wasn't originally tacked to the door, it doesn't refer to the Guiser's inability to perform and it doesn't mean young Ern will have to go on in his place."

There was a short silence.

"Speaking for self," Fox said, "I am willing to buy it, Mr. Alleyn." He raised his hand. "Wait a bit, though," he said. "Wait a bit! I've started."

"Away you go."

"The gardener's boy went down on Tuesday afternoon with a note for the Guiser telling him he'd got to sharpen that slasher himself and return it by bearer. The Guiser was in Biddlefast. Ernie took the note. Next morning—wasn't it?—the boy comes for the slasher. It isn't ready and he's told by Ernie that it'll be brought up later. Any good?"

"You're away to a pretty start."

"All right, all right. So Ernie does sharpen the slasher and, on the Wednesday, he does take it up to the castle. Now, Ernie didn't give the boy a note from the Guiser, but that doesn't mean the Guiser didn't write one. How's that?"

"You're thundering up the straight."

"It means Ernie kept it and pushed it over that tack and pulled it off again and, when he was sent down to fetch his dad, he didn't go near him. He dressed himself up in the Guiser's rig while the old boy was snoozing on his bed and he lit off for the castle and showed the other chaps this ruddy note. Now, then!"

"You've breasted the tape, Br'er Fox, and the trophy is yours."

iii

"Not," Alleyn said dubiously, observing his colleagues, "that it gets us all that much farther on. It gets us a length or two nearer, but that's all."

"What *does* it do for us?" Fox ruminated.

"It throws a light on Ernie's frame of mind before

the show. He's told us himself he went hurtling up the hill in their station-waggon dressed in the Guiser's kit and feeling wonderful. His dearest ambition was about to be realized: he was to act the leading role, literally to 'play the Fool,' in the Dance of the Sons. He was exalted. Ernie's not the village idiot: he's an epileptic with all the characteristics involved."

"Exaggerated moods, sort of?"

"That's it. He gets up there and hands over the note to his brothers. The understudy's bundled into Ernie's clothes, the note is sent in to Otterly. It's all going Ernie's way like a charm. The zeal of the folk dance sizzles in his nervous ganglions, or wherever fanaticism does sizzle. I wouldn't mind betting he remembered his sacrifice of our last night's dinner upon the Mardian Stone and decided it had brought him luck. Or something."

Alleyn stopped short and then said in a changed voice, " 'It will have blood, they say. Blood will have blood.' I bet Ernie subscribes to that unattractive theory."

"Bringing him in pretty close to the mark, aren't you, Mr. Alleyn?"

"Well, of course he's close to the mark, Br'er Fox. He's as hot as hell, is Ernie. Take a look at him. All dressed up and somewhere to go, with his audience waiting for him. Dr. Otterly, tuning his fiddle. Torches blazing. It doesn't matter whether it's Stratford-upon-Avon with all the great ones waiting behind the curtain or the Little Puddleton Mummers quaking in their borrowed buskins; no, by Heaven, nor the Andersen brothers listening for the squeal of a fiddle in the snow: there's the same kind of nervous excitement let loose. And, when you get a chap like Ernie—well, look at him. At the zero hour, when expectation is ready to topple over into performance, who turns up?"

"The Guiser."

"The Guiser. Like a revengeful god. Driven up the hill by Mrs. Bünz. The Old Man himself, in what the boys would call a proper masterpiece of a rage. Out he gets, without a word to his driver, and wades in. He didn't say much. If there was any mention of the hanky-panky with the written message, it didn't lead to any explanation. He seems merely to have launched himself at Ernie, practically lugged the clothes off him, forced him to change back to his own gear and herded them on for the performance. All right. And how did Ernie feel? Ernie, whose pet dog the old man had put down, Ernie, who'd manoeuvred himself into the major role in this bit of prehistoric pantomime, Ernie, who was on top of the world? How did he feel?"

"Murderous?" Thompson offered.

"I think so. Murderous."

"Yes," said Fox and Bailey and Thompson. "Yes. Well. What?"

"He goes on for their show, doesn't he, with the ritual sword that he's sharpened until it's like a razor: the sword that cut the Guiser's hand in a row they had at their last practice, which was first blood to Ernie, by the way. On he goes and takes it out on the thistles. He slashes their heads off with great sweeps of his sword. Ernie is a thistle whiffler and he whiffles thistles with a thistle whiffler. Diction exercise for Camilla Campion. He prances about and acts the savage. After that he gets warmed up still more effectively by dancing and going through the pantomime of cutting the Fool's head off. And, remember, he's in a white-hot rage with the Fool. What happens next to Ernie? Nothing that's calculated to soothe his nerves or sweeten his mood. When the fun is at its height and he's looking on with his sword dangling by its red cord from his hand, young Stayne comes creeping up behind and collars it. Ernie loses his temper and gives chase. Stayne hides in view of the audience and Ernie plunges out at the back. He's dithering with rage. Simon Begg says he was incoherent. Stayne comes out and gives him back the whiffler. Stayne re-enters by another archway. Ernie comes back complete with sword and takes part in the final dance. If you consider Ernie like that, in continuity, divorced for the moment from the trimmings, you get a picture of mounting fury, don't you? The dog, the Guiser's cut hand, the decapitated goose, the failure of the great plan, the Guiser's rage, the stolen sword. A sort of crescendo."

"Ending," Fox mused, "in what?"

"Ending, in my opinion, with him performing, in deadly reality, the climax of their play."

"*Hey?*" Bailey ejaculated.

"Ending in him taking his Old Man's head off."

"*Ernie?*"

"Ernie."

"Then—well, cripes," Thompson said, "so Ernie's our chap, after all?"

"No."

"Look—Mr. Alleyn—"

"He's not our chap, because when he took his Old Man's head off, his Old Man was already dead."

iv

Mr. Fox, as was his custom, glanced complacently at his subordinates. He had the air of drawing their attention to their chief's virtuosity.

"Not enough blood," he explained, "on anybody."

"Yes, but if it was done from the rear," Bailey objected.

"Which it wasn't."

"The character of the wound gives us that," Alleyn said. "Otterly agrees and I'm sure Curtis will. It was done from the front. You'll see when you look. Of course, the P.M. will tell us definitely. If decapitation was the cause of death, I imagine there will be a considerable amount of internal bleeding. I feel certain, though, that Curtis will find there is none."

"Any other reasons, Mr. Alleyn? Apart from nobody being bloody enough?" Thompson asked.

"If it had happened where he was lying and he'd been alive, there'd have been much more blood on the ground."

Bailey suddenly said, "Hey!"

Mr. Fox frowned at him.

"What's wrong, Bailey?" Alleyn asked.

"Look, sir, are you telling us it's not homicide at all? That the old chap died of heart failure or something and Ernie had the fancy to do what he did? After? Or what?"

"I think that may be the defence that will be raised. I don't think it's the truth."

"You think he was murdered?"

"Yes."

"Pardon me," Thompson said politely, "but any idea *how*?"

"An idea, but it's only a guess. The post mortem will settle it."

"Laid out cold somehow and then beheaded," Bailey said, and added most uncharacteristically, "Fancy."

"It couldn't have been the whiffler," Thompson sighed. "Not that it seems to matter."

"It wasn't the whiffler," Alleyn said. "It was the slasher."

"Oh! But he was dead?"

"Dead."

"Oh."

CHAPTER XI Question of Temperament

CAMILLA sat behind her window. When Ralph Stayne came into the inn yard, he stood there with his hands in his pockets and looked up at her. The sky had cleared and the sun shone quite brightly, making a dazzle on the window-pane. She seemed to be reading.

He scooped up a handful of fast-melting snow and threw it at the glass. It splayed out in a wet star. Camilla peered down through it and then pushed open the window.

" 'Romeo, Romeo,' " she said, " 'wherefore art thou Romeo?' "

"I can't remember any of it to quote," Ralph rejoined. "Come for a walk, Camilla. I want to talk to you."

"O.K. Wait a bit."

He waited. Bailey and Thompson came out of the side door of the pub, gave him good morning and walked down the brick path in the direction of the barn. Trixie appeared and shook a duster. When she saw Ralph she smiled and dimpled at him. He pulled self-consciously at the peak of his cap. She jerked her head at him. "Come over, Mr. Ralph," she said.

He walked across the yard to her, not very readily.

"Cheer up, then," Trixie said. "Doan't look at me as if I was going to bite you. There's no bones broke, Mr. Ralph. I'll never say a word to her, you may depend, if you ax me not. My advice, though, is to tell the maid yourself and then there's nothing hid betwixt you."

"She's only eighteen," Ralph muttered.

"That doan't mean she's silly, however. Thanks to Ernie and his dad, everybody hereabouts knows us had our bit of fun. The detective gentleman axed me about it and I told him yes."

"Good God, Trixie!"

"Better the truth from me than a great blowed-up fairy-tale from elsewhere and likewise better for Camilla if she gets the truth from you. Here she comes."

Trixie gave a definite flap with her duster and returned indoors. Ralph heard her greet Camilla, who now appeared with the freshness of morning in her cheeks and eyes and a scarlet cap on her head.

Alleyn, coming out to fetch the car, saw them walk off down the lane together.

"And I fancy," he muttered, "he's made up his mind to tell her about his one wild oat."

"Camilla," Ralph said, "I've got something to tell you. I've been going to tell you before and then—well, I suppose I've funked it. I don't know what you feel about this sort of thing and—I—well—I—"

"You're not going to say you've suddenly found it's all been a mistake and you're not in love with me after all?"

"Of course I'm not, Camilla. What a preposterous notion to get into your head! I love you more every minute of the day: I adore you, Camilla."

"I'm *delighted* to hear it, darling. Go ahead with your story."

"It may rock you a bit."

"Nothing can rock me really badly unless—you're *not* secretly married, I *hope!*" Camilla suddenly ejaculated.

"Indeed I'm not. The things you think of!"

"And, of course (forgive me for mentioning it) you didn't murder my grandfather, did you?"

"Camilla!"

"Well, I know you didn't."

"If you'd just let me—"

"Darling Ralph, you can see by this time that I've given in about not meeting you. You can see I've come over to your opinion: my objections were immoderate."

"Thank God, darling. But—"

"All the same, darling, *darling* Ralph, you must understand that although I go to sleep thinking of you and wake in a kind of pink paradise because of you, I am still determined to keep my head. People may say," Camilla went on, waving a knitted paw, "that class is *vieux jeu,* but they're only people who haven't visited South Mardian. So what I propose—"

"Sweetheart, it is I who propose. I do so now, Camilla. Will you marry me?"

"Yes, thank you, I will indeed. Subject to the unequivocal consent of your papa and your great-aunt and, of course, my papa, who, I expect, would prefer an R.C., although I'm not one. Otherwise, I can guarantee he would be delighted. He fears I might contract an alliance with a drama student," Camilla explained and turned upon Ralph a face eloquent with delight at her own absurdities. She was in that particular state of intoxication that attends the young woman who knows she is beloved and is therefore moved to show off for the unstinted applause of an audience of one.

"I adore you," Ralph repeated unsteadily and punctually. "But, sweetest, darling Camilla, I've got, I repeat, something that I ought to tell you about."

"Yes, of course you have. You began by saying so. Is it," Camilla hazarded suddenly, "that you've had an affair?"

"As a matter of fact, in a sort of way, it is, but—"

Camilla began to look owlish. "I'm not much surprised by that," she said. "After all, you are thirty and I'm eighteen. Even people of my vintage have affairs, you know, although, personally, I don't care for the idea at all. But I've been given to understand it's different for the gentlemen."

"Camilla, stop doing an act and listen to me."

Camilla looked at him and the impulse to show off for him suddenly left her. "I'm sorry," she said. "Well, go on."

He went on. They walked up the road to Yowford and for Camilla, as she listened, some of the brightness of the morning fell from the sky and was gone. When he had finished she could find nothing to say to him.

"Well," Ralph said presently, "I see it has made a difference."

"No, not at all," Camilla rejoined politely. "I mean, not really. It couldn't, could it? It's just that somehow it's strange because—well, I suppose because it's here and someone I know."

"I'm sorry," Ralph said.

"I've been sort of buddies with Trixie. It seems impossible. Does she mind? Poor Trixie."

"No, she doesn't. Really, she doesn't. I'm not trying to explain anything away or to excuse myself, but they've got quite a different point of view in the villages. They think on entirely different lines about that sort of thing."

" 'They'? Different from whom?"

"Well—from us," Ralph said and saw his mistake. "It's hard to understand," he mumbled unhappily.

"I ought to understand, oughtn't I? Seeing I'm half 'them.' "

"Camilla, *darling*—"

"You seem to have a sort of predilection for 'them,' don't you? Trixie. Then me."

"That *did* hurt," Ralph said after a pause.

"I don't want to be beastly about it."

"There was no question of anything serious—it was just—it just happened. Trixie was—kind. It didn't mean a thing to either of us."

They walked on and stared blankly at dripping trees and dappled hillsides.

"Isn't it funny," Camilla said, "how this seems to have sort of thrown me over on 'their' side? On Trixie's side?"

"Are you banging away about class again?"

"But *you* see it in terms of class yourself. 'They' are different about that sort of thing, you say."

He made a helpless gesture.

"Do other people know?" Camilla asked.

"I'm afraid so. There's been gossip. You know what—" He pulled himself up.

"What *they* are?"

Ralph swore violently.

Camilla burst into tears.

"I'm so sorry," Ralph kept repeating. "I'm so terribly sorry you mind."

"Well," Camilla sobbed, "it's not much good going on like this and I daresay I'm being very silly."

"Do you think you'll get over it?" he asked anxiously.

"One can but try."

"Please try very hard," Ralph said.

"I expect it all comes of being an only child. My papa is extremely old-fashioned."

"Is he a roaring inverted snob like you?"

"Certainly not."

"Here comes the egregious Simmy-Dick. You'd better not be crying, darling, if you can manage not to."

"I'll pretend it's the cold air," Camilla said, taking the handkerchief he offered her.

Simon Begg came down the lane in a raffish red sports car. When he saw them he skidded to a standstill.

"Hullo-ullo!" he shouted. "Fancy meeting you two. And how are we?"

He looked at them both with such a knowing air, compounded half of surprise and half of a rather debased sort of comradeship, that Camilla found herself blushing.

"I didn't realize you two knew each other," Simon went on. "No good offering you a lift, I suppose. I can just do three if we're cozy."

"This is meant to be a hearty walk," Ralph explained.

"Quite, quite," Simon said, beaming. "Hey, what's the gen on this show this afternoon? Do you get it?"

"I imagine it's a reconstruction, isn't it?"

"We're all meant to do what we all did on Wednesday?"

"I should think so, wouldn't you?"

"Are the onlookers invited?"

"I believe so. Some of them."

"The whole works?" Simon looked at Camilla, raised his eyebrows and grinned. "Including the ad libs?"

Camilla pretended not to understand him.

"Better put my running shoes on this time," he said.

"It's not going to be such a very amusing party, after all," Ralph pointed out stiffly, and Simon agreed, very cheerfully, that it was not. "I'm damn' sorry about the poor Old Guiser," he declared. "And I can't exactly see what they hope to get out of it. Can you?"

Ralph said coldly that he supposed they hoped to get the truth out of it. Simon was eying Camilla with unbridled enthusiasm

"In a moment," she thought, "he will twiddle those awful moustaches."

"I reckon it's a lot of bull," Simon confided. "Suppose somebody did do something—well, is he going to turn it all on again like a good boy for the police? Like hell, he is!"

"We ought to move on, Camilla, if we're to get back for lunch."

"Yes," Camilla said. "Let's."

Simon said earnestly, "Look, I'm sorry. I keep forgetting the relationship. It's—well, it's not all that easy to remember, is it? Look, Cam, hell, I *am* sorry."

Camilla, who had never before been called Cam, stared at him in bewilderment. His cheeks were rosy, his eyes were impertinent and blue and his moustache rampant. A half-smile hovered on his lips. "I *am* a goon,'" said Simon, ruefully. "*But,* still—"

Camilla, to her surprise, found she was not angry with him. "Never mind," she said. "No bones broken."

"Honest? You *are* a pal. Well, be good, children," said Simon and started up his engine. It responded with deafening alacrity. He waved his hand and shot off down the lane.

"He is," Ralph said, looking after him, "the definite and absolute rock bottom."

"Yes. But I find him rather touching," said Camilla.

ii

The five Andersen boys were in the smithy. The four younger brothers sat on upturned boxes and stools. A large tin trunk stood on a cleared bench at the far end of the smithy. Dan turned the key in the padlock that secured it. Sergeant Obby, who was on duty, had slipped into a light doze in a dark corner. He was keen on his job but unused to late hours.

"Wonderful queer to think of, hearts," Dan said. "The Guiser's savings. All these years." He looked at Chris. "And you'd no notion of it?"

"I wouldn't say that," Chris said. "I knew he put it by, like. Same as grand-dad and his'n, before him."

"I knew," Ernie volunteered. "He was a proper old miser, he was. Never let me have any, not for a wireless nor a telly nor nothing, he wouldn't. I knew where he put it by, I did, but he kept watch over it like a bloody mastiff, so's I dussn't let on. Old tyrant, he was. Cruel hard and crankytankerous."

Andy passed his great hand across his mouth and sighed. "Doan't talk that way," he said, lowering his voice and glancing towards Sergeant Obby, who had returned to duty. "What did we tell you?"

Dan agreed strongly. "Doan't talk that way, you, Ern. You was a burden to him with your foolishness."

"And a burden to us," Nat added, "as it turns out. Heavy and anxious."

"Get it into your thick head," Chris advised Ernie, "that you're born foolish and not up to our level when it comes to great affairs. Leave everything to us chaps. Doan't say nothing and doan't do nothing but what you was meant to do in the beginning."

"Huh!" Ernie shouted. "I'll larn 'em! Whang!" He made a wild swiping gesture.

"What'll we do?" Andy asked, appealing to the others. "Listen to him!"

Ernie surveyed his horrified brothers with the greatest complacency. "You doan't need to fret yourselves, chaps," he said. "I'm not so silly as what you all think I am. I can keep my tongue behind my teeth, fair enough. I be one too many for the coppers. Got 'em proper baffled, I 'ave."

"Shut up," Chris whispered savagely.

"No, I won't, then."

"You will, if I have to lay you out first," Chris muttered. He rose and walked across to his youngest brother. Chris was the biggest of the Andersens, a broad powerful man. He held his clenched fist in front of Ernie's face as if it were an object of virtue. "You know me, Ern," he said softly. "I've give you a hiding before this and never promised you one but what I've kept my word and laid it on solid. You got a taste last night. If you talk about—you know what—or open your silly damn' mouth on any matter at all when we're up-along, I'll give you a masterpiece. Won't I? *Won't I?*"

Ernie wiped his still-smiling mouth and nodded.

"You'll whiffle and you'll dance and you'll go where you went and you'll hold your tongue and you'll do no more nor that. Right?"

Ernie nodded and backed away.

"It's for the best, Ernie-boy," the gentle Andy said. "Us knows what's for the best."

Ernie pointed at Chris and continued to back away from him.

"You tell him to lay off of me," he said. "I know *him*. Keep him off of me."

Chris made a disgusted gesture. He turned away and began to examine the tools near the anvil.

"You keep your hands off of me," Ernie shouted after him. Sergeant Obby woke with a little snort.

"Don't talk daft. There you go, see!" Nat ejaculated. "Talking proper daft."

Dan said, "Now, listen, Ern. Us chaps doan't want to know nothing but what was according to plan. What you done, Wednesday, was what you was meant to do: whiffle, dance, bit of larking with Mr. Ralph, wait your turn and dance again. Which you done. And that's *all* you done. Nothing else. Doan't act as if there was anything else. There *wasn't*."

"That's right," his brothers counselled, "that's how 'tis."

They were so much alike, they might indeed have been a sort of rural chorus. Anxiety looked in the same way out of all their faces; they had similar mannerisms; their shared emotion ran a simple course through Dan's elderly persistence, Andy's softness, Nat's despair and Chris's anger. Even Ernie himself, half defiant, half scared, reflected something of his brothers' emotion.

And when Dan spoke again, it was as if he gave expression to this general resemblance.

"Us Andersens," he said, "stick close. Always have and always will, I reckon. So long as we stay that fashion, all together, we're right, souls. The day any of us cuts loose and sets out to act on his own, agin the better judgment of the others, will be the day of disaster. Mind that."

Andy and Nat made sounds of profound agreement.

"All right!" Ernie said. "All right. I never said nothing."

"Keep that way," Dan said, "and you'll do no harm. Mind that. And stick together, souls."

There was a sudden metallic clang. Sergeant Obby leapt to his feet. Chris, moved by some impulse of violence, had swung his great hammer and struck the cold anvil.

It was as if the smithy had spoken with its own voice in support of Dan Andersen.

iii

Mrs. Bünz made a long entry in her journal. For this purpose she employed her native language and it calmed her a little to form the words and see them, old familiars, stand in their orderly ranks across her pages. Mrs. Bünz had an instinctive respect for regimentation—a respect and a fear. She laid down her pen, locked away her journal and began to think about policemen: not about any specific officer but about the genus *Policeman* as she saw it and believed it to be. She remembered all the things that had happened to her husband and herself in Germany before the war and the formalities that had attended their arrival in England. She remembered the anxieties and discomforts of the first months of the war when they had continually to satisfy the police of their innocuous attitude, and she remembered their temporary incarceration while this was going on.

Mrs. Bünz did not put her trust in policemen.

She thought of Trixie's inexplicable entrance into her room that morning at a moment when Mrs. Bünz had every reason not to desire a visit. Was Trixie, perhaps, a police agent? A most disturbing thought.

She went downstairs and ate what was, for her, a poor breakfast. She tried to read but was unable to concentrate. Presently, she went out to the shed where she kept the car she had bought from Simon Begg and, after a bit of a struggle, started up the engine. If she had intended to use the car she now changed her mind and, instead, took a short walk to Copse Forge. But the Andersen brothers were gathered in the doorway and responded very churlishly to the forced bonhomie of her greeting. She went to the village shop, purchased two faded postcards and was looked at sideways by the shopkeeper.

Next, Mrs. Bünz visited the church but, being a rationalist, received and indeed sought no spiritual solace there. It was old but, from her point of view, not at all interesting. A bas-relief of a fourteenth-century Mardian merely reminded her unpleasantly of Dame Alice.

As she was leaving, she met Sam Stayne coming up the path in his cassock. He greeted her very kindly. Encouraged by this manifestation, Mrs. Bünz pulled herself together and began to question him about the antiquities of South Mardian. She adopted a somewhat patronizing tone that seemed to suggest a kind of intellectual unbending on her part. Her cold was still very heavy and lent to her manner a fortuitous air of complacency.

"I have been lookink at your little church," she said.

"I'm glad you came in."

"Of course, for me it is not, you will excuse me, as interestink as, for instance, the Copse Forge."

"Isn't it? It's nothing of an archaeological 'find,' of course."

"Perhaps you do not interest yourself in ritual dancing?" Mrs. Bünz suggested with apparent irrelevance but following up her own line of thought.

"Indeed I do," Sam Stayne said warmly. "It's of great interest to a priest, as are all such instinctive gestures."

"But it is pagan."

"Of course it is," he said and began to look distressed. "As I see it," he went on, choosing his words very carefully, "the Dance of the Sons is a kind of child's view of a great truth. The Church, more or less, took the ceremony under her wing, you know, many years ago."

"How! Ach! Because, no doubt, there had been a liddle license? A liddle too much freedom?"

"Well," he said, "I daresay. Goings-on, of sorts. Anyway, somewhere back in the nineties, a predecessor of mine took possession of 'Crack's' trappings and the Guiser's and the Betty's dresses and 'props,' as I think they call them in the theatre. He locked them up in the vestry. Ever since then, the parson has handed them out a week or so before the winter solstice to be looked over and repaired and used for the final practices and performance."

Mrs. Bünz stared at him and sneezed violently. She said in her cold-stricken voice, "Id is *bost* peculiar. I believe you because I have evidence of other cases. But for these joyous, pagan and, indeed, albost purely phallig objects to be lodged in an Aglicud church is, to say the least of it, adobalous." She blew her nose with Teutonic thoroughness. "Rebarkable!" said Mrs. Bünz.

"Well, there it is," he said, "and now, if you'll excuse me, I must go about my job."

"You are about to hold a service?"

"No," he said, "I've come to say my prayers."

She blinked at him. "Ach, so! Tell me, Mr. Stayne, in your church you do not, I believe, pray for the dead? That is dot your customb?"

"*I* do," Sam said. "That's what I'm here for now: to say a prayer or two for old William's soul." He looked mildly at her. Something prompted him to add, "And for another and unhappier soul."

Mrs. Bünz blew her nose again and eyed him over the top of her handkerchief. "Beaningk?" she asked.

"Meaning his murderer, you know," the Rector said.

Mrs. Bünz seemed to be so much struck by this remark that she forgot to lower her handkerchief. She nodded her head two or three times, however, and said something that sounded like "No doubt." She wished the Rector good morning and returned to the Green Man.

There she ran into Simon Begg. Alleyn and Fox witnessed their encounter from behind the window curtain. Simon contemplated Mrs. Bünz with, apparently, some misgiving. His very blue eyes stared out of his pink face and he climbed hurriedly from his car. Mrs. Bünz hastened towards him. He stood with his hands in his pockets and looked down at her. Alleyn saw her speak evidently with some urgency. Simon pulled at his flamboyant moustaches and listened with his head on one side. Mrs. Bünz glanced hastily at the pub as if she would have preferred not to be seen. She turned her back towards it and her head moved emphatically. Simon answered her with equal emphasis and presently with a reassuring gesture clapped his great hand down on her shoulder. Even through the window, which was shut, they heard her yelp of pain. It was clearly to be seen that Simon was making awkward apologies. Presently he took Mrs. Bünz by the elbow—he was the sort of man who habitually takes women by the elbow—and piloted her away towards the car she had bought from him. He lifted the bonnet and soon they had their heads together talking eagerly over the engine.

Fox said dubiously to Alleyn, "Is *that* what it was all about?"

"Don't you believe it, Br'er Fox. Those two are cooking up a little plot, the burden of which may well be, 'For, O, for, O, the hobby-horse is forgot.' "

"Shakespeare," Fox said, "I suppose."

"And why not? This case smacks of the Elizabethan. And I don't altogether mean *Hamlet* or *Lear*. Or nine-men's morris, though there's a flavour of all of them, to be sure. But those earlier plays of violence when people kill each other in a sort of quintessence of spleen and other people cheer each other up by saying things like, 'And now, my lord, to leave these doleful dumps.' Shall you be glad to leave these doleful dumps, Fox?"

"So, so," Fox said. "It's always nice to get a case cleared up. There's not all that much variety in murder."

"You've become an epicure of violence, which is as much as to say a 'bloody snob.' "

Fox chuckled obligingly.

Mrs. Bünz had drawn away from the car. She now approached the pub. They stood back in the room and they watched her. So did Simon Begg. Simon looked extremely worried and more than a little dubious. He scowled after Mrs. Bünz and scratched his head. Then, with the sort of shrug that suggests the relinquishment of an insoluble problem, he slammed down the bonnet of her car. Alleyn grinned. He could imagine Simon saying out loud, *"But,* still," and giving it up.

Mrs. Bünz approached the pub and, as if she felt that she was observed, glanced up at the windows. Her weathered face was patchy and her lips were set in a determined line.

"It's a very odd temperament," Alleyn muttered. "Her particular kind of Teutonic female temperament, I mean. At her sort of age and with her sort of background. Conditioned, if that's the beastly word, by violence and fear and full of curiosity and persistence."

"Persistence?" Fox repeated, savouring the idea.

"Yes. She's a very thorough sort of woman, is Mrs. Bünz. Look what she did on Wednesday night."

"That's right."

"Rubbed her fat shoulders raw, prancing round the dolmen in 'Crack's' harness. Yes," Alleyn repeated, more to himself than to Fox, "she's a thorough sort of woman, is Mrs. Bünz."

iv

The sun continued to shine upon South Mardian and upon the surrounding countryside. The temperature rose unseasonably. Bigger and bigger patches emerged, dark and glistening, from the dismantled landscape. Dr. Curtis, drving himself across country, slithered and skidded but made good time. At noon he rang through to say he expected to be with them before three. Alleyn directed him to Yowford, where the Guiser waited for him in the cottage-hospital mortuary.

At half past one a police car arrived with five reinforcements.

Alleyn held a sort of meeting in the back parlour and briefed his men for the afternoon performance. Carey, who had been down at Copse Forge, came in and was consulted with fitting regard for his rank and local importance.

"We haven't the faintest notion if we'll make an arrest," Alleyn said. "With luck, we might. I'd feel much happier about it if the results of the P.M. were laid on, but I've decided not to wait for them. The chances of success in a reconstruction of this sort rest on the accuracy of the observers' memories. With every hour they grow less dependable. We're taking pretty considerable risks and may look damn' silly for damn' all at the end of it. However, I think it's worth trying and Mr. Fox agrees with me. Now, this is what happens."

He laid out his plan of action, illustrating what he said with a rough sketch of the courtyard at Mardian Castle.

Dame Alice, Dulcie Mardian and the Rector would again sit on the steps. The rest of the audience would consist of Trixie, her father, Camilla, Carey, Sergeant Obby and Mrs. Bünz. The events of Wednesday night would be re-enacted in their order. At this point it became clear that Superintendent Carey was troubled in his mind. Seeing this, Alleyn asked him if he had any suggestions to make.

"Well! Naow!" Carey said. "I was just asking myself, Mr. Alleyn. If everybody, in a manner of speaking, is going to act their own parts over again, who would—er—who would—"

"Act the principal part?"

"That's right. The original," Mr. Carey said reasonably, "not being available."

"I wanted to consult you about that. What sort of age is the boy—Andy's son, isn't it?—who was the understudy?"

"Young Bill? Thirteen—fourteen or thereabouts. He's Andrew's youngest."

"Bright boy?"

"Smart enough little lad, far's I know."

"About the same height as his grandfather?"

"Just, I reckon."

"Could we get hold of him?"

"Reckon so. Andrew Andersen's farm's up to Yowford. Matter of a mile."

"Is Andy himself still down at the forge?"

"Went home for his dinner, no doubt, at noon. There's been a great family conference all morning at the smithy," Carey said. "My sergeant was on duty there. Obby. I don't say he was as alert as we might prefer: not used to late hours and a bit short of sleep. As a matter of fact, the silly danged fool dozed off and had to admit it."

The Yard men were at pains not to catch each other's eyes.

"He came forward, however, with the information that a great quantity of money was found and locked away and that all the boys seem very worried about what Ern may say or do. Specially Chris. He's a hot-tempered chap, is Chris Andersen, and not above using his hands, which he knows how to, having been a commando in the war."

"Hardly suitable as a mild corrective technique," Alleyn said drily.

"Well, no. Will I see if I can lay hold of young Bill, Mr. Alleyn? Now?"

"Would you, Carey? Thank you so much. Without anything being noticed. You'll handle it better than we would, knowing them."

Carey, gratified, set about this business.

They heard him start up his motor-bicycle and churn off along Yowford Lane.

"He's all right," Alleyn said to the Yard men. "Sound man, but he's feeling shy about his sergeant going to sleep on duty."

"So he should," Fox said, greatly scandalized. "I never heard such a thing. Very bad. Carey ought to have stayed there himself if he can't trust his chaps."

"I don't think it's likely to have made all that difference, Br'er Fox."

"It's the principle."

"Of course it is. Now, about this show—here's where I want everyone to stand. Mr. Fox up at the back by the archway through which they made their exits and entrances. Bailey and Thompson are coming off their specialists' perches and keeping observation again: there"—he pointed on his sketch—"by the entrance to the castle, that is to say, the first archway that links the semi-circular ruined wall to the new building, and here, by its opposite number at the other end of the wall. That's the way Ralph Stayne came back to the arena. The bonfire was outside the wall and to the right of the central archway. I want three men there. The remaining two will stand among the onlookers, bearing in mind what I've said we expect to find. We may be involved with more than one customer if the pot comes to the boil. Carey will be there, with his sergeant and his P.C., of course, and if the sergeant dozes off at *this* show it'll be because he's got sleeping sickness."

Fox said, "May we inquire where you'll be yourself, Mr. Alleyn?"

"Oh," Alleyn said, "here and there, Br'er Fox. Roaring up and down as a raging lion seeking whom I may devour. To begin with, in the Royal Box with the nobs, I daresay."

"On the steps with Dame Alice Mardian?"

"That's it. Now, one word more." Alleyn looked from Fox, Bailey and Thompson to the five newcomers. "I suggest that each of us marks one particular man and marks him well. Suppose you, Fox, take Ernie Andersen. Bailey takes Simon Begg as 'Crack,' the Hobby. Thompson takes Ralph Stayne as the Betty, and the rest of you parcel out among you the boy in his grandfather's role as the Fool and the other four sons as the four remaining dancers. That'll be one each for us, won't it? A neat fit."

One of the newcomers, a Sergeant Yardley, said, "Er—beg pardon."

"Yes, Yardley?"

"I must have lost count, sir. There's nine of us, counting yourself, and I understood there's only eight characters in this play affair, or dance, or whatever it is."

"Eight characters," Alleyn said, "is right. Our contention will be that there were nine performers, however."

"Sorry, sir. Of course."

"I," Alleyn said blandly, "hope to keep my eye on the ninth."

v

Young Bill Andersen might have sat to the late George Clauson for one of his bucolic portraits. He had a shock of tow-coloured hair, cheeks like apples and eyes as blue as periwinkles. His mouth stretched itself into the broadest grin imaginable and his teeth were big, white and far apart.

Carey brought him back on the pillion of his motor-bicycle and produced him to Alleyn as if he was one of the natural curiosities of the region.

"Young Bill," Carey said, exhibiting him. "I've told him what he's wanted for and how he'll need to hold his tongue and be right smart for the job, and he says he's able and willing. Come on," he added, giving the boy a business-like shove. "That's right, isn't it? Speak up for yourself."

"Ar," said young Bill. He looked at Alleyn through his thick white lashes and grinned. "I'd like it," he said.

"Good. Now, look here, Bill. What we want you to do is quite a tricky bit of work. It's got to be cleverly done. It's important. One of us would do it, actually, but we're all too tall for the job, as you can see for yourself. You're the right size. The thing is: do you know your stuff?"

"I know the Five Sons, sir, like the back of me yand."

"You do? You know the Fool's act, do you? Your grandfather's act?"

"Certain-sure."

"You watched it on Wednesday night, didn't you?"

"So I did, then."

"And you remember exactly what he did?"

"Ya-as."

"How can you be so sure?"

Bill scratched his head. "Reckon I watched him, seeing what a terrible rage he was in. After what happened, like. And what was said."

"What did happen?"

Bill very readily gave an account of the Guiser's arrival and the furious change-over: "I 'ad to strip off Uncle Ern's clothes and he 'ad to strip off Grandfer's. Terrible quick."

"And what *was* said?"

"Uncle Ern reckoned it'd be the death of Granfer, dancing. So did Uncle Chris. He'll kill himself, Uncle Chris says, if he goes capering in the great heat of his rages. The silly old bastard'll fall down dead, he says. So I was watching Granfer to see."

Bill passed the tip of his tongue round his lips. "Terrible queer," he muttered, "as it turned out, because so 'e did, like. Terrible queer."

Alleyn said, "Sure you don't mind doing this for us, Bill?"

The boy looked at him. "I don't mind," he declared and sounded rather surprised. "Suits me, all right."

"And you'll keep it as a dead secret between us? Not a word to anybody: top security."

"Ya-as," Bill said. "Surely." A thought seemed to strike him.

"Yes?" Alleyn said. "What's up?"

"Do I have to dress up in them bloody clothes of his'n?"

"No," Alleyn said after a pause.

"Nor wear his ma-ask?"

"No."

"I wouldn't fancy thik."

"There's no need. We'll fix you up with something light-coloured to wear and something over your face to look like a mask."

He nodded, perfectly satisfied. The strange and innocent cruelty of his age and sex was upon him.

"Reckon I can fix that," he said. "I'll get me a set of pyjammers and I got a ma-ask of me own. Proper clown's ma-ask."

And then, with an uncanny echo of his Uncle Ernie, he said, "Reckon I can make proper old Fool of myself."

"Good. And now, young Bill, you lay your ears back and listen to me. There's something else we'll ask you to do. It's something pretty tricky, it may be rather frightening and the case for the police may hang on it. How do you feel about that?"

"Bettn't I know what 'tis first?"

"Fair enough," Alleyn said and looked pleased. "Hold tight, then, and I'll tell you."

He told young Bill what he wanted.

The blue eyes opened wider and wider. Alleyn waited for an expostulation, but none came. Young Bill was thirteen. He kept his family feeling, his compassion and his enthusiasms in separate compartments. An immense grin converted his face into the likeness of a bucolic Puck. He began to rub the palms of his hands together.

Evidently he was, as Superintendent Carey had indicated, a smart enough lad for the purpose.

CHAPTER XII The Swords Again

THE afternoon had begun to darken when the persons concerned in the Sword Wednesday Morris of the Five Sons returned to Mardian Castle.

Dr. Otterly came early and went indoors to present his compliments to Dame Alice and find out how she felt after last night's carousal. He found the Rector and Alleyn were there already, while Fox and his assistants were to be seen in and about the courtyard.

At four o'clock the Andersens, with Sergeant Obby in attendance, drove up the hill in their station-waggon, from which they unloaded torches and a fresh drum of tar.

Superintendent Carey arrived on his motor-bike.

Simon appeared in his breakdown van with a new load of brushwood for the bonfire.

Ralph Stayne and his father walked up the hill and were harried by the geese, who had become hysterical.

Trixie and her father drove up with Camilla, looking rather white and strained, as their passenger.

Mrs. Bünz, alone this time, got her new car half-way up the drive and was stopped by one of Alleyn's men, who asked her to leave the car where it was until further orders and come the rest of the way on foot. This she did quite amenably.

From the drawing-room window Alleyn saw her trudge into the courtyard. Behind him Dame Alice sat in her bucket chair. Dulcie and the Rector stood further back in the room. All of them watched the courtyard.

The preparations were almost complete. Under the bland scrutiny of Mr. Fox and his subordinates, the Andersens had re-erected the eight torches: four on each side of the dolmen.

"It looks *just* like it did on Sword Wednesday," Dulcie pointed out, "doesn't it, Aunt Akky? Fancy!"

Dame Alice made a slight contemptuous noise.

"Only, of course," Dulcie added, "nobody's beheaded a goose this time. There is that, isn't there, Aunt Akky?"

"Unfortunately," her great-aunt agreed savagely. She stared pointedly at Dulcie, who giggled vaguely.

"What's that ass Ernie Andersen up to?" Dame Alice demanded.

"Dear me, yes," the Rector said. "Look at him."

Ernie, who had been standing apart from his brothers, apparently in a sulk, now advanced upon them. He gesticulated and turned from one to the other. Fox moved a little closer. Ernie pointed at his brothers and addressed himself to Fox.

"I understand," Alleyn said, "that he's been cutting up rough all the afternoon. He wants to play the Father's part."

"Mad!" Dame Alice said. "What did I tell you? He'll get himself into trouble before it's all over, you may depend 'pon it."

It was clear that Ernie's brothers had reacted in their usual way to his tantrums and were attempting to silence him. Simon came through the archway from the back, carrying "Crack's" head, and walked over to the group. Ernie listened. Simon clapped him good-naturedly on the shoulder and in a moment Ernie had thrown his customary crashing salute.

"That's done the trick," Alleyn said.

Evidently Ernie was told to light the torches. Clearly mollified, he set about this task, and presently light fans of crimson and yellow consumed the cold air. Their light quivered over the dolmen and dramatized the attentive faces of the onlookers.

"It's a strange effect," the Rector said uneasily. "Like the setting for a barbaric play—*King Lear*, perhaps."

"Otterly will agree with your choice," Alleyn said and Dr. Otterly came out of the shadow at the back of the room. The Rector turned to him, but Dr. Otterly didn't show his usual enthusiasm for his pet theory.

"I suppose I'd better go out," he said. "Hadn't I, Alleyn?"

"I think so. I'm going back now." Alleyn turned to Dulcie, who at once put on her expression of terrified jocosity.

"I wonder," Alleyn said, "if I could have some clean rags? Enough to make a couple of thick pads about the size of my hand? And some first-aid bandages, if you have them?"

"Rags!" Dulcie said. "Fancy! Pads! Bandages!" She eyed him facetiously. "Now, I *wonder*."

" 'Course he can have them," Dame Alice said. "Don't be an ass, Dulcie. Get them."

"Very well, Aunt Akky," Dulcie said in a hurry. She plunged out of the room and in a surprisingly short space of time returned with a handful of old linen and two bandages. Alleyn thanked her and stuffed them into his overcoat pocket.

"I don't think we shall be long now," he said. "And when you're ready, Dame Alice—?"

"*I'm* ready. Haul me up, will yer? Dulcie! Bundle!"

As this ceremony would evidently take some considerable time, Alleyn excused himself. He and Dr. Otterly went out to the courtyard.

Dr. Otterly joined his colleagues and they all took up their positions offstage behind the old wall. Alleyn paused on the house steps and surveyed the scene.

The sky was clear now and had not yet completely darkened: to the west it was still faintly green. Stars exploded into a wintry glitter. There was frost in the air.

The little party of onlookers stood in their appointed places at the side of the courtyard and would have almost melted into darkness if it had not been for the torchlight. The Andersens had evidently strapped their pads of bells on their thick legs. Peremptory jangles could be heard offstage.

Alleyn's men were at their stations and Fox now came forward to meet him.

"We're all ready, Mr. Alleyn, when you are."

"All right. What was biting Ernie?"

"Same old trouble. Wanting to play the Fool."

"Thought as much."

Carey moved out from behind the dolmen.

"I suppose it's all right," he murmured uneasily. "You know. Safe."

"Safe?" Fox repeated and put his head on one side as if Carey had advanced a quaintly original theory.

"Well, *I* dunno, Mr. Fox," Carey muttered. "It seems a bit uncanny-like and with young Ern such a queer excitable chap—he's been saying he wants to sharpen up that damned old sword affair of his. 'Course we won't let him *have* it, but how's he going to act when we don't! Take one of his fits, like as not."

"We'll have to keep a nice sharp observation over him, Mr. Carey," Fox said.

"Over all of them," Alleyn demanded.

"Well," Carey conceded, "I daresay I'm fussy."

"Not a bit," Alleyn said. "You're perfectly right to look upon this show as a chancy business. But they've sent us five very good men who all know what to look for. And with you," Alleyn pointed out wickedly, "in a key position I don't personally think we're taking too big a risk."

"Ar, no-no-no," Carey said quickly and airily. "No, I wasn't suggesting we were, you know. I wasn't suggesting *that*."

"We'll just have a final look round, shall we?" Alleyn proposed.

He walked over to the dolmen, glanced behind it and then moved on through the central arch at the back.

Gathered together in a close-knit group, rather like a bunch of carol singers, with lanthorns in their hands, were the five Andersens. As they changed their positions in order to eye the new arrivals, their bells clinked. Alleyn was reminded unexpectedly of horses that stamped and shifted in their harness. Behind them, near the unlit bonfire, stood Dr. Otterly and Ralph, who was again dressed in his great hooped skirt. Simon stood by the cylindrical cheese-shaped body of the Hobby-Horse. "Crack's" head grinned under his arm. Beyond these again, were three of the extra police officers. The hedge-slasher, with its half-burnt handle and heat-distempered blade, leant against the wall with the drum of tar nearby. There was a strong tang of bitumen on the frosty air.

"We'll light the bonfire," Alleyn said, "and then I'll ask you all to come into the courtyard while I explain what we're up to."

One of the Yard men put a match to the paper. It flared up. There was a crackle of brushwood and a pungent smell rose sweetly with smoke from the bonfire.

They followed Alleyn back, through the archway, past the dolmen and the flaring torches and across the arena.

Dame Alice was enthroned at the top of the steps, flanked, as before, by Dulcie and the Rector. Rugged and shawled into a quadrel with a knob on top, she resembled some primitive totem and appeared to be perfectly immovable.

Alleyn stood on a step below and a little to one side of this group. His considerable height was exaggerated by the shadow that leapt up behind him. The torchlight lent emphasis to the sharply defined planes of his face and gave it a fantastic appearance. Below him stood the five Sons with Simon, Ralph and Dr. Otterly.

Alleyn looked across to the little group on his right.

"Will you come nearer?" he said. "What I have to say concerns all of you."

They moved out of the shadows, keeping apart, as if each was anxious to establish a kind of disassociation from the others: Trixie, the landlord, Camilla and, lagging behind, Mrs. Bünz. Ralph crossed over to Camilla and stood beside her. His conical skirt looked like a giant extinguisher and Camilla in her flame-coloured coat like a small candle flame beside him.

Fox, Carey and their subordinates waited attentively in the rear.

"I expect," Alleyn said, "that most of you wonder just why the police have decided upon this reconstruction. I don't suppose any of you enjoy the prospect and I'm sorry if it causes you anxiety or distress."

He waited for a moment. The faces upturned to his were misted by their own breath. Nobody spoke or moved.

"The fact is," he went on, "that we're taking an unusual line with a very unusual set of circumstances. The deceased man was in full sight of you all for as long as he took an active part in this dance-play of yours and he was still within sight of some of you after he lay down behind that stone. Now, Mr. Carey has questioned every man, woman and child who was in the audience on Wednesday night. They are agreed that the Guiser did not leave the arena or move from his hiding place and that nobody offered him any violence as he lay behind the stone. Yet, a few minutes *after* he lay down there came the appalling discovery of his decapitated body.

"We've made exhaustive inquiries, but each of them has led us slap up against this apparent contradiction. We want therefore to see for ourselves exactly what did happen."

Dr. Otterly looked up at Alleyn as if he were about to interrupt but seemed to change his mind and said nothing.

"For one reason or another," Alleyn went on, "some of you may feel disinclined to repeat some incident or occurrence. I can't urge you too strongly to leave nothing out and to stick absolutely to fact. 'Nothing extenuate,' " he found himself saying, " 'nor set down aught in malice.' That's as sound a bit of advice on evidence as one can find anywhere and what we're asking you to do is, in effect, to provide visual evidence. To *show* us the truth. And by sticking to the whole truth and nothing but the truth, each one of you will establish the innocent. You will show us who *couldn't* have done it. But don't fiddle with the facts. Please don't do that. Don't leave out anything because you're afraid we may think it looks a bit fishy. We won't think so if it's not. And what's more," he added and raised an eyebrow, "I must remind you that any rearrangement would probably be spotted by your fellow performers or your audience."

He paused. Ernie broke into aimless laughter and his brothers shifted uneasily and jangled their bells.

"Which brings me," Alleyn went on, "to my second point. If at any stage of this performance any one of you notices anything at all, however slight, that is different from what you remember, you will please say so. There and then. There'll be a certain amount of noise, I suppose, so you'll have to give a clear signal. Hold up your hand. If you're a fiddler," Alleyn said and nodded at Dr. Otterly, "stop fiddling and hold up your bow. If you're the Hobby-Horse"—he glanced at Simon—"you can't hold up your hand, but you can let out a yell, can't you?"

"Fair enough," Simon said. "Yip-ee!"

The Andersens and the audience looked scandalized.

"And similarly," Alleyn said, "I want any member of this very small audience who notices any discrepancy to make it clear, at once, that he does so. Sing out or hold up your hand. Do it there and then."

"Dulcie."

"Yes, Aunt Akky?"

"Get the gong."

"The gong, Aunt Akky?"

"Yes. The one I bought at that jumble-sale. And the hunting horn from the gun-room."

"Very well, Aunt Akky."

Dulcie got up and went indoors.

"You," Dame Alice told Alleyn, "can bang if you want them to stop. I'll have the horn."

Alleyn said apologetically, "Thank you *very* much, but, as it happens, I've got a whistle."

"Sam can bang, then, if he notices anything."

The Rector cleared his throat and said he didn't think he'd want to.

Alleyn, fighting hard against this rising element of

semi-comic activity, addressed himself again to the performers.

"If you hear my whistle," he said, "you will at once stop whatever you may be doing. Now, is all this perfectly clear? Are there any questions?"

Chris Andersen said loudly, "What say us chaps won't?"

"You mean, won't perform at all?"

"Right. What say we won't?"

"That'll be that," Alleyn said coolly.

"Here!" Dame Alice shouted, peering into the little group of men. "Who *was* that? Who's talkin' about will and won't?"

They shuffled and jangled.

"Come on," she commanded. "Daniel! Who was it?"

Dan looked extremely uncomfortable. Ernie laughed again and jerked his thumb at Chris. "Good old Chrissie," he guffawed.

Big Chris came tinkling forward. He stood at the foot of the steps and looked full at Dame Alice.

"It was me, then," he said. "Axcuse me, maam, it's our business whether this affair goes on or don't. Seeing who it was that was murdered. We're his sons."

"Pity you haven't got his brains!" she rejoined. "You're a hot-headed, blunderin' sort of donkey, Chris Andersen, and always have been. Be a sensible feller, now, and don't go puttin' yourself in the wrong."

"What's the sense of it?" Chris demanded. "How can we do what was done before when there's no Fool? What's the good of it?"

"Anyone'd think you wanted your father's murderer to go scot-free."

Chris sank his head a little between his shoulders and demanded of Alleyn, "Will it be brought up agin' us if we won't do it?"

Alleyn said, "Your refusal will be noted. We can't use threats."

"Namby-pamby nonsense," Dame Alice announced.

Chris stood with his head bent. Andy and Nat

looked out of the corners of their eyes at Dan. Ernie did a slight kicking step and roused his bells.

Dan said, "As I look at it, there's no choice, souls. We'll dance."

"Good," Alleyn said. "Very sensible. We begin at the point where the Guiser arrived in Mrs. Bünz's car. I will ask Mrs. Bünz to go down to the car, drive it up, park it where she parked it before and do exactly what she did the first time. You will find a police constable outside, Mrs. Bünz, and he will accompany you. The performers will wait offstage by the bonfire. Dr. Otterly will come onstage and begin to play. Right, Mrs. Bünz?"

Mrs. Bünz was blowing her nose. She nodded and turned away. She tramped out through the side archway and disappeared.

Dan made a sign to his brothers. They faced about and went tinkling across the courtyard and through the centre archway. Ralph Stayne and Simon followed. The watchers took up their appointed places and Dr. Otterly stepped out into the courtyard and tucked his fiddle under his chin.

The front door burst open and Dulcie staggered out bearing a hunting horn and a hideous gong slung between two tusks. She stumbled and, in recovering, struck the gong smartly with the horn. It gave out a single and extremely strident note that echoed forbiddingly round the courtyard.

As if this were an approved signal, Mrs. Bünz, half-way down the drive, started up the engine of her car and Dr. Otterly gave a scrape on his fiddle.

"Well," Alleyn thought, "it's a rum go and no mistake but we're off."

ii

Mrs. Bünz's car, with repeated blasts on the horn, churned in low gear up the drive and turned to the right behind the curved wall. It stopped. There was a final and prolonged hoot. Dr. Otterly lowered his bow.

"This was when I went off to see what was up," he said.

"Right. Do so, please."

He did so, a rather lonely figure in the empty courtyard.

Mrs. Bünz, followed by a constable, returned and stood just within the side entrance. She was as white as a sheet and trembling.

"We could hear the Guiser," Dame Alice informed them, "yellin'."

Nobody was yelling this time. On the far side of the semi-circular wall, out of sight of their audience and lit by the bonfire, the performers stood and stared at each other. Dr. Otterly faced them. The police hovered anonymously. Mr. Fox, placidly bespectacled, contemplated them all in turn. His notebook lay open on his massive palm.

"This," he said, "is where the old gentleman arrived and found *you*"—he jabbed a forefinger at Ernie—"dressed up for his part and young Bill dressed up for yours. He grabbed *his* clothes off *you*"—another jab at Ernie—"and got into them himself. And you changed with young Bill. Take all that as read. What was said?"

Simon, Dr. Otterly and Ralph Stayne all spoke together. Mr. Fox pointed his pencil at Dr. Otterly. "Yes, thank you, Doctor?" he prompted.

"When I came out," Dr. Otterly said, "he was roaring like a bull, but you couldn't make head or tail of it. He got hold of Ernie and practically lugged the clothes off him."

Ernie swore comprehensively. "Done it to spite me," he said. "Old bastard!"

"Was any explanation given," Fox pursued, "about the note that had been handed round saying Ernie could do it?"

There was no answer. "Nobody," Fox continued, "spotted that it hadn't been written about the dance but about that slasher there?"

Ernie, meeting the flabbergasted gaze of his brothers, slapped his knees and roared out, "I foxed the lot of you proper, I did. Not so silly as what I let on to be, me!"

Nat said profoundly, "You *bloody* great fool."

Ernie burst into his high rocketing laugh.

Fox held up his hand. "Shut up," he said and nodded to one of his men, who came forward with the swords in a sacking bundle and gave them out to the dancers.

Ernie began to swing and slash with his sword.

"Where's mine?" he demanded. "This'un's not mine. Mine's sharp."

"That'll do, you," Fox said. "You're not having a sharp one this time. Places, everyone. In the same order as before, *if* you please."

Dr. Otterly nodded and went out through the archway into the arena.

"Now," Dulcie said, "they *really* begin, don't they, Aunt Akky?"

A preliminary scrape or two and then the jiggling reiterative tune. Out through the archway came Ernie, white-faced this time instead of black but wearing his black cap and gloves. His movements at first were less flamboyant than they had been on Wednesday, but perhaps he gathered inspiration from the fiddle, for they soon became more lively. He pranced and curvetted and began to slash out with his sword.

"This, I take it, is whiffling," Alleyn said. "A kind of purification, isn't it, Rector?"

"I believe so. Yes."

Ernie completed his round and stood to one side. His brothers came out at a run, their bells jerking. Ernie joined them and they performed the Mardian Morris together, wearing their bells and leaving their swords in a heap near Dr. Otterly. This done they removed their bells and took up their swords. Ernie threaded his red ribbon. They stared at each other and, furtively, at Alleyn.

Now followed the entry of the hermaphrodite and the Hobby-Horse. Ralph Stayne's extinguisher of a skirt, suspended from his armpits, swung and bounced.

His man's jacket spread over it. His hat, half topper, half floral toque, was jammed down over his forehead. The face beneath was incongruously grave.

"Crack's" iron head poked and gangled monstrously on the top of its long canvas neck. The cheese-shaped body swung rhythmically and its skirt trailed on the ground. "Crack's" jaws snapped and its ridiculous rudiment of a tail twitched busily. Together these two came prancing in.

Dulcie again said, "Here comes 'Crack,'" and her great-aunt looked irritably at her as if she too were bent on a complete pastiche.

"Crack" finished his entry dead centre, facing the steps. A voice that seemed to have no point of origin but to be merely *there* asked anxiously:

"I say, sorry, but do you want *all* the fun and games?"

"Crack's" neck opened a little, rather horridly, and Simon's face could be seen behind the orifice.

"Everything," Alleyn said.

"Oh, righty-ho. Look out, ladies, here I come," the voice said. The neck closed. "Crack" swung from side to side as if the monster ogled its audience and made up its mind where to hunt. Camilla moved closer to Trixie and looked apprehensively from Alleyn to Ralph Stayne. Ralph signalled to her, putting his thumb up as if to reassure her of his presence.

"Crack's" jaws snapped. It began to make pretended forays upon an imaginary audience. Dr. Otterly, still fiddling, moved nearer to Camilla and nodded to her encouragingly. "Crack" darted suddenly at Camilla. She ran like a hare before it, across the courtyard and into Ralph's arms. "Crack" went off at the rear archway.

"Just what they did before," Dulcie ejaculated. "Isn't it, Aunt Akky? Isn't it, Sam?"

The Rector murmured unhappily and Dame Alice said, "I do wish to goodness you'd shut up, Dulcie."

"Well, I'm sorry, Aunt Akky, but—*ow!*" Dulcie ejaculated.

Alleyn had blown his whistle.

Dr. Otterly stopped playing. The Andersen brothers turned their faces toward Alleyn.

"One moment," Alleyn said.

He moved to the bottom step and turned a little to take in both the party of three above him and the scattered groups in the courtyard.

"I want a general check, here," he said. "Mrs. Bünz, are you satisfied that so far this was exactly what happened?"

Bailey had turned his torchlight on Mrs. Bünz. Her mouth was open. Her lips began to move.

"I'm afraid I can't hear you," Alleyn said. "Will you come a little nearer?"

She came very slowly towards him.

"Now," he said.

"*Ja*. It is what was done."

"And what happened next?"

She moistened her lips. "There was the entry of the Fool," she said.

"What did he do, exactly?"

She made an odd and very ineloquent gesture.

"He goes round," she said. "Round and round."

"And what else does he do?"

"Aunt Akky—"

"No," Alleyn said so strongly that Dulcie gave another little yelp. "I want Mrs. Bünz to show us what he did."

Mrs. Bünz was, as usual, much enveloped. As she moved forward, most reluctantly, a stiffish breeze sprang up. She was involved in a little storm of billowing handicraft.

In an uncomfortable silence she jogged miserably round the outside of the courtyard, gave two or three dejected skips and came to a halt in front of the steps. Dame Alice stared at her implacably and Dulcie gaped. The Rector looked at his boots.

"That is all," said Mrs. Bünz.

"You have left something out," said Alleyn.

"I do not remember everything," Mrs. Bünz said in a strangulated voice.

"And I'll tell you why," Alleyn rejoined. "It is because you have never seen what he did. Not even when you looked through the window of the barn."

She put her woolly hand to her mouth and stepped backwards.

"I'll be bloody well danged!" Tom Plowman loudly ejaculated and was silenced by Trixie.

Mrs. Bünz said something that sounded like "—interests of scientific research—"

"Nor, I suggest, will you have seen what the Guiser did on his first entrance on Wednesday night. Because on Wednesday night you left the arena at the point we have now reached. Didn't you, Mrs. Bünz?"

She only moved her head from side to side as if to assure herself that it was on properly.

"Do you say that's wrong?"

She flapped her woollen paws and nodded.

"Yes, but you know, Aunt Akky, she *did*."

"Hold your tongue, Dulcie, do," begged her great-aunt.

"No," Alleyn said. "Not at all. I want to hear from Miss Mardian."

"Have it your own way. It's odds on she don't know what she's talkin' about."

"Oh," Dulcie cried, "but I *do*. I *said* so to *you*, Aunt Akky. I said, 'Aunt Akky, do look at the German woman going away.' I said so to Sam. Didn't I, Sam?"

The Rector, looking startled and rather guilty, said to Alleyn, "I believe she did."

"And what *was* Mrs. Bünz doing, Rector?"

"She—actually—I really had quite forgotten—she *was* going out."

"Well, Mrs. Bünz?"

Mrs. Bünz now spoke with the air of a woman who has had time to make up her mind.

"I had unexpected occasion," she said, choosing her words, "to absent myself. Delicacy," she added, "excuses me from further cobbent."

"Rot," said Dame Alice.

Alleyn said, "And when did you come back?"

She answered quickly, "During the first part of the sword-dance."

"Why didn't you tell me all this yesterday when we had such difficulty over the point?"

To that she had nothing to say.

Alleyn made a signal with his hand and Fox, who stood in the rear archway, turned to "Crack" and said something inaudible. They came forward together.

"Mr. Begg," Alleyn called out, "will you take your harness off, if you please?"

"What say? Oh, righty-ho," said Simon's voice. There was a strange and uncanny upheaval. "Crack's" neck collapsed and the iron head retreated after it into the cylindrical body. The whole frame tilted on its rim and presently Simon appeared.

"Good. Now, I suggest that on Wednesday evening, while you waited behind the wall at the back, you took off your harness as you have just done here."

Simon began to look resigned. "And I suggest," Alleyn went on, "that when you, Mrs. Bünz, left the arena by the side arch, you went round behind the walls and met Mr. Begg at the back."

Mrs. Bünz flung up her thick arms in a gesture of defeat.

Simon said clumsily, "Not to worry, Mrs. B.," and dropped his hands on her shoulders.

She screamed out, "Don't touch me!"

Alleyn said, "Your shoulders *are* sore, aren't they? But then 'Crack's' harness is very heavy, of course."

After that, Mrs. Bünz had nothing to say.

iii

A babble of astonishment had broken out on the steps and a kind of suppressed hullabaloo among the Andersens.

Ernie shouted, "What did I tell you, then, chaps? I said it was a wumman what done it, didn't I? No good comes of it when a wumman mixes 'erself up in this gear. Not it. Same as curing hams," he astonishingly added. "Keep 'em out when it's men's gear, same as the old bastard said."

"Ah, shut up, Corp. Shut your trap, will you?" Simon said wearily.

"Very good, sir," Ernie shouted and flung himself into a salute.

Alleyn said, "Steady now, and attend to me. I imagine that you, Begg, accepted a sum of money from Mrs. Bünz in consideration of her being allowed to stand-in as 'Crack' during the triple sword-dance. You came off after your tearing act and she met you behind the wall near the bonfire and you put your harness on her and away she went. I think that, struck by the happy coincidence of names, you probably planked whatever money she gave you, and I daresay a whole lot more, on Teutonic Dancer by Subsidize out of Substitution. The gods of chance are notoriously unscrupulous and, without deserving in the least to do so, you won a packet."

Simon grinned and then looked as if he wished he hadn't. He said, "How can you be so sure you haven't been handed a plateful of duff gen?"

"I can be perfectly sure. Do you know what the Guiser's bits of dialogue were in the performance?"

"No," Simon said. "I don't. He always mumbled whatever it was. Mrs. B. asked me, as a matter of fact, and I told her I didn't know."

Alleyn turned to the company at large.

"Did any of you ever tell Mrs. Bünz anything about what was said?"

Chris said angrily, "Not bloody likely."

"Very well. Mrs. Bünz repeated a phrase of the dialogue in conversation with me. A phrase that I'm sure she heard with immense satisfaction for the first time on Wednesday night. That's why you bribed Mr. Begg to let you take his part, wasn't it, Mrs. Bünz? You were on the track of a particularly sumptuous fragment of folklore. You didn't dance, as you were meant to do, round the edge of the arena. Disguised as 'Crack,' you got as close as you could to the Guiser and you listened in."

Alleyn hesitated for a moment and then quoted, " 'Betty to lover me.' Do you remember how it goes on?"

"I answer nothing."

"Then I'm afraid I must ask you to act." He fished in his pockets and pulled out the bandages and two handfuls of linen. "These will do to pad your shoulders. We'll get Dr. Otterly to fix them."

"What will you make me do?"

"Only what you did on Wednesday."

Chris shouted violently, "Doan't let 'er. Keep the woman out of it. Doan't let 'er."

Dan said, "And so I say. If that's what happened 'twasn't right and never will be. Once was too many, let alone her doing it again deliberate."

"Hold hard, chaps," Andy said, with much less than his usual modesty. "This makes a bit of differ, all the same. None of us knew about this, did we?" He jerked his head at Ernie. "Only young Ern seemingly. He knew the woman done this on us? Didn't you, Ern?"

"Keep your trap shut, Corp," Simon advised him.

"Very good, sir."

Chris suddenly roared at Simon, "You leave Ern alone, you, Simmy-Dick. You lay off of him, will you? Reckon you're no better nor a damned traitor, letting a woman in on the Five Sons."

"So he is, then," Nat said. "A bloody traitor. Don't you heed him, Ern."

"Ah, put a sock in it, you silly clots," Simon said disgustedly. "Leave the poor sod alone. You don't know what you're talking about. Silly bastards!"

Dan, using a prim voice, said, "Naow! Naow! Language!"

They all glanced self-consciously at Dame Alice.

It had been obvious to Alleyn that behind him Dame Alice was getting up steam. She now let it off by means literally of an attenuated hiss. The Andersens stared at her apprehensively.

She went for them with a mixture of arrogance and essential understanding that must derive, Alleyn thought, from a line of coarse, aristocratic, overbearing landlords. She was the Old Englishwoman not only of Surtees but of Fielding and Wycherley and Johnson: a bully and a harridan, but one who spoke with authority. The Andersens listened to her, without any show of servility but rather with the air of men who recognize a familiar voice among foreigners. She had only one thing to say to them and it was to the effect that if they didn't perform she, the police and everyone else would naturally conclude they had united to make away with their father. She ended abruptly with an order to get on with it before she lost patience. Chris still refused to go on, but his brothers, after a brief consultation, overruled him.

Fox, who had been writing busily, exchanged satisfied glances with his chief.

Alleyn said, "Now, Mrs. Bünz, are you ready?"

Dr. Otterly had been busy with the bandages and the pads of linen, which now rested on Mrs. Bünz's shoulders like a pair of unwieldy epaulets.

"You're prepared, I see," Alleyn said, "to help us."

"I have not said."

Ernie suddenly bawled out, "Don't bloody well let 'er. There'll be trouble."

"That'll do," Alleyn said, and Ernie was silent. "Well, Mrs. Bünz?"

She turned to Simon. Her face was the colour of lard and she smiled horridly. "Wing-Commander Begg, you, as much as I, are implicated in this idle prank. Should I repeat?"

Simon took her gently round the waist. "I don't see why not, Mrs. B.," he said. "You be a good girl and play ball with the cops. Run along, now."

He gave her a facetious pat. "Very well," she said and produced a sort of laugh. "After all, why dot?"

So she went out by the side archway and Simon by the centre one. Dr. Otterly struck up his fiddle again.

It was the tune that had ushered in the Fool. Dr. Otterly played the introduction and, involuntarily, performers and audience alike looked at the rear archway where on Sword Wednesday the lonely figure in its dolorous mask had appeared. The archway gaped enigmatically upon the night. Smoke from the bonfire drifted across the background and occasional sparks crossed it like fireflies. It had an air of expectancy.

"But this time there won't be a Fool," Dulcie pointed out. "Will there, Aunt Akky?"

Dame Alice had opened her mouth to speak. It remained open, but no voice came out. The Rector ejaculated sharply and rose from his chair. A thin, shocking sound, half laughter and half scream, wavered across the courtyard. It had been made by Ernie and was echoed by Trixie.

Through the smoke, as if it had been evolved from the same element, came the white figure: jog, jog, getting clearer every second. Through the archway and into the arena: a grinning mask, limp arms, a bauble on a stick, and bent legs.

Dr. Otterly, after an astonished discord, went into the refrain of "Lord Mardian's Fancy." Young Bill, in the character of the Fool, began to jog round the courtyard. It was as if a clockwork toy had been re-wound.

Alleyn joined Fox by the rear archway. From here he could still see the Andersens. The four elder brothers were reassuring each other. Chris looked angry, and the others mulish and affronted. But Ernie's mouth gaped and his hands twitched and he watched the Fool like a fury. Offstage, through the archway, Alleyn was able to see Mrs. Bünz's encounter with Simon. She came round the outside curve of the wall and he met her at the bonfire. He began to explain sheepishly to Alleyn.

"We'd fixed it up like this," Simon said. "I met her here. We'd plenty of time."

"Why on earth didn't you tell us the whole of this ridiculous story at once?" Alleyn asked.

Simon mumbled, "I don't expect you to credit it, but I was cobs with the boys. They're a good shower of bods. I knew how they'd feel if it ever got out. And, anyway, it doesn't look so hot, does it? For all I knew you might get thinking things."

"What sort of things?"

"Well, *you* know. With murder about."

"You have been an ass," Alleyn said.

"I wouldn't have done it, only I wanted the scratch like hell." He added impertinently, "Come to that, why didn't you tell us you were going to rig up an understudy? Nasty jolt he gave us, didn't he, Mrs. B.? Come on, there's a big girl. Gently does it."

Mrs. Bünz, who seemed to be shattered into acquiescence, sat on the ground. He tipped up the great cylinder of "Crack's" body, exposing the heavy shoulder straps under the canvas top and the buckled harness. He lowered it gently over Mrs. Bünz. "Arms through the leathers," he said.

The ringed canvas neck, which lay concertinaed on the top of the cylinder, now swelled at the base. Simon leant over and adjusted it and Mrs. Bünz's pixie cap appeared through the top. He lifted the head on its flexible rod and then introduced the rod into the neck. "Here it comes," he said. Mrs. Bünz's hands could be seen grasping the end of the rod.

"It fits into a socket in the harness," Simon explained. The head now stood like some monstrous blossom on a thin stalk above the body. Simon drew up the canvas neck. The pixie cap disappeared. The top of the neck was made fast to the head and Mrs. Bünz contemplated the world through a sort of window in the canvas.

"The hands are free underneath," Simon said, "to work the tail string." He grinned. "And to have a bit of the old woo if you catch your girlie. I didn't, worse luck. There you are. The Doc's just coming up with the tune for the first sword-dance. On you go, Mrs. B. Not to worry. We don't believe in spooks, do we?"

And Mrs. Bünz, subdued to the semblance of a prehistoric bad dream, went through the archway to take part in the Mardian Sword Dance.

Simon squatted down by the bonfire and reached for a burning twig to light his cigarette.

"Poor old B.," he said, looking after Mrs. Bünz. "*But,* still."

iv

Camilla had once again run away from the Hobby into Ralph Stayne's arms and once again he stayed beside her.

She had scarcely recovered from the shock of the Fool's entrance and kept looking into Ralph's face to reassure herself. She found his great extinguisher of a skirt and his queer bi-sexual hat rather off-putting. She kept remembering stories Trixie had told her of how in earlier times the Betties had used the skirt. They had popped it over village girls, Trixie said, and had grabbed hold of them through the slits in the sides and carried them away. Camilla would have jeered at herself heartily if she had realized that, even though Ralph had only indulged in a modified form of this piece of horseplay, she intensely disliked the anecdote. Perhaps it was because Trixie had related it.

She looked at Ralph now and, after the habit of lovers, made much of the qualities she thought she saw in him. His mouth was set and his eyebrows were drawn together in a scowl. "He's terribly sensitive, really," Camilla told herself. "He's hating this business as much in his way as I am in mine. And," she thought, "I daresay he's angryish because I got such an awful shock when whoever it is came in like the Guiser, and I daresay he's even angrier because Simon Begg chased me again." This thought cheered her immensely.

They watched young Bill doing his version of his grandfather's first entry and the ceremonial trot round the courtyard. He repeated everything quite correctly and didn't forget to slap the dolmen with his clown's bauble.

"And *that's* what Mrs. Bünz didn't know about," Ralph muttered.

"Who is it?" Camilla wondered. "He knows it all, doesn't he? It's horrible."

"It's that damned young Bill," Ralph muttered. "There's nobody else who does know. By Heaven, when I get hold of him—"

Camilla said. "Darling, you don't think—?"

He turned his head and looked steadily at Camilla for a moment before answering her.

"I don't know what to think," he said at last. "But I know damn, well that if the Guiser had spotted Mrs. Bünz dressed up as 'Crack' he'd have gone for her like a fury."

"But nothing *happened*," Camilla said. "I stood here and I looked and nothing *happened.*"

"I know," he said.

"Well. then—how? Was he carried off? Or something?" Ralph shook his head.

Dr. Otterly had struck up a bouncing introduction. The Five Sons, who had removed their bells, took up their swords and came forward into position. And through the central archway jogged the Hobby-Horse, moving slowly.

"Here she comes," Camilla said. "You'd never guess, would you?"

Alleyn and Fox reappeared and stood inside the archway. Beyond them, lit by the bonfire, was Simon.

The Sons began the first part of the triple sword-dance.

They had approached their task with a lowering and reluctant air. Alleyn wondered if there was going to be a joint protest about the re-enactment of the Fool. Ernie hadn't removed his gaze from the dolorous mask. His eyes were unpleasantly brilliant and his face glistened with sweat. He came forward with his brothers and had an air of scarcely knowing what he was about. But there was some compulsion in the music. They had been so drilled by their father and so used to executing their steps with a leap and a flourish that they were unable to dance with less than the traditional panache. They were soon hard at it, neat and vigorous, rising lightly and coming down hard. The ring of steel was made. Each man grasped his successor's sword by its red ribbon. The lock, or knot, was formed. Dan raised it aloft to exhibit it and it glittered in the torchlight. Young Bill approached and looked at the knot as if at his reflection in a glass.

A metallic rumpus broke out on the steps. It was Dame Alice indulging in a wild cachinnation on her hunting horn.

Dr. Otterly lowered his bow. The dancers, the Betty and the Hobby-Horse were motionless.

"Yes, Dame Alice?" Alleyn asked.

"The Hobby ain't close enough," she said. "Nothin' like. It kept sidlin' up to Will'm. D'you 'gree?" she barked at the Rector.

"I rather think it did."

"What does everybody else say to this?" Alleyn asked.

Dr. Otterly said he remembered noticing that "Crack" kept much closer than usual to the Fool.

"So do I," Ralph said. "Undoubtedly it did. Isn't that right?" he added, turning to the Andersens.

"So 'tis, then, Mr. Ralph," Dan said. "I kind of seed it was there when we was hard at it dancing. And afterwards, in all the muck-up, I reckon I forgot. Right?" He appealed to his brothers.

"Reckon so," they said, glowering at the Hobby, and Chris added angrily, "Prying and sneaking and none of us with the sense to know. What she done it for?"

"In order to hear what the Fool said when he looked in the 'glass'?" Alleyn suggested. "*Was* it, Mrs. Bünz?" he shouted, standing over the Hobby-Horse and peering at its neck. "Did you go close because you wanted to hear?"

A muffled sound came through the neck. The great head swayed in a grotesque nod.

" '*Once for a looker,*' " Alleyn quoted, " '*and all must agree/If I bashes the looking-glass so I'll go free.*' Was that what he said?"

The head nodded again.

"Stand closer then, Mrs. Bünz. Stand as you did on Wednesday."

The Hobby-Horse stood closer.

"Go on," Alleyn said. "Go on, Fool."

Young Bill, using both hands, took the knot of swords by the hilts and dashed it to the ground. Dr. Otterly struck up again, the Sons retrieved their swords and began the second part of the dance, which was an exact repetition of the first. They now had the air of being fiercely dedicated. Even Ernie danced with concentration, though he continually threw glances of positive hatred at the Fool.

And the Hobby-Horse stood close.

It swayed and fidgeted as if the being at its centre was uneasy. Once, as the head moved, Alleyn caught a glimpse of eyes behind the window in its neck.

The second sword-knot was made and exhibited by Dan. Then young Bill leant his mask to one side and mimed the writing of the Will and the offer of the Will to the Sons.

Alleyn quoted again:

" 'Twice for a Testament. Read it and see/If you look at the leavings then so I'll go free.' "

The Betty drew nearer. The Hobby and the Betty now stood right and left of the dolmen.

The Sons broke the knot and began the third part of the dance.

To the party of three on the steps, to the watching audience and the policemen and to Camilla, who looked on with a rising sensation of nausea, it seemed as if the Five Sons now danced on a crescendo that thudded like a quickening pulse towards its climax.

For the last and the third time their swords were interlaced and Dan held them aloft. The Fool was in his place behind the dolmen, the hermaphrodite and the horse stood like crazy acolytes to left and right of the stone. Dan lowered the knot of swords to the level of the Fool's head. Each of the Sons laid hold of his own sword-hilt. The fiddling stopped.

"I can't look," Camilla thought and then, "But that's not how it was. They've gone wrong again."

At the same time the gong, the hunting horn and Alleyn's whistle sounded. Ralph Stayne, Tom Plowman and Trixie all held up their hands and Dr. Otterly raised his bow.

It was the Hobby-Horse again. It should, they said, have been close behind the Fool, who was now leaning across the dolmen towards the sword-lock.

Very slowly the Hobby moved behind the Fool.

"And then," Alleyn said. "came the last verse. '*Here comes the rappers to send me to bed/They'll rapper my head off and then I'll be dead.*' Now."

Young Bill leant over the dolmen and thrust his head with its rabbit-cap and mask into the lock of swords. There he was, grinning through a steel halter.

"Betty to lover me
Hobby to cover me
If you cut off my head
I'll rise from the dead."

The swords flashed and sang. The rabbit head dropped on the dolmen. The Fool slid down behind the stone out of sight.

"Go on," Alleyn said. He stood beside the Hobby-Horse. The Fool lay at their feet. Alleyn pointed at Ralph Stayne. "It's your turn," he said. "Go on."

Ralph said apologetically, "I can't very well without any audience."

"Why not?"

"It was an ad lib. It depended on the audience."

"Never mind. You've got Mr. Plowman and Trixie and a perambulation of police. Imagine the rest."

"It's so damn' silly," Ralph muttered.

"Oh, get *on*," Dame Alice ordered. "What's the matter with the boy!"

From the folds of his crate-like skirt Ralph drew out a sort of ladle that hung on a string from his waist

Rather half-heartedly he made a circuit of the courtyard and mimed the taking up of a collection.

"That's all," he said and came to a halt.

Dame Alice tooted, Dulcie banged the gong and Chris Andersen shouted, "No, it bean't all, neither."

"I mean it's all of that bit," Ralph said to Alleyn.

"What comes next? Keep going."

With rather bad grace he embarked on his fooling. He flirted his crinoline and ran at two or three of the stolidly observant policemen.

His great-aunt shouted, "Use yer skirt, boy!"

Ralph made a sortie upon a large officer and attempted without success to throw the crinoline over his head.

"*Yah!*" jeered his great-aunt. "Go for a little 'un. Go for the gel."

This was Trixie.

She smiled broadly at Ralph. "Come on, then, Mr. Ralph. I doan't mind," said Trixie.

Camilla turned away quickly. The Andersens stared, bright-eyed, at Ralph.

Alleyn said, "Obviously the skirt business only works if the victim's very short and slight. Suppose we resurrect the Fool for the moment."

Young Bill got up from behind the dolmen. Ralph ran at him and popped the crinoline over his head. The crinoline heaved and bulged. It was not difficult, Alleyn thought, to imagine the hammer blows of bucolic wit that this performance must have inspired in the less inhibited days of Merrie England.

"Will *that* do?" Ralph asked ungraciously.

"Yes," Alleyn said. "Yes, I think it will."

Young Bill rolled out from under the rim of the crinoline and again lay down between dolmen and "Crack."

"Go on," Alleyn said. "Next."

Ralph set his jaw and prepared grimly for a revival of his Ernie-baiting. Ernie immediately showed signs of resentment and of wishing to anticipate the event.

"Not this time yer won't," he said showing his teeth

and holding his sword behind him. "Not me. I know a trick worth two nor that."

This led to a general uproar.

At last when the blandishments of his brothers, Dame Alice's fury, Alleyn's patience and the sweet reasonableness of Dr. Otterly had all proved fruitless, Alleyn fetched Simon from behind the wall.

"Will you," he said, "get him to stand facing his brothers and holding his sword by the ribbons, which, I gather, is what he did originally?"

"I'll give it a whirl if you say so, but don't depend on it. He's blowing up for trouble, is the Corp."

"Try."

"Roger. But he may do *anything*. Hey! Corp!"

He took Ernie by the arm and murmured wooingly in his ear. Ernie listened but, when it came to the point, remained truculent. "No bloody fear," he said. He pulled away from Simon and turned on Ralph. "You keep off."

"Sorry," Simon muttered. "N.b.g."

"Oh, well," Alleyn said. "You go back, will you?"

Simon went back.

Alleyn had a word with Ralph, who listened without any great show of enthusiasm but nodded agreement. Alleyn went up to Ernie.

He said, "Is that the sword you were making such a song about? The one you had on Wednesday?"

"Not it," Ernie said angrily. "This'un's a proper old blunt 'un. Mine's a whiffler, mine is. So sharp's a knife."

"You must have looked pretty foolish when the Betty took it off you."

"No, I did not, then."

"How did he get it? If it's so sharp why didn't he cut his hand?"

"You mind your own bloody business."

"Come on, now. He ordered you to give it to him and you handed it over like a good little boy."

Ernie's response to this was furious and unprintable.

Alleyn laughed. "All right. Did he smack your hand or what? Come on."

"He wouldn't of took it," Ernie spluttered, "if I'd seen. He come sneaking up be'ind when I worn't noticing, like. *Didn't* you?" he demanded of Ralph. "If I'd held thik proper you wouldn't 'ave done it."

"Oh," Alleyn said offensively. "And how *did* you hold it? Like a lady's parasol?"

Ernie glared at him. A stillness had fallen over the courtyard. The bonfire could be heard crackling cheerfully beyond the wall. Very deliberately Ernie reversed his sword and swung it by the scarlet cord that was threaded through the tip.

"*Now!*" Alleyn shouted and Ralph pounced.

"Crack" screamed: a shrill wavering cry. Mrs. Bünz's voice could be heard within, protesting, apparently, in German, and the Hobby, moving eccentrically and very fast, turned and bolted through the archway at the rear. At the same time Ralph, with the sword in one hand and his crinoline gathered up in the other, fled before the enraged Ernie. Round and round the courtyard they ran. Ralph dodged and feinted, Ernie roared and doubled and stumbled after him.

But Alleyn didn't wait to see the chase.

He ran after the Hobby. Through the archway he ran and there behind the old wall in the light of the bonfire was "Crack," the Hobby-Horse, plunging and squealing in the strangest manner. Its great cylinder of a body swung and tilted. Its skirt swept the muddy ground, its canvas top bulged and its head gyrated wildly. Fox and three of his men stood by and watched. There was a final mammoth upheaval. The whole structure tipped and fell over. Mrs. Bünz, terribly dishevelled, bolted out and was caught by Fox.

She left behind her the strangest travesty of the Fool. His clown's face was awry and his pyjama jacket in rags. His hands were scratched and he was covered in mud. He stepped out of the wreckage of "Crack" and took off his mask.

"Nice work, young Bill," Alleyn said. "And that, my hearties, is how the Guiser got himself offstage."

v

There was no time for Mrs. Bünz or Simon to remark upon this statement. Mrs. Bünz whimpered in the protective custody of Mr. Fox. Simon scratched his head and stared uncomfortably at young Bill.

And young Bill, for his part, as if to clear his head, first shook it, then lowered it and finally dived at Simon and began to pummel his chest with both fists.

Simon shouted, "Hey! What the hell!" and grabbed the boy's wrists.

Simultaneously Ernie came plunging through the archway from the arena.

"Where is 'e?" Ernie bawled. "Where the hell is the bastard?"

He saw Simon with the Fool's figure in his grip. A terrible stillness came upon them all.

Then Ernie opened his mouth indecently wide and yelled, "Let 'im have it, then. I'll finish 'im."

Simon loosed his hold as if to free himself rather than his captive.

The boy in Fool's clothing fell to the ground and lay there, mask upwards.

Ernie stumbled towards him. Alleyn and the three Yard men moved in.

"Leave 'im to me!" Ernie said.

"You clot," Simon said. "Shut your great trap, you *bloody* clot. Corp! *Do you hear me? Corp!*"

Ernie looked at his own hands.

"I've lost my whiffler. Where's 'tother job?"

He turned to the wall and saw the charred slasher. "Ar!" he said. "There she is." He grabbed it, turned and swung it up. Alleyn and one of his men held him.

"Lemme go," he said, struggling. "I got my orders. Lemme go."

Mrs. Bünz screamed briefly and shockingly.

"What orders?"

"My Wing-Commander's orders. Will I do it again, sir? Will I do it, like you told me? Again?"

Looking larger than human in the smoke of the bonfire, five men moved forward. They closed in about Simon.

Alleyn stood in front of him.

"Simon Richard Begg," he said, "I am going to ask you for a statement, but before I do so I must warn you—"

Simon's hand flashed. Alleyn caught the blow on his forearm instead of on his throat. "Not again," he said.

It was well that there were five men to tackle Simon. He was experienced in unarmed combat and he was a natural killer.

CHAPTER XIII The Swords Go In

"HE's a natural killer," Alleyn said. "This is the first time, as far as we know, that it's happened since he left off being a professional. If it *is* the first time it's because until last Wednesday nobody had happened to annoy him in just the way that gingers up his homicidal reflexes."

"Yes, but *fancy!*" Dulcie said, coming in with a steaming grog tray. "He had *such* a good war record. You know he came down in a parachute and killed *quantities* of Germans with his bare hands all at once and escaped and got decorated."

"Yes," Alleyn said drily, "he's had lots of practice. He told us about that. That was the last time."

"D'you meantersay," Dame Alice asked, handing Alleyn a bottle of rum and a corkscrew, "that he killed Will'm Andersen out of temper and nothin' else?"

"Out of an accumulation of spleen and frustrated ambition and on a snap assessment of the main chance."

"Draw that cork and begin at the beginnin'."

"Aunt Akky, shouldn't you have a rest—"

"No."

Alleyn drew the cork. Dame Alice poured rum and boiling water into a saucepan and began to grind up nutmeg. "Slice the lemons," she ordered Fox.

Dr. Otterly said, "Frustrated ambition because of Copse Forge and the filling station?"

"That's it."

"Otters, don't interrupt."

"I daresay," Alleyn said, "he'd thought often enough that if he could hand the old type the big chop, and get by, he'd give it a go. The boys were in favour of his scheme, remember, and he wanted money very badly."

"But he didn't plan this thing?" Dr. Otterly interjected and added, "Sorry, Dame Alice."

"No, no. He only planned the substitution of Mrs. Bünz as 'Crack' and she gave him, she now tells us, thirty pounds for the job and bought a car from him into the bargain. He'd taken charge of 'Crack' and left the thing in the back of her car. She actually crept out when the pub was bedded down for the night and put it on to see if she could support the weight. They planned the whole thing very carefully. What happened was this: at the end of his girl-chase he went offstage and put Mrs. Bünz into 'Crack's' harness. She went on for the triple sword-dance and was meant to come off in time for him to change back before the finale. La Belle Bünz, however, hell-bent on picking up a luscious morsel of folksy dialogue, edged up as close to the dolmen as she could get. She thought she was quite safe. The tar-daubed skirts of the Hobby completely hid her. Or almost completely."

"Completely. No almost about it," Dame Alice said. "I couldn't see her feet."

"No. But you would have seen them if you'd lain down in a shallow depression in the ground a few inches away from her. As the Guiser did."

"Hold the pot over the fire for a bit, one of you. Go on."

"The Guiser, from his worm's viewpoint, recognized her. There she was, looming over him, with 'Crack's' carcass probably covering the groove where he lay and her rubber overshoes and hairy skirts showing every time she moved. He reached up and grabbed her. She screamed at the top of her voice and you all thought it was Begg trying to neigh. The Guiser was a very small man and a very strong one. He pinioned her arms to her body, kept his head down and ran her off."

"That was when Ralph pinched Ernie's sword?" Dr. Otterly ventured.

"That's it. Once offstage, while he was still, as it were, tented up with her, the Guiser hauled her out of 'Crack's' harness. He was gibbering with temper. As soon as he was free, a matter of seconds, he turned on Begg, who, of course, was waiting there for her. The Guiser went for Begg like a fury. It was over in a flash. Mrs. Bünz saw Begg hit him across the throat. It's a well-known blow in unarmed combat, and it's deadly. She also saw Ernie come charging offstage without his whiffler and in a roaring rage himself. Then she bolted.

"What happened after that, Ernie demonstrated for us to-night. He saw his god fell the Guiser. Ernie was in a typical epileptic's rage and, as usual, the focal point of his rage was his father—the Old Man, who had killed his dog, frustrated his god's plans and snatched the role of Fool away from Ernie himself at the last moment. He was additionally inflamed by the loss of his sword.

"But the slasher was there. He'd sharpened it and brought it up himself and he grabbed it as soon as he saw it.

"He said to-night that he was under orders and I'm sure he was. Begg saw a quick way out. He said something like this: 'He tried to kill me. Get him, Corp!' And Ernie, his mind seething with a welter of emotions and superstitions, did what he'd done to the aggressive gander earlier that day."

"Gracious! Aunt Akky, fancy! *Ernie!*"

"Very nasty," said Mr. Fox, who was holding the saucepan of punch over the drawing-room fire.

"A few moments later, Ralph Stayne came out with Ernie's whiffler. He found Ernie and he found 'Crack,' squatting there, he says, like a great broody hen. Begg was hiding the decapitated Guiser with the only shield available—'Crack.'

"He told Stayne that Ernie was upset and he'd better leave him alone. Stayne returned the whiffler and went on round the wall to the O.P. entrance.

"Begg knew that if the body was found where it lay Stayne would remember how he saw him squatting there. He did the only thing possible. He sent Ernie back to the arena, threw the slasher on the fire and overturned the drum of tar to obliterate any traces of blood. It caught fire. Then he hitched 'Crack's' harness over his own shoulders and returned to the arena. He carried the body in his arms and held the head by the strings of its bag-like mask, both ends of which became bloodstained. All this under cover of the great canvas body.

"At this time the final dance was in progress and the Five Sons were between their audience and the dolmen. 'Crack' was therefore masked by the stone and the dancers. Not that he needed any masking. He dropped the body—laid it, like an egg, in the depression behind the dolmen. This accounts for the state it was in when the Andersens found it. Begg leapt with suspicious alacrity at my suggestion that he might have tripped over it or knocked it with the edge of 'Crack's' harness."

"Oh, dear, Aunt Akky!"

"He was careful to help with the removal of the body in order to account for any bloodstains on his clothes. When I told him we would search his clothes for bloodstains, he made his only mistake. His vanity tripped him up. He told us the story of his ferocious exploit in Germany and how, if a man was killed as the Guiser was supposed to have been killed, his assailant would be covered in blood. Of course we knew that, but the story told us that Begg had once been involved in unarmed combat with an old peasant and that he had been saved by one of his own men. A hedge-slasher had been involved in that story, too."

Alleyn glanced at Dame Alice and Dulcie. "Is this altogether too beastly for you?" he asked.

"Absolutely *ghastly,*" Dulcie said. "Still," she added in a hurry, "I'd rather *know.*"

"Don't be 'ffected, Dulcie. 'Course you would. So'd I. Go on," Dame Alice ordered.

"There's not much more to tell. Begg hadn't time to deliberate, but he hoped, of course, that with all those swords about it would be concluded that the thing was done while the Guiser lay behind the dolmen. He and Dr. Otterly were the only two performers who would be at once ruled out if this theory were accepted. He's completely callous. I don't suppose he minded much who might be accused, though he must have known that the only two who would really look likely would be Ernie, with the sharp sword, and Ralph Stayne, who pinched it and made great play slashing it round."

"But he stuck up for Ernie," Dr. Otterly said. "All through. Didn't he?"

Fox sighed heavily. Dame Alice pointed to a magnificent silver punch bowl that was blackening in the smoke on the hearth. He poured the fragrant contents of the saucepan into it and placed it before her.

Alleyn said, "Begg wanted above all things to prevent us finding out about Ernie and the slasher. Once we had an inkling that the Guiser was killed offstage his improvised plan would go to pot. We would know that *he* was offstage and must have been present. He would be able, of course, to say that Ernie killed the Guiser and that he himself, wearing 'Crack's' harness, was powerless to stop him. But there was no knowing how Ernie would behave: Ernie filled with zeal and believing he had saved his god and wiped out that father-figure who so persistently reappeared, always to Begg's and Ernie's undoing. Moreover, there was Mrs. Bünz, who had seen Begg strike his blow, though she didn't realize he had struck to kill. He fixed Mrs. Bünz by telling her that we suspected her and that there was a lot of feeling against her as a German. Now he's been arrested, she's come across with a full statement and will give evidence."

"What'll happen?" Dame Alice asked, beginning to ladle out her punch.

"Oh," Alleyn said, "we've a very groggy case, you know. We've only got the undeniable fact, based on medical evidence, that he was dead before Ernie struck. Moreover, in spite of Ernie, there may, with luck, be evidence of the actual injury."

"Larynx," Dr. Otterly said.

"Exactly."

"What," Dr. Otterly asked, "will he plead?"

"His counsel may plump for self-defence: the Guiser

went for him and his old unarmed-combat training took over. He defended himself instinctively."

"Mightn't it be true?"

"The Guiser," Alleyn said, "was a very small and very old man. But, as far as that goes, I think Begg's training *did* re-assert itself. Tickle a dog's ribs and it scratches itself. There's Begg's temperament, make-up and experience. There are his present financial doldrums; there are his prospects if he can start his petrol station. There's the Guiser, standing in his path. The Guiser comes at him like an old fury. Up goes the arm, in goes the edge of the hand. It was unpremeditated, but in my opinion he hit to kill."

"Will he get off?" Dr. Otterly asked.

"How the bloody hell should I know!" Alleyn said with some violence. "Sorry, Dame Alice."

"Have some punch," said Dame Alice. She looked up at him out of her watery old eyes. "You're an odd sort of feller," she remarked. "Anybody'd think you were squeamish."

ii

Ralph took Camilla to call on his great-aunt.

"We'll have to face it sooner or later," he said, "and so will she."

"I can't pretend I'm looking forward to it."

"Darling, she'll adore you. In two minutes she'll adore you."

"Come off it, my sweet."

Ralph beamed upon his love and untied the string that secured the wrought-iron gates.

"Those geese!" Camilla said.

They were waiting in a solid phalanx.

"I'll protect you. They know me."

"And the two bulls on the skyline. The not very distant skyline."

"Dear old boys, I assure you. Come on."

"Up the Campions!" Camilla said. "If not the Andersens."

"Up, emphatically, the Andersens," Ralph said and held out his hand.

She went through the gates.

The geese did menacing things with their necks. Ralph shook his stick and they hissed back at him.

"Perhaps, darling, if you hurried and I held them at bay—"

Camilla panted up the drive. Ralph fought a rear-guard action. The bulls watched with interest.

Ralph and Camilla stumbled breathless and handfast through the archway and across the courtyard. They mounted the steps. Ralph tugged at the phoney bell. It set up a clangour that caused the geese to scream, wheel and waddle indignantly away.

"That's done it," Ralph said and put his arm round Camilla.

They stood with their backs to the door and looked across the courtyard. The snow had gone. Grey and wet were the walls and wet the ground. Beyond the rear archway stood a wintry hill, naked trees and a windy sky.

And in the middle of the courtyard was the dolmen, very black, one heavy stone supported by two others. It looked expectant.

" '*Nine-men's morris is filled up with mud,*' " Camilla murmured.

"There *were* nine," Ralph said. "Counting Mrs. Bünz."

"Well," she said under her breath, "that's the last of the Mardian Morris of the Five Sons, isn't it? *Ralph!* No one, not the boys or you or Dr. Otterly can ever want to do it again: ever, ever, ever. Can you? *Can* you?"

Ralph was saved from answering by Dulcie, who opened the great door behind them.

"How do you do?" Dulcie said to Camilla. "Do come in. Aunt Akky'll be delighted. She's been feeling rather flat after all the excitement." Ralph gently propelled Camilla into the hall. Dulcie shut the door.

"Aunt Akky," she said, "does so like things to happen. She's been saying what a long time it seems to next Sword Wednesday."